JUDGE STONE

JUDGE STONE

VIOLA DAVIS

JAMES PATTERSON

CENTURY

UK | USA | Canada | Ireland | Australia
India | New Zealand | South Africa

Century is part of the Penguin Random House group of companies
whose addresses can be found at global.penguinrandomhouse.com

Penguin Random House UK,
One Embassy Gardens, 8 Viaduct Gardens, London SW11 7BW

penguin.co.uk

First published 2026
001

Copyright © Viola Davis and James Patterson, 2026
Produced in association with JVL Media

The moral right of the authors has been asserted
The characters and events in this book are fictitious. Any similarity to real persons,
living or dead, is coincidental and not intended by the authors.

Penguin Random House values and supports copyright. Copyright fuels creativity,
encourages diverse voices, promotes freedom of expression and supports a vibrant culture.
Thank you for purchasing an authorised edition of this book and for respecting intellectual
property laws by not reproducing, scanning or distributing any part of it by any means
without permission. You are supporting authors and enabling Penguin Random House to
continue to publish books for everyone. No part of this book may be used or reproduced
in any manner for the purpose of training artificial intelligence technologies or systems.
In accordance with Article 4(3) of the DSM Directive 2019/790, Penguin Random House
expressly reserves this work from the text and data mining exception.

Printed and bound in Great Britain by Clays Ltd, Elcograf S.p.A.

The authorised representative in the EEA is Penguin Random House Ireland,
Morrison Chambers, 32 Nassau Street, Dublin D02 YH68

A CIP catalogue record for this book is available from the British Library

ISBN: 978–1–529–94362–7 (hardback)
ISBN: 978–1–529–94363–4 (trade paperback)

Penguin Random House is committed to a sustainable future
for our business, our readers and our planet. This book is made
from Forest Stewardship Council® certified paper.

For Nancy Allen and the late Robert Barnett, brilliant lawyers who helped in so many ways with the research, story, and much-needed encouragement to get this right.

PART
ONE

CHAPTER 1

Dr. Bria Gaines

UNION SPRINGS, ALABAMA

Bria Gaines stood at the back door of the small brick office building she rented in Union Springs, Alabama, population 3,314. She pulled her phone from her pocket to check the time. Six minutes past midnight. They were late.

Maybe they weren't coming.

Maybe she'd be spared.

It was dark out, mostly quiet except for frogs, the spring peepers, singing in the narrow creek that wove through trees leafing out for the season.

She heard the rattle of an approaching vehicle before the flash of its brights signaled the arrival of the old Toyota SUV.

Pulling up onto the gravel space that served as a parking lot, the driver cut the engine, killed the headlights.

Bria's nerves were strung tight, heart pounding. She knew the risk when she'd agreed to do this thing. Nobody had forced her into it. Sometimes, she'd realized, a person has to take a stand.

Bria tried hard not to let fear overcome her certainty. But when she flipped on the back door light, panic sent her pulse racing. Something was wrong already. Only two people emerged from the car. Bria had expected three.

She recognized the driver. It was Cocheta Bass, the nurse practitioner who worked at Union Springs Middle School. The passenger was a female wearing a hoodie that left her face in shadow.

Bria watched Cocheta pat the girl's shoulder as they climbed the back steps together. She pushed the door wide, to let them in, then immediately flipped off the outdoor light. Pulled the door shut and turned the dead bolt. They needed to be locked up tight.

Bria led them into her office waiting room, toward the table lamp that dimly lit the space around the reception desk. Checking to see that the blinds were shut, Bria flipped the overhead light on.

The school nurse spoke in a whisper, as if fearful of being overheard. "Dr. Gaines, this is Nova."

The girl pulled the hood off her head and pushed her hair away from her face to reveal cheeks and a forehead glistening with sweat.

Nova Jones was tall, standing five feet, eight inches, and her body had already matured. Bria recognized the frightened girl as the attentive big sister who chased around town after a brood of younger siblings.

She smiled and said, "Hi, Nova. I've seen you at church, over at Victory Baptist. How old are you now?"

Nova looked down at the floor and whispered, "Thirteen."

So. This was actually happening. A first for Bria Gaines, that was certain.

She'd never committed a felony before.

But a key person was missing. Bria couldn't overlook that. She glanced from Nova to the school nurse. "So where's Ms. Jones, Nova's mom?"

Nova's breath caught. She took a step backward, like she might bolt. "No! No, ma'am, Mama can't know. Never!"

Bria spoke gently to the girl. "You need your mother's support. She'll need to care for you, help you through this."

Nova's voice shook as she said, "She'll be so mad. She'll think I'm a bad girl. That I was out there being fast." The girl's chest heaved, like her distress was combusting, getting ready to explode.

Bria had the uneasy feeling that she was walking straight into a predicament—a precarious situation even more out of control than she'd been led to believe.

Bria didn't let her agitation show as she walked over to a supply cupboard. She pulled a clean hospital gown from a stack of linens and handed it to Nova. "The exam room is right over here," she said, opening another door and flipping the interior light switch. "You can change in there. Take everything off, okay? Even your bra and panties. Let me know when you're done."

She used her doctor voice—encouraging, brisk, professional. The girl wiped her wet eyes with her sleeve as she stepped into the examination room, shutting the door behind her.

Cocheta pressed her hand against her chest. "How you doing, Doctor? I'm so nervous, it's making me lightheaded. I was afraid I'd keel over, just from walking up those stairs."

Bria turned to the nurse, taking care to keep her voice low. "You said her mother would be here with her."

Cocheta heaved a deep breath. "I tried, I did! Nova won't tell her mother about it. Absolutely won't budge on that. She's scared to death about what her mother will do if she finds out."

"Cocheta, I'd feel a lot better about this if she had family support."

The nurse darted a look at the exam room door before she

responded. "That girl got her first period when she was nine years old. You know what her mother did? Gave her a pad and told her if she ever brought any babies home, she'd kick her ass out."

"Oh, my God." It was a tragic situation, but it also scared her. She turned away from the nurse, wishing she had time to think it through.

The nurse said in an urgent whisper, "If you don't fix this tonight, I can't guarantee what the outcome's gonna be. That poor child actually threatened to try a coat hanger. Lord! I swear, I thought those days were history."

The suggestion terrified Bria. She rubbed her eyes, taking a moment to compose herself. There was only one reasonable solution. The stakes, though, were enormous. "Who got her pregnant, who's the father? Did you get her to open up about that?"

Sounding rueful, Cocheta said, "I asked. She still won't say. So legally, I'm supposed to call the Division of Human Resources, or the police. As you know."

Bria did know. "Mandated reporter statute."

"Yeah, we're mandated reporters under Alabama law. But I grew up on the Creek reservation in Poarch. So I never really felt like state law governed me, because my tribe had a treaty with the feds. Does that make sense?"

"No." The discussion made Bria's head hurt. Cocheta's interpretation of her legal liability was flat wrong. "We're both mandated reporters in Alabama. Both subject to Alabama state law."

"Okay, right. But if we call the police or DHR, you know what's going to happen, what they'll force her to do. She's just thirteen, Dr. Gaines. Barely thirteen."

Bria knew what the child's fate would be. She also knew that the assistance that Nova Jones and Cocheta Bass wanted her to provide could end her medical practice and send her to prison.

Alabama had the toughest anti-abortion law in the country, and it placed criminal liability squarely on the backs of doctors. Under the Alabama Human Life Protection Act, intentionally performing an abortion was a Class A felony.

Maybe Cocheta could read her mind. She said, "Doctor, I know the spot I'm putting you in. Good Lord! We're both putting our lives on the line for this girl. I threw up twice today, just from nerves. Thought about backing out. But I couldn't live with myself if I did that." Her voice cracked when she added, "If she ends up trying to kill herself or butcher herself—"

Cocheta didn't finish the sentence, because the door to the examination room opened. Nova stepped out with bare feet, clutching the loose ends of the blue hospital gown behind her back. Nova's toes curled up on the tile. But it wasn't the cold from the air-conditioning that made the girl tremble.

Nova's voice was shaking when she said, "Please, Doctor. Help me."

Bria caught her breath. Everything fell into place inside her head. She smiled as she reached out and wiped away the tears under Nova's eyes. "I'm going to take care of you, sweetheart. Gonna do what's right. Everything will be okay, don't you worry."

CHAPTER 2

Judge Mary Stone

STONE FAMILY FARM
BULLOCK COUNTY, ALABAMA

One day, I'm going to strangle that goddamn rooster. Maybe I'll strangle him today.

That was my first thought after being rudely—no, savagely—awakened on a Monday morning in late March.

The night before, I'd spent the wee hours staring up at the farmhouse ceiling. I grew up on this farm in rural Alabama. So I never developed a habit for sleeping in because farm life is too hard to afford that luxury. My daddy used to say he couldn't take a vacation day until the livestock agreed to take one, too.

It's not so different for judges. Pending cases take up residence in the mind.

I'd been agonizing over a decision I'd be called on to make. It was no exaggeration to say I'd been dreading this cursed day for weeks. Counting down the hours until I had to choose between life and death. And trying to determine the wisest course.

I rolled out of bed, pulling a long-sleeved T-shirt over my head and fastening the suspenders of my overalls. Didn't bother to glance at my reflection in the mirror while I brushed my teeth. At that hour, it didn't much matter how I looked.

Inside the mudroom door, I stepped into a pair of rubber chore boots. Stuffed my pant legs into the boots to discourage ticks from latching onto me. Then I exited the farmhouse just as the sky overhead was lightening from black to indigo blue.

I crossed the hard, bare ground of the side yard, heading to the weathered barn my great-grandfather had built with his own hands. The rooster followed along, scolding me. I was not having it.

"Don't mess with me, Foghorn Leghorn. I'm in no mood," I said. When he continued to squawk, I resorted to threats. "I'll chop you into pieces and fry you up in a pan. You hear?"

My quarter horse, Tornado, trotted up to meet me. She was my pride, a cross-rein-trained mare that was a joy to ride. But not these days. Tornado was swelling with a new foal. I wasn't about to mount the pregnant mare to ride the rounds. She wasn't livestock. She was dear to me.

Inside the barn, I climbed onto the John Deere tractor and drove it to the east pasture, where I keep bales of hay stored under a plastic tarp. Used the pallet fork on the tractor to carry hay to the spot where my cattle grazed. I had twenty head of Charolais, including a bull that I rented out for stud. My cows were high-breed beef cattle, some of the best in the region.

As I drove the tractor across the field, the cattle looked up, eager to eat. I called out to them, just like my mama and daddy used to do.

The cattle lowed in response as they ambled toward me. I fed them the hay, mixed with barley and oats from a burlap sack. While I scattered the feed, one of the cows brushed up against me. I stroked her neck behind the ears before climbing back on the tractor.

As I drove back, the sun had risen high enough to turn the sky pink, casting a rosy glow on my land. The sight of that early light generally gave me pleasure. On that morning, though, it served as a reminder. Nothing could stop this day from coming.

Just contemplating the terrible task ahead sent a zing into my lower back. I ignored it. I had no time for back trouble. I needed to muck out my horse's stall before I got into the shower.

After twenty minutes of shoveling shit, replacing it with fresh wood shavings, and setting out food and water for my mare, I left the barn and headed back to the house. Foghorn scuttled up to squawk at me again as I crossed the yard. He hushed up when I tossed a handful of seed for him to peck.

I quickly showered and dressed. Chugged a cup of coffee while I stared at my reflection in the mirror, just thinking. I almost shoved the cosmetic bag out of my way, tempted to forgo that process. But at fifty, a woman can't rely on the glow of youth. So I did the bare minimum. Rubbed in some moisturizer, applied foundation. A lick of blush and a swipe of lipstick.

I was aware that I might be facing an audience. The press.

Before I left through the front door, I picked up my briefcase and pulled the black judicial robe off the coatrack, draped it over my arm.

CHAPTER 3

BULLOCK COUNTY COURTHOUSE
UNION SPRINGS, ALABAMA

I pulled into my designated spot in the Bullock County Courthouse parking lot. One of the sweetest perks of my elected position was that nine-foot-by-twenty-foot slice of asphalt directly under the window of my chambers on the second floor. Marked by two white stripes and a small sign that clearly stated: RESERVED FOR CIRCUIT JUDGE MARY STONE.

I left that beautiful sight for a familiar one.

Aurora Freeman, a member of the custodial staff, was smoking a cigarette by the back door. As I passed by, toting my bright red leather briefcase and black robe, she blew out a cloud of smoke and said, "Morning, Judge Mary."

"Morning, Aurora." I pulled the door open, pausing to say, "How's your hip? Seems like you should be home with your feet up."

She waved off the suggestion with a flip of her hand, sending ashes flying. "Don't you worry about me, honey, I'm good. You run along now."

Aurora is well over seventy, old enough to be my mother. Back when I was a student at Union Springs Elementary School, Aurora was as influential as any teacher. She worked in the lunchroom and she ruled that cafeteria with an iron hand. Aurora regularly threatened to whoop our butts, and it was not an empty threat.

Now I spend a fair amount of my life in the confines of this courthouse, a three-story brick structure topped by two towers. The National Register of Historic Places recognizes it as one of the finest courthouses in the state of Alabama, and the only one built in the Empire style. I'm a circuit judge, not a student of architecture, so I'm not sure what all that entails. But it's a pretty building, the centerpiece of the historic district in our small town.

No debating that. Nor the weight of the past.

Every day I climbed the double curved staircase toward the courtroom where I presided at the oak bench. Hearing and deciding cases inside that historic structure where my people weren't permitted to vote for damn near one hundred years after the courthouse was built in 1871. My great-grandpa and great-great-grandpa couldn't vote because the Klan wouldn't let them. One grandpa couldn't afford to pay the poll tax they imposed; the other's vote was blocked by a literacy test. None of the women in my family could cast a vote in my current workplace before the passage of the Voting Rights Act of 1965.

At nine thirty this morning, I would be handing down a sentence.

My administrative clerk, Luna Young, lingered in the open doorway, her mouth turned down in a worried frown. She was young, barely thirty, but I'd observed her air of maturity when I hired her. She'd also demonstrated a gift for handling people in tough situations. A judge's clerk has to conduct communications with attorneys, law enforcement, and the public. I was lucky that Luna possessed more tact than I generally exhibited.

When I walked past Luna's desk, she said, "Judge Mary, you've got the sentencing set in *State v. Gray* today."

Luna didn't need to provide a reminder of the murder charges against Ferrell Gray, the contentious jury trial over a case where the evidence of guilt was overwhelming.

At trial, the defendant had been hard to control, disrupting the proceedings with violent outbursts on more than one occasion. I was tempted to remove him from the courtroom. Threatened to do it at least twice, informing him that he could watch the case unfold on a monitor inside the county jail.

The jury had found him guilty and recommended punishment, but imposing sentence is the judge's job. That was the dilemma that had kept me awake the night before. Trying to decide whether I should impose the penalty that the jury recommended.

The death penalty.

CHAPTER 4

I stepped into chambers, dropped my briefcase beside the desk. Through the door, I called to the clerk. "Get the sheriff on the line for me, Luna. I'm going to request some extra security at the sentencing hearing today."

Luna sped into chambers and was standing beside my desk before I had time to hang up my robe. "The sheriff's already been here," she said. "He told me to give you this letter. Warned me not to look at it. He said you should read it before you go into court."

Luna handed me a plastic bag protecting a plain paper envelope. My name was scrawled on the front, below a distinctive return address: Ferrell Gray, Bullock County Jail.

Settling into my chair, I opened the envelope and saw a sea of blue ink scribbled across the front and back of two sheets of paper.

I scanned the letter quickly. And then I set both pages on my desk pad and slowly reread it. Gave it a thorough review.

"Sweet Jesus," I muttered.

Luna said, "Is it something terrible? I never saw the sheriff bring a letter to the courthouse before."

That was true. It was a harbinger of ill tidings. Mick Owens and I went way back. He was the sheriff of Bullock County and did not, as a rule, deliver the mail.

Hastily, she added, "You can tell me to mind my own business. But I can't believe someone about to be sentenced would have the nerve to write a personal letter to you." Her head shook in disbelief. "That man's crazy."

"Yeah, it's to me, no question. The salutation reads: 'To Judge Stone, you fucking whore.'"

Luna slapped her hand over her mouth. When she remained in the doorway, I asked, "You want to hear more?"

She shook her head no. Then changed her mind, I guess, because, with her mouth still covered, she nodded at me.

I summarized the high points. She'd be making copies in a minute and could read the whole thing from start to finish.

"He devotes an entire page to my personal appearance. Unflattering comments, you feel me? The description 'ugly bitch' is repeated in three places, and he spells it differently every time. *Damn.*" I clicked my tongue in disapproval.

"He says I'm too dumb to be a judge—even though his spelling and grammar would shame a third grader. Attributes my incompetence to my race, which he describes with the old-time slur." That word, he could spell.

"It's a scandal, Judge," Luna said.

I turned to the second sheet of paper. "Well, there's more. He informs me that he has made a deal with the devil. Satan himself is now Ferrell Gray's ally, apparently. And that forms the basis for his threat."

"He threatened you? Oh, no, he did not."

"He did. He says if I follow the jury's recommendation and sentence him to death, the devil will see to it that I die a gruesome death. Which the defendant describes in some detail."

I winced as I read the second page a final time. Recalling the brutality of the deaths the defendant had inflicted on the elderly couple he'd murdered when the old folks interrupted his burglary of their home, I knew that Ferrell Gray didn't require the devil's assistance to commit unspeakable acts.

I blew out a deep breath. Our system places tremendous power in the hands of the judiciary. The delicate balance can get thrown off when personal emotions come into play.

Luna lingered in the door of my chambers. I picked up the envelope and letter. Extended the documents across my desk for her to take.

"I need three copies, Luna. Be sure to get the front and back of both those pages. Envelope, too."

I was glad she pulled the door shut behind her. I had some thinking to do.

CHAPTER 5

Every courtroom has its own vibe. I learned that as a trial lawyer in Alabama, but it's true everywhere. That vibe produces an atmosphere inside the courtroom, like an electrical charge in the air. Everyone in the gallery can almost smell it.

The judge is responsible, you understand. Whether the atmosphere in court is good or bad is determined by the person in charge. If the courtroom is relaxed and people are courteous to one another and to the public, the judge has set a standard for that behavior. On the other hand, if a court operates with a bailiff who's a bully, and a docket that never starts on time, and a court reporter who's surly to lawyers and snaps at witnesses? That's the judge, too. Shit's rolling downhill, staff is copycatting the judge's attitude.

In most US courtrooms, all interested parties are in place before the judge arrives. The judge's appearance is announced with pomp and ceremony. The bailiff shouts "All rise!" and people jump to their feet. That's how it's done.

But it's not necessarily standard procedure in my courtroom. Not always. Sometimes, I like to be the first person to the party. Helps me get in the right headspace.

So when folks started drifting into court, taking their seats in the spectators' gallery, I was already seated. In the big rolling chair at the raised wooden bench, I was suitably attired in my black robe zipped up and topped with a bright yellow scarf—my substitute for a man's necktie.

Bullock County Courthouse has a huge courtroom, designed when it served a wide variety of purposes. Back in the day, there was a function in addition to upholding law and order by enforcing the criminal law and serving up justice in civil cases. Because the courtroom also provided entertainment to the masses. The public would turn out for jury trials to see the show. Jury trials are live theater, in which the script is written as the drama unfolds.

The defendant didn't have a cheering section, no family willing to claim him, not that we'd seen at trial. But journalists had picked up on the sympathy for the childless murder victims and wanted to report on the sentencing to curiosity seekers inside and outside the courtroom.

The defense attorney, Bradley Tyler, was a member of the death penalty team in the Birmingham public defender's office. He walked in with a stoop that was probably related to the weight of his occupation.

I called out to him. "Good morning, Mr. Tyler."

He was startled to see that I already occupied my perch. Still clutching his briefcase, he took a step toward the bench. "Am I late, Your Honor?"

"Late? No! I'm early."

That comment generated a chuckle from my bailiff, Ross Carr, who'd put up with my idiosyncrasies for almost six years.

"Mr. Tyler, you're from out of town. You don't know all my quirks."

The lawyer set down the briefcase. "No, ma'am. But I appreciate the restraint and professionalism you've shown in this case. I know it's been a tough one. I understand why you're held in such high regard. I'm familiar with your reputation. Before we tried this case in Bullock County, I asked around."

First-class bullshitter. Trying to butter me up. Hopes I'll show some mercy today. That will not happen.

That suspicious voice in my head was familiar. A symptom of the impostor syndrome I couldn't shake. I was among the first Black women in the state to be elected to the circuit bench. And in law school at the University of Alabama, even though I ranked at the top of the class, it never felt like I got the respect I deserved. Yeah, I still suffered from self-doubt. The habit had a way of sticking with me.

I worked hard to conceal it. Particularly when the DA was in court.

Robert Reeves, district attorney for the 3rd Judicial Circuit of Alabama, walked in late. As he set his laptop on the prosecution counsel table, he didn't apologize. Didn't even meet my eye. I was debating whether to call him out for it.

My bailiff interrupted my thoughts. "You ready for me to bring the defendant in, Judge?"

I nodded, rising from my chair. Decided that the morning called for ceremony. "Ross, I'll be in chambers. Let me know when everyone's ready."

A few minutes later, I walked back into court as Ross called out, "All rise! Circuit Court of Bullock County is now in session, Judge Mary Stone presiding."

The public defender jumped to his feet. All of the people gathered in the gallery stood up. Even the DA waited for leave to sit down.

"Y'all be seated," I said. "We're here in the matter of *State v. Ferrell Gray,* Case No. CR193878. The State appears by District

Attorney Robert Reeves. Defendant appears in person and by counsel Bradley Tyler."

Two uniformed deputies sat within snatching distance of the defendant. I was glad to see it. Ferrell Gray was the kind of dude who could put a courtroom at risk.

I gave the folks in court a minute to get settled before I made my announcement.

"I received a letter from the defendant this morning. I have copies of the correspondence to share with the parties."

When I picked up the folder containing the copies Luna had stapled together, my bailiff stepped up to take it from me. I signaled to him with a shake of my head as I descended from the bench. I didn't need Ross's assistance.

I personally hand-delivered the copies: one to the DA, one to the defense. I was glad to have an excuse to leave the bench. I prefer to move around the courtroom, like I did as a trial lawyer. Thinking on my feet was always my strong suit.

After the public defender skimmed the letter, he turned to his client, demanding in a stage whisper, *"Did you write this?"*

I leaned against the empty jury box, curious to learn Gray's response, but he didn't reply to his lawyer. He twisted in his seat and directed a question to me.

"How come I don't get a copy?" the defendant asked. "You got a problem with me taking a look at it? This is my trial, ain't it?"

Ferrell Gray would test the patience of a saint.

And I was no saint.

CHAPTER 6

I fought back the urge to approach the table where the defendant sat. Had the sound judgment to stand back. "Mr. Gray, I suspect you already know what the letter says. You wrote it, didn't you?"

"Hell yeah," Gray said, just as his lawyer snapped, "Don't answer that."

Bradley, the defense attorney, shook his head with some combination of frustration and disgust. Couldn't blame the man for that, not in his position. Bradley stood and said, "Judge, in light of this information, it's obvious that the sentencing can't proceed."

"It's not obvious to me," I said.

Bradley remained on his feet, but he started to look panicky. "Respectfully, Your Honor, the defense requests that you recuse yourself."

"Why would I do that?" I reached around and rubbed my lower back. It was still bothering me.

"Because your receipt of the letter—a letter purporting to be from the defendant in this case, though his responsibility for the document hasn't been proven—will make it impossible for you to be fair and impartial."

I stared the man down for a moment before I asked, "And why do you think I won't be fair?"

I heard the rattle of chains as the defendant lifted his handcuffed wrists to flip me the bird with both hands. As he tried to stand up—his belly chain appeared to cause some difficulty—he proclaimed, "I want a new judge! I'm a white man. I can't get any justice from this affirmative action bitch they hired!"

The defendant was unfamiliar with the judicial process. I wasn't hired. I was elected. In Alabama, circuit judges are elected to six-year terms of office by the registered voters of the counties in their circuit.

As the deputies jumped up to ensure that Gray remained in his seat, the public defender said, "Judge Stone, I apologize for that outburst."

The outburst wasn't over, not yet. While the deputies wrestled Gray back into his seat, the defendant continued to utter insults that were, thankfully, mostly incomprehensible. His lawyer appeared to be sincerely distressed.

"It's not your fault," I told the public defender. I felt the urge to move, so I stepped closer to the defense counsel table, but took care to keep a safe distance from the criminal defendant when I addressed him. "Mr. Gray, you need to quiet down. You're not helping your cause."

That was when the DA decided to weigh in. "Your Honor, the law on this matter—"

I swung around to face him. "You think I'm not acquainted with the law on this issue?"

He blinked, continued in his nasal voice, "I just want to contribute the State's position—"

"I don't recall asking for your opinion."

The DA was getting under my skin, as he tended to do. It was time to create some distance. I strode back to the bench. Climbing up the three wooden steps that led to my chair was well-timed in this instance. It demonstrated my authority.

As I sat, I said, "Defendant's motion is overruled."

Ferrell Gray snatched his attorney's copy of the letter and flung it to the floor. "The devil gonna burn you alive! You'll be screaming when your flesh is on fire!"

To the court reporter, I said, "Marlena, did you get all that?"

When she nodded, I said, "I have ruled. The law is on my side. In Alabama, judges are obligated to recuse themselves when they've behaved badly. To be clear: That's when the *judge* has behaved badly."

"You're an ugly whore!" Gray shouted. His lawyer grimaced, looking away. He was embarrassed.

I said, "This is just what I'm talking about. See? In this case, the wrongful behavior is all on Mr. Gray's part. The defendant has behaved badly, but I won't permit him to use that as a basis to go judge shopping. If you have any dispute on this issue, I recommend that counsel check out *ex parte Bentley*, an Alabama appellate decision that's on all fours with our situation in court today."

The DA smirked, looking satisfied. Well, that would be short-lived.

"Mr. Gray, please stand," I said.

The defendant snarled. "Why?"

"Because I'm going to pronounce sentence in your case."

The defense attorney stood and whispered an entreaty to his client to do likewise. But the defendant didn't want to comply with traditional procedure at sentencing. It required the assistance of both deputies to pull Ferrell Gray into a standing posture.

"In the case of *State of Alabama v. Ferrell Gray,* on counts 1 and 2, I hereby sentence you to life imprisonment without possibility of parole."

I didn't drag it out, didn't make long pauses for dramatic effect. But the statement packed a punch. The defendant lost his balance and fell back against the chair with his mouth sagging open.

And the prosecutor's face had turned scarlet. "Your Honor, the sentence doesn't reflect the jury's recommendation."

"That's true, Mr. Reeves. Because it's my decision to make. As the prosecution is well aware. And Mr. Gray, lest you're confused by today's events, you can't tempt me to sentence you to death with threats and insults and abuse. Because I believe in the sanctity of human life. Even your despicable life is sacred."

I keep a good-sized wooden gavel on the bench. Sometimes I hit harder than I should, just for personal satisfaction. This was one of those occasions.

"You'll be transferred to the Alabama Department of Corrections to serve out your sentence for the remainder of your natural life. Court is adjourned."

CHAPTER 7

STONE FAMILY FARM
BULLOCK COUNTY, ALABAMA

Saturday morning, 4:30 a.m. My alarm went off while the rooster was still sound asleep with his head tucked all snug under his wing.

I jabbed that snooze button, thinking: *I. Do. Not. Want. To. Get. Up.*

No.

As I stared up in the darkness, the cussing started. I muttered, "Son of a bitch."

And then I lay there, waiting, bracing myself for the alarm. Knowing it would shriek again in a couple of minutes.

"Shit. Shit. Son of a *bitch*." Louder that time, with feeling.

I couldn't abide the wait. Grabbed my phone and turned off the alarm, because snoozing wouldn't save me. I dragged myself out of bed and into the kitchen. Filled the industrial-sized copper-bottomed pot with water and put it on to boil before I drank my first cup of coffee. Made that pot of coffee strong, inky black. I had work to do.

Weekly breakfast at the farm was my mama and daddy's tradition, and I'd made it my own. In a matter of hours, there'd be a long line at the food table and every seat would be filled, with the younger folks eating on the grass, picnic style.

Hopefully, I'd be smiling then, instead of grumbling and cussing. That was the goal. I intended to give a warm welcome to each soul who showed up. Even if we'd never met, or I'd encountered them in unhappy circumstances. In my courtroom, for instance.

No one was ever turned away from Saturday breakfast. So long as the guests behaved themselves, they were welcome.

If, however, they took advantage of the Stone family hospitality, well. I knew how to enforce my house rules. The rules were well-known, just common sense. No fighting, no drinking or drugs, no harassment. We didn't see many problems, honestly. I couldn't remember the last time I'd had to instruct someone to leave.

By sunrise, I had my big pots of grits and oatmeal ready, and the first three pounds of sausage patties fried and draining on paper towels. I set the burners to warm and took off for the barn.

Foghorn chased after me, bitching like he thought I'd forgotten all about him. I tossed the seed just to hush him up. "Lazy man! Can't you find a worm or a bug? Look around, Foghorn, you've got the whole yard to yourself."

By the time my chores were done, I exited the barn and saw both of my sisters' cars parked on the gravel drive. With Mama and Daddy gone, there were three of us left. I was oldest, Nellie was the middle child, Jordan was the baby. When I reentered the kitchen, Nellie was standing at Jordan's elbow, giving her grief.

"Jordan, you're burning that bacon. It won't be fit to eat," Nellie said.

Jordan shoved Nellie aside with her hip. "Quit bossing me, Nellie." She made a face and rolled her eyes as she turned the knob, adjusted the heat.

I walked up and inspected the skillet. "That bacon looks fine to me."

"Mary, you always do that," Nellie said, her voice rising. "Treat Jordan like a baby, even though she's past forty. Saint Jordan could set the kitchen on fire and you'd be fine with it."

"That's true. Jordan's so much nicer than you, Nellie."

The three of us toiled side by side over the gas stove in the kitchen. When Jordan's husband, Trayvone, showed up, my brother-in-law and their two girls got to work setting up tables and chairs. So by the time the battered bus from Victory Baptist rolled up the road in a cloud of exhaust, we were ready for them.

The gears of the old bus ground together before the engine rumbled a final time. After it fell silent, the doors opened and folks climbed out of the vehicle and fanned across my yard.

Some of them were the unhoused. In Union Springs, the homeless population consisted primarily of single men who took shelter at night in abandoned buildings. But there were also women, families, too. A lot of people came for a free meal. Members of the Baptist church arrived in their own cars, bearing dishes covered in aluminum foil, to fill out our table. And friends from town, some courthouse folks, dropped in, just to be social.

Jordan sailed into the yard, waving an arm. "Welcome, y'all! Who needs a cup of coffee or a cold drink?"

The last person to step off the church bus was the Reverend Curtis Erskine. He drove the vehicle, ferrying a busload of hungry people to my farm every Saturday morning.

He stepped up to my brother-in-law, Trayvone. As the men shook hands, Nellie sidled up to me at the screen door. She said, "The rest of us grow older. But the pastor never ages a day."

Nellie was right. Erskine was several years older than I was. Didn't look it. "Clean living, I reckon."

"Maybe that's it. Or it could be that way he has, the charisma. Our congregation keeps growing. Church membership has doubled since you used to attend on Sundays."

"Good. He's doing his job, then." My voice was clipped. Nellie cut her eyes at me.

"You've never told me why you quit going."

"That's because it's my own business." I moved away, into the kitchen pantry, to get sugar for the oatmeal. Poured sugar from the bag into the sugar bowl and stuck a clean spoon inside.

Walked back to the kitchen door where Nellie stood, staring out into the yard through the screen.

Nellie made a humming noise in her throat. "Yes, ma'am, that's one fine-looking man," she said as she wiped her hands on the flour sack dish towel she'd tied around her waist. "His wife doesn't deserve him. That Doreen Erskine is cold as a Popsicle. Just look at her! Acts like she'd rather be anywhere but here."

Through the kitchen screen, I saw Doreen Erskine. She hadn't arrived on the bus. And she was standing away from the crowd, listening stone-faced to a small cluster of the female pillars of the Baptist church.

My sister kept on talking about her. "Doreen's a looker, can't deny that. Keeps her figure. But someday, Pastor's going to stray. Just to find communion with a warmhearted soul. I'd bet money on it. What do you think, Mary?"

"I don't care what the man does. He's not my business," I said. And I meant it.

CHAPTER 8

The preacher never made it to the kitchen door. He was stalled midway, brought to a halt by a young woman dressed in a tight pair of well-worn jeans. When the woman buttonholed Reverend Erskine, Nellie made a scornful noise.

She nudged me. "Mary, check her out. You see that one? Pastor would be wise to turn and run. Run for his life."

I did look, just to see what Nellie was going on about. The woman smiled up at Erskine, talking a mile a minute. She was laser-focused on the preacher until a child toddled up and grabbed her around the leg.

Without looking down at the child, the woman whirled around and called out, "Nova!"

Beside me, Nellie made a disapproving click with her tongue. "I can tell you who she's hollering for. Nova, that's her oldest. I see the girl at school. I'll have her in my math class next year. She's finishing seventh grade."

Nova ran up to her mother. The girl had a child in her arms, two more trailing behind her.

Nellie kept talking as she grabbed a gallon of milk from my

refrigerator and carried it back to the door. "That girl Nova looks a lot older than she is. You'd think the child was in high school, she's so big. Really stands out. She's taller than most of the boys."

The revelation stirred memories. "I was a big girl. It's not easy." I still recalled exactly how it felt to tower over everyone, to be the first girl to wear a bra. What it was like to explain to the teacher that I desperately needed to run to the restroom in the middle of class.

My sister and I stood together, watching Nova peel her sibling away from her mother's leg. Nellie said, "That mother's still in her twenties. Has five children, no man at home. But she runs up to the church every time the pastor opens the door. What do you think about that?"

My voice was neutral. "I don't think I should judge."

Nellie's laugh sounded like a hoot. "You judge people all day long. It's your job."

Hugging the plastic milk jug, she shouldered her way through the screen door. As it banged shut, I checked the clock over the stove.

It was past time to feed my guests. Still holding the sugar bowl, I made my way out of the house and into the yard, stopping to greet people as I passed them. We'd lucked out with the weather, had a brilliant blue sky overhead. The late March sun was just right, not too hot. People were comfortable, whether they stayed in the shade of the porch, or in the middle of the yard, or under the old birch trees laden with Spanish moss.

As I set the sugar by the oatmeal pot, Reverend Erskine came over. "Always a pleasure to break bread at your table, Judge Mary."

"Thank you, Reverend. Will you lead us in prayer?"

He did a creditable job, knew when to wrap it up. I was glad of that. Hungry people don't appreciate a mealtime grace that runs overlong.

Keeping dishes filled while folks went through the line was a group effort. Jordan ladled the oatmeal while Nellie served bacon and sausage and I dished up the eggs and grits. People helped themselves to biscuits, rolls, the covered dishes neighbors had shared. A separate table held a coffee urn, milk, cold water, and juice. I had to keep an eye trained on how the food was holding out. I had Jordan's husband take my place while I ran into the kitchen for more butter and juice.

Walking back out, I got a rush of satisfaction seeing all those folks enjoy the breakfast. Every seat on the porch was filled, and clusters of people sat on old sheets spread across the yard in the shade. I saw Nova and her mom struggling to keep all those little children corralled. The youngest was a baby who kept crawling off the sheet and into the grass.

I walked over and scooped him up. He was a pretty boy, with eyes like buttons.

Nova started to rise. I shook my head, to keep her seated. "You eat your breakfast, hon. I'll hold this big boy for a bit."

Nova looked at her mother for permission before she sat back down and spooned up oatmeal for her little sister. I caught her looking over her shoulder, across the field. In a voice so soft I could barely catch it, she said, "You got a lot of pretty trees."

The dogwoods were blooming, redbuds starting to fade. I said, "It's been a good year for dogwoods. Weather must be just right for them."

She looked up at me. "How'd you plant so many?"

"Oh, honey, they grow wild on my farm. Dogwood trees have been growing here as long as I can remember."

The young mother spoke up. "Is she bothering you about the trees? That child is always going on about them. Showing off how she knows so much about flowers and all."

The woman shaded her eyes with her hand and smiled up at me. "You're the judge, aren't you? Judge Mary? I'm Starla Jones. These are my kids. We've been going to Victory Baptist, that's how we heard about your Saturday picnic."

I knew every soul in that town, but I rarely encountered her. "Welcome, Starla. I'm happy y'all could come."

Her little boy bounced on my hip, chewing on his fist. I whispered to him, talking baby talk. Starla glanced at the child in my arms and said, "Nova, did the baby eat his cereal? I don't want him crying in an hour."

Nova scurried around, looking for the little boy's foam dish of oatmeal. I took it from her. Plopped myself down on the tattered sheet and balanced the baby in my lap.

The girl looked hesitant, like I might not be up to the task.

I said, "Nova, I had two little sisters. I used to feed Jordan oatmeal just like this. You sit down and eat. Do you have a plate?"

Nova shook her head and whispered, "I don't want any breakfast. Thank you, though."

Starla's voice rose. "All this food out here, and you didn't get nothing to eat? What's the matter with you?"

She answered in a voice even softer than before. "I don't feel good, Mama."

"You got nothing to feel bad about. I bring you to a judge's house, and she invited you to eat. Don't give me any attitude. Get you a plate."

"I said I'm not hungry." I could hear tears in the girl's voice.

"Nova, you fix your face right now."

Oh, Lord, I thought. *Here it comes.*

Scooting sideways, I put my back to them, gave the baby another spoonful of cereal and scraped the excess off his chin. Tried to pretend I couldn't hear Starla fussing with her daughter about breakfast.

But it was impossible to ignore. Nova whispered, "My stomach hurts. I need to go to the bathroom."

"Are you kidding me? You're thirteen years old. You know better. You're supposed to pee before you get on the church bus."

I had to intervene. "Y'all, it's fine. Nova, you go in the house through that screen door, and the bathroom's just beyond the kitchen."

Starla wanted to argue with me, but I was insistent. Nova sat unmoving on the ground, looking miserable.

That's where I was—sitting on the ground holding a baby—when a news van pulled into my yard. I watched the vehicle pull up within yards of my house.

"What the hell?" I said. I should've watched my language. One of Starla's children repeated it. I heard a child exclaim, "What the hell?"

CHAPTER 9

I sat there in the grass, slack-jawed, as a TV team emerged from the van. The camera crew spotted me. I saw one of them point me out to a reporter before the camera turned my way.

The reporter, a young white man, was easy to identify. He wore orange pancake makeup on his face and held a microphone as he approached the house.

I passed the baby off to Nova and scrambled to my feet. As I hurried across the yard, I called out to the young reporter.

"What's going on?" I demanded.

I could see that the camera was already taking footage, zooming in on the sunken faces of ragged men who sat on my front porch, accepting my charity. I saw one man bow his head in shame.

My temper flared. My sisters had stepped away from the food table to watch the TV team. When I caught Nellie's eye, her chin lifted in defiance. I marched up to her. "Now what the hell is this? Nellie! Is this your doing?"

She didn't deny it. "I'm trying to help you! I got a TV news team interested in doing a feature on Saturday breakfast. To help you out!"

"Don't help me. I don't want it."

"Why are you so stubborn? This is free advertising for your reelection campaign."

I strode right over to the camera team. The young reporter with the mic gave me a once-over as he stepped up to greet me. "Judge Stone, I'm Reese Wilson, with WYLR in Birmingham."

His starched white oxford shirt was tucked into pressed khaki pants. I resisted the urge to brush food splatters from my faded T-shirt. When I gave him a tight smile, my tone was all business. "Nice to meet you, Mr. Wilson. Y'all need to turn right back around. Put your equipment back in the truck. There's no story here today. Nothing to see."

The camera crew looked to the reporter for guidance. When Wilson spoke, his voice carried barely a hint of his regional Southern accent, but his native arrogance hadn't been erased.

He said, "Really? Nothing to see? Judge, it's right here in front of me, I can see it with my own two eyes. We were invited to do a feature on you. We drove two hours to get here."

I tried to keep it civil. Even though something in the young man's face as his eyes swept over my home triggered a defensive reaction in me. "Sorry for your inconvenience, Mr. Wilson. But I didn't invite you. And it's my private property."

The reporter flatly ignored me. He turned to his crew, gestured toward the house. "Set up down there, with the porch in the background."

This kid had picked the wrong woman to mess with. I was mad enough to spit.

"I'm not playing." My voice had a hard edge. "You are trespassing. I'm ordering you to leave."

"You're not serious," he said.

I shot a look at my breakfast guests, seated on the porch and scattered across the grass. Some of them watched the confrontation furtively, others had turned their heads away. I didn't blame them. I wished I could turn away from it.

I dropped my voice. "My guests deserve their privacy. I'm going to protect it. You understand me?"

He didn't bother to lower his voice. "You're a public figure, an elected official. As a journalist, I'm entitled, and obligated, to cover you. I also have a lot of influence over how you'll be perceived. You understand? I'm entitled to do this."

"Oh, I understand you, better than you might imagine. And one thing we agree on—you're entitled. You're an entitled little ass."

His eyes widened. I thought I heard the cameraman snicker. Maybe I imagined it.

I pulled my phone from my pocket. Held it up. "I've already informed you that you're trespassing. And I have the sheriff's department on speed dial. Sheriff Owens is a quick responder. He'll be out here in a flash." The sun was in my eyes. I squinted at him, to make sure my words hit home. "Want to see me in court on Monday morning?"

He hesitated. I gave him a moment to think it over. I would prevail, no doubt about that. The only question was how far the battle would go.

He exchanged a glance with the cameraman. I saw the reporter curl his lip. But he'd backed down. I could sense it.

I followed them back to the van and watched them load their equipment. I waited until they started the van up and put it in reverse. As they departed down the gravel drive, I waved at the van and called out, "Y'all drive safe!"

When the news van disappeared, I started picking up empty

plates and cups. It was time to wrap up the breakfast. If folks started leaving soon, I might have everything cleaned up around two in the afternoon.

Not trying to blow my horn. That's the way it's always been on our farm. Just a typical Saturday.

CHAPTER 10

Nova Jones

UNION SPRINGS, ALABAMA

Nova Jones ran down the cracked concrete steps and headed across a weedy strip of green yard. She'd barely made it to the sidewalk when the door to their apartment building flew open.

"Nova! Get back here!"

She turned, squinted up at the figure of her mama. Mama was standing in the doorway, frowning down on her, like Nova done something wrong.

Nova said, "You told me to go to the dollar store, Mama!"

"You get back here and take your brother. I can't have him underfoot."

Nova walked back up the steps, moving slow and dragging her feet. "He won't mind me, Mama."

"You make him mind. Caden, get over here! You're going with your sister!"

Mama opened the door, pulled Caden through the opening. Squatting on her haunches, she shook a finger in the toddler's face. "When you go in the store, you don't touch nothing. You hear me?"

Nova wanted to scream. She just couldn't do it. No way she could carry Caden all that way. She'd been cramping again, pain coming and going, and spotting blood. Dr. Bria said it might happen. Told her to come back to see her if it did. But how was Nova supposed to do that? How would she explain it to her mama?

"Mama!" Nova's voice rose to a whine. "I can't carry him. It's too far!"

"Take the wagon!"

Her mama pointed at an ancient toy wagon, its red body covered with a coat of rust. Nova sighed as she climbed back up the steps, picked up her brother, and carried him to the wagon.

"Don't you fall out," she said, giving him a glare.

Mama called from the door. "Don't be lazy, pick up your feet! I don't want to wait all day for you to get back here."

"Yes, ma'am."

"If they give you any trouble about using my EBT card, you ask for Sherree. She knows you're just helping me out."

Nova kept her mouth shut. It wasn't that easy, using Mama's card when she wasn't there to approve it. More than once, the women working at the store had refused, saying Nova wasn't authorized. And how could Nova argue with that? It was Mama's card, not hers.

No point in fighting about it with Mama. Nova had a better chance winning an argument with the cashier at Dollar General. Mama didn't put up with any back talk.

She picked up the handle, gave it a pull. Her baby brother had to grab both sides of the wagon to keep from spilling out. He didn't cry, though, didn't complain. He crowed with laughter, giggling like a crazy boy.

Nova smiled. It was hard to stay mad at Caden. Not his fault Mama was acting so cross.

Not Caden's fault that Nova was feeling bad, either. He was a sweet baby, a funny little guy. Nova loved babies. She hoped the Lord would understand that, when she stood before him on Judgment Day. God would know it wasn't all her fault. God saw everything, so he knew what got done to her.

Nova tugged on the wagon. She wasn't going to think about that. Going to push that memory clean out of her head.

She talked to Caden over her shoulder. "You want me to show you something pretty? Pretty trees and flowers?"

He let out a happy squeal. "Pretty!"

Her spirits lifted. She took a right at the intersection, taking the long way. So there'd be more to see.

An old run-down house up the block had the biggest lilac bush in town. The bush sat in full sun on the corner of the property, crowding the sidewalk. No telling how old it was. When they reached it, Nova stopped the wagon. Picked her brother up and propped him on her hip.

"See those purple flowers? That's old-fashion lilac. Old Missy Mabel, who used to live here, she told me so. And it smell sweeter than anything."

She pulled a branch toward them, tickled the boy's nose with a lilac bloom. "Smell it," she whispered.

He sniffed, then wrinkled his nose and rubbed it. Nova clicked her tongue, dropped him back in the wagon.

"Boys don't know nothing about perfume. Lilac is the sweetest thing there is."

As she pulled the wagon away, the boy made a grab for the bush.

"Mine!" he cried, indignant.

"No, Caden. That lilac ain't ours. We got to leave it alone. These flowers belong to somebody else. We just get to look."

She felt a sharp twinge of discomfort in her belly. It made her pause. Felt like the cramping that had started up yesterday, when she was at the big breakfast at Missy Mary's farm. Nova wondered whether something was bad wrong with her, maybe she should turn the wagon around and go home.

Then an image of her mother's face appeared in her head. She pulled the wagon onward.

Nova stepped onto the strip of green around a telephone pole. Plucked three plants and showed them to her brother.

"This is the plain old dandelion. Just a weed, folks say. But it's pretty, right?"

"Yellow."

"Yes! And it has a nice smell. You try it."

She let him hold the yellow head while she showed him another plant. "This is white clover. Grows all over, animals eat it. And I think it smells sweet, too. I'll make you a necklace sometime. Tie the stems together. And look at this."

She held up a three-leafed clover. Popped it into her mouth, chewed and swallowed.

"You can eat it! An old auntie at church told me. Clover is good for you. She said it cleans the blood."

Nova took the white clover and yellow dandelion back from the baby—because she knew that Caden would chew down on them, if he took the notion. "You can have all the dandelions and clover you want. They're wild, see?"

She picked up the handle, started pulling the wagon again. Noted the pink and white dogwoods, still in full bloom. *Cornus florida.*

Nova learned the fancy name for dogwoods when she looked it up on the computer at school. They'd always been her very favorite trees, as long as she could remember. Judge Mary had lots of dogwoods. It made Nova happy, knowing that they grew wild at Missy Mary's farm. If Nova could find a wild dogwood, she'd break off a blooming branch, put it in a jar of water by her bed. Her very own sprig of flowers and green leaves.

As she pulled the wagon along, the pain in her belly got worse. Like yesterday, but stronger this time. Felt like menstrual cramps. Bad ones.

She stopped, bent over, grabbed her knees for support. Caden started to fuss. Making loud noises that threatened to turn into full-out wailing.

Nova straightened up, walked over to a patch of clover. She picked a handful of white clover, tossed it in the wagon. "You can have all that. It's yours. When the weather gets hot and school is out, I'll take you to the railroad tracks. We'll pick pink coneflowers. They grow wild, all summer long. And black-eyed Susans, as many as we want. We'll fill this wagon with wildflowers. They don't belong to nobody, so they're for everybody."

The baby was distracted. He clapped his hands, picked up a clover and waved it.

Nova tried to carry on, pulling the wagon down the road. But she couldn't stand up straight. She was doubled over with the cramping pain.

When the blood stained her shorts, she didn't know what to do. She was in agony, couldn't go on to the store, didn't have the strength to go back.

She pulled the wagon off the road, into someone's yard. Got the baby out of the sun, under the shade of a tree. A dogwood tree.

She sat in the grass, panting. Tears started running down her face, she hurt so bad. Nova had to get home, some way. But she couldn't just lie there in the grass. Caden could crawl out of that wagon, get into the street.

Nova got on hands and knees, then got to her feet. Grabbed the handle of the wagon, then started walking. She stumbled down the sidewalk, bent over, pulling the wagon behind her.

Seemed like it took years before she made it back to her street and dragged the wagon up the walk. Nova sobbed as she clutched Caden's hands to tug him up the steps. Kept on putting one foot in front of another until she made it inside the front door of their apartment.

Caden toddled off, crying, "Mama!"

Nova dropped to the floor of the front room and curled up in a ball. Mama stepped out of the bedroom. The minute she saw Nova, Mama screeched like she saw a snake ready to strike.

"Nova! What you up to? Where's them things I told you to go get?"

Nova could barely whisper the answer. "I'm sick, Mama."

"Quit putting on a show. You just lazy! You not sick when you got up this morning. Now get up and go on back to the dollar store, like I told you."

Nova knew she couldn't do it. Couldn't stand up and walk, not even if someone set the house on fire. She closed her eyes, wailing with the pain.

Her little sister had crawled under the table. She called out to Mama. "Nova making the floor dirty, Mama. Making a big mess!"

The blood flow was heavy, making a big swipe of red on the floor. Dirty, like her sister said, but Nova couldn't clean it up. She clutched her belly while she moaned and cried.

All the noise made a neighbor come across the hall, to see about the commotion. Nova heard old Missy Potter squawk in the doorway. "Starla Jones! You got to call for help!"

"Mind your business! She just playing."

"That girl needs the doctor. Call 911!"

Nova didn't know how much time passed before she heard the siren out in the street. She was certain she was dying, waiting for either the angels or the devil to come. When two men came instead, and put her on a stretcher, she thought she was dreaming.

CHAPTER 11

Bria Gaines

UNION SPRINGS, ALABAMA

The flushed, feverish child tried to clamber off the examination table in Dr. Gaines's office. She caught him before he escaped.

"Arlene, you'll need to hold him while I get a look inside that ear."

The child's mother stepped up to the padded table and held him snugly against her chest. Bria was able to get a good look at the inflammation. The boy had another ear infection, his third in the past two months.

"You were right about the ear, Arlene. A lot of moms are excellent diagnosticians."

"Dr. Gaines, why does he keep getting these ear infections? Are the antibiotics not working?"

Bria was sidetracked before she could answer, distracted by

noise in the outer office. Raised voices were making a ruckus right outside her door. She heard her receptionist, Sonya, arguing with a man. He was demanding to see Bria immediately.

The office got noisy sometimes. People who were sick, or in pain, or advocating for loved ones, could become agitated. But this sounded different. Something about the exchange set off warning bells in Bria's head.

Made her stomach clench with dread.

Sonya commenced rapping at the door of the examination room. "Dr. Gaines!" she said. "Dr. Gaines, we have a problem."

Bria stepped away from the exam table, whispering an apology to the little boy's mother as she carefully set her otoscope on the instrument table. She held herself together, walking to the door with an appearance of equanimity.

When she opened it and saw the uniformed deputy standing close behind her frightened employee, Bria didn't let them see how shaken she was. She put on a brave face. Poised, professional.

Sonya sounded breathless when she said, "Dr. Gaines, I told the officer I'm not supposed to interrupt your appointments. Deputy Simmons said I had to."

The young deputy wasn't one of Bria's patients, but he was familiar. She had seen him around town. He was generally affable and courteous with her.

But not today. "Bria Gaines, I have a warrant for your arrest."

A pair of handcuffs dangled from his belt. Bria's eyes followed the movement as he unlocked the cuffs.

"Hands behind your back," he said. The deputy's manner was abrupt, rude. He'd never addressed Bria in that tone, ever.

He sounded like he was giving an order to a criminal.

The waiting room was crowded with people, patients with appointments on her busy afternoon schedule. They had watched the events unfold, shocked into silence. But as the deputy handcuffed Bria's wrists, they started to whisper among themselves. Some of the patients even ventured a protest.

An elderly woman Bria was treating for diabetes struggled to rise with the assistance of her walker. "What's happening here? Deputy Simmons! Where you taking my doctor?"

The deputy ignored the woman. He grasped Bria's arm and pulled her toward the door.

A shout of alarm followed, and a young mother holding an infant launched out of her seat in the waiting room. She rushed up behind them and snatched at the hem of Bria's white coat. "My baby's sick! Ran a fever all night! I don't know what he's got. What am I supposed to do?"

The deputy scowled down at the mother. "Are you trying to interfere with an arrest? You want to go to jail, too, Della?"

The woman let go of the coat and backed away. Clutching the baby tightly, she said, "But what do I do?"

"Take it to the ER," the deputy said.

The woman cried out in frustration. "Officer, that hospital gonna make me wait for hours until they look at him! Some days, the doctor ain't even there, or they want money up front. This baby sick. How am I supposed to take care of my baby?"

Bria knew that Della wasn't overstating the circumstances. The baby needed to be examined. Bria tried to reason with the officer. "Let me see the baby. Just for a minute, Deputy. I won't take long."

Deputy Simmons behaved as if he hadn't heard her speak. He pulled a sheet of paper from his pocket. "Bria Gaines, you're under arrest for the Class A felony of performing an abortion. A Class A felony carries a minimum sentence of ten years, a maximum imprisonment of ninety-nine years to life."

Bria was aware of the law. She'd read the penalty before, multiple times. Hearing the range of punishment stated aloud, though, gave it a different weight. It conjured up the image of that vast stretch of prison time, swallowing up the remaining years of her life.

The deputy pulled her into the vestibule and rapped on the glass of the front door. The sheriff of Bullock County, Mick Owens, was standing guard outside. He pulled the door open and stepped into the vestibule with them.

Owens glanced at Bria, checked to see that her handcuffs were secure. Then the sheriff said to the deputy, "Read her her rights yet?"

The deputy's face reddened under the brim of his hat. "I was about to, but some of the patients started getting disorderly."

Sheriff Owens cast a withering look at his deputy. Then he cleared his throat. "Bria Gaines, you have the right to remain silent. Anything you say will be used against you in a court of law. You have the right to have a lawyer present during questioning. If you can't afford a lawyer, one will be appointed for you."

When the sheriff recited the words of the Miranda warning, the language was a wake-up call, like someone had doused her with a glass of ice water.

"I have an attorney." Her throat was tight, but her speech was audible, perfectly clear.

The sheriff didn't acknowledge her announcement. He studied his own reflection in the glass door. He was a tall Black man, just over fifty, with an athletic build. He straightened his hat, adjusted his sunglasses, and then spoke to the deputy. "Let's go."

Deputy Simmons slipped through the door of the clinic and held it wide open. Bria saw people gathered outside, heard voices rise in a shout. But she persisted, saying to the sheriff, "I have an attorney. Chuck Rich, he has an office across the street from the courthouse. I want to contact him immediately. It's my constitutional right."

The sheriff grabbed her upper arm in a tight hold. "You don't sound like a doctor to me. More like a professional agitator, all that talk about lawyers and rights." He pulled her across the threshold.

One news van was parked outside her office, with a cameraman waiting to film the perp walk. But a handful of local people had also gathered, drawn by the patrol car. Handheld phones were raised in the air as Bria was marched to the waiting vehicle, with its light bar already flashing red and blue.

People are recording this, Bria thought. *Making a video. Of me, being walked to a police car in handcuffs.*

She hoped it wouldn't be seen by anyone she knew.

Bria didn't realize that the footage would be downloaded before she arrived at the sheriff's department. That thousands of views would be recorded before nightfall.

She just concentrated on walking, moving her feet down the pavement, step-by-step. Trying not to collapse in front of the camera.

A thought drummed in her head. *Can't be happening. It can't be happening. Not to me.*

But it was.

She felt the sheriff's hand cradle the back of her head before he shoved her into the back seat of the patrol car.

CHAPTER 12

Mary Stone

BULLOCK COUNTY COURTHOUSE
UNION SPRINGS, ALABAMA

I opened the file that had been placed squarely in the center of the bench. Looked down at the top sheet of paper and read the charge in the case of *State of Alabama v. Fergus Pitt.*

Fergus Pitt was on trial for committing the misdemeanor offense of posing a nuisance to public health by maintaining and using an unsanitary sewage collection and disposal facility on his property in Bullock County.

I sat back and gazed out over the courtroom. The DA and the defense attorney sat at their respective counsel tables. The accused, Fergus Pitt, sat at his lawyer's left hand. Fergus is a neighbor. He lives on a tiny farm not far from my own. But we didn't grow up together, not really. He is a half generation younger than I am.

I directed a question to both of the lawyers seated before me. "What's a misdemeanor jury trial doing in my court?"

I'm no snob, Lord knows. And I'm not a judicial officeholder who's all puffed up with her own importance. But I'm a circuit judge. I preside over circuit court and follow the judicial structure for criminal cases in Alabama state court. Felonies are tried in circuit court. Misdemeanors are tried in district court, by the district judge.

The DA rose halfway out of his seat. "Your Honor, the district judge is tied up in court over in Clayton this week. The parties — the prosecution and defense — agreed that you could preside over the case. Isn't that right, Chuck?"

Chuck Rich, the defense counsel, nodded. "Yes, Judge. My client—"

Reeves talked over him. "And you'd called up a jury panel for the week. You have the prospective jurors sitting inside the courthouse today. They're here. So you can't claim that it will inconvenience you."

There. That's what I've put up with for nigh on six years. A DA shouldn't be telling the judge whether she has been inconvenienced. It's a reversal of the power roles.

He went on. "And it's not like you're unqualified to hear a misdemeanor case. I know you don't generally hear misdemeanors, but this is a court of general jurisdiction. You may exercise jurisdiction over legal matters filed in district court."

Reeves liked to toss his opinions at the bench, just like that. Speaking with more arrogance than propriety required. Just a little too sure of himself, acting like his knowledge was broader than my own. I wasn't imagining the attitude. The DA was an ass.

Someday, he and I were going to throw down. And that particular morning was shaping up to supply the necessary push.

I was about to pop off. To kick the misdemeanor out of my court. Kick it so high it might fly all the way over to Barbour County in Clayton, Alabama, where they could take it up with the district judge. But before I opened my mouth, I caught a glimpse of the defendant, Fergus Pitt.

Pitt sat at the defense table, twisting an ink pen over and over in work-hardened hands. He looked nervous. And scared — scared to death, which you don't generally see in misdemeanor cases.

I glanced down at the charge a second time. Read it over again, from start to finish. Considered airing my opinion about the criminal allegation made by the State. Decided against it.

Instead, I smiled and said, "I see. All right, then. Gentlemen, if y'all have agreed to have me preside over this case, let's get started."

Ross Carr, my bailiff, stood at the back of the courtroom. I said, "Bailiff, bring the jury panel into court for voir dire. We'll start jury selection now."

We had the jury picked and seated before noon. After the parties made brief opening statements, we took a one-hour lunch break.

Back in court at 1 p.m., I told the DA to call his first witness. Reeves led with his expert, Marcus Lindsey. Lindsey had come from Montgomery to appear. He was a good witness, made an impressive appearance on the stand. Articulate but not stuffy. And it was clever of the white DA to use a Black engineer in his case against a Black defendant. Our jury was three-quarters Black, a pretty fair representation of the county's racial breakdown.

"And what is your occupation, Mr. Lindsey?"

"I'm an environmental engineer."

"What's your educational background?"

"I got my bachelor's degree at Tuskegee University. Then studied engineering at University of Alabama."

I didn't betray any reaction when the witness revealed he'd received his degree at the very same HBCU where I'd done my undergraduate studies. I was tempted to gaze at the jury box, see whether any of them were wrestling with the question that had occurred to me. How many of us were wondering why that engineer was testifying for the prosecution in this case?

The DA's voice oozed courtesy when he spoke to the witness. More courtesy than he'd ever shown to me. "Directing your attention to March 17 of this year, did you have occasion to be in Bullock County, Alabama?"

"I did travel to Bullock County, yes."

"For what reason?"

"To determine whether raw sewage was contaminating private property and threatening public health."

I sneaked a look at the defense table. The defense attorney was fidgeting in his chair. I tried to send him a mental message. *Get out of that chair! Stand up and fight!*

The attorney didn't pick up my vibes.

Meanwhile, the DA's direct examination continued. "Where did you go on that date?"

"To a rural property located a mile north of the city limits of Union Springs. The address was 37 Farm Road 164 in Bullock County, Alabama."

"Did anyone accompany you?"

"A sheriff's deputy. The sheriff's department had hired me to make the inspection."

What the hell? The sheriff had laid out funds from our impoverished county to pay for a private-sector engineer? What was Mick Owens thinking? It took tremendous fortitude to remain in my seat. Had to put my hands in my lap, out of sight. My clenched fists would give me away.

I stared at Chuck Rich again. Saw him sigh as he wrote something on his legal pad.

The DA edged over to the jury box as he asked the next question. "What did you observe on the property at the location, Mr. Lindsey?"

"There was a mobile home on the property, about fifty yards from the road. I observed a long white PVC pipe, running from the trailer to a trench in a pasture behind the home."

"What, if anything, did you observe in the trench?"

"It was filled with raw sewage from the trailer. The owner of the property was straight-piping his sewage to a hole in the nearby field."

"Objection, Your Honor!"

Finally. It had taken him long enough. The defense attorney was on his feet. "Grounds?" I said.

The defense attorney, Chuck Rich, was sweating. Perspiration trickled down his face, making dark spots on the collar of his blue shirt. "Judge, they can't do this. The DOJ put a stop to it when they were prosecuting people in Lowndes County."

The DA leveled a look at me. "This isn't Lowndes County. We're in Bullock County."

Rich gawked in disbelief before he turned back to me and said, "Judge, what he's trying to do is outrageous, this is an environmental equity issue!"

Reeves extended an arm to the jury, so they'd know he was addressing them. "I don't disagree with the last half of that statement. The environmental quality of this county is an important issue. And it's equitable and fair that we keep people in the county safe. I think that it's in the interest of every citizen of Bullock County that we eliminate these pools of raw sewage before they make everybody sick. Hope people in this jury haven't caught anything yet."

That statement caused an outcry and a flurry of rustling in the jury box, as jurors scooted in their seats to ensure they weren't in physical contact with anyone else.

A rivulet of sweat rolled down Chuck Rich's cheek. "Objection, Your Honor! The prosecution hasn't offered evidence of any disease!"

"Sustained," I said, adding, "The DA's statements are out of order. The jury is instructed to disregard his comments."

"I'll tie it up later, Judge." Reeves smirked at me.

Two reasons: He knew the jury couldn't disregard the suggestion of disease; it was too shocking. And he also knew he was right—and probably had evidence to back up the statement.

The pools of raw sewage that polluted nearly every county in the Black Belt of Alabama caused a host of infectious diseases. I'd read up on it, after I heard a DOJ presentation on the topic at a judges' conference. The guy from the DOJ said that we're not supposed to have hookworm disease in the United States anymore. He also said that almost one-third of people tested over in Lowndes County were positive for hookworm. It's found in underdeveloped countries that don't have indoor plumbing. Or toilets that flush away human waste. You catch hookworm through contact with the stool of an infected person, or infected soil.

The Black Belt of Alabama is my ancestral home. Fergus Pitt's land—his soil—was a stone's throw from my own.

My skin began to itch. I had to suppress the urge to reach under my robe and scratch.

CHAPTER 13

"No further questions," the DA said.

The defense attorney consulted with his client. Appeared to me that he was reassuring the man. Privately, I've always thought Chuck Rich's intentions were good.

It was the execution that was faulty.

Like, for example, his very first cross-examination question.

Rich rose and stepped toward the witness stand. "Mr. Lindsey, have you read the interim agreement that the Justice Department has reached with the Alabama Department of Public Health?"

"No."

Rich hesitated. As if he hadn't expected that answer and didn't know quite what to do next. "Well, are you familiar with it?"

The DA eased out of his chair and called out, "Objection, Your Honor, irrelevant."

I checked out the jury, wondering whether they were familiar with it and knew what the defense attorney was referring to. They needed to be aware. "Mr. Reeves, I think it's entirely relevant. Overruled."

The DA regarded me with hooded eyes. Like he didn't want to reveal his true assessment of me. "Judge, do I need to point out that neither the federal Justice Department nor the state Department of Public Health is a party to this lawsuit?"

I was running low on patience. "Counsel, approach the bench."

Both attorneys walked over to my right side, so that the jury wouldn't overhear. As soon as they stood before me, I snapped.

"Gentlemen, why is this federal civil rights matter being bandied about in state court?"

Reeves wore an innocent expression, phony as hell, as he said, "I'm just doing my job as prosecutor in this district, Judge."

Chuck Rich had a desperate tone. "Judge, I told the DA he couldn't proceed with this prosecution. This case violates the agreement that Public Health reached with the feds. The DA should never have filed this charge. The government is supposed to help people who are too poor to have sanitation systems."

I flipped through the file. "So where's your motion to dismiss, Mr. Rich? I don't find any pretrial motions from the defense. Not one."

"The DA told me not to file it! He said we'd resolve the issue at trial."

Lord have mercy. "Mr. Rich, do you think it's smart to take advice from the opposing party? Let's clear that up right now. It's not wise. He is your enemy."

Reeves was smirking, and that pushed me into the red zone. I had to act.

As a rule, I tried to remain in my seat during jury trials. Truly I did. But sometimes it just wasn't possible. I found myself rising, stepping down the stairs, with the black robe billowing behind me.

I approached the witness stand. "Mr. Lindsey, did you have any conversation with Fergus Pitt regarding the direct piping of sewage on his land?"

"I did."

"What did he tell you?"

"He said that a septic tank had been installed on the property at one time. But the system failed. That's when he installed the straight-piping system."

"In your experience, have septic tank systems been known to fail in this region of Alabama?"

The engineer glanced at the DA. I caught him at it. I pressed closer to the witness stand. "Answer the question, Mr. Lindsey."

He shrugged. He knew the jig was up. "Yes, they often fail."

"It's because of our soil, isn't it, Mr. Lindsey?"

I'd switched on the lightbulb. The jury knew what I was talking about. Half of them were nodding.

The engineer said, "The soil in the Black Belt region of Alabama—soil that gave the region its name, because the rich, black soil was great for growing cotton. Unfortunately, the dense, claylike soil isn't conducive to septic systems."

"What would a septic tank cost that would withstand the soil we have here?"

He stopped to think. Looked off in the distance, calculating a figure. "Three times as much as an ordinary system."

The witness was telling the truth about that. I'd had the system on my farm replaced a few years back.

"In your experience, the people in the Black Belt who are living without basic sanitation systems—is it because they prefer to be exposed to raw sewage?"

He was quiet for a moment. Maybe I'd shamed him. "No, Your Honor."

"In your opinion, why have these residents failed to install sanitary systems?"

He shifted uncomfortably in the chair. Maybe he was coming around. "Because they can't afford the cost."

"Yes," I said, placing my hand on my chest and taking a deep breath. We'd solved the puzzle. "They can't afford to pay for it, because if they could, they would."

I was on a roll, all fired up. "Anyone who's lived with these conditions—or had family exposed, had an auntie living in a home where the system failed—knows what we're talking about. Human waste bubbling up in the sink and into the bathtub when the heavy rains come. Kids can't play out in the backyard, because the dirt will make them sick. And the smell!"

I was dizzy, just remembering. When I was a child, our septic tank failed. It happened in a bad year, when crops were poor, and we were poorer. The backup got so bad, we couldn't use indoor plumbing. Had to use the ancient outhouse on the farm. Mama said we were lucky to have it.

The DA was sitting at his counsel table, disgruntled with me for taking over his witness. I figured I had uncovered the necessary information. So I climbed back up to my seat. Nodded at the defense attorney. Frankly, he appeared to be somewhat confused.

"Mr. Rich, you may continue cross-examination of the State's witness."

Chuck Rich whispered to his client. Fergus Pitt shook his head. Rich said, "No more questions, Your Honor."

The State wrapped its case up pretty fast after that. And Chuck Rich put the defendant on to testify on his own behalf. Fergus did a good job of explaining how the system broke down over time. Described his efforts to seek repairs. He'd installed the straight-piping as a last resort, a Band-Aid while he tried to save up money to buy a new system, one that would work in Black Belt soil. But saving up thirty thousand dollars was an impossible task for a man whose annual income was around twenty-seven thousand dollars.

"The defense rests," Chuck Rich said.

"Any rebuttal witnesses for the prosecution?"

"No, Your Honor." Reeves's voice was icy.

I shifted in my seat, leaned on my elbow to glare down at the defense attorney. "Does the defense have any motions?"

He was quiet—it worried me for a minute. Then Rich stood up and said, "The defense moves for a judgment of acquittal."

I waved the attorneys up to the bench. "Please approach." We'd need to argue the matter outside the hearing of the jury.

We waited for the court reporter to join us, so the discussion would be on the record. As soon as she was settled, the DA said, "I haven't received a copy of any motion for judgment of acquittal."

"Not required," I said. "The motion under Alabama Criminal Rule 20 can be made orally or in writing." I focused on Chuck Rich. "Mr. Rich, what are the grounds for your motion?"

His brow wrinkled. After a brief pause, he said, "The evidence that the DA presented isn't sufficient to support a finding of guilt beyond a reasonable doubt."

Those were the magic words.

I said, "Defendant's motion is sustained. The State's evidence was insufficient to support a conviction. We will dispense with closing arguments. I'm not submitting the case to the jury. I hereby find the defendant not guilty."

I swiveled the chair to face the jury. "Ladies and gentlemen, I want to thank you for your time and attention today. It will not be necessary for you to retire to the jury room for deliberation."

I'd hoped to get the jury free before the DA came out swinging. Wasn't going to happen.

Reeves barely made it back to the counsel table before he got mouthy. "I object! What's going on here? I have the right to a jury verdict!"

He most certainly did not. Furthermore, Reeves knew better. Under the Rules of Criminal Procedure, I had the power to throw the case out with a judgment of acquittal before it reached the jury. "Mr. Reeves, don't be ridiculous."

"I made a submissible case." He actually pounded on the wooden counsel table with his fist. "I provided evidence from an independent third party licensed in Alabama. The engineer's testimony proved up the allegations of the criminal complaint."

I frowned down on him from my seat at the bench. "Where was the proof of criminal intent? You should be thanking me, Mr. DA. The State of Alabama got their butt kicked by the DOJ for doing exactly what you're trying to do. And you think you have the power to defy the United States Justice Department, with an action down here at the county level? You're familiar with the Supremacy Clause, right? I just saved you from some excruciating embarrassment."

"Yeah, here we go. Because it's always about you, isn't it, Judge Stone?" Reeves was pale as death. I recognized his expression; it was one he'd displayed from time to time over the years. I anticipated that he would launch an attack on me without weighing the consequences.

He went on. "Every case has to be decided on the basis of your life, your personal history, the way it makes you feel. And you just take over the courtroom. You're the defense attorney, the judge, and the jury, right? Well, I'm still the prosecutor in this district, and I'm sick of this game."

I was shaking with anger. I had to tuck my hands inside the sleeves of my robe so that he wouldn't see it. "One more word, Mr. Reeves. Just one more word. And I'll hold you in contempt."

I settled back in my seat, waiting to see which way it would go. He wanted to back-talk me, that was obvious. Reeves struggled to swallow it. Looked like he was going to lose the battle.

I gave him some incentive. Said to the bailiff, "Ross, when I say the word, you'll escort Mr. Reeves to the county jail."

That extinguished the DA's fire. Reeves dropped back into his chair. He kept his mouth shut while I dismissed the jury. But I could feel the heat of his fury as I left the bench and went into chambers.

CHAPTER 14

That raw sewage misdemeanor flat wore me out. My mind was troubled. Though I had saved Fergus Pitt from criminal consequences, the inequity of this situation hadn't changed. That trench of raw sewage still sat in his pasture. It was a weighty problem—one I couldn't solve.

I trudged into chambers, wrestling with the zipper on my robe. Needed to get the heavy garment off my shoulders.

My clerk followed me into chambers. Luna said, "Judge, something's happened. You need to know about it."

The zipper had caught in the fabric of the seam. I tugged at it but couldn't work it free. "Damn! I'm stuck."

Luna stepped up, nimbly fixed the zipper without ripping a hole in the robe—which I was likely to do. I'd torn it before, in a fit of impatience.

"Luna, thank you—you saved me again. Is there anything you can't do?" I shrugged off the robe and hung it on the coatrack that stood in the corner.

When I turned back around, I was shocked to see that her mouth was trembling. She looked like she was about to cry.

"Luna, what's the matter? Is it your daddy?"

Her father was battling lymphoma, and his condition was grave.

She shook her head. "Something terrible has happened to our doctor."

Luna croaked the words out in a whisper. I didn't follow her meaning, didn't know who she was referring to, until she added, "She's been arrested."

Well. That cleared it up. Union Springs had only one female doctor. Bria Gaines, who ran a family clinic.

"What on earth?" I asked. I didn't know the woman well. She was new to town, much younger than I was. And I wasn't her patient. But it was a shock, nonetheless. I would've bet cash money on Bria Gaines being an upstanding, law-abiding citizen. "What did she do? Run a stop sign?"

"Abortion," Luna whispered. "She performed an abortion."

The pronouncement was shocking. It took me a moment to absorb it. I assumed the abortion had been performed in Bullock County, which meant that I would be presiding over the highly controversial criminal case.

I was still getting my head around it when the DA strolled into my chambers. Which never happens. We don't hang out under the best of circumstances. And that day had been a stormy one. Reeves and I had just knuckled up and started swinging in court, not ten minutes prior.

But there he stood. Right in front of my desk. He smiled at me, showing a mouthful of teeth. "Have you heard the news?"

Sniffling, Luna turned on her heel and left the office. Reeves and I were alone. I eyed him with some trepidation. Wondered what he wanted. And how long he'd linger.

Reeves gestured at one of the chairs facing my desk. "May I?"

I thought about discouraging him. Telling him I was running late for an appointment, that I had to leave. But it's important to keep your enemies close. I needed to learn what the purpose of the visit might be.

"Sure. Have a seat." I sat in my own chair, pushing my knees squarely under the desk and folding my hands on the leather desk pad. Didn't want to look relaxed or chummy. We weren't pals.

But the DA demonstrated an amazing change in his mood since we'd left court. He was chatty, even garrulous. "You know this Bria Gaines, right? She bounced into town two years ago and set up a clinic on Blackmon Avenue. Just a couple blocks over. Have you been in there?"

I had my guard up. "Well, I'm not her patient. So, no."

"Me neither, no way. I have an internist in Montgomery—excellent doctor, by the way, in case you're looking. I'd be glad to give you his contact info."

"Thanks. But it's not necessary." I didn't take my eyes off him. It was almost as if I feared he'd make a sinister move if I glanced away.

"Yeah, I don't know her personally. Just what I read in the probable cause statement attached to the arrest warrant. But it's shocking, I guarantee you. The girl she performed the abortion on? Thirteen years old."

The information made my stomach hurt. I took deep breaths, trying to gain control over my emotional reaction. I didn't ask for more details, but the DA wouldn't shut up.

"The PC statement said the abortion was performed in Gaines's clinic. She did it in the middle of the night. And the girl's mother wasn't there. Get this—the mother didn't even know she was pregnant! Nobody thought the mother of a thirteen-year-old girl was entitled to know? Have you ever heard anything like it?"

I asked a question. Maybe I shouldn't have. "How did they find out about it? Did the girl tell somebody?"

"She got sick! Just last weekend, started bleeding, hemorrhaging all over the floor. Cramps so bad she thought she was dying. The mother got scared, called 911, and the sheriff's department came and took her to the nearest ER. The ER nurses thought she was having a miscarriage."

So sad. Such an old story. My eyes started to burn. I sat up straight. I wouldn't reveal my weakness to Reeves.

"Did the girl tell them? At the ER?"

He slid down in the chair like he was getting comfortable. Crossed his legs. "Yeah. She got scared. Fessed up. Said Dr. Bria Gaines did it. Then the mother pitched a fit. Can't really blame her for that. Can you?"

I had my armor on at that point. "I don't think we can discuss this any further, Mr. Reeves. You know why."

He knew. I'd be presiding over the case. He was trying to coerce me into revealing my personal judgment.

"Sorry, Judge. I didn't mean to overstep. I should think before I speak, isn't that right? You know that I forget that sometimes." He grinned at me, showing those teeth again.

He looked down at his sleeve and picked at an invisible thread. Like he was about to say something of no significance. "I mean, you probably know the Jones family. It's Nova Jones who had the abortion. She goes to your church, right?"

Oh, there it was. Finally, I could see it clearly. I said, "I don't go to church."

"Is it your sisters', then? Are they members at Victory Baptist? I've heard about that tradition of yours, fixing breakfast for poor people every Saturday. I figured you were doing it because you were part of the church. Shoot, I guess you could be putting on a feed to get votes."

Son of a bitch. I didn't say it out loud. Instead, I pushed my chair back from the desk and rose. "I have an appointment."

It was a lie. Maybe he guessed, because he made no move to depart. He shifted in his seat but didn't stand. "Nova Jones has been seen at your house. In your own front yard, for that potluck breakfast. So if she's been a guest at your house, well, that creates a conflict. Your acquaintance with the witnesses creates bias. It will render you unable to preside over the trial. Surely you can see that. It's a different issue from the sentencing in the murder case, where Ferrell Gray wrote you a threatening letter."

I stared him down. "There are no conflicts that amount to a damn, and you know it. A State's witness ate oatmeal on my lawn. That's the basis of your claim? Most of the town has breakfasted there, one time or another. I can be fair and impartial. It's my job."

I stepped away from the desk. Picked up my red briefcase. "I'll walk you out of my chambers now, because I have to go. But I'm not walking away from this case. After six years, you should know that."

He lurched out of the chair, as if my words had thrown him off balance. "You're running for office this year. You've got a strong opponent. That man is going to put up a hell of a race for your seat in the general election. You know how much money he's raised?"

I knew. He could outspend me by a wide margin. My support came from a different demographic than his.

Reeves followed me into the hallway. "I tried to provide you with an out. This case will bury you. And that will be all your fault. You just remember that."

I was so eager to get away from Reeves that I slipped on the stairs, barely stopped from plunging headfirst down that long, curved stairway.

My story could have ended right there.

Some people probably wish that it had.

CHAPTER 15

I didn't break my neck on the staircase, not that day. And I managed to lose the DA when he paused on the stairway to speak to a local lawyer. At the bottom of the stairs, I made a dash down the central lobby and pushed through the back door. Straight to the parking lot.

I had my key fob in hand, my car unlocked. Pulled the driver's door open just as an older-model SUV with a rattle in the engine roared into the lot, blocking me.

Nellie. My sister rolled down the car window. "Get in," she said.

Nellie is not the boss of me. I'm the firstborn child, the one who had to babysit two little sisters so Mama could work the farm. But the expression she wore that day made me climb into the passenger seat without argument.

"Where we going?" I asked.

"For a drive. Maybe get a Coke at the McDonald's."

She gripped the wheel so hard that I could see the tendons stand out on her hands. Her voice was grim. "The sheriff came to school today. Mick Owens waltzed into the office like he owns the building. Didn't even take off his shades."

I've known Mick Owens since high school. He was my date to senior prom, in fact.

Mick drove us to the gym in his daddy's pickup. Mama sewed my prom dress herself. We cut out early from the dance, for the usual teenage reasons, and went to the local make-out spot by the river, where we engaged in what the health teacher would have described as "heavy petting."

Back at school on Monday, Mick implied to everybody that we'd done a lot more. He was generally believed. I'm still pissed off about that. Maybe I'll get over it after another thirty-four years.

The image of the sheriff shaking up the school troubled me. "He's pulling Nova Jones out of class, in front of her peers? That's a clumsy way to investigate. Seems like he'd want to approach her at home, to respect her privacy. He needs to be careful with a child witness."

"Not Nova. He came for the school nurse. Cocheta Bass. You know her?"

Sure, I knew everybody. In a town of three thousand, you do. "Our paths cross. At the Piggly Wiggly or the Dollar General."

"He took her out of the building in handcuffs. She was crying, begging the office to call her son, let him know what's happening."

I was speechless. What the hell kind of role did the school nurse play in the scenario? The case was becoming more outlandish with each additional detail.

Nellie pulled up to the speaker in the McDonald's drive-through lane and ordered a large Diet Coke. Glanced my way. "You want something?"

I shook my head. We didn't speak again until Nellie had her drink in hand and rolled the window up.

"I guess everyone at school is freaking out," I said.

She took a pull on the straw before she set her drink in the cupholder. "It's wild. They're already picking sides."

"What?"

"Dividing into camps. For and against." Nellie took her eyes off the road to give me a look. "Sure, there's some people who are loyal to Cocheta and Dr. Gaines. But there's other people saying they committed cold-blooded murder. That they killed a baby. A baby in the womb of a girl too young to know her own mind. A lot of people are saying it."

"Damn." My throat had gone dry. Wished I had ordered a big Diet Coke. I needed that cold carbonation to burn the ache away.

Nellie's voice was flat. "You're gonna have to pass on this one, Mary."

"Oh, stop." I picked up her drink. Lifted the lid and took a gulp from the side of the cup. Made me feel better, to tell the truth.

She grabbed the cup away from me, just like we were squabbling kids again. "Damn it, Mary! Why didn't you order one for yourself? I don't want your germs."

"You never did like to share, Nellie."

She scoffed at me. "Mary, you listen to me. I'm serious. Let some other judge handle this. Someone who doesn't live right here in Bullock County. We're going to see people all eaten up by this case, totally obsessed. The crazies will come out. Mark my words, Mary. This case will destroy you."

"You're being dramatic." I turned away from her, looked out the window at the buildings as we passed. Our town was dwindling. People kept moving out, businesses shut down. But we still had a church on every street corner.

Nellie raised her voice, determined to be heard. "This is a losing proposition. Call it abortion, pro-life, pro-choice, women's reproductive health. Doesn't matter how you label it, there is no middle ground. None. Not here in Alabama. The issue fires people up, makes them unhinged. Whatever the outcome in that criminal case, a whole lot of people will be mad. You know who they're gonna blame?"

Silence in the car. It wasn't until she elbowed me that I realized. She expected an answer.

"Yeah, I know."

"Good. You tell me. Who are they going to blame? Who will people be mad at?"

I sighed. She was right on that one. "The judge."

She repeated it. "The judge! That's what I'm saying!"

She picked up her big cup of Diet Coke again. Our eyes met while she drank more down. I was shocked to see tears welling up in her eyes.

Quickly, I reassured her. "Nellie, I hear you. Consider your words marked."

A tear ran down her face, and she wiped her nose. Her voice shook as she said, "I'm scared for you, Mary. I keep thinking about what happened to Daddy that time. You know what I'm talking about."

My chest tightened. I did know what Nellie meant. And I didn't like being reminded. Nellie and I had been grade-school age, Jordan wasn't born yet. We'd been driving to Birmingham when our car was pulled over and Daddy had to get out of the car. The deputy didn't like it when Daddy argued and insisted he hadn't been driving too fast, hadn't veered out of his lane. I won't ever forget the sight of Daddy's head getting split open while Nellie and I screamed and cried in the back seat. Mama was scared for us, said we had to quit making so much noise. She crawled halfway over the seat, trying to cover our mouths with her hands while the deputy beat my daddy by the side of the road.

But that was almost half a century ago. Times had changed since then. I squeezed Nellie's shoulder. "Don't be upset, Nellie. It's going to be okay."

She whispered, "I hope you're right. Because I've got this bad feeling. Like everything is about to change."

I wished she hadn't confided that. I was starting to get that feeling, too.

CHAPTER 16

We had a homegrown scandal. After that day, people in Union Springs couldn't stop talking about it. Bria Gaines; Nova Jones; the abortion; the arrest. Everyone breathless with anticipation to see what might happen next.

I tried my best to bow out of those conversations, truly I did. Damn near impossible. There was no place to hide. The criminal case against Dr. Gaines was top of mind in every corner of the community.

On Friday, I had a reprieve written into my schedule, and I was looking forward to it. I had plans to get out of town, out of the county. I'd be driving my car up highway AL-110 to I-85, because I had a standing appointment with an old friend. Twice a month, we met up at the Oyster House in downtown Montgomery.

To be honest, I was tempted to duck out early that day. The clock moved so slowly after lunch, I was wild to cut out at three.

I held off. Didn't let myself slack. Maybe that was the wrong choice.

Because at five past three, Reverend Curtis Erskine strolled into the front office. I heard him say to Luna, "If Judge Stone's in, I'd like to speak with her."

Luna ushered him right through my door. She should've checked with me first, to get a green light. Must've slipped right out of her head. She assumed that the standard rules didn't apply to Erskine. He's got that old magic, like my sister said. Works on all women—with the possible exception of his wife.

I rose from my seat and extended my hand across the desk. "Reverend! What business are you doing at the courthouse this afternoon?"

Frankly, I was curious to see whether he'd tell a lie. Nothing happens at the Bullock County Courthouse on Friday afternoons. Same could be said of most any courthouse, anywhere, for that matter.

He smiled, grasping my hand in a warm grip. "No business. Just wanted to talk with you, Judge, if you're not tied up."

So he wasn't a liar. But he was crafty. He'd handpicked the time, knowing I'd be free.

Luna shut the door, closing me in with the preacher. I stared at the landline phone on my desk, half inclined to pick it up and tell Luna to keep the door cracked open. But I couldn't think of a rational justification. I certainly didn't believe the preacher was bent upon inflicting physical harassment. He hadn't come to my chambers to throw a punch, or to steal a kiss.

As he sat across from me, I stared him down, wondering, *Just what does he intend to accomplish?*

He didn't make me wait. "Judge Mary, you won't be surprised to learn that I've heard about the abortion case. It's weighing on me. A heavy burden." He paused. When I didn't speak, he sighed and said, "You know I'm Nova Jones's pastor. I'm ministering to the whole Jones family. And Bria Gaines has also attended my church from time to time."

I cleared my throat. "I really can't talk about this, you understand."

"I do! I do understand, Judge. I'm not here to force any confessions or guarantees out of you. Just here in my capacity as a man of God."

The audacity of that man shouldn't have surprised me. I cut him off. "You wanting to pray over me, Reverend? I'd rather skip that. Not comfortable with it in this setting."

"Hear me out, Judge. I want to counsel you. To tell you this." He made eye contact, held it. "Do the right thing or don't do it at all."

"What did you say to me?"

"You know exactly what I'm saying. What the right thing to do would be. If you can't do that, well, don't do it at all."

Anger surged, making sparks blur my vision. "You got a lot of nerve, Reverend. Trying to influence a judge."

He raised both hands in a defensive gesture, like he was saying *Don't shoot!* "Don't take it wrong."

"How am I supposed to take it?"

"Judge, I'm a pastor, it's my job to advise people."

A pulse was beating in my head. I had to work hard to hold on to my temper. "Well, here's some advice for you. You want to be a preacher, stay out of politics."

"I'm not talking about politics."

"The hell you say."

His eyes widened. Probably because he wasn't used to people cussing around him. He dropped his voice. "I'm talking about God's word. The Sixth Commandment. 'Thou shalt not kill.'"

"And I'm talking about your nonprofit status. Your church doesn't pay taxes."

It startled him. I could see it in his face. I drove the point home.

"Getting involved in political matters can threaten your tax-exempt status. You know the IRS rules. 501(c)(3). You want to use your position and pulpit to play with politics, your church can start paying taxes, just like the rest of us."

He scowled at me. I could see he wasn't ready to quit.

So I finished it for him. Stood up, grabbed my bag, walked to the door and pulled it open. "I have someplace I need to be. Let's put a stop to this conversation before you go too far, Reverend."

He was fuming as he launched out of the chair and left my chambers. But he didn't say another word. I watched him go. After the door slammed shut behind him, Luna turned to me with her eyes wide. "Are you all right?"

"I'm fine," I said. My tone was brusque. I eased off; none of this was Luna's fault. "We're getting out of here, Luna. Taking off early. I have to get out of this town."

CHAPTER 17

MONTGOMERY, ALABAMA

A couple of hours later, I was in Montgomery. Sitting in a waterfront restaurant that looked out on the Alabama River. I studied the menu like I'd never seen it before.

After carefully reviewing the list of dinner entrées, I looked up at the waitress and said, "I believe I'll have the low country boil."

My dinner companion, Loucilla Payne, scoffed and said, "That's a shocker."

She was just trying to devil me. I ignored it and smiled politely at the waitress, as if Loucilla hadn't spoken a word.

Loucilla crossed her arms and leaned on the table. She gave the young waitress a confiding look over her round-framed eyeglasses. "Save yourself a trip. She'll want extra red cocktail sauce for her shrimp. And double butter for her corn and potatoes."

Loucilla held up the bottle of Crystal Hot Sauce they'd set with the salt and pepper shakers. "Can you bring a fresh bottle? This one's all used up."

I let the waitress walk away before I said, "Just because you're my best friend doesn't mean you can order my food."

She laughed at me. "We've been meeting up twice a month for years. You pick the same restaurant every time. And you always order the same damn thing. You're entirely predictable."

It wasn't surprising that Loucilla Payne could anticipate my selection from the menu at the Oyster House in downtown Montgomery. We went way back. We'd had each other's back since we were undergrads at Tuskegee University.

And now, thirty years later, Loucilla was a tenured professor of political science at the University of Alabama at Birmingham. I said, "Whatchu got good? Anything happening this week?"

"Mary, please." She gave me that no-bullshit glare over the glasses. "I lectured about global politics, attended faculty meetings, graded papers. Meanwhile, you were *in* the papers, first with the murder sentencing, then that criminal case against the man piping raw sewage. And then Bullock County topped that, made the national news—never thought I'd see that day. Tell me about it."

I took a swallow of lemonade. Loucilla had a frosty glass filled with lager beer, which I'd have preferred. But a woman who's running for reelection as circuit judge has no business trifling with alcohol when getting behind the wheel.

Loucilla was impatient. "Come on! Quit dragging your feet. I want to hear about that thirteen-year-old girl, and the poor doctor they're determined to crucify."

I'd tried to avoid the topic all week. But I couldn't dodge it with Loucilla. She was my confidant, the one person with whom I could unburden myself and be vulnerable.

I dropped my voice. "She'll be arraigned in circuit court next week. It's on my Tuesday docket. But you know nothing happens at arraignment. I just read the charge to her. Her lawyer will enter a plea of not guilty and that's it. Simple. Nothing much to it. So maybe we won't attract too much media attention."

"You kidding me? *Really?* It's the biggest case in the country. Media's going to be on it like flies on shit. And you're right in the middle of the controversy. You watch your back, Mary."

"I think you're being dramatic."

When she rolled her eyes, I doubled down, saying, "I know it's a high-profile case, no question about that. But you're exaggerating my importance. The case isn't about me. I'm just the judge. The arbiter up behind the bench. Nobody pays attention to the judge in these sensational cases."

Loucilla gave me a dark look. Shaking her head at me, she said, "Are you just lying to me? Or actually deceiving yourself, too? You can't honestly believe what you're saying here. Remember that judge in Las Vegas who got knocked flat when a defendant leaped over the bench like Superman?"

I did remember that. At the time, I had to make myself stop playing that clip over and over on social media. But Union Springs wasn't Vegas. "The defendant in this case will not fly over the bench to attack me. I guarantee it."

"It's not her I'm worried about." She was getting worked up, starting to raise her voice. "It's a miracle you haven't been assaulted already, the way you sashay around the courtroom in that black robe. Like a bullfighter waving a red cape."

"Oh, stop. And for God's sake, lower your voice. You'll get us thrown out."

"You stop. I'm serious." She was giving me a searching look. "There's a lot of talk on campus. They're already organizing. Students are planning to head to Bullock County when it goes to court, to protest."

I tried to envision it. Protesters on both sides of the issue, clashing in the street in front of the courthouse. The sheriff might want to get involved, and the result could get ugly.

I reached for her beer and took a sip from the bottle. When she saw me steal a swallow, Loucilla squawked. "Get your own bottle! You're a grown woman, why you always do that?"

I didn't try to explain my actions. Loucilla knew I grew up with two little sisters. I didn't get to have a Coke all to myself until I went away to college. "It will be a long time before the case goes to trial. College students will have a new cause célèbre by then."

"You can't seriously believe that."

I didn't, not really. But I wasn't disposed to admit it, even to my best friend.

I said, "Well. If people want to voice their opinions on the public sidewalk, that's their right." The waitress walked up, bearing a tray. My dinner was a steaming dish of shrimp and Andouille smoked pork sausage with red potatoes and corn on the cob. I was glad to see generous helpings of butter and red sauce. And the waitress set a brand-new bottle of hot sauce on the table.

Loucilla cut into her steak but wouldn't back off. "What you're going to face won't be a friendly debate, a simple difference of opinion. People are not going to be civil, Mary. Is the county prepared? You need security."

"Loucilla, it's a courthouse. I have a bailiff. We're protected by the sheriff's department."

She snorted at that. "Jesus, Mary. Anybody can bypass security at the Bullock County Courthouse, it's so full of holes. They barely monitor the metal detector at the front door. And the back door—they still keeping it propped open?"

They were, but I was too ashamed to admit it. The employees wanted a shortcut from the parking lot for their breaks. That would have to change. There was an elementary school behind the courthouse. If hell ever broke loose, those kids could be in danger. I needed to talk to the County Commission.

Loucilla tipped back her beer. When she set it down, I was ready to change the subject. Thought we could talk about her life for a bit, rather than mine. I said, "So tell me about your ex. Has she recovered from her broken heart? Or is she still calling in the middle of the night?"

"You think you can distract me that easily? I'm not done with you yet."

I considered a restroom run, just to create a break in the conversation. "I don't want to talk about it anymore."

"You think you can avoid this topic?" My friend laughed in my face, didn't try to hide it. "You're sitting on the biggest case Alabama's ever seen. This could be the most significant court decision on individual rights and science since the Scopes Monkey Trial in Tennessee in the 1920s."

For the moment, I was speechless. The parallel was daunting. Was I ready to rise to the challenge?

Loucilla wasn't put off by my silence. "Of course you can't go into specifics. You have an ethical obligation. But just let me say this." She pierced me with a look through her eyeglasses. "You can make history. *Do the right thing.*"

My shoulders sagged. Within the space of a couple of hours, I'd been instructed to do the right thing by two people with opposing views who devoutly believed they were on the ethical and decent side of the issue.

I lifted the ear of corn from my dish and bit into it, hoping to silence the discussion. But my friend kept talking. "But maybe it's too much, more than you signed on for. You know, Mary, that's okay. You know you can dodge it altogether. Make it someone else's problem. You could drop out of the judge's race right now."

I dropped the corn onto my plate. Couldn't protest, because my mouth was full.

She said, "If you withdraw from the election, you know what would happen? Your term ends, new judge gets elected and takes your place. Someone else, some other judge, would try that criminal abortion case. It doesn't have to be you. Girl, you could let that cup pass."

I just shook my head, wondering, *How many times will I be advised to step away from the Bria Gaines case?*

Loucilla was trifling with me, willfully misunderstanding my situation. She couldn't have been serious when she suggested that I drop out of the judge's race. I had an obligation to the citizens of Bullock County. I'd sworn an oath to faithfully discharge my duties as judge of my Alabama circuit. I took that responsibility seriously. It was sacred to me. Who would take care of the people of Union Springs if I just dropped out?

When I could speak, I said, "I never quit anything in my whole damn life."

She hid a smile. "Hmmm. I guess that's true."

Our dinner talk was subdued afterward, even stilted. We split the bill, as was our custom. I was afraid my reticence had erected a wall between us, but as we walked out of the restaurant, she linked her arm through mine.

When we paused on the sidewalk, I saw the figure in his hiding place. A man standing deep in the shadows across the street had his phone pointed directly at the two of us—certainly appeared to be taking photos. I nudged Loucilla.

She dropped my arm. Squinted through her round glasses, took a step toward the curb. "Hey!" she called out.

The guy darted away, disappearing into an alleyway. Loucilla turned toward me, wearing an expression that said *What the hell?*

"Was that my imagination?" she asked.

It wasn't. But I couldn't explain it. "Looked like he was taking our picture."

"Damn, Mary. It's starting. Paparazzi are already chasing after you."

"Nobody's chasing after me. Must be a mistake." I was serious. In my years as a lawyer and a judge, no one had ever snapped a picture of me outside the courthouse. "I don't think he wanted my picture. Maybe they mixed us up with somebody else."

"No, ma'am. You're an influencer, an overnight sensation. You'll have to get used to the attention." She teased me about it as we walked to the parking garage. "You're going to need to buy some new clothes, Mary. Something with style, clothes that make a statement. You have to be camera-ready."

I laughed along with her.

When we fell silent, an uneasiness, even tension, arose. We both carried that constant sense of watchfulness, the notion that things could go bad at any time.

All the way home, I caught myself looking in the rearview mirror. Like I thought someone might be following me.

CHAPTER 18

Tuesday morning, nine o'clock.

It was time to go to court.

But before I left chambers, I checked my reflection in the mirror hanging on the back of the door. And decided that my bright yellow scarf didn't strike the right note. Too cheery, I thought. Quickly, I unknotted it and tossed the scarf on my desk.

I pushed the door open. My bailiff was already on his feet. Ross Carr called out, "All rise!"

I heard rustling sounds and muted voices as I ascended the steps. But I didn't look out at the courtroom until I sat behind the bench. *Good Lord.* Without question, we'd set a new record for attendance. My spacious courtroom—which was huge by modern standards—was beyond capacity, standing room only.

I scanned the crowd. Some faces were familiar to me. But most weren't. Highly unusual occurrence, for me to look out at my Bullock County courtroom and see the old wooden benches filled with people who were strangers to me. Well, I shouldn't have been surprised. As predicted, we had attracted a lot of attention.

And this was only the arraignment.

"You may be seated," I said.

It was Dr. Gaines's first appearance in circuit court. Her first appearance before me, as circuit judge. She sat alone at the defense table, wearing a high-necked, long-sleeved dress with a conservative hemline. A dress like that was categorized as "church clothes" back in the day. In law school, we were taught that it was crucial to make our clients wear church clothes to court. It was sound advice, and when I started out in my law practice, trying mostly criminal cases, I urged my clients to follow it. That was twenty-five years ago, and people didn't necessarily dress up for church or court anymore. I wondered where Bria Gaines was getting her wardrobe advice.

Because she was sitting alone, no lawyer in sight.

It didn't make sense that she was alone in court. She should have a lawyer at her side. The woman was charged with a felony.

"Dr. Gaines," I said. She sat up straight with a jolt, raised her eyes to meet mine. "Are you represented by counsel?"

"Yes, Your Honor." When she spoke, her hands clutched involuntarily, like she was looking for something to hold on to. She hid them in her lap. Clearly, the doctor was petrified; I could see fear etched in her face and hear it in her voice, though she tried to hide it. "He was here, said he'd be back in a second."

The courtroom door opened, and he trotted down the aisle. "Apologies, Your Honor. I had to step out. I'm representing Dr. Gaines."

Well, shit. It was Chuck Rich.

Like I've always said, Chuck's intentions are good. I admired his willingness to take on clients whom other attorneys turned away. But I was reminded of his lackluster performance in Fergus Pitt's misdemeanor trial. And this case was no misdemeanor.

Chuck Rich was in over his head.

And he probably was aware of it. It would explain why a lawyer would have to run out of court to answer nature's call right as his big case was about to be heard.

While he joined his client at the counsel table, I opened the file and read the docket sheet. One of the notations was shocking. Almost made me shake my head in disgust, right in front of everybody. Chuck Rich had waived a preliminary hearing in the case. By doing that, he had squandered his chance to obtain an early look at the DA's evidence and get the witnesses' testimony under oath, so they couldn't change it down the road.

The opportunity was gone, the defense couldn't get it back. I wondered why Chuck Rich had taken such a foolish step. I looked out at the prosecution counsel table. Stealing a glance at the smug face of Reeves, it occurred to me that the DA might have talked Rich into it. Even though I'd tried to remind Chuck Rich when he was last in my courtroom: The DA is not the ally of the defense.

"Mr. Rich, are you ready?" When he nodded, I said, "In the case of the *State of Alabama v. Bria Gaines,* the defendant appears in person and with her attorney, Chuck Rich. Dr. Gaines, you are charged with the Class A felony of intentionally performing an abortion. Shall I read the language of the charge aloud?"

Chuck Rich stood and said, "We waive formal reading of the felony charge."

"All right. Dr. Gaines, how do you plead?"

Again, Chuck Rich spoke. "The defendant pleads not guilty."

I nodded. Uncapped an ink pen, made a notation in the file. It only took a second. But that momentary pause was all that was needed.

It gave a man in the courtroom the time to stand up in the crowded room and shout, "Liar! You're guilty as hell, you murdering witch! God will make you pay!"

CHAPTER 19

When the man shouted out from the courtroom gallery, I dropped my ink pen. It rolled off the bench and fell to the floor.

A crazy impulse tempted me to duck down and pick it up. I resisted the urge. I had a situation in my court.

"Liar!" he cried out again, even louder this time. "We all know what you done!"

The man was about my age, wearing an ill-fitting suit coat that didn't cover his belly. Not a local white guy, or I'd know him. And he'd know better than to act out in my courtroom.

Voices began buzzing in the benches, people exclaiming as they shifted in their seats, turning toward the speaker. I had to put a lid on the disturbance. If I didn't, it could become explosive.

Grabbing the wooden gavel, I struck it three times, to ensure that I had everyone's attention.

My bailiff was in position. Ross Carr had made his way to the aisle where the incorrigible citizen stood, and he was waiting for me to say the word. I pointed the gavel directly at the disrupter. To

Ross, I said, "Bailiff, escort this individual out of my courtroom. Immediately."

The guy appeared compliant, but the process was slow. In part, because the bench was crowded and the man was stout. A woman cried out when he stepped on her.

But also, I suspected that the shouter was in no hurry to depart. He wanted to air more of his opinions before he left the courtroom. As he lumbered past the people packed into his row, his statements were audible, even where I sat. "Everybody knows she done it. I saw it on TV! The girl's mother told the reporter what happened!"

That sent the room into another buzz of reaction. Apparently, lots of folks watched the interview. I didn't catch the broadcast, but Luna told me about it. She said that Nova Jones's mother had permitted a TV news reporter into her home. They didn't show Nova, but Starla was willing to be interviewed. The reporter recorded Starla Jones with his phone, and she'd had a lot to say.

Unbelievable. I wondered whether the DA had known about it in advance. Surely not. It was unethical to try the case in the press before it went to trial. In my opinion, it reflected poorly on the prosecutor, whether he had plotted it or not. The DA should have his witnesses under control.

The bigmouthed out-of-towner had finally reached my bailiff, but he still wouldn't shut up. "We all know that doctor done it. She can't take it back now!"

Dr. Gaines's face twisted. Bowing her head, she edged lower in her seat. The courtroom spectator was robbing her of the dignity she'd fought hard to maintain.

"That's it," I said, rising. I'd been itching to jump out of my chair since he first opened his mouth.

I hurried down those steps and out onto the courtroom floor.

"You are in contempt of court, sir, for disrupting these proceedings. Bailiff, take the man to the county jail."

It was a gamble. A contempt citation ordinarily would dump cold water on courtroom misbehavior, and everyone would simmer down. Folks would get the message. No one wanted to be the second person sent to jail.

But the current climate was hard to predict. Taking a hard line against the dude could incite sympathizers to jump to his support, and then I'd be screwed. Because we were not prepared for a major revolt. We were understaffed. My miscalculation. I had failed to predict that a brief arraignment would command this level of response.

Ross got the big guy out of the aisle and under control. When the bailiff cuffed his hands behind his back, it took the wind out of him. I stood in front of my bench and watched until the two men disappeared through the door.

Then I walked down the center aisle of the spectators' gallery and addressed everyone present. "Due process of law is guaranteed in this courtroom. I don't know what your prior experience has been in state court in Alabama. Tell you the truth, I don't care. Don't care what you've seen before, or what you watched on television, or what you think the legal system should be. The Fifth Amendment states that no person shall be deprived of life, liberty, or property without due process of law. That's a sacred guarantee."

I was just warming up, honestly. When I got on a roll about the constitutional rights of the accused, I could go on indefinitely. I'd made my share of closing arguments as a trial lawyer, and the words rolled out with ease. And I thought this gathering of citizens could benefit from hearing what I had to say.

But as I reached the very last bench in the courtroom, the one near the exit, I spotted a familiar face. It was that journalist, the arrogant young TV reporter who'd crashed Saturday breakfast at my farm.

Reese Wilson. With WYLR in Birmingham.

He was recording my Fifth Amendment lecture on his telephone. Smirking at me while he did it. *Son of a bitch.*

It threw me, seeing him holding out that phone. Phones weren't allowed in my court; they were supposed to be collected when people went through the metal detector. More security gaffes. I broke off midsentence. Turned on my heel and walked back up to the bench. Scooted back into my chair. During my return, the murmur of voices in court started up again. I silenced the whispers with a polite tap of the gavel.

I glanced down at my file, trying to recall where we'd been in our stage of proceedings, before things got out of control.

My handwritten notation steadied me and triggered my recall. "The record will reflect that the defendant has entered a plea of not guilty to the charge." I paused to glare at the courtroom spectators, daring them to act out. My bailiff had returned with miraculous efficiency, providing backup.

Other than the rustle of scores of bodies shifting on hard wooden benches, the courtroom was quiet.

To the attorneys, I said, "I see that the defendant is currently out on bond."

Reeves, the DA, stood. "I wish to address the matter of bond, Your Honor."

After I gave him a nod, he stepped away from the counsel table. Which indicated that he was about to put on a show for the benefit of the citizens gathered in the gallery.

Reeves said, "The district judge set an initial bond amount of ten thousand dollars, which the defendant easily met. The judge didn't seek my input or recommendation when he let this woman out with such a ridiculously low bond. Why he didn't consult me, I can't guess."

Oh, I could. I knew I was able to correctly guess the reason. I folded my hands on the bench. Gave him another minute to talk.

"This defendant has been charged with an offense that carries a penalty of ninety-nine years to life imprisonment. She is a flight risk, Your Honor, because she has the motivation to flee and the financial means to do so. Moreover, this woman is a danger to the community. The crime she's been charged with is akin to murder, the taking of human life!"

Objection Objection Objection. I cut my eyes at Chuck Rich. The man remained seated on his butt in that damned chair. He looked distressed, but still. He should've been on his feet, raising hell. The word *murder* should never have been uttered in this hearing.

I hadn't intended to take over. They gave me no choice. I looked down at the defense table and met the young woman's eye. "Dr. Gaines," I said, "please describe for the court your ties to this community."

She paused, stole a look at her lawyer. He gave her an encouraging nod and whispered something.

The defendant cleared her throat as she rose from her seat. "Your Honor, I moved to Union Springs after completing my residency. I have a family practice, a medical office here in town."

"How many patients?"

"Oh, gosh." She took a moment to think. "Just under four hundred, I believe."

"Do you own property in the community?"

"I lease the building where I conduct my medical practice. But I own a house, a residence up on the hill."

I nodded at that. Everyone knew about the hill. Our town was poor, but the prettiest houses were built on the high land to the east of town.

"Dr. Gaines, do you understand your obligation to appear in person at the trial of your case?"

"I do, Your Honor."

"And are you affirming that you will be present in person for all hearings and matters scheduled by this court?"

"I will, Your Honor. I swear it." She was gripping the counsel table with both hands.

"Bond remains at ten thousand dollars." I picked up the gavel. Gave it a tap rather than a bang. No need to raise a ruckus this time.

Looked down at the DA just in time to catch his expression.

The man was livid.

CHAPTER 20

After the arraignment of Bria Gaines, I made my escape. Ran from that courthouse like a coward.

Didn't exit through the front door, though. I'm no fool. I figured the press would be jockeying for prime position in front of the courthouse, hungry for some footage of the key figures in the case of *State v. Bria Gaines*. I'd come to terms with my new reality, understood that I was more newsworthy than I used to be.

That's why I headed for the back door, keeping my head down. Almost made it. Stood an arm's length away from the exit when Earl Hodge, the mayor of Union Springs, popped out of the probate office.

"Judge Mary! Hold on, I need a minute!"

He hustled up to me and grabbed my arm, right above the elbow.

What the hell?

I stared at his hand for a moment and then raised my eyes, fixed them on his. He got the message. Let go of me, took a step back. Thrust his offending hand into a pocket.

"Sorry, Judge, but I've been meaning to talk to you. About this abortion case."

I literally groaned, couldn't help it. Took a breath and repeated my go-to line. "I can't discuss this matter with you."

"Not the facts. Nothing like that. Just the situation, you understand?"

I didn't. He must have read it on my face; he quickly added, "I need to lay out the situation it's putting us all in. You know, the city."

I didn't ask for any details on the city's situation. I was itching to get away. "It's a felony case, Earl. We see them all the time. And this isn't the ugliest set of facts I've heard in my courtroom. Isn't the most horrific crime I've presided over this year."

"But it's the most sensational, Judge. Don't you get that?"

As he spoke, he used both hands to fiddle with his bow tie, like he wanted to make sure it was straight. I took a closer look at him. Earl was all dolled up, wearing a flashy suit and a striped bow tie. The man was camera-ready.

I should've anticipated it. The mayor of Union Springs was a social-climbing tool who was not content to abide in our community. Earl Hodge had higher ambitions. He'd made it clear, on multiple occasions, that he would do anything to get a bigger job in Birmingham or Montgomery.

"Earl, I don't know what you expect me to do. We're the county seat, and the DA has filed the case in Bullock County, alleging that the crime occurred here. He has to file his suit in the correct venue. In a criminal case, the proper venue is the place where the crime occurred. If you don't believe me, go talk to the DA."

I stepped toward the back door, opened it, and glanced around. Didn't appear that the press or public was waiting to pounce. I stepped across the threshold.

Judge Stone

Earl Hodge followed me out. "I already talked to the DA. Reeves was the one who told me it's going to be a really big deal. With national press. Did you see how many people turned out today?"

Did I see? I didn't respond. The question was too ridiculous for words. I'd had the best seat in the house for the day's events.

The mayor dogged my heels as I made my way to my car, parked in my personal space.

In a loud whisper, Hodge said, "He told me something in confidence, but it doesn't need to be a secret from you. You'll be the first to know."

I had the key fob in my hand. But that statement made me pause. What secrets about the case was the DA sharing with the mayor? "Tell me."

"He's bringing in the Alabama attorney general's office to serve as co-counsel. To balance the scales, he said."

"Balance the scales?" I echoed. "Against Chuck Rich? He thinks he needs more muscle to litigate against Chuck Rich?"

Hodge grimaced. His eyes cut to the right. I've seen the eye dart, it's a giveaway. Deciding whether to lie or not.

He looked down at his shoes and kicked at some loose chunks of asphalt in the worn parking lot. "I guess he means you, Judge Mary."

"What?" My voice was sharp enough to make the man scoot back.

He said, "I'm just repeating Reeves's words. He told me you rule against him all the time. He needs somebody to back him up. That it will even the scales."

It would reveal weakness—vulnerability, insecurity—to let on that I was offended. So I didn't give any indication that the words had wounded me.

But I was curious. Wanted to know just who Reeves had chosen as his bodyguard. "Any idea who's going to rep the AG's office?"

"Yeah, he told me. It's Eleanor Lindquist. You ever run across her in court before?"

Oh, my Lord. Eleanor Lindquist. Yeah, I'd seen her in action. Things were about to get worse for Bria Gaines.

CHAPTER 21

That was a long old day. When I reappeared at the courthouse in the afternoon, I had to make up for cutting out in the morning. It was past suppertime and dark outside when I finally left the courthouse for good. And I had more work—farm chores—waiting for me at home. By the time I finally pulled off my chore boots and shucked my overalls, I was spent.

I stood on the kitchen floor in my stocking feet, wondering what I should eat. I didn't have enough ambition to microwave a frozen dinner, much less cook from scratch. So I pulled a box of Ritz crackers and a jar of peanut butter from the shelf. Ate standing up, dropping crumbs on the kitchen counter, until I decided that spreading the peanut butter required too much effort. Carried the cracker box with me into my bedroom.

I had to shower; no skipping that step, regardless of how worn out I might be. The hot water felt good on my tired muscles, therapeutic. I dried off, pulled a clean T-shirt over my head, and crawled into bed.

With the cracker box.

I appreciated the irony, you feel me? Eating crackers in bed. But no one was around to appreciate the joke.

I had my phone in bed with me, because I intended to check the news online, to see whether the Gaines arraignment had generated an uproar. Didn't quite make it. My eyes drooped, head nodded. I fell asleep with the phone in my hand.

Later that night, the ringtone jerked me from a restless sleep. My sheets were tangled into a jumble. I must've been kicking them while I slept.

I grabbed the phone, squinted at the screen. The caller had an Alabama area code, but the number was unfamiliar. Definitely not anybody in my contacts.

Still fuzzy from sleep, I debated whether I should go ahead and answer. Just swipe my thumb across that screen, see what was up. Maybe there was an emergency in one of the counties in my circuit.

The ringtone jangled again while I stared at the number.

As a judge, I get an occasional wake-up call in the middle of the night. Sometimes—rarely, but it's happened—a detective needs me to sign off on a search warrant, and believes it can't wait until morning, because time is of the essence. I'm always available in such a circumstance.

Or sometimes an old client of mine from my criminal defense days gets in trouble and thinks that if he can reach me, I'll wave a magic wand and tell the cops to set him free. Those calls don't end happily.

But the search warrant scenario, that was possible. It was reasonable to suppose that a cop in my circuit was calling from a cell phone. A number I didn't have in my contacts.

I decided to answer just as it went to voicemail.

Too late. I set the phone down. Tried to convince myself that it was probably nothing important. And if it was a crucial matter, they'd try again. Maybe come out to my house and bang on the door.

I was considering pulling on some pants just in case I received a visitor. That's when I heard the ding, notifying me: The caller had left a message.

I sighed out as I grabbed the phone, relieved to know I wouldn't be forced to wonder all night about the reason for the call. I was happy to know someone had left a message.

Until I played it.

"Judge, I'm calling you because I just can't sleep. I've been in a terrible state, ever since I saw that woman on the news. That negro woman in court who killed the little girl's baby."

Her voice was thin and wavering over the phone. Sounded like an old white lady, and not one I knew. I lifted my thumb, ready to pause, to delete. But she caught her breath and went on talking.

"That doctor is going to hell for what she done. The girl, I can't say. Maybe the Lord will forgive her if she repents. Or might be she'll burn in hell, too, for killing her own child. I felt called to tell you something, though, and it couldn't wait. The Lord moved me. He commanded me to give this message to you."

I shivered as the old woman delivered her warning. "Judge, don't you follow them. You have the choice, you understand me? Don't you follow those women into hell. The devil may be at your shoulder, tempting you, whispering in your ear—"

That was enough. I cut the voice off and then I swiped it, made the message disappear. As I leaned back against the pillows, gripping the phone, I had second thoughts. Maybe I should have kept the recording instead of deleting it. If that little old lady showed up at the courthouse with a long gun and a plan to hurry me into the afterlife, the recording would be good evidence of premeditation.

But it was too late. I closed my eyes, hoping I'd be able to ease back into the deep fog of sleep. The phone rang again.

I checked the number. Not an Alabama area code, so I didn't even consider picking up. When the message appeared, I played the audio. This one sounded less crazy. Just an impassioned statement of support for the prosecution, a lament for the number of children whose lives had been ended before birth. Some statistics, an offer to send me the information.

Delete.

Between 1 and 3:25 a.m., I received roughly a half dozen calls. The ringtone would rouse me from a light slumber. I'd wait for the message. Calculate the crazy factor, the odds that the caller was capable of actual harm.

And I'd wonder how the hell people were getting their hands on my private cell number. Exactly who was giving that information away?

The seventh call was the game changer. The caller was no reedy-voiced church lady. It was a man who sounded like he was in his prime, speaking in a deep baritone. He got right to the point.

"I saw you on the news. Big Black bitch in a big black robe, sitting up all high and mighty in that courtroom, like you got a right to be there. Time was when you people knew your place."

I slid down and pulled the covers to my chin. But I kept listening.

"You poison this case, you're gonna be put right back in your place again. You might just wish somebody killed *you* in the womb. Trust me, when I catch you, you'll be licking my fine leather boots and begging for your goddamn life!"

The message ended.

I didn't delete that one. It had to be preserved. But I knew that I couldn't tolerate another night caller. I muted my phone but didn't put it on the bedside table. Kept it in a tight grip, ready to dial 911 if necessary.

I lay awake for a long while, tossing in bed, watching the minutes tick closer to morning. Gave me time to think. Too much time, arguably. I grew maudlin, and commenced a nostalgic fit of longing for ordinary days. For times when I faced the obligations and labor of the farm and my judicial seat without this new level of exposure and drama.

My last conscious thought before I dropped into a deep sleep was a somber realization. That there would be no more normal days for me, not for a long while.

When I slipped into a nightmare, I couldn't tell if I was asleep or awake.

CHAPTER 22

Bria Gaines

UNION SPRINGS, ALABAMA

Didn't take long for Bria Gaines to discover a basic fact. Being charged with a felony was bad for business.

The destruction of her medical practice was an overnight phenomenon. Bria hadn't expected it, couldn't have foreseen the cancellations, the no-shows that left her pacing her empty office. She'd sent the receptionist home. Indefinitely.

When it became apparent that the downturn wasn't a temporary blip, but would continue, she cut her hours of operation. Open Monday, Wednesday, and Friday, 8 a.m. to noon. The sign she printed for her office door said WALK-INS WELCOME! in bold print.

That's why Bria was sitting at home on Monday afternoon at two thirty, parked in front of her television. A reality TV program was playing out on the screen, two people engaged in some ridiculous argument. Bria didn't know what they were fighting about, hadn't paid sufficient attention. She kept it on for background noise. When the house was silent, she was left to her own thoughts. And currently, she preferred the sound of battling strangers to the voice in her own head.

The doorbell rang.

It startled her. She still had some friends left in town. They had reached out, and she was grateful for that. But nobody would be stopping in on a Monday to have a friendly chat over a glass of tea.

On the other hand, since she'd been doxxed online by pro-life vigilantes, some crazy people had been pounding on the door. Shouting out of car windows as they drove past. Somebody scrawled *Murderer* across her garage door in red spray paint. Bria had made a quick repair as soon as she discovered the vandalism the next day, but it needed a do-over. She fancied that she could see the red letters bleeding through the coat of white paint she'd slapped on the door.

When the bell rang again, she tiptoed to the door to look through the peephole. A young white man was standing on her front porch. He was wearing a dark blue suit, paired with a bright purple tie.

Sharp dresser. Probably a journalist, she thought. She definitely didn't want to talk to the press. No effing way.

Bria didn't open the door. She called to him through the crack. "Go away, please. I don't want to see anybody."

She squinted back through the peephole, to watch him depart. She wanted to be certain he'd understood her, that he needed to walk away. But he was still standing on the welcome mat. She saw him reach out toward her door.

He knocked. A nice knock, not too loud. But not timid, either.

So the guy was persistent. But not frightening. Bria took a deep breath and unlocked the dead bolt. When she pulled the front door open, she kept her screen door latched, to keep a barrier between them.

As soon as the door opened, he broke into a brilliant smile.

Definitely a journalist, she thought. *TV, not print, from the look of him.*

"Dr. Gaines!" he said through the screen door. "Thank you for seeing me."

"I'm not seeing you. You heard what I said two seconds ago. I'm not talking to anybody. Just making that clear."

"I'm here to help you."

At that, she choked out an involuntary laugh. And she hadn't laughed in a long while. "Yeah, I bet. Really, I need for you to leave me alone. Just turn and go. Please."

Her voice wobbled on the word *Please*. It embarrassed her. She would have to toughen up if she intended to survive this ordeal in the months ahead.

"May I give you my business card?"

He pulled a white card from a pocket inside his jacket and held it out. Bria kept the screen door closed, thinking: *No way am I letting him in.* She shook her head in the negative, to make it clear.

The man had a lot of confidence, she had to give him that. He pressed the card to the screen and said, "Take it. Check me out. I think you'll like what you find. You can google me. I graduated from Duke Law School. Top of my class. Not number one. But close."

Through the screen mesh, Bria read the embossed black lettering: *Benjamin C. Meyers, Attorney-at-Law.* So. A lawyer, not a reporter from Fox or CNN.

He still wasn't getting past her door. "You carry your diploma around with you? To impress people?"

He laughed, flashing the megawatt smile again. "Hey, I'm proud of going to Duke, I won't lie. A family tradition. My mother went there. Back when women were just breaking into the legal profession."

Bria liked him a little better for that. But not enough to lift the latch on the screen door that kept him out of her house.

He said, "Dr. Gaines, I came over here today because I want to represent you."

"No, thanks." Bria backed away a step and started to swing the front door shut. "I already have a lawyer."

"I know—Chuck Rich. I just came from his office."

She hadn't expected that. Maybe it was why she didn't slam the door in his face.

"We had a long conversation, a good talk. In fact, Chuck encouraged me to come by. Gave me your home address. He thought I should introduce myself."

That sent Bria's anxiety into overdrive. What was Chuck thinking, sending people to her front door? She was going to let him know exactly what she thought about having a lawyer who made free with her personal information.

And then Benjamin Meyers put a hand on the frame of her screen door, like he thought she was about to invite him inside her house. She was determined to disabuse him of that notion.

She was curt. "I don't know you, and I'm not in the market for a defense attorney. Chuck is a friend of mine. I trust him."

Benjamin Meyers dropped the cheesy grin. His face was somber as he said, "Do you trust that lawyer with your life, Dr. Gaines?"

Bria didn't have an easy answer for that.

"You understand that if the jury finds you guilty, they can send you to prison for the rest of your life?"

Bria nodded slowly.

"Well, you're looking at the man who can get you off."

CHAPTER 23

Mary Stone

STONE FAMILY FARM
BULLOCK COUNTY, ALABAMA

I heard the rumble of the pickup truck before the vehicle came into view, ground to a stop. Then I heard the voice of the driver.

"I hope you know, Mary, nobody but you would have the gall to drag me out here before sunrise."

That was probably true.

"Morning, Troy."

A man dressed in tan coveralls opened the driver's door and hopped out near my front porch, where I'd been pacing the wooden floorboards, waiting.

"You got a flashlight?" he muttered. "Can't see my hand in front of my face. Sun's not even up yet."

So much for pleasantries. I held up my work lantern and flipped it on.

Troy winced and covered his eyes. "Damn it, Mary! You trying to blind me now?"

I aimed the beam at the gravel under our feet. "Quit griping, you big baby. You should be used to strange hours by now."

Dr. Troy Nelson had been serving Bullock County as a veterinarian for about as long as I'd been in the law. He'd grown up on a farm just down the road. We went through school together, not always that friendly. But we'd shared a similar path. A couple of Black farm kids determined to get into college and break into a profession.

I turned in my rubber boots to head for the barn and he fell into step beside me.

"Thanks for coming out," I said. "I know it's early in the day for a prenatal visit."

"Damn right."

As we opened the barn door, I could hear Tornado stirring in her stall.

When I walked up, she nickered and nuzzled me, resting her head on my shoulder. I nuzzled her right back. "And good morning to you, too, Mommy-to-be."

I kept sweet-talking Tornado while Troy pressed his stethoscope against her abdomen.

"Hush, Mary," he said. "It's hard enough to hear a heartbeat over the gut noise. Can't hear nothing with you chattering."

I was not accustomed to being told to hush, but I complied. Because I was invested in the outcome of the examination. Hell, you'd think the baby was mine.

And in a way, it was.

After a few minutes, Troy stood upright, grunting as he rubbed his back. "Is her appetite off?"

"No, she seems to be eating just fine."

"Well, she looks all right to me. Didn't hear anything inside to be concerned about."

I nodded, still on edge. Afraid he might drop a nugget of bad news.

Troy scratched the back of his neck, frowning. "There'd be no reason to worry at all, except for what happened last time. When was that? About a year and a half ago?"

"Closer to two."

"That's right," said Troy. "She lost the foal around twenty weeks." He patted Tornado's flank before he stepped out of the stall.

I followed, kicking up straw and wood shavings. "What are the odds? That she'll have a good outcome this time."

"There's no way to know if she'll carry it to term. The fact that she lost a foal in an earlier pregnancy is the indicator that it could happen again. But you just don't know."

My eyes pricked with tears. Quickly, I blinked them back, embarrassed by my reaction. I'm not a crier, never have been. I work hard to keep that urge under tight control.

"There's got to be something I can do for her," I said.

"What you want to look for, Mary, are signs of distress. Placentitis is the typical risk for a mare. It's caused by bacteria contaminating the cervix and entering the uterus. That's probably what caused the miscarriage last time."

"So tell me what I can do for her now."

"You want to look for premature udder development, bagging up, long before the due date. Also look for streaming milk and vaginal discharge. Okay?"

"Yeah, absolutely. I'll keep an eye out, contact you if I see anything that's off. Are there any other tests to make sure she's okay?"

"I know a vet in Macon County who can do an ultrasound. But I don't necessarily recommend it. I'm not an advocate of bothering the mare with sonograms. If she develops an infection, we'll treat it. Otherwise, just let nature take its course."

My throat was tight. I coughed, to clear it. "Right."

"You call me if something happens. But Mary, don't be getting me out of bed again. Not unless it's a damn emergency."

"No promises," I said.

When Troy left the barn, I stayed behind. I had my morning chores to attend to. Needed to feed Tornado and the cattle, and Foghorn Leghorn would be demanding my attention any minute. Before I started working, I went back to Tornado. Scratched behind her ears.

"It's going to be all right, Mommy," I told her. "Everything is going to be just fine."

I wasn't sure whether I was comforting her or reassuring myself.

CHAPTER 24

Bria Gaines

UNION SPRINGS, ALABAMA

Unbelievable.

Friday morning, 11:55. Bria stepped into the reception area of her office after another slow morning, keys in hand. She was ready to lock up and go home.

There he stood, inside her office. Bold as brass, wearing another expensive suit. That arrogant lawyer, Benjamin Meyers.

He flashed that big smile at her. "Surprised to see me again?"

Was she? Maybe not. He'd been calling nonstop for the past few days.

But she hadn't expected to see her lawyer—Chuck Rich, the defense attorney she'd formally retained—standing directly beside him.

Bria addressed Chuck, because it was clear that Benjamin Meyers wouldn't listen to her. "Chuck, would you please tell this man to leave? And to quit calling. I told him on Monday, I already hired a lawyer."

Chuck just stood there, while Benjamin said, "Just give me five minutes."

Bria took care to sound firm, decided. "Nope. Sorry. I don't have five minutes."

Meyers put his hand over his heart. "You can't spare me five minutes? Really? What are you afraid of?"

Bria wouldn't confess it. But when he came to her home on Monday, Benjamin Meyers's words scared her. Especially the part about trusting her lawyer with her life.

Still, she had no cause to place any trust in him. He'd done nothing to earn her regard. The man was from out of town, a total stranger. Plus, he was white. Not an automatic disqualifier. After all, Chuck was a white man. But it wasn't a trait that inspired immediate confidence.

"You have to go." Making sure she didn't convey any doubt, she appealed to her lawyer a second time. "Chuck, please tell this guy y'all are leaving. Now."

Chuck lifted his shoulders in an apologetic shrug. "I think we ought to hear him out. He's come all this way, Bria, from his office in Atlanta."

"Atlanta?" Bria almost sputtered when she spoke. "You never told me you were from Atlanta!"

Meyers said, "You didn't give me a chance to tell you much of anything."

"Oh, great—that's all I need. Some out-of-state lawyer who lives three hours away from here. Are you even licensed to practice in Alabama?"

"Would I be standing here if I wasn't licensed to practice in Alabama courts?"

"Hell, I don't know. I don't know anything about you." It was beyond belief that some white stranger would feel compelled to come across the state line to save her. She turned to Chuck again, willing him to step up. "Chuck, we don't know this guy."

Chuck said, "I want you to listen to him, Bria."

Her shoulders sagged. She couldn't keep on fighting; it was wearing her out. "Okay," she said, walking over to the waiting room chairs that lined the wall. She dropped into one of the seats, slumped down in it. "You can have five minutes."

An old-fashioned wall clock hung behind the reception desk. She took note of the time as Chuck sat next to her. It was 12:03. At 12:08, she would toss him out.

Meyers walked to the middle of the room. "I'm going to make an opening statement. For your criminal trial. It's a rough version of what I'd say in the courtroom."

Bria shrugged. "Okay. Go ahead."

He didn't launch into the speech immediately. He took some time, maybe thirty seconds. In that span of half a minute, she watched him undergo a transformation. Physical changes in his posture, demeanor, expression. Bria was glued to the spectacle, couldn't look away.

He made eye contact. "Ladies and gentlemen of the jury, I'd like to thank you for your service in this trial. You know, Abraham Lincoln said, 'The greatest service of citizenship is jury duty.'"

Brief pause. In a wry tone, he added, "You notice, President Lincoln didn't say anything about jury duty being convenient. Or easy. Or lucrative."

Okay, Bria thought. *That was funny.* It took some effort to keep a straight face. Which, considering the circumstances, was preposterous. Crazy.

After the icebreaker, he segued to the next part. He talked

about the burden of proof, how it was the State's job to prove Bria guilty, and not Bria's job to prove herself innocent.

Bria knew all that, was certainly aware. However, she suspected that the average citizen of Union Springs might be unaware of those basic precepts of criminal justice. She thought it was probably wise to give a reminder.

"You watch out for that DA, for how he tries to frame this case. What did he just try to tell you in his opening statement? 'This is a simple case,' he said. The sheer insolence of that statement shocks the conscience! The man presumes to characterize a case of this magnitude as 'simple'? Oh, no complexity here—is that right, Mr. DA? Not like we're talking about the rights of women, or women's bodily autonomy, or their reproductive health, or the future of medicine, or right to privacy and constitutional guarantees. The DA would have you believe that none of those crucial issues are present in this case."

While she listened, Bria started nodding, though she was barely conscious of the movement. It was as if he'd cast a spell, demanding her acquiescence. And getting it, too.

He stepped closer. "The DA told you that the defendant in this case is Dr. Bria Gaines, but he left out a lot of pertinent information. Facts that you need to know about Bria. Bria Gaines was born in Tuscaloosa to a family with seven kids. Her mama and daddy stressed academic excellence, and Bria was top of her class all the way from K through 12 in Tuscaloosa public schools. Valedictorian of her senior class, and she got a full ride to Xavier University of Louisiana, in New Orleans. After graduating with highest honors— summa cum laude—she was accepted into medical school, University of Alabama at Birmingham."

Bria was surprised that he knew so many specifics. The man had done his homework.

"She could've remained in Birmingham, where there are lots of attractions for young people. Could have left the state of Alabama, gone back to New Orleans, or anywhere, to go into practice. What did she choose to do? She looked for a community in dire need of a family doctor. Found it right here in Union Springs, Alabama, and set up her office. Just think what she has done for your community since she arrived. The changes she's made in access and quality of health care. Care for children, the poor, the elderly.

"Let's consider the State's case for a minute. Did y'all listen when the DA talked about his State's witnesses? He named Nova Jones, we all heard that. And he mentioned that she was pregnant at thirteen. But it seemed like he glossed over a crucial fact."

The mention of the name Nova Jones made her chest tighten. Bria was devastated to know that the girl was forced to endure unrelenting public scrutiny. As a doctor, she was worried about Nova's health and welfare, and the toll that the case would have on the child.

It was a weird jumble of emotions. Confusing, sometimes, to feel overwhelming sympathy and concern for the prosecution witness whose testimony would send her to prison.

The lawyer was still giving his speech. Wearing a thoughtful expression, Meyers raised his index finger, shook it at the ceiling. "When a thirteen-year-old girl becomes pregnant, there's a story there. Not a love story. Not Cinderella at the ball. No happily-ever-after. Y'all know this is true. A tragic fact of life. Did the DA bother to tell you that story? Ladies and gentlemen, he did not."

He took a breath and released it before he said, "What else is he keeping from you?"

Bria had heard enough. He hadn't finished his opening statement, but she was impressed. He'd shown what he could do. The man was good. Really good. She felt obliged to be up-front with him.

She needed to be direct. He had just started up again when she interrupted him.

"Mr. Meyers, you're extremely talented, there's no question about that. And you've clearly done your homework. But the idea of handing over this case, and my life, my fate, to a complete stranger? It scares me."

She turned to Chuck, sitting in the seat beside her. "Chuck, you're the first friend I made when I moved to town. I know you're sincerely dedicated to helping people with legal problems. I admire that. I trust you to have my best interest at heart."

Bria's life had been upended. She didn't want to go to prison, God knows; she wanted the best representation she could afford. But she had to cling to the true friends who stood by her.

He smiled at her, a rueful grin. Chuck said, "We're good friends, Bria, and I'm proud to have your trust. So you should trust me when I tell you, you need to let me withdraw so you can hire this guy."

She glanced from Chuck to Meyers, and back to Chuck again. Her friend said, "I'm dead serious."

That did it.

Bria rose from her seat, extended her hand to Meyers. When he gripped it in a firm handshake, she said, "Okay, Mr. Meyers. If you really want this hopeless case, it's yours."

He was smiling at her again. It made Bria feel edgy. She said, "I don't even know if I can afford you."

Meyers said, "I'd take your case for nothing. Do it for free."

And the crazy thing about that? He actually sounded like he meant it.

CHAPTER 25

Mary Stone

BULLOCK COUNTY COURTHOUSE
UNION SPRINGS, ALABAMA

I was sitting at the bench, taking a guilty plea from a local miscreant who habitually broke into parked vehicles by busting the windows in the wee hours of the morning. Then he'd get inside the vehicle, take a backpack, laptop, jacket. Or dig in the console, take something from the glove box. Steal whatever he could find, even if it was just a handful of change. Take a nap, maybe. Jerk off, if he had the urge.

In Alabama, that's a felony. Property crimes are strictly enforced. The law of FAFO. Fool around, find out.

"Mr. Wagner, you've been charged with seven counts of the Class C felony of unlawful breaking and entering a vehicle. Are you withdrawing your plea of not guilty and entering a plea of guilty to these charges?"

"Yes, Judge." He sounded sulky, resentful. Bad attitude. I made a mental note.

"And you are pleading guilty because you are guilty?"

"Yeah."

The public defender nudged the defendant, whispered something. Likely advising him to speak respectfully in court.

"Mr. Wagner, please describe for the record what happened on the thirty-first of August of last year."

His eyes rolled up to the ceiling, as if he was asking the Lord to give him strength. That man should have started praying some years back. This wasn't the first time I'd seen him in my courtroom.

"So me and a friend was hanging at his place. We didn't have no money, wasn't doing nothing. He thought we ought to go out, bip some cars. Maybe make some cash."

Make some cash. Like he was engaging in honest work. "You used an expression: bip. Tell us what that means. For the record."

"Bip. Bipping cars. You bust out the window. So you can open the door, get in there, and get what's inside."

"How many cars did you 'bip' on the early morning of August 31?"

"I don't know. A lot." The attorney whispered in his ear again. "Seven. We hit seven cars."

I folded my hands on the bench. Asked a follow-up question, to check all the boxes. "When you broke the car windows and entered into those seven vehicles on August 31, did you do so with the consent of the owners of those vehicles?"

"Huh?"

"The people who owned those cars. Did they consent to you breaking the windows, getting inside to steal? They give you permission to do it?"

"Oh. Nah, no. We didn't have nobody's consent."

I looked at the DA. "Is there a plea bargain agreement in this case?"

Reeves was present. His mood had improved in recent days; he wasn't sending me any deadly looks. He stood up, holding a legal pad. "There is, Your Honor. In exchange for his plea of guilty to counts 1 to 4, the State has agreed to dismiss counts 5 to 7 and recommends a three-year sentence of imprisonment."

The door behind the bench opened. No way to ignore it — that was my chambers door. I glanced over. Luna was leaning out, peering at me. Which is not something I'd usually see. Luna doesn't interrupt court proceedings. She knows better.

I turned my attention back to Reeves. "What is the State's position on probation?"

"We stand silent, Your Honor. The State takes no position."

So. It would be up to me. Without any argument from the prosecution, one way or another. I'd ultimately decide whether the man would go to prison or go home. But there were preliminary procedures in this situation. I would need to order a pre-sentence investigation by the Office of Probation and Parole.

I heard a whisper.

"Judge Mary!"

I swiveled in the chair. "Luna? What on earth?"

She grimaced with embarrassment, gripping the edge of the wooden door. "You have a phone call!"

I dropped my voice; no need to shout at my clerk in front of the whole courthouse. "Luna. I'm in the middle of a felony guilty plea. Take a message."

I swiveled back, facing the courtroom. The attorneys were exchanging a look. I saw the DA shrug, as if asking *Who knows?*

That whisper again. "It's the governor!"

Wow. That was a first.

I paused for a moment, trying to decide. What was proper

procedure in a situation like this? I didn't have personal experience contending with high state officials.

Then I caught the defendant, Ray Wagner, rolling his head back, like he was bored.

This was my courtroom. Where justice was served. And I was dealing with the specific crime and punishment of a man standing before me.

"Luna, tell the governor I'm on the bench," I said. I sat up straight. Adjusted the gavel so that the handle was within easy reach, as it should be.

I looked over my shoulder at my administrative clerk. She was pretty flipped out. She'd recover. The governor would recover, too.

"He can leave a number. I'll call him back."

CHAPTER 26

After I wrapped up the guilty plea and left the bench, I was breathing hard. Like I'd just run up two flights of stairs. Or had stepped on a copperhead in the barn.

I charged into chambers, with Luna at my heels. She said, "Oh, Judge — thank the Lord, you got here in time. The governor's office is calling back in just a few minutes."

"Already?" I'd never spoken to the man before, now he was calling me every ten minutes. I closed the door and checked my face in the office mirror, to make sure I didn't look a sight. "Is it a Zoom call?"

"No, a conference call. On the landline. With you and the governor and the Alabama attorney general."

The state attorney general? *Shit.* It was getting worse and worse.

I unzipped the robe. No need to stay in uniform for an old-fashioned conference call, where no one could see me. "What's the number, the ID info?"

"His secretary is setting it up. Very old-school. We don't dial. They call us."

"Wow." It had been a while since I'd had a meeting that way. "Okay, then. I'll wait."

Judge Stone

Luna left my office and was back at her desk before I had the presence of mind to ask. I called out, "Luna, what's the governor calling about?"

She didn't shout out the answer. She stepped back to my doorway and whispered, "*State v. Bria Gaines.*"

I tipped back in the big chair and closed my eyes. I wanted to take a moment to center myself, but I didn't have that luxury. My desk phone rang. I hit the speaker and Luna's voice came through. "Governor's office on line two."

I pushed the line and said, "This is Circuit Judge Mary Stone."

A female voice responded. "I'll connect you."

A moment later, I heard two men laughing. About what, I had no clue. I coughed, to give them a heads-up, before I said, "Judge Stone here."

"Judge! This is Governor Bert Lamar, up in Montgomery. We've got General Dick Winston on the call—he's on the road, driving to Nashville for a meeting. You still with us, General?"

The dude wasn't a general. Never even served in the military. That was a phony courtesy title that some people used to buddy up to the state AG. I wasn't one of them. Dick Winston and I had some history. Of the bad variety.

"I'm here. How you doing, Mary?" Winston asked.

"Fine."

I didn't elaborate. There was an uncomfortable silence. The governor broke it off pretty swiftly.

"Judge Stone—may I call you Mary? I feel like I already know you. Because I've heard so many excellent things about you."

Really? Privately, I was skeptical. But I behaved myself, answered politely. "Thank you, Governor, that's very gratifying. Sure, you can call me Mary."

"And you call me Bert."

I said, "Right." But it was BS. I wasn't calling the man nothing.

"I'm serious, now. I know what's going on in your circuit, the talk gets back to me. What a fine job you're doing on the bench. Folks say you're fair. Your courtroom is orderly, because you're no-nonsense! Making efficient use of the limited facilities y'all got in your circuit. Everyone gives you high marks, Mary. Five gold stars!"

It was flattering. I'd have liked to believe that he was sincere. But I'd been an outsider in Alabama's power circles too long to be fooled.

My suspicions were confirmed when the AG chimed in. "Mary, I was telling the governor you do a hell of a job with what you've got. Hell of a job! But there's limitations, you know what I mean."

The governor's voice boomed through the speaker. "That's it, limitations. Some matters outside of your control. Up here at the capital, we've had serious discussions regarding those problems. That's why we think it would be best for you to recuse yourself from that abortion case—*State v. Gaines*. Seems like the trial should be moved to Montgomery or Birmingham."

I kept my voice steady. "Explain to me exactly why y'all believe I'm not qualified to preside over *State v. Gaines*."

"Not qualified?" "Nooo! It's not that!" "Nobody's saying that!"

They were both speaking at once, garbling their fervent denials. The governor backed off and let the AG take over. Dick Winston had been a trial lawyer, back in the day. He talked fast, trying to make his case.

"It's got nothing to do with your qualifications or your legal background, Mary. Your record is stellar, stellar! It's just that doggone county you're stuck in. You know what I'm talking about. Your courthouse hasn't been updated, your security can't provide the protection you need. And the town lacks the necessary amenities for an event like this is shaping up to be."

Governor Lamar jumped back in. "You've got no hotel! Where will the media stay? How can you sequester a jury? Union Springs hasn't got a decent goddamned hotel anywhere in the city limits!"

They were giving me a headache. I rubbed my temples. "We've got a motel to house a jury. It's not part of a major chain, but—"

The governor cut me off. "Where will folks eat? All you've got to offer is one little ole McDonald's. They gonna run out of Big Macs the first day!"

The AG piled on. "It will create a hardship for the community, Mary. They'll be overwhelmed. And it will be a burden on your judicial circuit. You know this case is going to be a hot potato. It will eat up all your time."

I opened my mouth to speak, but the governor was faster. "Isn't there a school located near the courthouse? An elementary school? That's problematic."

I glanced out the window: There it sat, Union Springs Elementary School. The kids were out for recess. If I cracked the window open, I'd hear them on the playground.

The governor's voice became warm, persuasive. Buttery, almost. "Let us take this burden off your back. You recuse, and we'll bring it up here."

"To Montgomery," the AG said. Made sense he'd want it at the Alabama State Capitol building, where he had his office. He could keep the case tucked in his vest pocket.

The governor went on. "You can see the advantages, Mary. The merits of making the switch. In Montgomery, we have circuit judges with more years on the bench. More experience with major cases."

I'd still been watching the little kids on the school playground. That comment pulled my eyes away from the window. "I appreciate your concern, gentlemen. Thanks for the offer. I'm turning it down."

A moment of shocked silence before the governor said, "Don't you want to take some time to think about it, Mary?"

"Don't need to. My mind's made up. It's set." I let them hear it in my tone. Firm, decided. *I'll show you who's no-nonsense,* I thought.

I heard a disgruntled sigh blow through the speaker. The governor said, "Well, then. If that's your final word. I guess we can end this call, right?"

"Right," I echoed. "Y'all have a good day."

I would've cut off the call. But my cell phone was sitting on my desk, right in front of me. I was distracted when the cell phone screen lit up with a text, looked like it was from my friend Loucilla. So I reached for the cell phone instead of punching the button to end the call on the landline.

I heard the governor say, "You still there, Dick?"

"Yep."

One second passed, maybe two. "Goddamn! That fucking bitch!"

Psychic abilities weren't necessary to realize the governor was talking about me.

Dick Winston replied, "I tried to warn you, Bert. I've put up with shit from that uppity bitch for years."

I decided it was time to speak up. "Umm, guys? I'm still here."

Neither of the men spoke. No apology, reply, regrets. I heard two metallic clicks as they individually terminated the call.

There was a tentative knock on the door. I composed my face, sat up straight in the chair. "Yes?"

Luna peeked in. "I saw the light go out, from your call with the governor. Everything okay?"

"Sure."

She grimaced. "They were pretty loud, Judge. I couldn't help hearing it. You all right? You sure?"

"Yeah, I'm fine."

She looked doubtful. I was going to have to convince her. "Seriously, Luna, I'm fine. It's good to know where you stand with people. They asked me to do something. I turned them down. So they called me names. That's nothing new. Same old shit."

"But it's terrible!"

I waved a hand in dismissal. "It's over, and I'm glad. What else can they do to me?"

CHAPTER 27

After that telephone scuffle with the governor, I was on high alert, poised for trouble to start. But May passed without any kind of major incident. School let out, and it appeared that we might have an ordinary summer in Bullock County.

Traditionally, the courthouse is quiet in June and July. The temperature heats up and people slow down. Folks don't have the energy to duke it out in court. Their kids are running the streets of town all day, and those summer days are long. The sun doesn't set until eight o'clock and twilight keeps the sky lit past nine.

It was a Friday afternoon in the middle of June, and the end of the workweek had me in good spirits—except that I was missing the Oyster House.

Since the Bria Gaines case had put me on people's radar, Loucilla and I had to switch up our long-standing meeting day. Changed locations, too, moving around and trying out new restaurants. A change of habit is healthy, Loucilla claimed, but the novelty didn't hold much charm for me, and I wondered whether we might hazard a return visit without attracting unwanted attention.

As I turned off the farm road and into my gravel drive, Foghorn trotted out of the barn to greet me. Before I reached the farmhouse, I had to hit the brakes and let the car idle while he picked his way across the path. Damned rooster thought he owned the place. You know what people say about cats. Same thing was true with Foghorn: He was just letting me live in the house rent-free.

While I waited for the rooster to pass, I gazed over at the farmhouse. The pots of red geraniums I'd planted lent a bright pop of color to the front porch. The place looked good, tidy and neat, with a recent coat of paint and a fairly new roof. I take pride in the little house that has stood on this spot for a century. I tell anyone who'll listen that the place is structurally sound, thanks to craftsmanship and materials — minus the ancient wiring and plumbing — that are just plain superior to what builders use now. They don't make them like that anymore.

While I was admiring my house, I noticed another spot of color. A yellow note had been left on the doorframe. The paper that fluttered in the warm breeze was an ominous sign.

"What the hell?"

I parked the car, ran across the hard-packed dirt, and hurried up the porch steps. The printed message from the US Postal Service — *Sorry we missed you while you were out* — was as regulation as my old-fashioned metal mailbox, the kind that allows the rural-route postman access without leaving his vehicle.

But a return-receipt legal notification required the dude to leave Farm Road 164, drive up to my house, get out, and knock on my door.

For a quarter century, I'd been engaged in the legal profession — a profession that dealt in bad news.

Somebody was fucking with me.

The handwritten notations on the form revealed my assailant: the Pearce Law Firm in Union Springs.

A spurt of anger sent my heart racing. Arch Pearce called himself a lawyer, but he was a glorified collection agent, one of the unscrupulous, overreaching shysters who made a living as a landgrabber. His brand of legal practice, targeting poor real estate holders, was one of the reasons that landownership by Black people had dwindled to nearly nothing.

Whenever he appeared before me in my courtroom, I'd been inclined to lock him up in jail with the other crooks and thieves. But the law isn't written that way, and I don't abuse my power, regardless of what the DA may claim. So I tried to intervene by taking measures under my control. Like reining him in by ruling against him whenever possible.

And now, in an ugly shift of circumstances, I was the target of an Arch Pearce certified letter. I crumpled the note in my hand. Paced up and down the porch, listening to the pine boards creak under my shoes.

"I've got nothing to worry about." I said it out loud, to a limited audience: the rooster and the insects buzzing around. "This is my land. I take care of what's mine, always have."

It didn't sound convincing enough. I raised my voice, letting it ring out. "Pearce won't win. I'm bulletproof. No one can take it from me."

Pearce handled a lot of collection cases. I took care of expenses, paid my debts, paid my bills, leaving no basis for one. But if Pearce wasn't bringing a collection action, that only left one other alternative.

He was after the farm.

The Stone family farm had been handed down from generation to generation. My sisters and I inherited the land from our parents.

Neither Mama nor Daddy ever made a will. Not uncommon in this area. My parents died intestate. So did my grandparents. That meant that the farm in Bullock County was technically "heirs' property." Land owned by the descendants of the deceased as tenants in common.

And heirs' property is a can of worms.

Shitttt. I should have taken care of it. Should have dug through our ancestry, taken time to file a quiet title action. Bought my sisters out, had them sign a quitclaim deed.

Because I knew the facts. Over the past few decades, 90 percent of Black Americans had lost their farmland. Through partition sales, foreclosures, deceptive tactics. Their property interests were vulnerable because of the history of heirs' property and the cloud it casts over title.

I wanted to storm the post office and demand to see the correspondence. I was wild to know what that letter would say.

But the letter wasn't even there. The postman still had it in the postal truck that was bumping over a farm road somewhere in Bullock County. And the postal notice stated that I could pick the letter up at the post office in Union Springs in two days.

Two days? That was a damned lie. It was Friday; the post office was closed on Sunday. I'd have to wait until Monday. And if they insisted on hanging on to it for two business days, it could be Tuesday before I'd be able to collect the letter and see what the hell this was all about.

I leaned against the painted beam holding up the porch and looked out at my property. Seeing it with fresh eyes—the trees, weathered barn, green fields. The sight as familiar as my own face in the mirror.

No one was going to take it. I wouldn't permit that to happen.

I walked over to my wicker rocking chair and sat. Tried to calm myself by rocking back and forth.

Right.

Good luck with that.

Friday through Tuesday? I couldn't wait it out. No damn way.

I lunged out of the chair so fast that it rocked so far back that it tipped against the window frame. Any more force and I'd have busted out the glass pane.

I charged across the yard and pulled open the driver's door, climbed inside. Didn't even check the clock. Because it didn't matter what time it was.

There was someone I had to see.

CHAPTER
28

I wanted to burn the rubber off my tires. Tear the asphalt off those country roads. It required all the restraint I could claim, but I kept my foot from stomping on the accelerator and stayed within the speed limit.

Back in the city limits of Union Springs, I headed downtown and wheeled into a parking spot close to Arch Pearce's law office. After I slammed my car door shut, I was disposed to break into a run. But I held back, as a matter of dignity. I was trying like hell to hold on to mine.

When I stepped up to the entrance of the office building, I caught a glimpse of my reflection in the glass. I paused, taking a longer look. Determined, yes. Intimidating? Sure. Just wanted to make sure that I didn't appear to be crazy or wild-eyed.

A buzzer sounded when I opened the door and stepped inside. *Fancy*, I thought. *Very twenty-first century.* Moreover, alerting Arch Pearce to arrivals would be a practical necessity in that office. Odds were good that a person walking in was someone he had pissed off.

After all, he was in the business of taking advantage of people who were vulnerable. Bringing them to their knees. Taking what was rightly theirs.

Well. He'd picked the wrong woman to mess with.

It was getting close to five o'clock. The reception area was empty except for one lone employee, a young administrative assistant occupying a desk. As I marched up, she watched with some trepidation, shrinking back in her chair.

That might've been a result of my intense facial expression.

I stood in front of her desk, eyeing the closed door directly behind her, bearing a brass nameplate.

"I'm here to see Arch Pearce."

The young woman gave me an apologetic grimace. "Judge Mary, do you have an appointment?"

Of course she knew who I was. Everyone in town knew me. Unfortunately, I couldn't place her. So I cheated, peeked down at her desk and faux-wood nameplate: Crystal Corbett. Aw, hell. I knew her mother, from our school days.

I kept my voice level—for auld lang syne, you see. "Crystal, I don't need an appointment. He contacted me. Tell him I'm here."

She picked up the desk phone. Glancing away, she cleared her throat and whispered into the receiver.

"Judge Mary Stone here to see you, sir."

If I hadn't been so worked up, I probably would've felt sorry for the girl. People shouldn't work for a thief like Pearce. But she was young, and I knew her background. Nobody was packing up the car to send this girl off to college at eighteen. She was probably just getting by, like most people in town.

But she was in bed with the devil. And probably wise to the scam. He'd probably made her print out the correspondence he'd sent to me. She may have folded the paper and licked the envelope.

"Yes, sir," she said. Pinching her lips together with a pained expression, she put the receiver back in place on the desk phone. Handling it delicately, as if it were made of glass.

She knew why I was at the office. Addressing a point over my left shoulder, she said, "Mr. Pearce is busy right now."

The fucking nerve? I almost laughed; it was so absurd. "He's busy? Really?"

"Tied up. Mr. Pearce is tied up."

She met my eye then, with a pleading look. The girl was terrified.

I didn't jump on her. There was no cause for that. My argument was with her boss. As I moved on past her desk, I bent down to say, "When he asks, just tell him you tried. But there was nothing you could do to stop me."

I twisted the knob of his office door and discovered that Pearce was underestimating the opposition. Apparently, he'd believed that little Crystal Corbett could shoo me away.

I swung the door wide and stepped right in. "Mr. Pearce! I understand you have some business with me."

He hopped out of the chair. "Judge Stone! I wasn't expecting you."

I ignored his outstretched hand. "Is that right? But you sent this, didn't you?"

I had the crumpled sticker in my pocket. I pulled it out, stuck it on his desk, smoothed it out. "That's your name, your business address. When I saw the notice on the front door of my house, I came right on over. I'd like for you to produce a copy of the correspondence so that we can discuss it."

He was wary. "You haven't received the letter through the mail?"

"I wasn't home. That's why the postman left this." I tapped it with an index finger. "But I'm very curious about the contents of your letter. Let's see it."

I dropped into the chair across from his desk. Sat back, crossed my legs. I was prepared to wait, if necessary.

He didn't pretend to hunt for the file. It was within easy reach, sitting on the credenza behind his chair. He opened the file folder, pulled out a copy of the letter, and slid it across the desktop.

I picked it up. I was careful to keep a neutral face as I read. It was tough to do.

Dear Mary Stone,

This letter serves to advise you that our client, Mr. Caleb Wilton, recently acquired a common interest in the sixty-acre tract of land in Bullock County, Alabama, where you currently reside.

He acquired his interest through a certain Mr. Abraham Stone, who inherited his heir's interest as a direct descendant of your late grandfather, Luke Stone.

It was a phony, a sham. Had to be. We knew our family tree. Even though the babies prior to my generation had been delivered at home and birth certificates didn't exist. But they were recorded in the family Bible.

I kept reading. The next line jumped out at me. I should have anticipated it, but the words shook me, nonetheless.

Mr. Wilton desires that the subject real estate be sold at auction to monetize his duly acquired interests.

Alternatively, if you wish to acquire Mr. Wilton's interests, the appraised value for his share is $190,000.

I had to read it twice. Just to be sure it wasn't a typo. I was careful not to let my face betray me. Looking up, I deadpanned.

"One hundred ninety thousand. You kidding me, Arch?"

He shifted in his chair. "It's valuable property. I shouldn't have to convince you of that. You've lived on it all your life."

"Yeah, it's valuable to me. But no legitimate expert would appraise the value of a one-fourth share of the property at one hundred ninety thousand dollars. That's astronomical."

He sighed. Looked at his wristwatch — the guy still wore one, a real watch. It was a theatrical prop. Immediately after checking the time, he said, "I hate to rush this impromptu meeting, Judge Stone. But, like the saying goes, I got someplace I gotta be."

"Is that right?" I gripped the arms of the chair. Wanted to show him I wasn't going anywhere. "Business? Or pleasure?"

"Ummm." He tapped an ink pen against his chin. Like he was thinking it over. "A combo, I guess? A political event. In Montgomery."

"Ah." The clouds disappeared, and I could see clearly. "Think you'll run into the governor?"

He gave me a sheepish grin. "It's likely. He's the keynote speaker."

"How lucky for you. To get to hear him speak."

I stood, seized by a sudden urge to get the hell out of that office. Didn't even want to breathe the air in there.

Felt like the atmosphere was toxic. Poisonous. Burning my lungs.

I leaned over the desk and peeled my yellow sticker off the surface. Held up Pearce's letter and said, "I see you've given me thirty days from receipt of this letter to elect to purchase the interest."

He looked guarded. "Yes. That's standard."

"Thirty whole days. I bet that demand typically cuts Black people off at the knees. They get confused, think they're at your mercy. And then you buy them out. At a fraction of the property's actual worth."

"Well, I don't know about that."

"Oh, I do. I know all about it."

He didn't respond. That was okay, I didn't need for him to explain his game plan. "If I don't buy the interest, you're going to sue. That right, you want to sue me? Go ahead, do it. Waste your time and resources."

"I don't consider it a waste of my time."

I shook my head in disbelief. "But you know I'm gonna win. You can't claim adverse possession. I've occupied that property for over twenty years. Whereas I can successfully make a case of adverse possession under color of title. But you know that."

"We don't need to make an adverse possession claim. This property interest was obtained from a member of your family, a direct descendant of Luke Stone."

"Bullshit!"

And suddenly I was ten-year-old Mary again in the face of Stanley the school bully who decided to single me out because my hair was kinky and my skin was too dark, and he couldn't make sense of it. He singled me out because he could. I was scared then but not now, and like an eight-hundred-pound bull being taken down by four lions...I roared.

"You want to bring me down? You think you have the balls, you cowardly piece of horseshit? You just woke up the lion!"

I fired a parting shot. "Get ready, Pearce. I'm going to disprove your claim, even if I have to dig my granddaddy up to do it. Don't think I won't. I know where the bones are buried."

CHAPTER 29

Back in the driver's seat of my car, with windows rolled all the way up, I let loose.

"Stupid! Stupid, stupid!"

I beat the heel of my hand against the steering wheel hard enough to hurt. Because I was mad as hell. But my ire wasn't only directed at the shyster Arch Pearce and his lying client. I also wanted to beat my own head against a wall.

A lot of Black folks lose their land because they don't understand the law. I didn't have that excuse. I knew better.

"Idiot!"

We could lose everything Mama and Daddy died for.

One final slam against the steering wheel. People passing by on the sidewalk were looking spooked. Guess I was making more noise than I intended.

I can carry a lot. That's why I stay so busy, work so hard. I can shoulder everything. But not my own pain.

After I started the ignition, I hit Nellie in my contacts. She picked right up.

"What's up?" she said. Her voice was cheery, with that upbeat "Friday afternoon" sound.

"Meet me at Jordan's. I'm on my way over there right now."

I could tell that I'd stolen the shine right off her day when she answered. "Is something wrong? You sound like somebody just died."

I blew out a breath, tried to chill. It wouldn't help to scare my family out of their wits. "Nothing that bad. Serious, though. Jordan's home, isn't she?"

"Yeah, I just talked to her. What is this all about?"

"I'll see you over there." Cut off the call, didn't even say good-bye. I could hear Nellie's voice in my head: *Why do you have to be so rude?* But I was trying to spare her. There's some news you don't want to break over the phone.

It only took a few minutes to drive to Jordan's house from the commercial area of town. Nellie got there before me, though. The call must've lit a fire under her. I pulled up behind Nellie's car on the curb.

I walked up to the front door of the neat one-story, ranch-style house where Jordan and Trayvone lived with their two daughters. The front door was open. I could see Jordan and Nellie through the screen door, waiting for me.

When the door banged shut behind me, the questions started raining down.

Nellie was quicker. "What the hell is going on? Damn! You do realize you hung up on me, right?"

"Nellie! Don't start cussing, the girls will hear you. Mary, what's wrong? Nellie said you're sounding like the world is coming to an end."

"Let's sit down, okay?"

Jordan led us into the kitchen. I pulled the copy of Pearce's letter from my bag. It was wrinkled, but not so bad that they couldn't read it. Jordan sat and smoothed the paper on the wooden table. Nellie leaned on the chair behind her, reading over her shoulder.

Jordan gave her head a shake, like she was trying to clear it. "I don't understand. What's it mean?"

Nellie wasn't as naïve. "They're taking the farm." She looked up, met my eye. "That's right, isn't it? That's what they want."

I pulled out a chair. Sat down. "That's what they're trying to do."

"No." Jordan was genuinely confused. "They can't. It's been in the family for generations."

"That's true. But—there was no will, you understand."

"But we own it."

I put my elbows on the table, propped up my chin in my hand. Suddenly felt so weary, I had to hold my head up.

I said, "Nellie, that's just it. No one in the family ever made out a legal will. So the farm, the sixty acres our great-grandfather bought back in 1917, it's heirs' property. When a person in Alabama dies without a will, their heirs own the property as tenants in common."

Jordan wasn't a believer, not yet. "But we're the last. The only surviving generation. Everybody knows that. So it belongs to us."

Nellie put her finger on the sheet of paper for emphasis. "Apparently, this motherfucka Wilton is not convinced. He's claiming that he bought a share from Abraham Stone—whoever the hell that is."

In complete disbelief, we three sisters exchanged glances, our voices rising, each speaking over the other now, not in anger, but in urgency—to get our points across, as if the volume directly correlated with the others' understanding of the words.

Jordan said, "Daddy ain't had but two brothers and one died

when he was one year old. Direct descendants? Make that make sense."

"Shit, Jordan! It doesn't have to. Wilton is just a name." Nellie nudged my shoulder.

I interjected, my voice overpowering theirs, "Nellie's right. Somebody who claims to be a descendant sold his interest to this Wilton."

"But what the fuck, Mary? You pay the taxes! You've paid them every year since Mama died." Jordan swiped the paper off the table. She looked like she was about to cry.

"It's not enough that I pay the taxes. Not if he's an heir."

"He's lying, though." Nellie grabbed the sheet of paper off the floor and slid it across the table at me, like I needed to see it again. "He's obviously a crook. Look at the dollar amount in this letter. No way his claim could possibly be worth that kind of money. One hundred and ninety thousand, for his one-fourth share? That would make the farm worth over three-quarters of a million dollars." She broke into a rusty laugh. "Damn, girls! We're millionaires!"

I snickered, couldn't help myself. "I feel better already. Now that I know I'm so rich."

Nellie slapped the tabletop. "I'm gonna go buy me a Lexus!"

We laughed together. It felt like Nellie and I were schoolgirls again, trying to put on a brave face and shrug off something that was bringing us down.

Jordan stared at both of us like we were crazy. Well, she was the baby. Our little Saint Jordan. The relationship dynamic was different with her.

Our laughing got the kids' attention. They came running into the kitchen. "What's funny?" Stella asked. She was the youngest. Jordan's first daughter was named Rose, for our mama.

Jordan turned into strict Mama. "Out into the backyard, you two. I told you we were talking about grown-up business in here."

"But y'all was laughing, Mama."

"You gonna make me tell you again?"

That did it. We waited until they slipped out the patio door into the back. Watched while they ran across the yard and climbed onto the swing set. Jordan lingered by the window, then turned to me. "What do we do, Mary?"

I'd already started to map it out. "We'll be prepared to go to court. We get all of the documentation we can put together. I'll get the deed from the safe-deposit box at the bank. Jordan, you've still got the family Bible?"

She sputtered, indignant. "Of course I've still got it!"

"I'll do a title search. Nellie, did you ever find anything when you were going onto that ancestry website?"

She shook her head. "Girl, there wasn't much I could find. It's hard to document our family history, even after our people were free. We just didn't have many official papers. No birth certificates or death certificates. No government documents."

"I think I've got Mama's and Daddy's death certificates. There are some old obituaries somewhere."

"Yeah, I think I've got those," Nellie said.

"We'll put it all together. You know, another name for heirs' property is 'tangled property.' We need to straighten it out."

We fell silent for a long minute. Jordan reached across the table, clutched both our hands. I gave hers a squeeze.

My baby sister's voice wavered when she asked, "We won't let them take the farm, will we?"

"No!" I answered. I didn't repeat my vow to Arch Pearce: that we'd dig up Luke Stone, if need be. Sounded gruesome.

Nellie wasn't put off. "I told you, Mary. They're coming after you." She shook off Jordan's hand, walked away from the table. Her voice sounded bitter when she spoke.

"That goddamn court case."

I didn't deny it.

She wasn't wrong.

PART
TWO

CHAPTER 30

Nova Jones

BULLOCK COUNTY COURTHOUSE
UNION SPRINGS, ALABAMA

It was around eleven o'clock on a hot Monday morning in late August, and Nova Jones was wishing she was somewhere else.

Whenever Nova had a rare opportunity for alone time, she would walk to the nearby pond.

Nova once read that trees and plants benefit from being spoken or sung to, so one day she tried it with the ones surrounding the still water. It was a relief for her to lay her soul bare to these beautiful beings. She found peace in their presence. She felt them listening to her confidences with patience and love, which was something she hadn't experienced with people since Granny died.

Nova missed her granny dearly. She missed her wrinkled hands. Her favorite days were when she wore her blue cotton dress with the yellow daisies. Her granny had embroidered the flowers for her when she was alive. The dress was tight on her now, but she didn't care.

Her love of nature and the library was born from her granny, who had read to her at night and guided Nova's hands in the dirt to search for roly-poly bugs and pick cherry tomatoes in the summer.

Nova felt closest to her granny when she was at the library or sitting in the grass reading the books she'd checked out about gardening, herbs, and other natural phenomena. Nova's favorite books were about Indigenous practices in plants and healing. She learned to propagate and identify different varieties of hibiscus. She read about the Creek people who once roamed the lands she walked on. They cared for the earth and nurtured it with their mind, body, and soul. *How beautiful to love and be loved in this way,* she thought.

Nova felt alone all the time — at school, with her family, and at church. When she walked into a room, she could feel everyone's eyes on her, like a caged animal at the zoo. She heard their whispers, saw them furrow their brows and shake their heads in disapproval. This small pond was the only place where Nova felt truly seen, away from the people who called her names like *heifer* and *slut,* away from the parental responsibilities that came with being the oldest child.

She'd rather be with the wind and the trees than where she was now. Waiting on a hard wooden bench in the courthouse, right in the middle of town, where everyone could see her.

Nova could tell that people walking by her in the courthouse knew who she was. They gave her nosy looks and nudged each other as they passed by. She slid down in her seat, ducked her head, wouldn't look at them.

They all thought she was a heifer—that's what her mama would say. A whorish heifer. Nova wanted to hide, but she didn't have a chance of going unnoticed. Not a prayer. Not here.

On top of that, her baby brother was screaming his head off.

Her sisters, Arbonne and Reba, and her other brother, Tre, were all over at the elementary school right behind the courthouse. But Mama couldn't find anyone to watch Caden. She'd called a few women from church, but not one stepped up. That didn't seem very Christian to Nova.

And now Caden was pitching a fit. Big tears rolled down his chubby cheeks, snot running from his nose.

"You get him to hush up," Mama said. "Or I'm going to give him something to cry about."

Nova bounced her brother on her knees. She wiped his nose and whispered, "You better be good, you hear?"

Caden stuck his thumb in his mouth and sucked on it, looking around him with those big wet eyes. They sat that way for a while. Nova could tell that her mama was nervous, jiggling her foot like she always did when she was edgy.

The door at the end of the hallway opened up and a man in a suit walked out. Nova recognized him right away. It was Mr. Reeves, the man who told her she'd need to be part of the trial—the one about the abortion. Nova had been scared when he said it. And Mama had flipped out. "Are they gonna put my child in jail?"

Mr. Reeves said no, nobody was trying to put Nova in prison. She wasn't in any trouble, he said. So long as she cooperated.

He said the only person who was going to prison was Dr. Gaines. That scared Nova, too. Because it didn't seem right.

How could they put a doctor in jail for helping somebody?

As Nova twitched on the hard bench, Mr. Reeves walked right up to where they were sitting. "Morning, Nova." Then he looked at her mama. "Ms. Jones, thanks so much for bringing Nova in today."

Mama gave him a bright smile, the smile she gave to people who were in charge—school principals, cops, welfare investigators. Especially if they were men.

"Glad to help out. Me and Nova, we available anytime, anything you need us to do."

Nova jiggled Caden on her knee as a woman walked up and stood beside Mr. Reeves. White woman. Pretty. Wearing a nice blue outfit. Nova had never seen her before.

"Morning, y'all," she said.

Mr. Reeves nudged her forward. "Eleanor, I'd like you to meet Nova Jones and her mother, Starla. Ladies, this is Miss Eleanor Lindquist. Eleanor is an assistant attorney general with the office in Montgomery."

Nova stared at the two fancy-pants lawyers while she tugged on her worn T-shirt, a hand-me-down from her mama. Mr. Reeves was nice-looking in an ordinary way, but Miss Lindquist looked like she'd walked right out of a TV show. She sure as hell didn't look like anyone Nova knew in Union Springs.

As Nova was staring up at her, Miss Lindquist bent down. "I'm looking forward to getting acquainted, Nova. I've heard a lot about you."

Nova wondered what she meant. For sure, everybody was talking about her. But they weren't saying anything good.

"Yes, ma'am," Nova whispered. "Nice to meet you."

The baby pulled his thumb from his mouth with a pop and started talking. Just nonsense sounds, mostly.

While he babbled, the pretty lawyer looked at him real close, like she was examining a flower. "What a pretty baby!" she exclaimed with a smile on her face. She smiled at Caden. She smiled at Nova.

But Nova saw something else on Miss Lindquist's face. She knew what the lawyer really thought. She thought Nova was dirty. Nova kept telling herself that wasn't true and could no longer tell what was real anymore.

Her mama tried to settle Caden down, but his patience was all used up. He started up crying again.

Nova watched her mama bend him over her shoulder and swat his bottom. "You stop that!"

That made Caden cry even louder. Nova could've told her that would happen, but nobody was asking for her opinion.

Miss Lindquist turned to Mr. Reeves. "Robert, tell your clerk she needs to take this mama and her baby to a restaurant. Somewhere they can get something for the baby to eat."

Nova's mama didn't argue. "He eats McDonald's. Love those nuggets and fries."

"Perfect. What is it now, eleven thirty? You go have a nice lunch and come back in about an hour. We'll be all done by then."

Mr. Reeves made a quick call on his cell phone. A few seconds later, Nova saw a young woman coming down the hallway. She walked right up to her mama and Caden. Ignored the fact that the baby was wailing like crazy. Just patted him on the head like he was a puppy. "Hi! I'm LuAnne. You two ready to go?"

Nova watched as her mother walked out with the baby and the clerk.

When she looked up, Miss Lindquist winked at her. "Nova, I'm pretty sure I know what you're thinking. You're wishing that you were going to McDonald's, too."

Nova ducked her head and looked down at the floor, embarrassed.

She wasn't sure what to say, so she nodded because it seemed like something she should do. Nova hadn't eaten all morning. She knew she should be hungry. But she hadn't been able to keep anything down since what happened to her.

The silence in the room was heavy as they all stood there and waited for Nova to give her order.

"Chicken nuggets and fries?" Nova Jones said.

Nova kept waiting for someone to notice that she wasn't really there. She felt off balance, like she'd stepped out of her body and forgot where she put it.

She still remembered the pain in her stomach, and the chunks of blood that came after. She remembered it so often, it was like the pain never went away. The pain stole all the breath from Nova's body. She was still waiting to get it back, so she could breathe again.

"Come with me," Miss Lindquist said. Nova stood up and followed her through the door into a big office. Mr. Reeves came in right behind them.

"Don't you worry, Nova," said Miss Lindquist. "I'm going to take care of everything you need." And then came out with a little laugh. "What kind of lawyer do you think I am, starving my star witness? Do you think I'd do that?"

Did she expect an answer to the question? She had no idea what a star witness was. She'd never felt like the star of anything.

"Nova, you're a VIP in this courthouse—a very important person—are you aware of that?"

Nova didn't feel important. She often felt like a rabbit being chased by a coyote. Her heart was pounding through her chest so hard, she thought surely people could see it thump-thumping through her T-shirt.

Nova shook her head. "No, ma'am. Never thought I was important."

"Well, you are. You're making history, Nova. And so we're going to take very good care of you. Okay? Starting with McDonald's. Anything you want." She turned to Mr. Reeves.

"Hey, Robert? Can you do a McDonald's run? Just hit the drive-through."

Nova sucked in a breath. Mr. Reeves looked busy. And he seemed like he was the boss around here. Nova expected him to come back at Miss Lindquist with a smackdown. Instead, he just pulled out his car keys. He looked at Nova.

"Nuggets and fries."

Nova nodded.

"And maybe a Diet Coke?" said Miss Lindquist.

As Mr. Reeves walked out, Miss Lindquist called down the hallway to him. "Bring it to the war room, we'll be in there."

War room? Nova felt a chill run through her. "War?"

Miss Lindquist smiled. "It's just an expression. But I'm glad you asked. Anything you want to know, anything you get confused about, any question you have, you come straight to me."

Did she mean it? Because Nova *did* have a question, one that kept her awake at night.

"Can I ask a question about Dr. Gaines?"

"Sure you can."

"Is she gonna be okay?"

Miss Lindquist got a funny look on her face. "What do you mean, Nova?"

Nova was frozen in place, like she was short-circuiting. Staring into space. It seemed impossible to answer. What *did* Nova mean? She was searching for words but instead heard herself repeat.

"Is she gonna be okay?"

She saw Miss Lindquist's eyes widen. "What a strange thing to ask." Miss Lindquist searched the room, looking for an answer to

Nova's question. After a moment passed, she smiled and replied, "Bria Gaines will get a fair trial."

Nova didn't trust Miss Lindquist, but she really, *really* wanted to believe her.

She felt the strongest urge to run out of that room and straight to her pond. She needed to ask the trees and plants for guidance. If she closed her eyes real tight and listened to the wind in the leaves, she could hear their answer.

CHAPTER 31

Mary Stone

BULLOCK COUNTY COURTHOUSE
UNION SPRINGS, ALABAMA

On the third Monday in September, I was struggling to get matters under control.

Monday is generally the toughest day of my workweek. Whether that holds true for every member of the bench, I can't say. Maybe the judges who sit on appellate courts, or federal courts, or judges in courts of limited jurisdiction, like bankruptcy and probate, have a different experience. Those folks may cruise through Monday with ease. Privately, I suspect that's possible, and I can explain the reason why. They don't work as hard as the circuit judges who preside over state court. That's just a fact.

Even though I didn't have a criminal or civil jury week, just a normal Monday docket, I was scrambling. Apparently, it had been a wild weekend in Bullock County. Too many people drinking to excess. And invariably, the intoxication resulted in ugly behavior. Which led to women showing up at the courthouse on Monday to seek protection orders under the Alabama Protection from Abuse Act.

On that particular Monday, I heard from a young woman who'd just filed for an ex parte protection order against her fiancé in the case of *King v. Stuart*. Ms. King needed that order entered, without delay. I could see that before she uttered a word. Her eye was swollen shut, and her lip was split, still oozing. She kept dabbing at it with her finger.

I had a box of tissues on the bench. When I held the box out to her, she approached the bench and pulled one out.

"Take some more," I said. When she reached again, I handed it off. "Take the box."

I held the form she'd filled out in the circuit clerk's office. Walked her through it.

"Ms. King, you state on this form that you live with the defendant, LeRoy Stuart. That y'all have been living together for over a year."

"Yes, ma'am." She corrected herself. "I mean, yes, Judge."

"And you indicated that when the defendant inflicted harm upon you, the weapon used was his fists and feet."

She hung her head — as if the beating was cause for her to feel shame and chagrin. "That's right. He punched me. Kicked me, when I was down on the floor. Got me in the stomach and the ribs. When I rolled over, pulled up my knees to protect my gut? He kicked my back, kicked me in the butt."

Her skin tone was as dark as mine. Bruising is harder to see, and it shows up red or purple, instead of blue. But even from the distance of the bench, I could see it. On her face, arms, neck. He'd whaled on that woman without mercy.

I softened my voice. Asked a question that wasn't on the form. "Did you get any medical attention? See a doctor or go to a clinic?"

She shook her head. "I don't have a doctor. I used to see Dr. Gaines, but she's mostly shut down her office now."

In past months, I'd heard the same refrain from a number of folks in my courtroom. Medical care took a hit in our town when the DA filed his felony case against Bria Gaines.

I was concerned for the woman in court, worried about her physical condition. Felt compelled to come down from the bench, to take a closer look. I couldn't take the chance that she was neglecting a serious injury.

She looked nervous as I approached. I inspected the marks that were visible, took note of swelling and discoloration, the reddish hue on her battered skin.

"Did you take pictures of yourself? Pictures that show the injuries covered by your clothes? I'll need to see them, if you have them."

She nodded. Pulled them up on her phone and handed it to me.

I flipped through the images. My head started pounding as I looked at the pictures. My eyes grew hot. Quietly, I asked, "Did you call the police?"

"No, ma'am. I was too scared, shook up. I just got out, me and my two boys."

"I see." That was the plain truth. I did see. "Kids in school right now?"

"Yes, the grade school behind the courthouse."

I studied her. She looked like she was about to drop, she was so spent. I wanted to show emotional support, to give her a hug, but I didn't dare. I was afraid I'd hurt her anywhere I touched her.

Gently, I reached for her hand and held it. "I'm worried he might've broken something," I said. "Damaged you more than you know. I sure do think you ought to go to the hospital. And file a police report, too."

"Yes, ma'am. Maybe so."

"This is not your fault. You know that, right? There's no reason in the world why he'd be entitled to do this to you. No justification."

"Thank you, Judge. I understand that."

Her eyes wouldn't meet mine when she said it, though. She took a breath and said, "Mostly, I just need to get me a court order. So he'll know to leave me alone."

Maybe, I thought, *we can revisit the issue after the order is entered.* I returned to my seat at the bench and continued asking the standard questions.

"Is the defendant the father of the children?"

"No, ma'am—Judge. They not his."

"All right." I glanced at Luna, to let her know I was ready to enter the order. "I hereby find that this court has jurisdiction. And that a temporary order is necessary to prevent abuse. That the defendant represents a credible threat to the physical safety of the plaintiff."

The courtroom door opened, then slammed shut. I ignored it. I was filling in the boxes on the ex parte protection order form. "This court hereby orders that defendant LeRoy Stuart is restrained from committing or threatening to commit acts of abuse; and that the defendant is restrained from any contact with the plaintiff, Ada King. This order will be effective until further order of the court."

I had my eyes on the paper in front of me, was signing my name in blue ink. I heard the footfalls pounding on the wooden floor. Looked up.

He was stomping down the middle aisle of the courtroom. The defendant, without doubt. Walking with a swagger with his eyes fixed on his fiancée. The young woman was scooting away from him. She clearly believed he posed a threat. I shot a look at my bailiff. Ross was already on his feet.

The chip on the dude's shoulder was almost visible to the naked eye. Stuart swung his gaze from the fiancée to me. In a belligerent voice, he demanded, "Did I hear you say I can't have any contact with my own woman?"

"That's right, Mr. Stuart. You cannot." I held the form aloft. "You'll get a copy of this, so you can read the contents."

"Don't I get a trial?"

"Nope."

He stepped closer, pointing a finger at me. "I know the law. You can't do nothing to me without a trial."

My voice was sharp. "You gonna tell me about the law? This is an ex parte protection order. If you wish, you can request a hearing at a later date. It's all set out on the form. I recommend that you read it thoroughly as soon as I give you your copy."

He turned, gave his battered fiancée the evil eye. Then he turned that eye on me again. "So I'm supposed to read the paper? Don't get to say anything in my own defense?"

"That's right." In my no-bullshit tone.

That man was itching for a fight, I could tell. And he couldn't punch Ms. King, not in court. So he wanted to fight with me. He raised his voice—way too loud for a court of law. More like a volume he'd use in a barroom.

He said, "So you better explain this to me. How am I supposed to not have any contact with her when we live in the same house?"

I stood up. Because I was getting that urge, the one that frequently pushes me out of my chair and down from the bench. "Mr. Stuart, I have ordered that you be removed and excluded from the residence."

He flat-out shouted, "I own that house! It's mine!"

I was losing my cool. I could feel it slipping. My own voice made an echo in the big courtroom when I replied. "It doesn't matter who owns it. You are removed from the residence until I order otherwise."

"You can't do that!"

"I already did!"

I was getting hot. In the figurative sense, my temper was getting out of hand. But the anger heated me up, making me perspire under the black robe. A trickle of sweat made a path between my shoulder blades and down my back.

He was hot, too. "You can throw that piece of paper in the goddamn trash! I'm not afraid of you!"

"You should be! If you're not afraid, you're a damn fool!"

Ross, the bailiff, had taken a position between the angry defendant and the battered plaintiff. There was nothing to be gained by my entering the fray. But I was itching to climb down those steps and get into his face.

I almost went down there. Had to stop myself.

I grabbed the gavel instead. Pounded it three times before I pointed it directly at the defendant. "Violation of this order is a Class A misdemeanor. You'll do a year in jail for that. I promise that you will serve every single day of that time. I don't want you within three hundred feet of this woman or her home, or place of work, or the children or their school. I'm not just talking about punching and kicking, you understand. You are restrained from harassing her, stalking her, threatening or annoying her."

At that juncture, he wouldn't look at me. He had his head turned toward her, was scowling at his fiancée.

"You understand me?" I demanded. I wanted to hear him acknowledge it.

He lifted his chin. Didn't answer, didn't look my way. Kept

eyes on his fiancée while she backed away, like she thought he'd punch her out again in a court of law.

As part of standard courtroom equipment, I have a microphone at the bench. But I don't actually need one. I raised my voice to maximum volume. "Mr. Stuart! Do you hear me?"

I knew he did. They could hear me across the street.

He gave a sullen nod. Muttered an acknowledgment. It wasn't until Luna made copies of the order and they were served to both parties that I collected myself.

Sat back down in my chair and surveyed the back of the courtroom. As I pulled out a fresh box of tissues and used one to dab at my neck, I observed that we had an audience.

The DA was there, with a blond-haired woman wearing a sharp business suit. She had her arm around the shoulders of a young Black girl. I knew that girl on sight: Nova Jones.

Thirteen-year-old Nova Jones was in my courtroom. And it appeared that I'd just scared her to death.

CHAPTER 32

Tell the truth and shame the devil. I was mortified.
Not that I regretted taking the wife-beating maggot in hand. He needed the slap-down I'd just delivered. But I didn't intend to give it in front of an audience.

Not that audience, anyway. I didn't want to frighten a child, a vulnerable young girl.

The DA ambled down the aisle toward me. "Do you have a minute, Judge?"

There was nothing wrong in the words he used. It was the air he always had—like he owned that courtroom. Owned the whole county, everyone in it. Makes me mad as hell! Because I promise you, I care more about the community than that self-serving ass does.

I was in danger of self-combusting that morning, but Reeves hadn't noticed that anything was amiss. "I'd like to make some introductions," he said, in that flat voice.

Luna and Ross had separated the battered woman and her fiancé and had ushered Ada King and LeRoy Stuart out of court. I descended from the bench and approached the DA, hoping to ease the courtroom experience for the child he'd brought along.

"Good morning, Mr. Reeves. Who all do you have with you today?" I cut my eyes at Nova and smiled. Inside my head, I was calling out to her: *Are you okay? I'm here for you. I got you, Nova.* Trying hard to convey to her that I wasn't the Wicked Witch, or Cruella, or Ursula. Whoever she thought was the scary lady.

Reeves didn't introduce Nova, not then. "Judge, this is Eleanor Lindquist, she's with the attorney general's office. Maybe you've heard of her?"

"I believe I have," I said, nodding at her. "I read about a case you handled in Selma."

She extended her right hand, gave me a brisk handshake. "Honored to meet you, Judge Stone."

"Likewise. What brings you to Bullock County, Eleanor?"

The woman exchanged a glance with Reeves. He did the talking. "Ms. Lindquist is going to assist as co-counsel in the Gaines case. That's why we're making the rounds today. Eleanor wanted to be introduced to courthouse personnel, meet the law enforcement involved in the case."

"That's right," she said. She patted Nova Jones's shoulder. "And I wanted to get acquainted with this young lady. We'll be spending a lot of time together."

Really? That's pretty sus, I thought. The prosecution didn't need a personal relationship with a young and vulnerable State's witness. A professional relationship, certainly. But the chumminess she was displaying seemed a little off. Smacked of coercion, almost.

When the woman started patting Nova's shoulder like she was somebody's pet, it made my hackles rise.

And she kept on talking. "Your Honor, I've had some cases with young witnesses. And I've found that it's crucial to introduce them to the process. Give them an orientation that goes beyond a verbal description of what to expect at trial. I want my witnesses to feel at ease. So I take them on a tour of the courthouse. First on the agenda: Make sure they know where the restrooms are. That's an important thing to know, right?"

Laughing, she nudged Nova, like they were just having a good time. The woman was full of shit. That thirteen-year-old was facing public testimony in a case that exposed her most painful, intimate secrets. It was going to be an excruciating experience.

I watched Nova Jones, to see whether the AAG's sales pitch worked. Maybe not. Nova's eyes were shuttered, her muscles appeared taut—like she was prepared to cut and run, if necessary. Smart kid; she wasn't fooled. Testifying in a court of law ain't no fun for nobody.

I picked up the vibe; the girl wanted to get out of the room. I couldn't keep my mouth shut. "Is this some holiday I've forgotten? Shouldn't Nova be in school right now?"

The queen of the AG's litigation division chattered on. "Judge, it's a school day. But it was imperative that we schedule this session. This is a valuable part of the orientation. I want to give Nova access to the courtroom. So she can see what it's like in here. Where she'll stand to take the oath, and then sit while she testifies." She grasped Nova right above the elbow and ushered her down the aisle. "See, Nova, where Judge Stone was standing when we walked in? That's the bench. She sits up there. And the chair beside her, that's the witness stand. That's where you'll sit. The jury is in that box." She pointed at the jury box with its twelve empty seats.

Then with a sweep of her arm, she showed her the counsel tables for the prosecution and the defense. "I'll be right here, with Mr. Reeves. Unless I'm up by the witness stand, talking to you."

She paused, looking expectantly at Nova. Nova picked up the cue, gave a quick nod.

The woman flashed a broad smile. "I haven't made the most important introduction! Judge Stone, I'd like to introduce Nova Jones."

I opened my mouth to speak, but Lindquist was still talking. "Nova, Judge Stone will be in charge of your case. Whenever she speaks to you, you'll call her 'Judge' or 'Your Honor.' Can you remember that?"

"Stop!" I had to shut her up or I was gonna lose my mind.

Lindquist caught her breath, as if I'd choked her. Honestly, I kinda wanted to.

I said, "No need for introductions. Miss Jones and I have met before."

"Is that right?" The woman sounded surprised, but it was a shade overdone. I wondered whether she already knew about Saturday breakfast when she'd planned this whole exchange. "Nova, you never mentioned this. How long have you known the judge?"

Nova looked confused and a little frightened—like a kid who thinks she's in trouble but doesn't know what she's done wrong.

I had to cut that scene short. Lindquist would need to learn; I didn't play. "Miss Jones probably doesn't remember me; it was a brief meeting, and I wasn't wearing my robe."

Eleanor Lindquist wouldn't let it go. "Is that true, Nova? Do you remember meeting the judge or not?"

Nova lifted her eyes and briefly inspected me. "We go to Saturday breakfast sometimes. Mom says it's at Missy Mary's house. And Mama told me she was a judge. But she didn't look like it. Not at the farm." Nova lifted her shoulders in a shrug. "She just look like everybody else."

"Yeah, it's the robe that does it. Nice to see you again, Nova. I'll let y'all continue your courtroom tour. I have some work to do in chambers." I turned to go. Needed to escape before I snapped at the prosecution. I didn't want to scare Nova a second time.

Didn't make it through the door before I heard that woman call my name.

"Judge Stone, just a heads-up! General Winston's going to be in town today. He'll probably want to talk to you."

Shitttt. Dick Winston was coming to sit his butt down in one of my office chairs. The prospect made me want to spit. I'd have to be polite. Smile when I really wanted to snatch him bald.

Goddamn Mondays.

CHAPTER 33

The offhand comment from Eleanor Lindquist was all the notice I received heralding the AG's visit. He never let me know he was coming. No call from a secretary requesting an appointment.

Fortunately, I wasn't fated to spend the whole day dreading his arrival. The attorney general sailed into Luna's office right before we shut down for lunch.

My door was open, so I witnessed his entrance. Watched him flash a benevolent smile at my administrative assistant.

"Tell Judge Stone an old classmate of hers from University of Alabama is here."

Luna wasn't in on the game. I hadn't alerted her. "Sir, it's twelve o'clock. I'm about to lock up for the lunch hour. Do you have an appointment?"

I had to cover my mouth. Didn't want him to see me grinning. I knew it was a blow to his ego when Luna didn't recognize him on sight. The man thinks he's a star, always has.

The schmoozing politician disappeared. His voice was tight when he replied. "I'm Dick Winston, the attorney general of the state of Alabama. Go ask Judge Stone if she'll spare me a moment of her valuable time."

I was quick to come to Luna's rescue. I rose from my chair, called through the door. "Luna's just trying to keep me on schedule. Come on back, Dick. You don't need an appointment to see me."

Luna was flustered. She followed him, lingering in the doorway. "I'm really sorry, sir. For not knowing you right off."

He didn't speak, wouldn't acknowledge her apology. *Asshole.* I wasn't going to let him freeze out my hardworking clerk. I said, "Luna, Dick has been in politics for a long while. He doesn't get his feelings hurt by folks who intend no insult. Do you, Dick?"

Dick unbuttoned his jacket before he sat down. Looked like he'd put on weight. "Certainly not."

I gave Luna a nod. "Close the door behind you, please."

Not because I was eager to be alone with the man. I wasn't.

But I figured he'd come to deliver a message. And he probably didn't want an audience to hear it.

He cleared his throat before he spoke. "Mary, I'm here to extend an olive branch. With regard to that telephone snafu. I hope you're not upset by the governor's slipup over the phone last spring. He's a hotheaded guy, runs off at the mouth sometimes. Doesn't mean anything by it."

Sure, I could've made it easy on him. But I wasn't disposed to. Tipped back in my chair, like I was thinking it over. "I wouldn't say I'm upset, exactly."

"Good, that's good to hear. But I did want to clear the air, just in case."

Deadpan, I said, "Sure. It's always good to clear the air."

"You're not the sensitive type. Hell, I've known that since University of Alabama, right? Remember how we battled it out in moot court, back in law school?"

I did recall. I beat him like a drum in those mock trials, but Dick always seemed to garner all the credit. Even when he cheated.

I wanted to shout: *I graduated summa cum laude, you bastard!*

He was waiting for me to respond. I made a neutral noise. Kept my mouth closed.

"Hey, I hear you met my assistant today. Eleanor? She's a tough competitor, I'll guarantee that. Powerful litigator. Lots of courtroom experience."

"I'm familiar with her rep." I was, actually. Eleanor Lindquist was becoming low-key famous in Alabama. Everyone in the law biz knew about the victories she'd won in high-profile cases.

I wondered whether he'd reveal the true reason for her presence on the case. Was sincerely curious. I said, "I know you send some trial lawyers from your litigation division to lend a hand to inexperienced county prosecutors. When they need help with big cases. But that situation doesn't apply to Robert Reeves, our DA. He's not a novice."

"True. But Eleanor Lindquist, well, she's got qualities that Reeves lacks. She'll add a different dimension to the trial. She's already establishing rapport with the State's primary witness."

"I see." Actually, I did see. Strategically, it was a smart move. "So y'all are thinking that a woman at the prosecution counsel table will counter sympathy for the doctor. Juries sometimes have a soft spot for female defendants. And when your thirteen-year-old witness testifies, being questioned by a woman will make the direct examination less awkward."

He nodded, shrugged. "You always had an instinct for strategy, Mary. One of your strengths."

"Hmmm." I was growing weary of the conversation. There was no pleasure in tripping down memory lane with Dick Winston.

"When are you heading back to Montgomery? I know you're a busy man."

Take the hint, I thought. Maybe he did. He cut the shit, got to the point.

"This case in your circuit is really blowing up, Mary. Isn't it? Eleanor and I were talking about it on the way down here today. It's not surprising, because feelings run high on the issue. I feel that, personally. I'm pro-life, I make no secret. I believe that abortion is murder."

I sat there. Didn't respond.

He said, "Eleanor's young, she's not as conservative as I am. She told me that she personally believes we could benefit from more leniency in our Alabama law. But it won't affect her ability to represent the State in this case." His voice was deliberately casual when he said, "What do you think?"

I sounded perfectly chill. "She's your employee. You know best."

"No, no, no—I mean, where do you stand on the issue? Of abortion?"

"Well. That's a personal question, Dick."

He edged forward in his seat. "Come on, Mary—it's a fair question. No one really knows your position on these issues! You're running as a Democrat on the ballot for your reelection campaign for circuit judge. But where do you stand? No one knows for sure what your position on abortion is. Hell, I don't know. And we're old friends."

I was getting hot. Didn't let it show, not then. "I'm a judicial candidate. I can't make statements about issues of law that will come before my court. Can't commit to ruling in a particular way on the bench. You're well aware of that."

"Mary, it's just the two of us sitting in here."

Lord, he was trying my patience. "Dick. I know what you're doing."

He sat back. Smiled at me. "What am I doing? I'm trying to have a conversation with you."

The condescension was biblical. It always has been, with him.

"No, you're not! You're trying to coerce me into making a statement that you can use to pry me out of my position as the judge overseeing this case. Even though you are perfectly aware of my obligation to remain politically neutral. You want a statement? Here it is: As circuit judge, I'll uphold the law. In the case of *State v. Gaines*, I will preside in a fair and impartial manner."

We had a brief standoff after that, a short period of strained silence. When the AG finally spoke, he'd dropped all pretense of civility. "Let me tell you what's gonna happen here, Mary. Dr. Gaines will be convicted. We both know that, don't we? It's open-and-shut. And the jury will recommend a sentence. I'm projecting nothing less than twenty years. Hell, they may give her life."

No easy exit. That was the problem with having a shithead like Dick Winston sitting in my chambers. It was my territory, so I couldn't just get up and walk out. I needed to kick him out of my office before I lost it. After all, he was the state AG.

I was devising a good line to get him up from that chair and out the door when he dropped the bomb. "After she's convicted, a lot of money will be spent—whatever it takes—to be absolutely certain you're no longer a circuit judge. You'll lose everything."

That did it. No point in fake civility. We were past that. I pushed away from my desk and stood up, because I was determined to get that man out of my space. Even if I had to haul him out by his shirt collar. "Well, at least I'll have the family farm."

"Careful, Mary. You might lose that, too."

Son of a bitch. "What's that? What you say about my farm?"

I don't want to hate anybody, truly. But I hated Dick Winston's guts. I stalked around the desk toward him, ready to smack that smirk off his face. Maybe he could see my intention, knew he'd gone too far.

He hustled out of the chair and threw the door open. "Mary, I'm just bullshitting you. Trying to push your buttons. Got to go now! Thanks for receiving me in your sanctum sanctorum."

I watched him run past Luna's desk. After the door shut behind him, I muttered, "We've had a reckoning coming for a long while. You'd best stay out of my sights, Winston."

My heart was so bitter, I could feel it burning inside my chest.

CHAPTER 34

Bria Gaines

UNION SPRINGS, ALABAMA

Bria read through the final page of the police report. Turned it upside down on top of a stack of documents resting on a rickety metal desk. She was sitting in an office Ben Meyers was renting, a small space in a mostly deserted strip center on the outskirts of Union Springs.

When Bria looked up, Meyers was watching her. "You made it through? Read all the way to the end?"

"Of course I did." Bria rubbed her eyes. She'd been reviewing police and medical reports through most of the afternoon.

"You buzzed through that file pretty fast. That's all." Meyers picked up the stack of paper and slid it into a folder. "I don't want you to miss anything that might make a difference to our defense."

"I've read that file so many times I could quote it back to you chapter and verse. Do you actually think I'd ignore the evidence against me? I'm not an idiot."

Meyers looked down. "Did I imply that? If I did, I apologize." He flashed a smile at her.

The man had a dangerous amount of charm. Bria knew it would be useful at trial, but she'd put up a wall against it. Getting a schoolgirl crush on her defense attorney would lead nowhere good.

She stood up, eager for a break from the unforgiving office chair. A coffee maker sat on a plastic table in a corner of the room. The pot held a scant inch of inky brew. Bria stepped over, poured it into a mug. She made a face.

"Sorry," said Meyers, "that's from this morning. Should I make a fresh pot?"

"Wouldn't hurt. I think this might have solidified."

Meyers walked over to the corner and pulled out a bag of Peet's.

"How come you haven't joined the coffee pod cult?" asked Bria.

"I like making coffee," said Meyers. "It's one of the few domestic skills that I've mastered." He measured the coffee into the basket and set the control to Brew, then leaned back against the counter. "So what do you think of Nova's story?"

Bria shook her head. "Tragic. Heartbreaking. I know I'm the one on trial, but you and I both know what's criminal about this whole thing—the fact that the law requires a child to bear a child." She leaned against the sink. "You want to know why I became a doctor?"

"I do. And if you're about to tell me that there was a time in your life when you had to terminate a pregnancy of your own, I absolutely understand. I'd never judge you."

Bria blinked. Meyers was being a little too presumptive. And way too personal. She decided to ignore it. Maybe it was just his way of saying he was on her side. She took a beat and plunged ahead.

"I grew up in Alabama. Working class, seven kids. I was number six. Churchgoing family. My mama and daddy tithed. Ten percent of their gross income — not net! — went into the collection plate. Didn't matter what we needed. The car broke down, shoes had holes, no difference. The church came first."

Meyers nodded. "I knew a lot of families like that growing up."

Bria went on. "My folks didn't have medical insurance. If we got sick, we had to suck it up. Don't make a fuss."

She took a deep breath. These were painful memories.

"I liked boys, but I was careful. Because I'd seen what could happen. My sister Bailey, three years older than me, she got pregnant in high school. Fifteen years old. Carried to term. Begged to keep her baby. Of course, that couldn't happen. And, oh, my Lord! You should have seen all those fine Christian friends of ours turn their backs on her."

"Is she okay now?" asked Meyers.

"She's alive. She functions in the world. But what happened back then did something to her, messed her life up, and she never really got it back. That's why I went to med school. I wanted to be on the side of young women. Especially poor women. No matter what their circumstances."

"Coffee's ready," said Meyers. He pulled the carafe from the base and poured Bria a fresh cup. "Sugar? Cream?" he asked.

"Nothing," said Bria. "I want to judge it on its own merits."

She took a small sip, then another. She smiled. "You're right, Benjamin Meyers. You *are* domestic."

Meyers poured a fresh cup for himself. "So what do you think of Nova's story, the one she gave to the cops? About how she got pregnant?"

Bria toyed with the handle of her mug. "I feel for that girl, you know that. I keep her in my heart, even with everything that's happening. But — that story doesn't ring true."

"How come?" asked Meyers. "In her statement to the police, she said she didn't know who got her pregnant. Says she was drinking at a high school party and passed out. That doesn't sound credible to you?"

"I think what she described is a common occurrence. But it's not what happened to Nova."

Meyers carried his coffee mug over to the desk. "Based on what?"

Bria followed him and sat down. "Based on what she said that night, in my office. During the procedure."

"I'm listening," said Meyers.

"During the physical exam, I asked Nova some basic health questions, explained the procedure to her, made sure she understood what was going to happen, got her consent. At that point, she wasn't volunteering much information. Pretty much just one-word answers."

Meyers didn't interrupt. Just gave an encouraging nod.

"The procedure I performed that night was an aspiration abortion, because Nova was less than fourteen weeks. She was just under the line. It took me about fifteen minutes, maybe a little longer."

"Wait," said Meyers. "You said she was talking during the procedure. Wasn't she sedated?"

"No. It's standard to perform that procedure without sedation or anesthetic. She was awake. A little uncomfortable, but not in pain."

Bria closed her eyes. It was all coming back, she could see it like a reel playing in her head. Nova in the stirrups, gripping the sides of the examination table with both hands. Tears running down her face.

"She kept saying, 'This ain't my fault! You done this! I hate you, I hate you!'"

"Hate *who*?" asked Meyers. "She never said a name?"

"No name. But she kept repeating that she should've fought back. I remember her saying: 'I shoulda kicked the way the Dora Milaje do it. Just like in *Black Panther*. Like a warrior.'"

Meyers shook his head, like he didn't get it. "Tell me what you're thinking."

Bria pushed her chair away from the desk. Stood up, paced the small office. "She didn't talk about it like a girl who had no memory of what occurred. To me, it sounded like she knew exactly who it was that assaulted her."

"Bria, even if you're right, and even if we had the name of the attacker, it wouldn't make any difference for you. It doesn't create a defense. There are no exceptions for abortion under Alabama law. Not even for age or rape or incest. You know that."

"We need to talk to Cocheta Bass. She was the one Nova talked to first. Maybe she knows something I don't."

Meyers shook his head. "Cocheta Bass isn't going to be any help to us."

"Of course she will. Cocheta and I have been friends since I moved to Union Springs."

Bria saw Meyers dip his chin toward his chest, like he didn't want to meet her eyes. "Ben! What's going on? What do you mean she won't be any help?"

Meyers looked up. "Bria, she's testifying against you. Cocheta is a witness for the State."

In shock, Bria dropped back into her chair. She clutched the edges of the desk, felt the metal dig into her fingers. "No! She wouldn't!"

"Reeves just notified me today. They offered her a deal for deferred prosecution on the mandated reporter charge in exchange for her testimony in the felony abortion case against you."

Bria couldn't speak. Cocheta had turned on her.

Just like everyone else in town.

She let go of the desk. Her hands dropped into her lap and lay there, inert.

Meyers scooted his chair closer to hers. "Bria? You all right?" He leaned in closer. "Look, I know it's a shock. It's okay to cry. People feel better after they cry, sometimes."

Bria lifted her chin and sat up straight in her seat. "No, thanks. I'm all cried out. Didn't make me feel any better."

CHAPTER 35

Twenty minutes later, Bria and Ben walked into a barbecue joint in Union Springs. Honestly, she didn't know why she'd agreed to go. She certainly wasn't hungry. After Ben dropped the bomb about Cocheta turning State's witness, Bria's stomach turned so sour, she didn't think she'd ever eat again.

But Ben said they needed to get out of the office, to have a change of scene. Get some air. He said it would give Bria a lift. Make her feel better.

He escorted her to a two-top table in the far corner, away from other customers. Ordered her a beer and a pulled pork sandwich.

Service was fast. The waitress delivered the food and drink in record time.

Bria ignored the sandwich. She drank the beer while they sat in silence.

When Bria drained the final swallow of beer, she spoke. "We can't win. I don't have a prayer."

Ben's shoulders relaxed. He breathed out, sliding down in his seat. "Thank God. You've regained the power of speech. I thought I'd lost you."

She glared at him. "Seriously? You were worried about my health. So you brought me to a bar?"

He chuckled. "I had a friend, he practiced law in Atlanta. Met him right after I got out of law school. When the chips were down, he'd say, 'It's a beautiful day! Let's go someplace dark.'"

Bria waited, assuming there'd be an uplifting sentiment in the story. But that was it.

She looked around. It was dark inside the bar. And the gloomy atmosphere was intentional. It was the kind of establishment that covered the windows, to prevent the light from shining in.

"We can sit here in privacy." Ben bit into his sandwich.

She scoffed. "There's no privacy in this town. Not for me."

After he swallowed, he said, "Okay, then—relative privacy." He nudged the plate that held her untouched sandwich. Pushed it an inch closer to her. "You should try it. It's delicious. Spicy. It'll put some fire in you."

"Not happening. The fire's out. Extinguished." She studied her empty beer glass. "I'd take another drink. That might make me feel better."

He looked doubtful. "Is that a medical opinion? Because in my experience, more alcohol isn't always better—"

"Oh, shut up." Bria raised her glass to signal the waitress. When a fresh beer appeared in front of her, she took a sip. Just to show him she was in control.

"I've made up my mind, Ben," she said. Her voice sounded thoroughly professional. One glass of beer couldn't shake that. "You've been extremely noble, coming in from Atlanta and taking this case on. But it's hopeless. We can't win, so what's the point of going to trial? There's no benefit, none that I can see. I may as well plead, I'm ready to go there. What's the best plea bargain offer you think you can get? I don't expect the DA to recommend probation, there's no chance he'd do that. The case is too political."

"Bria…"

She kept talking, couldn't stop. "But if he'd offer a reasonably low sentence, and take no position on probation? I think I'd have a shot. My record is clean, I've done a lot for the community. And Judge Stone, she'll be fair. I sincerely admire that woman. The judge seems genuinely compassionate."

"Bria, stop."

He didn't raise his voice. But when he spoke the words, her breath caught. He wore the expression she'd often seen in the medical profession. When a doctor had to break the terrible news.

He didn't sugarcoat it. Evenly, he said, "It's not an option for you. Reeves doesn't intend to offer us a deal. I already inquired, just raised it as a standard question, like I always do. He made it very clear. No plea bargain in this case."

The revelation shocked her into silence. Bria wasn't naïve. She knew that she faced an uphill battle in the case, and that the DA would never offer her a sweetheart deal. But the stark refusal to consider a plea bargain at all?

She picked up the beer. Didn't sip it, took a deep swallow. Wished it were something stronger.

When she started shaking, Ben put his hand on her arm. It steadied her. He said, "We're going to trial, Bria. There's no reasonable alternative. But we're going to fight this. I believe in you, and I'm going to do everything in my power to see that you get justice."

She couldn't look at him, didn't permit himself to meet his eye. She was afraid of what she'd see, what she might read in his face.

But she was regaining her self-control when she said, "Justice?

Don't bullshit me, I won't stand for that. There's no way you can tell me that I'm going to be all right when this is over."

He dropped his voice. "Come on, Bria, you're a doctor. You know no profession can guarantee results. I can't promise an acquittal any more than a doctor can guarantee a cure. But I'm going to be your advocate. Try with everything I've got."

It wasn't enough. She could feel disaster looming over her. Bria wanted to hear straight talk. Nothing less. "Ben, I'm going to lose. I know that. You have to know that, too. Why are you here?"

Ben didn't respond immediately. He paused, took a breath. "Because it's wrong, Bria. Everything that's happening, what they're doing to you. It couldn't be more wrong. The day the story broke, I read about the case. I just had to come."

He wadded up a paper napkin, tossed it on his plate. "Like I told you, I can't roll out guarantees. Except for this: Gonna do the best I can to make it right."

It was the best offer she'd receive. Bria knew that. "Okay. What now?"

His voice was reassuring. "We'll take it one step at a time. I'm going to talk to each of the State's witnesses. Take a statement. Analyze what they say."

She thought about that. "Nova? You're taking her statement?"

"Got to. Her mother's, too."

She opened her mouth, shut it. It hurt to think of inflicting distress on the girl, making her talk about the abortion. She wished she could prevent it. But it was inevitable. Bria had to let her lawyer do his job.

They talked about his pretrial prep, and her struggle with the pain of waiting. She asked him to advise her, how she could best survive until the trial. He advised Bria to try to stay calm, keep up her day-to-day activities. Work, home. Go to church if that was part of her routine.

"I don't know about that," she said. "I'm more comfortable in a seedy bar right now than sitting in a pew at the Baptist church."

Just then, the door opened, sending a burst of afternoon sunlight into the gloomy interior. The light blinded Bria for a moment. When her eyes adjusted, she saw that three men had sidled up to the bar. She knew one of them: Vic Fowler, a patient of hers. Though it was probably more accurate to classify him as a former patient.

Vic Fowler and his friends appeared to be getting rowdy, from the way they were calling for drinks. Sounded like they were all half lit.

"Let's go," she said, picking up her purse. It was time to leave. She just had that feeling.

Ben paid the waitress, and they made their way to the door. They didn't dawdle on the way out, but they weren't quick enough.

Fowler had spotted Bria, despite the dim lighting.

"Goddamn! It's Dr. Bria Gaines! You got a lot of nerve, showing your face in here."

Bria didn't break stride. She pushed the door open and hustled outside, with Ben right behind her. When they were on the sidewalk, Ben took her arm as they hurried toward his car.

But Vic Fowler followed. "Hey, Doc! Got a message for you. I think there ought to be the death penalty for what you done!"

Ben held the key fob, unlocked the doors. When they reached the vehicle, Fowler ran up and blocked the passenger door, to prevent them from leaving.

Bria tried to reason with him. "Vic, I can't believe you're acting like this. I'm your family doctor. I set your arm when you broke it. I cared for your wife during her pregnancy. I delivered your daughter."

"You're not our family doctor anymore, you bitch. You won't fool me again. You're a cold-blooded murderer. A baby killer."

When he called her a killer, he advanced on her, coming in so close, she could smell his hot breath. She stepped back, stumbling when her feet hit the curb. Ben kept her from falling.

Then he moved up to confront Fowler. Ben said, "Back off." And he shoved Fowler away.

The shove threw Fowler off balance for a moment; his arms flailed. When he recovered, he reared back and threw a punch that sent Ben face down onto the asphalt. Knocked Ben out cold.

"No!" Bria fell to her knees on the pavement, checking the injury. His nose was gushing blood.

Fowler stalked away, heading back to the bar. Before he ducked inside, he shouted a warning.

"You can't be no Christian, Dr. Gaines. Probably don't believe in God. Do you believe in omens? Well, there's your omen!"

CHAPTER 36

Mary Stone

BULLOCK COUNTY COURTHOUSE
UNION SPRINGS, ALABAMA

I hadn't set a trial date yet. Too damn early, I opined. Dr. Bria Gaines had hired a new attorney: Benjamin Meyers, from Atlanta, Georgia. He'd only entered his appearance in court a couple months prior. It was a major case. He needed time to prepare.

Especially since he was traveling to Union Springs from Atlanta. That's a long-ass round trip. It was a first for me, having an out-of-state lawyer throw his hat in the ring for one of my small-town Alabama trials. Had to wonder. What exactly was the motivation?

I'd done some investigation, just to satisfy my curiosity. Meyers was a native of Georgia, a graduate of Duke Law School. Went into a silk-stocking Atlanta firm after passing the bar but didn't stay long. Made his name taking on high-profile cases—and winning them.

A high-stepping white boy tearing down the highway to Union Springs, to defend a young Black woman? Maybe he was kindhearted, compassionate. A supporter of feminist causes.

Or it might be, he was ambitious. Trying to enhance his reputation as a high-powered litigator.

Could be something else. There was that, too.

I intended to keep a sharp eye out.

Because I knew that a case like the Gaines trial wouldn't die down or fade from public attention. Even though we had no hearings scheduled, no motions being heard, no jury panel scheduled. *State v. Bria Gaines* was top of mind. The public imagination had been kindled, with emotions running high.

It was an uneasy balance I had to strike. Needed to give the defense and the State adequate time to get their ducks in a row. But not too much time, lest public reaction spin out of control.

That was the goal. I thought my balancing act was working reasonably well.

I was wrong.

I heard Luna knock. "Judge?" she called.

"Yeah? Come on in."

She opened the door, stepped inside my office. She was holding her cell phone in her right hand. "Judge Mary, you got a minute? I need to show you something."

Luna came over beside the desk with her arm extended. Holding her phone so close to my face my eyes couldn't focus on the screen. But I did hear the scrambled sound of people fussing with one another.

I pushed back from my desk, wheeling my chair away from her. Didn't mask my disapproval as I asked, "Is that social media? You know I don't hold with that."

"Yes, it's Twitter. X, I mean. Judge, I know you don't usually follow it—"

"Luna, I never look at it. No 'usually' to it. I pay no attention to that, don't have the time or the patience to watch other people acting the fool."

She still had that damn phone aimed straight at me. "Really, Judge, you ought to—"

"Girl, you know me better than this. Haven't you heard me preach on the evils of TikTok and Twitter and Instagram? That stuff they post on there is toxic. It's a time waster. People get all worked up, watching fights between folks they've never met, happening a thousand miles away."

She wouldn't back off. "Judge Mary, it's not miles away. This video on X, it was shot right here. In Union Springs."

That shook me. "What have you got there? What are you looking at?"

She handed her cell phone to me, and this time, I took it. Looked down at a frozen image. I tapped the arrow with my thumb and the action started. Two people were having an argument, people I'd never seen before. A middle-aged white man held a big poster: ABORTION IS MURDER. A young white woman—college-age, maybe—was trying to grab the poster, pull it out of his hands. They struggled over the rectangle of poster board. After about half a minute, the girl shoved the protester, and he pushed back. They screamed at each other. I couldn't make out every word that they were saying. But the subject of the argument wasn't a mystery.

The controversy over abortion rights had never been hotter, not in my lifetime. That dispute captured by the video might be playing out in any city in the United States. But the video hadn't been filmed in some faraway place.

I tapped the screen. "That's Union Springs, for sure. They're on the sidewalk in front of Bria Gaines's medical office."

There was no mistaking it. Her name was still painted on the front window. The shiny black letters hadn't been obscured by the red paint vandals had flung on the building's exterior.

Luna nodded. "That's what I saw, too. Seemed like you needed to know about it. It's not the only fight I've heard about. Did you know that Vic Fowler punched out Bria's lawyer?"

I did not know that. "Where?"

"Outside of Uptown Barbecue."

"Shit." I muttered the word, though I wanted to shout it. Had to exercise some self-control, in the heart of the courthouse. "No, I hadn't heard that."

"Yeah, Bria had to take him to the hospital. His head hit the pavement, gave him a black eye and a bloody nose."

"Good Lord! Why am I the last person in town to hear this? That's an assault on defense counsel. I have the duty to provide oversight for the trial of this case."

Well. I couldn't pretend that it was a surprise, because I'd been expecting it. I capped my ink pen. My desk pad held a stack of motions I'd been reading, to enter rulings in other cases. I hastily returned the papers back to their respective file folders, shoved them to the side.

"Luna, get counsel for both sides of *State v. Gaines* on the phone, arrange a time for a conference. We need to have a serious talk about damage control."

"Okay." She started to head out, then lingered in the doorway. "One more thing, Judge. I heard it over at the sheriff's office. Can't swear that it's true."

I squeezed my eyes shut. "Lord help me. What did you hear?"

"The governor. He's threatening to send in the National Guard."

Okay, that announcement threw me. I was speechless. Opened my eyes to see Luna standing in the doorway, awaiting my response. When I recovered, I said, "We're going straight to hell. I don't suppose the governor's office tried to contact me? To give fair warning?"

Only Luna could provide that answer. She shook her head.

I took a breath. Released it. Turned to my keyboard, pulled up the court calendar. "Luna, after you make these calls, get back in here. We're setting that case for trial before they burn this town to the ground."

CHAPTER 37

Luna hadn't managed to reach the DA. His clerk said he was taking a break at LuLu's, a diner about two blocks from the courthouse. He'd be back in a bit, she said.

I wasn't inclined to wait. Not in the mood.

I decided to run Reeves down myself. In person. Get things settled.

I shoved my laptop in my bright red leather briefcase, so I could access my court docket. I needed to move this train down the tracks, for the good of everyone involved.

I stepped out the front door of the courthouse and walked straight into a cloud of smoke.

Aurora Freeman, my former school lunch lady, was taking her morning cigarette break.

I waved the smoke out of my face. "Aurora, why aren't you in the parking lot? You know the mayor's gonna complain if he sees you smoking on the front sidewalk again."

Aurora was unmoved. She flicked an ash. Sucked on the filter, inhaled the smoke deep before blowing it out. "I just wanted to see what's going on out here." She pointed down Prairie Street. "Looks like the circus is in town."

Aurora had the right of it. Just one block away from the courthouse, the sidewalks were crowded with people, swirling around the storefronts and surging into the street. Traffic was at a standstill. Drivers were laying on their horns, trying to get the crowd to part. No use.

Aurora pointed with her cigarette. "That's a sight, ain't it? I can't remember a crowd like this since the Christmas parade."

"That's not a crowd, Aurora. It's a mob. You should get back inside."

"What about you?"

"I'm heading over to LuLu's. I hear Reeves is holed up there."

Aurora fired up a fresh cigarette, lighting it with the cherry from her last one. "Hope you got your body armor on."

"Coming through!" A woman's voice. I looked to my left. A young mom was trying to steer a baby stroller past me. It was a two-seater, baby in front, toddler in back. I took a half step to the right, but not fast enough.

"I got babies here!" the woman shouted. Her oversized diaper bag clipped me in the chest. She seemed amped up, on a mission. As she passed by, I caught the lettering on the back of her T-shirt. LET LIFE HAPPEN.

I turned to Aurora. "I mean it. Get back inside."

She tossed her cigarette onto the pavement and crushed it with her heel. "You watch yourself, Judge Mary. These people ain't here to sing 'Silent Night.'"

I tightened my grip on my briefcase and headed down the street. Within half a block, I was surrounded by people, jostling me, crowding me, carrying me along like a stick in a stream. I couldn't have turned around if I wanted to.

I looked from side to side for people I knew. Didn't see anybody. Just a mix of unfamiliar faces, more white than Black. Some toted Bibles. Some carried posters.

BEFORE YOU WERE BORN, I CONSECRATED YOU said one. Another just said ISAIAH 49:1.

A thickset man in front of me held a little boy on his shoulders. The lettering on the back of the boy's T-shirt said FEARFULLY & WONDERFULLY MADE. Up ahead, I could hear a woman starting to whip a contingent into a chorus of shouts. "Life is precious! Save the babies!" I saw a row of vans parked by the curb. All from Christian churches. Some from Alabama, but most from out of state. Mississippi, Georgia, Louisiana. All over the South.

I didn't like crowds. Never a fan of big concerts. A mosh pit was my worst nightmare. And this was starting to feel like one. I was getting claustrophobic. My heart was racing. I could hardly breathe. And the farther I went, the worse it got. I wasn't even moving under my own power anymore. I was just getting swept along.

Somebody stepped on my heel. My right shoe came off. I shouted out, "Hey! Wait! Hold up!" But the crowd just kept moving, and me along with it. That shoe was gone. I grabbed my briefcase in both hands and held it against my chest. I started swinging my elbows, trying to make some room. But the crowd didn't pay me any mind. It had a mind of its own.

I realized that I had no power here. No robe or gavel. These people didn't know me from Adam. And they sure as hell didn't give a damn what I thought.

I spotted LuLu's about a half block up. Suddenly there was a man with a bullhorn behind me. The damn thing squeaked and squawked when he turned it on. Then he started shouting through it. "Human rights begin before birth! Human rights begin before birth!"

The people all around me took up the chant. I was the only silent one in the jostling mass. The energy was now at a whole different level. It was no longer just a moving crowd. It was a march.

I turned to the side, trying to avoid the blast of the bullhorn. With one shoe missing, I was off balance. I tripped over somebody else's feet and fell forward. My head hit somebody's hip on the way down. My briefcase landed hard on the pavement and I landed right on top of it.

"Stop!" I shouted, as if anybody could hear me.

Work boots and running shoes stomped by inches from my face. For a second, I thought I was about to be trampled to death. When I pressed my right hand onto the asphalt to push myself up, somebody stepped on it. I let out a howl. Felt like my fingers were broken.

At that moment, I felt a strong arm around my waist, and then somebody scooped me up and set me on my feet. It was a muscular white man, with tattooed arms and a thick beard. He stood like an oak, holding me in front of him as the mass surged around us. He leaned down and spoke right into my ear. "You okay?"

I nodded, out of breath. My knees were banged up. My blouse was dirty and torn.

When my rescuer stepped back, he kept his hands on my shoulders, steadying me. I could see a silk-screened image on his T-shirt. A Confederate flag draped over a crucifix, as if Jesus had left it there.

"Can you walk?" he asked.

"I'm fine. Thanks."

"Praise the Lord!" he said.

"Praise the Lord!" I said right back. At least that was one thing we could agree on.

I thanked him again, then shoved my way through the crowd until I was huddled in the entryway of LuLu's. Through the glass door, I could see Reeves inside at a table, talking to two of his associates. I couldn't imagine what he'd say when he saw me in this kind of shape.

As I tried to collect myself, I watched the marchers stomp past, waving their signs, chanting their chants, blocking out everything that was familiar on Prairie Street.

I was born in this town. Grew up here. But I didn't know it anymore.

Union Springs, Alabama, had gone batshit crazy.

CHAPTER 38

Cocheta Bass

HAPPY HAVEN NURSING HOME
UNION SPRINGS, ALABAMA

Cocheta Bass was working two jobs these days.

During the ten months of the school year, she was employed as a school nurse at Union Springs Middle School, where she screened adolescents for illness and treated injuries of all sorts. Served up no-nonsense maternal advice, along with bandages and disinfectants and sanitary napkins.

And there was that one time. When she landed in the middle of a student's major life crisis. Cocheta was still paying a high price for that decision.

But miraculously—it hadn't resulted in Cocheta getting fired. Because she was hard to replace. The county was short on licensed nursing professionals. A person with her background was in demand.

So, after her divorce from her no-good, deadbeat husband, she'd taken on a second job. Cocheta worked the swing shift at the Happy Haven Nursing Home, right outside the city limits of Union Springs. Cocheta didn't relish the sixteen-hour days. She took on the extra work because her son, Holden, had started college the year before. Holden was the first in her family line to attend college. Not a matter of importance to her ex, though. Despite all the promises that Karl Bass had made to step up and help fund their son's education, that man never had any money to spare when tuition was due, or the housing bill came up.

She sat at the computer in the nurses' station, recording her notes on the status of the residents on her floor. A coworker, one of the aides, walked up and leaned over the counter, watching her. Out of the blue, the young woman said to Cocheta, "You know what I think is crazy? That she wasn't on the pill. I mean, why wasn't she using birth control? That would've fixed everything."

Cocheta didn't answer. The explanation was so obvious, she wanted to scream. *Because she was thirteen!*

It was dark outside. Stars were starting to blink; she could make them out through the skylight overhead. Cocheta looked up, checked the time on the wall clock. Almost ten o'clock. She wouldn't be compensated for overtime. Cocheta typed faster.

The nurse's aide kept firing questions. "So how'd it go down? Did the girl come to you at school, tell you she was pregnant? Or did that Bria Gaines get you involved?"

The mention of Dr. Gaines made an ice pick go to work on Cocheta's brain. She winced as a band of pain tightened around her head. The product of a guilty conscience. Bria Gaines didn't get Cocheta involved. It was the other way around.

But they'd threatened her. Said she'd go to jail. Who would

take care of Holden? How would he remain in school if Cocheta was locked up?

"I can't talk about it" was all she said.

Finally, she wrapped up her reports. Unlocked a drawer and pulled out her purse.

"I'm heading out now," she told the aide. "When Shakira gets back, tell her to keep an eye on Iona Johnson in 21E. Her *C. diff* is acting up."

"Again?"

Cocheta walked to the side exit. Her departure was delayed when she encountered a roaming resident who was this close to placement in the memory care unit. After she walked the man back to his room, Cocheta made it to the parking lot.

She had a sinking feeling when she started up her Toyota SUV and saw that it was low on gas. That meant she'd need to go out of her way, to drive to the twenty-four-hour convenience store on the highway. Just a matter of minutes, but she wasn't happy about the delay. Cocheta felt like she was out of gas, too. Her energy supply was drained, she just wanted to get home.

She'd driven about half a mile from the nursing home when the glare of headlights shining in her rearview mirror started to bug her. She took a glance over her shoulder. Looked like a truck was following her, with its brights on. The headlights blinded her, so she couldn't tell much about the truck, couldn't guess the make or even the color.

Wasn't her husband, though. His truck was a clunker that ran on diesel; you could hear it a mile away.

She was relieved when the brightly lit QUICK SERVE sign came into view. She turned into the lot, releasing a huge breath as the truck picked up speed and drove on by.

She only pumped twenty dollars' worth of regular, because payday was a week away. Then she went inside the store, to kill a little time. Wandered the snack aisle, walked by the coolers of water, soda, and beer.

The cashier kept an eye on her. He called out, "Can I help you find something?"

Cocheta almost confided in him. Told him that a truck was following, making her paranoid. But the guy didn't look particularly sympathetic. These days, people around town were giving Cocheta short shrift, the cold shoulder.

So she just shook her head. "No thanks," she said as she headed out of the store.

Inside her car, she hit the lock button before she buckled her seat belt. Thought about calling somebody, asking for reassurance. But who could she call? It was well past ten o'clock. Nobody wanted to be bothered past ten at night.

As she pulled out of the lot and onto the highway, she wondered what her ex-husband was up to. Would Karl put someone up to this? Had she made him mad again? It didn't take much.

Had she ticked off someone else?

She'd driven a quarter mile when she saw it. A truck pulled off the side of the road, idling.

After she passed, its brights came on and it pulled onto the road behind her.

Cocheta hit the gas, picked up speed.

The truck stayed right on her tail.

CHAPTER 39

Benjamin Meyers

MAGNOLIA APARTMENTS
UNION SPRINGS, ALABAMA

Benjamin Meyers knew the ropes. Over the past decade, he'd taken countless witness statements. Scores of depositions. He knew how to talk to people. All kinds of people. Old, young. Friendly, neutral, hostile. He had a skill for turning hostile witnesses around. One of his superpowers, some said.

He stood at the door of a fourplex—an old house chopped into four apartment units. Ancient layers of lead paint cracked like crocodile hide, sloughing off the door's brass number. A makeshift label—masking tape and black marker—read APT. #3.

Nobody answered when he knocked, but he could hear people inside, a babel of high-pitched voices, children shouting, arguing, making demands. He knocked again, louder.

This time, he heard a woman's voice, her tone shrill: "Nova! You deaf? Get the door!"

Meyers waited. He heard footsteps, and a second later, the *thunk* when the dead bolt disengaged.

The door opened. A tall, Black teenage girl stood there in jeans and a T-shirt.

It was Meyers's first face-to-face meeting with the State's complaining witness. As the door creaked open, he wondered how he would be received.

One look gave Meyers his answer. *Hostile.* The girl clearly didn't want him there.

Meyers gave her his trademark grin. "Hey, it's Nova, right? I'm Benjamin Meyers. Pretty sure y'all are expecting me today."

The girl cracked the door just wide enough for Meyers to squeeze through. He stepped into the tiny living room — a hive of crawling, rassling, squalling young creatures. He counted four, plus Nova.

Meyers raised his voice above the din. "Is your mother around?"

At that moment, Nova's mom emerged from a bedroom, striking a pose in the doorway. Meyers did a quick assessment. Mom had taken pains with her appearance. Elaborate hairdo. Full makeup. Starla Jones was a remarkably attractive woman, and in admirable shape, especially considering she had birthed all the kids in the room.

With every witness, Meyers strove to be scrupulously polite, appropriate. "Good afternoon, Ms. Jones. I'm Benjamin Meyers. Counsel for Dr. Gaines."

Nova's mom was showing cleavage, and her jeans were tight. And she was barefoot, with toenails painted bright red.

She walked over and stuck out her hand. "Call me Starla."

Maintain eye contact, thought Meyers. *Don't look down.*

Don't. Look. It was a challenge. Starla Jones was built like a brick shithouse.

"Ma'am, I appreciate you letting me come by your home to visit with y'all today. Hope it's not an inconvenience."

"You coming here? No inconvenience at all. You understand why I couldn't come to your office with Nova. No way I could leave these other ones at home. They'd burn the house down."

"Mama, look!" Meyers turned toward the kitchen. One of the kids had clambered up onto the kitchen counter and was crawling across the stovetop. Proudly.

Starla smacked her hands together. "Tre! You get off that stove right this minute. You could burn your damn hide off! Nova, get that child down from there!"

"I'm hungry!" the boy wailed. "I want chips!"

"We don't got any chips. Nova, get him a cracker."

"I don't want a cracker!" the boy shouted.

"You can have nothing at all, then. Nova, put him to bed and lock that door."

To Meyers, Nova looked doubtful, like she didn't think lockdown was the answer. After she put the boy on her hip, Meyers saw her grab a Little Debbie pie from a shelf. She slipped the snack to the boy as she carried him down the hall.

The other kids were still romping in a corner of the room. But their mother's presence seemed to lower their volume a smidgen.

"Come sit," said Starla.

She led the way to a pair of sticky chairs at a round wooden table.

Meyers sat down and pulled out his iPhone. "Do you mind if I record our conversation?"

"No problem at all," said Starla. She seemed welcoming and

cooperative—unlike her daughter. Meyers got the distinct sense that Starla liked attention.

"Can I get your full name please?"

"Starla Simone Jones."

"Age?"

"You probably won't believe me. Twenty-eight."

"Why wouldn't I believe you?"

"Because I got all these kids, that's why. And a teenage daughter. A teenager! Of course, I was a teenager when I had her."

"How many altogether?" Meyers asked. He'd done a head count, but he wanted to be sure he wasn't missing anyone.

"Three girls, two boys. Nova's the oldest, she's thirteen. My baby Caden, he not two yet. I just love children. Always have."

"Starla, the district attorney has endorsed you as a witness for the State in the case against Dr. Bria Gaines."

"That's right, yes, sir."

"And you understand that Dr. Gaines has been charged with a felony."

"Oh, hell yeah, I do understand that. She aborted Nova's baby. Sucked it out, killed it, threw it out like trash. And didn't nobody ask me nothing about it. The mother! I'm Nova's mother! Nobody told me shit."

"Are you personally acquainted with Dr. Gaines?"

"Oh, I've seen her. Met her." Starla crossed her legs, leaned forward. Meyers kept his eyes on hers. Her eyes were pretty. Big and brown. Like Nova's.

Starla wrinkled her nose. "Dr. Gaines, she'd go to church once in a while. Over to the Victory Baptist. That's Pastor Erskine's church, where we belong. But she never helped out, didn't bring anything for bake sales, nothing like that. Some folks used to say that she thought she was too good for that kind of work. Because of her being a doctor."

"So you're a regular at Victory Baptist? You and your family?"

"Since Caden was born, yeah. They took care of me. Made a food train, brought a meal every night for weeks. I don't know what I'd have done if it hadn't been for Reverend Erskine. He got everyone to pitch in. That man has the true spirit."

Meyers made a mental note. *Baptist church assistance.*

"Starla, do you think your daughter Nova was physically prepared to bring a pregnancy to term?"

"Sure she was." She narrowed her eyes, like she thought it was a trick question. "I was just fifteen when I had Nova. Didn't hurt me none."

"But with your last child, you said you couldn't have handled it without church assistance, am I right?"

Starla was impatient, her answer clipped. "Look. I didn't say she was going to *raise* it. Nova's just a kid. No way she could've kept it. But she could've had it. Delivered the baby. Nova would've been fine with that."

Meyers glanced over Starla's shoulder. Nova was standing at the front of the hallway, one foot in the living room. He lowered his voice.

"Some experts might say that carrying a pregnancy to term at Nova's age would have negatively impacted her health."

"Bullshit." Starla tugged up on the neckline of her shirt. "I know what you're trying to do. The cops explained it to me. The only way they'll let Dr. Gaines off is if Nova's life was at stake. But Nova was never in danger. You saw her! She's a real sturdy girl."

Meyers looked over to see if Nova was still there. She was. She was listening.

"Nova's strong as an ox. And plenty big enough. She's been wearing my clothes since sixth grade. She's popping out the seams now. And her feet are too big for my shoes."

Meyers glanced up again. Nova was standing with her head down, like she was trying to pretend she wasn't even there.

CHAPTER 40

Nova Jones

MAGNOLIA APARTMENTS
UNION SPRINGS, ALABAMA

Nova stared at the rug. She was embarrassed. For herself. And for her mama.

She'd seen her leaning into the lawyer, trying to flirt with him. She hated when her mama acted that way. Being a Pick Me girl. Showing off her chest.

If Nova tried any of that, Mama would open up a can of whoop-ass on her.

Her mama turned around and pointed toward the kids in the corner. "Nova! Settle these rascals down. Get 'em something to eat."

"Yes, ma'am."

Nova walked into the kitchen and opened a full loaf of bread and a jar of peanut butter. There was grape jelly in the fridge; she got that, too. Ever since the DA brought the case about the abortion, they had all the food they needed. Church pantry showed up every week with plenty of groceries for all six of them. Treats, too. Like the Little Debbies and Hostess cupcakes.

Nova made three sandwiches, cut them into neat triangles and put them on a plate. She walked into the living room and waved the plate like a lure. "Ya'll want PB&Js?"

Arbonne ran over. Reba followed, dragging baby Caden along with her. They all piled into the tiny kitchen and grabbed for the sandwiches. Nova walked down the hall to release Tre from captivity.

"You behave," she whispered, walking him out, "or she'll make me lock you up again!" Tre nodded and ran into the kitchen to join his siblings.

Nova stood by the refrigerator watching them all eat. She wasn't hungry. Had a bad feeling in her stomach.

Then she saw the lawyer standing in the doorway.

"Nova? Can I ask you some questions?"

She looked past him to her mama, still sitting at the living room table. Her mama gave her a quick, impatient nod.

"Where?" asked Nova. "Here?"

"Come sit in the living room."

Nova followed him over to the table where her mama was sitting. She picked a chair across from the lawyer, as far away as possible. She felt awkward. She didn't know how to deal. Didn't have Mama's game. Didn't know how to play a grown man.

The lawyer put his iPhone in the middle of the table. "I'm going to record our conversation, Nova. That way, down the line, nobody can claim that either of us said something different. Is that okay with you?"

Nova thought about that. It made her nervous, being recorded. But the lawyer was right. It was better than somebody lying about it later.

The first questions weren't hard. Name, age, birthday, where she went to school. The lawyer was making notes on a pad. Then he put down his pen and looked straight at her.

"Nova, did you get pregnant in the past year?"

She closed her eyes tight. Couldn't look at him. Nodded.

"Nova, you have to say it out loud."

She breathed out, a heavy sigh. It was hard. She didn't want to talk about it. Hurt to think about it. "Yes."

"Thank you, Nova. Please remember to speak up."

She opened her eyes. The lawyer didn't look mad. Didn't sound impatient. But he could be making her the fool. She didn't trust him.

"The police report says you got pregnant in December. Is that correct?"

"Yeah."

Nova looked down. Couldn't bear his eyes on her. Or her mama's.

"And you told the police it happened at a party. With older kids?"

"Yeah."

She kept her gaze down on the table. Concentrated on a scorch mark, the black circle a hot pan had made. Wanted the lawyer to go away. Leave her house. Never come back.

"Do you know who got you pregnant, Nova?"

"It was dark." Her answer was loud, like it jumped right out of her. She felt like she could hear her heartbeat. "They gave me weed. And wine. And it was too dark to see."

"*Who* gave you weed and wine?"

"Older kids. I didn't know them. Driving around in a car. They not from here."

"What about the one you had intercourse with? What do you remember about him?"

"Nothing."

"Can you describe him? Size, race, voice?"

"I don't remember." Nova cut her eyes to the side, looking to her mama. Wanting her to help. Wanting her to forgive her. Wanting her to not hate her right now.

"I told him no, told him to stop. I said he was hurting me."

"So you can recall that? That it was painful, and you told him to stop. What did he say?"

Nova's breath caught. She wanted to run. Bolt from the room. The memories flooded into her head. What got done to her. What was taken from her. She could remember the pain, the bleeding, and her screaming and begging, please stop.

And she remembered something else. Crying for Mama. Over and over, she kept thinking while it was happening, *I want Mama.*

"Nova? What did he say?" It was the lawyer. Wanting an answer.

"I don't know. Can't remember."

"Do you recall when you suspected you were pregnant?"

"In March."

"And how do you remember that?"

"Dogwoods."

The lawyer's head tilted. "Dogwoods?"

Nova nodded. "The dogwoods were blooming. That's when I figured it out. That I didn't have a period."

The lawyer looked confused.

He didn't get it. How she always clocked the season by the flowers blooming. Forsythia, pansies, crabapple, redbud, dogwood. The pink and yellow and purple of spring flowering all around while she suffered through those terrible weeks. No one to talk to. Not a soul to rescue her.

"So when you realized that you'd missed your period, what did you do?"

Nova wanted to bury her head in her arms. She wanted the questions to stop. She could feel her mama's eyes on her. "I waited. To see if I'd start bleeding. Prayed."

"And you didn't tell anybody?"

Nova shook her head. "We got a nurse at school. She started asking me stuff. Because I'd get sick in class in the mornings. Go lie down in her office after I threw up."

"Was that Cocheta Bass?"

Nova nodded. "She got me a test. The kind where you go into the bathroom and pee on it. It turned blue."

"And Ms. Bass, the nurse—she was the one who took you to see Dr. Gaines?"

"Yeah."

"At her office."

"Yeah."

"How many times?"

"Just the one time. I was supposed to go back for a checkup, but I got sick and Mama called the ambulance. They took me to the hospital. That's when everybody found out."

"Okay," said the lawyer, "let me make sure I've got this. Before you went to the hospital, Nurse Bass knew you were pregnant. And Dr. Gaines knew. But nobody else?"

Nova's head jerked up. "Nobody. I never told nobody about it."

Nova's stomach hurt so much she was just about doubled over in the chair. She couldn't be honest with the lawyer. Or her mama. She couldn't say what really happened.

Because all hell would break loose if she did that.

CHAPTER 41

Mary Stone

BULLOCK COUNTY COURTHOUSE
UNION SPRINGS, ALABAMA

I was meeting with Arch Pearce. The collections attorney who tried to steal my family's land.

Circumstances were different this time around. We were still meeting in an office, across a desk.

But on this occasion, it was my office. My desk.

Pearce held up a manila folder. Which he'd described as the *Wilton v. Mary Stone* file. "So! I showed my client the documentation you provided. And the written statements from you and your sisters, and the neighbors. He found them to be pretty convincing."

I can keep a straight face. "Well, that's gratifying. I guess."

"Right! Caleb—Mr. Wilton—he's willing to unilaterally amend this offer. The one I made in the original letter, sent by registered mail. You first saw a copy of it at my office."

I raised my brows. "I'm familiar with it. You're talking about that part of the letter where you demanded one hundred ninety thousand dollars?"

He gave a sheepish chuckle. "Yeah. That feels out of range, in light of what you've shared. I'm authorized to settle for a payment of twenty thousand."

I didn't just laugh. I howled. The man was hilarious. "Arch, I'm not paying your client a damn dime. You know that."

"But it would resolve the issue, Judge. Wilton couldn't come back later to make another claim."

"Let him come. I'm ready to take him on. Arch, I think your client Wilton is a liar, who never had dealings with this mysterious Abraham Stone. Or alternatively, Abraham Stone is a phony who conned your client."

I leaned forward. Placed my elbows on my desk. Toyed with a letter opener shaped like a dagger. "Either way, it's not on me. In law school, I had this commercial law professor. He beat something into our heads. He'd say: 'He who deals with the bad actor is lost.'"

"Yeah, I had him, too."

"Then you know."

I wasn't blowing smoke. Wasn't just talk, trying to get a more attractive offer. Arch Pearce couldn't make an offer I'd accept. He and his client would never make me surrender, no matter what terms he laid out.

That being the case, I was ready for Pearce to dislodge himself from that chair and get out of my office. Wished I were wearing a wristwatch, so I could pull back my sleeve and stare at it. Toss that "gotta go" trick right back in his hungry face.

But I didn't need it. Luna saved me. The office line buzzed. When I picked up, Luna said, "Your sister's here, Judge."

Uh-oh. My sister? At the courthouse. "Which one?"

"Miss Jordan."

Took me by surprise. I wasn't expecting her, though the timing was ideal.

"Arch, we'll have to cut this off. Something's come up."

He took the hint. Picked up his file folder and left, passing my sister in the reception area.

Jordan sidled into my office, looking peaked. It worried me. I rose from my chair, half inclined to press my palm to her forehead, like I did when she was little. Check for fever.

She said, "Nellie told me to come. She can't leave school, or she'd be here herself."

"Sit on down," I said.

Jordan shut the door before she sat. Perched on the edge of her chair. Acting for all the world like there was trouble, that she was gonna break some terrible news.

I tensed up. "What's the matter with Nellie?"

"It's not Nellie, it's about the nurse. School nurse."

Gave my head a shake. Ashamed to admit, but I was wondering what awful thing they were going to say the woman had done.

"Yeah, so? What about her?"

"She's dead."

Jordan's voice was flat when she said it. Like she didn't believe it.

I could hardly believe it myself. "Dead? Cocheta Bass? The woman's just in her forties! Are you sure?"

"I'm sure. Nellie heard all about it. Cocheta didn't come to school this morning. And they couldn't get her on the phone. She's been living alone in that little house outside of town, since her divorce last year."

"Right." I was aware of the divorce. Not amicable. It was a bloodbath. I should know, it was filed in my court. I signed the judgment, divided the property. "I know the place. I drive right by there."

"They sent the assistant principal—Lyssa Simpson—to check on her. Because they were worried about Cocheta."

Another pause, while Jordan blinked back tears. I was getting agitated, running low on patience. "What, Jordan? Tell me what happened!"

Jordan grimaced. "Mary, Lyssa found her hanging. Cocheta was hanging from a tree behind her house."

I recoiled. "Sweet Jesus."

The news knocked me flat. Rendered me silent, too. Because the mental image of Cocheta Bass's demise was so triggering that words failed me.

CHAPTER 42

I knew for a fact that showing up at an active crime scene was the last thing I should be doing. Especially when the victim was a listed witness in a case before me.

But to hell with all that.

When I pulled up to Cocheta's house on the outskirts of town, two police cars were blocking the driveway. I parked at the edge of the yard and got out of my car. As I headed across the front lawn, a cop held up his hand to stop me. "Sorry, Judge. Sheriff says not to let anybody back there."

The cop was Buddy Hopkins. Rookie on the force. I went to school with his parents. Attended his baptism. I held up my hand. "Don't worry, Buddy. I'll tell him you tried to hold me back."

I walked up the gravel driveway past the garage. Behind the house was a thick stand of Alabama pines and red maples. Yellow scene tape was strung around four of the tree trunks, marking off a space about fifteen feet square. I saw Mick Owens, the local sheriff, talking with two deputies in the middle of the square. A police photographer was aiming his camera into the trees.

That's when I looked up and saw her.

My God!

Cocheta was still hanging there.

Mick saw me coming and hustled over to intercept me. "Mary! Damn it! You can't be back here! The ME hasn't even shown up yet."

Mick and I had history. One look at my face and he knew I wasn't going anywhere.

I ducked under the tape and walked straight over to the tree. It was one of the maples. Cocheta was hanging from a branch about ten feet up. Her feet were dangling in front of my face. She had one shoe on. The other was lying in leaves below her. Her neck was cocked to one side with a thick rope around it. The other end was tied around the trunk. Her face was twisted and ashy.

Her eyes were open and bulging. Her hands were tied behind her back.

This was no suicide. Somebody lynched her.

Somebody wanted to leave a message.

I turned into the brambles and threw up.

As I was bent over, I felt a hand on my back. It was Mick. "Mary, go back to town. Let me finish up here. I promise I'll give you the full report."

I stood up and wiped my mouth on my sleeve. "How long has she been up there?"

Mick looked up at Cocheta's corpse. "Probably since last night or real early this morning. People saw her at the Quick Serve between ten and eleven. We'll get a better time frame from the ME."

I shook my head. "I know this abortion case has people fired up. But who would do this?"

"Mary, we don't know this has anything to do with the case."

Mick was right. I was jumping to conclusions. Bad habit for a judge. "What about the ex?" I asked. "It was an ugly divorce."

"Macon PD informed him. And it looks like his whereabouts last night are accounted for."

"Hey, Sheriff! Take a look over here." It was the photographer. He had moved around the other side of the tree. The underbrush was thicker there.

Mick headed over. I followed right behind him.

The photographer pointed to the trunk of the tree.

At about eye level, I saw a marking in red spray paint.

It was a big *K*. The color of blood.

"Looks fresh," said Mick.

I looked down. Sure enough. Some excess spray had misted the leaves below.

I stared at the letter. Turned it over in my mind. What did it mean?

K for *Killer*? Maybe somebody blamed Cocheta for her part in the abortion.

K as in short for the Greek word *kilo,* meaning *thousand*? Did Cocheta owe somebody money?

Or maybe *K* for *Klan*? The group that's been stringing up people of color down here for more than a hundred and fifty years.

CHAPTER 43

Back in court. A week had passed, and Sheriff Owens was still investigating the death of Cocheta Bass. He'd called a press conference, a rare event in Bullock County—though it was becoming more common. The sheriff said they still had no suspects, but that he wanted to reassure the community: There was no cause for alarm.

People were not comforted by his rhetoric. Plenty of folks in the county were alarmed. I was included in that number. Because I was well acquainted with the sheriff, had the opportunity to observe his investigative skills over the years.

Mick Owens wasn't stupid. He did just fine handling a case that was open-and-shut. Where the suspect was caught red-handed or confessed during interrogation. But in a challenging case?

That man couldn't find his ass with both hands.

I sat at the bench the following Tuesday, looking down at the counsel tables. The DA, Robert Reeves, sat in his customary spot. On that occasion, he had AAG Eleanor Lindquist seated beside him.

At the defense table, Benjamin Meyers sat with Dr. Bria Gaines. She appeared to be composed, listening and nodding as Meyers spoke softly to her. She was changing, though. I could see it. Like she was aging before my eyes. Her face had the haggard look that comes from stress and uncertainty and sleepless nights. Didn't surprise me that she was suffering. If the doctor *wasn't* scared, I'd be concerned. Might have to question her intelligence.

But Dr. Gaines was smart. She knew what the stakes were.

I cleared my throat to get their attention. After all parties raised their eyes to the bench, I said, "I see that counsel for defendant has filed a motion in the case of *State of Alabama v. Bria Gaines*, Case No. CR194317. Defendant is here in person and with counsel, Benjamin Meyers. The State is represented by District Attorney Robert Reeves and Assistant Attorney General Eleanor Lindquist."

They were quiet. Waiting.

I said, "Mr. Meyers, you have filed a motion in limine to exclude witnesses. For the record, please identify the witnesses you allege should not be permitted to testify at trial in the instant case."

He stood. "Starla Jones and Nova Jones, Your Honor. For the reasons set forth in the motion."

I was entirely familiar with the substance of his motion. A motion in limine is a request made prior to trial to exclude certain evidence or testimony. He wanted to keep Nova and her mother off the stand. A helluva ask, you understand. I needed to hear his justification, to have it on the record. "And what are the grounds?"

"Your Honor, I've uncovered information confirming that the prosecution witnesses are being compensated in exchange for their testimony."

"Objection!" It was a female voice, ringing out in righteous indignation. The AAG, Lindquist, was on her feet, rather than Reeves. Which was interesting. Made me wonder who was in charge.

She spoke with the air of a person whose good name had been besmirched. "The defense is making grave allegations of misconduct, Judge. Allegations which are baseless. We're putting the defense on notice that the State will not permit opposing counsel to abuse our witnesses. The claims in the motion are highly inflammatory. The State believes that these false statements constitute defamation."

I focused on the defense table. Meyers appeared unaffected by Lindquist's accusations. His client, though, was troubled. Bria's mouth trembled, and she covered it with her hand.

The doctor was torn. And she was not alone. I had conflicting sympathies in this case, too.

I kept my manner brisk, all business. "Mr. Meyers, what evidence do you have to support the claim that the witnesses are being compensated for testimony?"

He opened a file folder. Pulled out two stapled documents. "Your Honor, to substantiate our claims, I submit witness statements from two individuals who have been endorsed as witnesses by the State. The first is the statement of Nova Jones, whose name appears in the charge against my client. And the second statement was taken from her mother, Starla Jones."

Lindquist took a step toward the bench. "Those statements are not sworn, Judge. Not taken under oath. And Mr. Meyers didn't ask our permission to speak with the clients. He didn't even let us know he'd contacted them. We should have had the opportunity to be present."

She was speaking out of turn. I ignored her. "Mr. Meyers, what did the witnesses tell you regarding compensation?"

"They said they were receiving donations. Food deliveries on a regular basis. Clothing donations. Even cash. To cover rent and sundry expenses."

That was a serious allegation. The DA's office couldn't provide its witnesses with cash support. If the claim was true, the prosecution had to answer for it.

I turned directly to the DA. "Mr. Reeves?"

Before the DA could reply, Benjamin Meyers stepped right up to the bench. "Judge, one more thing. The DA failed to disclose this. Neither Reeves nor Lindquist revealed this crucial information to the defense. That's a Brady violation, Judge!"

Damn.

It was getting deeper and deeper. The Brady rule requires the prosecution to disclose evidence favorable to the defendant's case. If the State suppresses exculpatory information, it's a violation of due process. Could be a basis for throwing out the whole damn case.

Reeves was on his feet. "We didn't know!"

Eleanor Lindquist echoed the words as she joined Benjamin Meyers in front of the bench. "We didn't know, Judge! Neither the DA's office nor mine had any idea that this was going on. After we received the defendant's motion, we looked into it. And apparently the Victory Baptist Church has been providing some assistance to Starla and her children. As part of the mission of the church. We had no part in it, Judge."

Reeves stepped up. "Judge, we asked Reverend Erskine to be present today, in case we need his testimony. He'll back us up, I assure you."

Lindquist said, "He's waiting just outside the courtroom, Judge."

Well, shit. *Erskine.* I was in no mood for that. Lindquist marched down the aisle to the courtroom entrance. Prepared to prove it, I expect.

The DA said, "And Starla and Nova Jones are waiting in my office. We can put them on the stand. They'll testify under oath that we have not provided any compensation whatsoever."

The AAG opened the courtroom door, and Erskine entered. Wearing his full pastoral regalia: the black suit, white clerical collar.

"He's prepared to testify, Judge," Lindquist said.

I looked to Benjamin Meyers. "Well? It's your motion."

Meyers walked back to the counsel table. Bent down to confer with Dr. Gaines.

That's when Pastor began to volunteer information. "Judge Stone, I apologize if my parishioners have caused any trouble in this court case. I assure you, that was not our intent. We were just trying to do the Lord's work. Looking out for the fatherless children."

I took a breath. Because I intended to cut the man off, shut him up.

He was too quick for me.

"Your Honor! We're humble Christians at Victory Baptist, we don't know all the twists and turns of the laws of the government. My parishioners just had one aim. They were trying to provide charity to a single mother. 'For now abideth faith, hope and charity, these three. But the greatest of these is charity.' That's the King James Version."

Jesus. I frowned down at Benjamin Meyers. Was he gonna make me do his job?

Apparently not. Meyers shot a look at Erskine, said, "Your Honor, defense objects and asks that this man's statements be removed from the record. This witness hasn't been sworn."

The sound of Erskine's laughter bounded off the courtroom

walls. "This man doesn't know me, Judge. I don't need to take an oath in order to speak the truth."

I did not intend to lose control of the courtroom. I'd be damned if I'd let Erskine drag his pulpit up to my bench. "Sustained. Reverend Erskine, if you wish to remain in court, you'll need to be seated. And you'll hush your mouth. Unless—does the prosecution intend to put the pastor on the stand in this hearing?"

The pastor did not sit his ass down. Erskine's voice boomed, drowning mine out. "Judge! I can fix this problem. My church made it, it's my responsibility to correct it." He gazed around the courtroom, staring at Dr. Gaines before turning back to me. "If Victory Baptist has offended the law by providing food and clothing and rent money to the Jones family, we'll cut it off. Immediately."

Well, shit.

It made me sick. I was forcibly reminded of the passel of small children eating breakfast on my farm. Starla Jones had so many, I couldn't keep all the names straight.

My job is tough. And some days are worse than others. I kept my tone flat when I addressed the defense attorney.

"Mr. Meyers? Is that what you want? Will the reverend's proposal satisfy the defense?"

I could catch her whisper when from the counsel table Bria Gaines said, "No!" Benjamin Meyers heard it, too. They consulted, a hushed exchange.

He stepped back to the bench. "The defense doesn't control the actions or decisions of the leadership at Victory Baptist Church. But the prosecution has permitted a coercive situation to develop, under which the State's witnesses are rewarded for their participation in this criminal case against my client. On that basis, their testimony should not be admitted."

I was torn, shredded. I didn't want to make the order that would dry up the Jones family's grocery supplies. Starla and her kids needed whatever support the church could provide.

But Bria deserved a fair trial. Her life was at risk.

I almost chickened out. Almost said, "I'll take it under advisement."

But that wouldn't resolve anything. So I made my decision. Announced it from the bench. Just like the judgment of King Solomon. In the Book of Kings, the Old Testament story of the two women who claimed the same baby.

"Defendant's motion in limine is overruled. The receipt of donations from the members of Victory Baptist is not a basis to exclude Starla Jones and Nova Jones from testifying in this case."

I stole a look at Dr. Gaines. She was staring at a blank legal pad. Seemed like she'd lost all hope. So I split the baby. Like King Solomon offered to do.

"But the defense raises a viable possibility that witnesses might be affected. The donations may continue, but the defense can use the facts regarding compensation in cross-examination at trial."

At that, the courtroom burst into a chorus of voices, all the lawyers talking at once.

"Objection!"

"This won't work, Judge, you need to rethink it—"

"This is an unreasonable ruling—"

"What's the church supposed to do? We need a firm decision!"

I pounded that gavel. "Order!"

Kept bringing the hammer down until the voices fell silent. I looked over at Marlena. "Did you get that ruling down?"

Marlena nodded as her hands flew over the keyboard, recording the ruling.

"Court is adjourned," I said. In my no-bullshit judge voice.

At the counsel tables, briefcases were slammed shut. Angry murmurs were just barely audible.

No surprise. I could read the room. If King Solomon was still around, he could've warned me.

When you split the baby—you make everybody mad.

CHAPTER 44

I was late to meet my sisters. Not my fault, there was no help for it. The discovery hearing in a personal injury case ran long. The lawyers put on a show for their clients, objecting to everything, making long, stuffy speeches.

So by the time I reached Coley's, a restaurant on the other side of town, my sisters were already there. I spotted them in a booth against the far wall. Jordan raised her hand and waved.

Coley's was busier than usual. I shouldered my way through the crush, trying to avoid stepping on feet. I slid into the red vinyl booth, next to Nellie.

They were dressed all in black, down to the toes of their church shoes.

"Nice service?" I asked.

They both nodded. I could tell Jordan had been crying.

"Well attended, I expect?"

Nellie put her napkin on her lap. "People were asking after you."

"Well, I hope you told them I had a full schedule at the courthouse. I had cases set. If I could've been there, I'd have gone. I feel terrible about Cocheta. Always liked her. I kept track of her after her divorce."

Jordan leaned forward. "He showed up. The husband."

I clapped my hand to my chest. "Oh, no, he did not."

Jordan lowered her voice to a whisper. "He threw himself on the casket. Carrying on and crying like a baby."

Nellie nodded. "Nobody believed it was for real. All for show. Pastor pulled him off."

I could picture the scene playing out. I'd seen Karl Bass's theatrics in my courtroom. "The son of a bitch."

"The man ought to be in jail," said Nellie.

I felt the same way. If not for murder, at least for decades of mistreatment and abuse.

To my sisters, I said, "I keep thinking about Cocheta's body. I can't put the sight out of my mind."

The three of us fell silent, experiencing a shared pain.

"What happened to Daddy that night on the way to Birmingham"—I stammered, then fell silent again until I could conquer my fears—"that ain't gonna happen to me."

Nellie said, "We never even said anything after what happened to Daddy. He just got back in the car and we went home."

I shivered at the memory.

"Jordan," I said. "You weren't born yet, so you never had to see Daddy getting beaten by that deputy who said he was driving too fast."

"I always hated that story," Jordan said. "Especially the part about how scared Mama was for our whole family."

The brass bell over the entrance jingled. I looked over as three white men entered the restaurant. My gut turned. The man in the lead was Mason Phelps, a notorious town troublemaker. He'd caused plenty of problems over the years. DWIs. Bar fights.

Disturbing the peace. He'd been in my courtroom more than once.

Phelps and his buddies all had the same basic wardrobe. Torn denim jeans, mesh snapback caps, gray T-shirts.

Phelps's tee bore the words SAVE OUR HERITAGE under the image of the Confederate flag. His companions' shirts had a different logo. GOD BLESS THE SOUTH was screened under a design of the rebel flag draped over the cross.

Wait. I'd seen that same design before. At the march in town. On the man who rescued me.

It was a hard image to forget.

Nellie nudged me. Nodded in Phelps's direction. "I swear I'd heard that Phelps had finally given up. Some folks at school were saying his Neo-Confederate Club disbanded."

Jordan gave a nervous glance over her shoulder as Phelps started putting up posters of the same Confederate flag he wore on his shirt.

"That's what Trayvone said. He heard the same thing. Folks were saying the white supremacists lost their nerve after Charlottesville."

I couldn't believe how naïve my sisters sounded, considering they'd both lived their whole lives in the Black Belt of Alabama.

"Are you kidding?" I asked. "They didn't disband. Just went underground for a while. Like hot coals under a layer of ash. People think the fire's out, but sooner or later it'll come back to life and burn the whole house down."

Phelps and his men chose a table with a clear view of us. They settled in and stared with an intensity in their gaze that sent fresh shivers down my spine.

"I don't like the way they're staring at us," Jordan remarked in a hushed tone.

"I don't like it, either," replied Nellie. "Best not to start something.

They want to get a rise out of us. They want a confrontation. It's not worth it."

My sisters tried their best to carry on our conversation and ignore the men.

I could still hear Phelps, though. Every word.

He was talking about Alabama's abortion law. It was a common topic these days. Everybody had an opinion. Sometimes I wondered whether folks ever talked about anything else.

I caught Mason Phelps staring directly at me. I slipped out of the booth and stepped into the aisle. Had a rage burning deep inside me. I wanted to smack the smirk off his ugly face. The fearsome image of Cocheta swinging from that tree stopped me.

Phelps stood. To make sure he had everybody's attention, he raised his arms, revealing a mark burned into his forearm. A symbol that looked like the letter *K*.

Apparently, he had one more announcement to make. He called it out in a booming voice.

"There's a protest coming up, folks! Biggest one anybody around here's ever seen! A mess of warriors are coming, they gonna open people's eyes in this town. Things are changing!"

Then he looked straight at me. "Shit's going back to how it used to be. God bless Alabama!"

We girls sat frozen at our table until Nellie rose and broke the silence. "Let's all walk out together."

I was taking care of the check when I heard Nellie emphatically whispering, "Jordan, *no!*"

Jordan was standing frozen at the doorway. Staring down the men who represented everything that was taken from her with no repercussions. Staring...almost daring them to be men, to stand up and fight.

Phelps took notice. He stopped his posturing. He stared back and took a bold step forward. His friends swayed as if slightly tipsy, though aware enough to see something big silently brewing.

Nellie walked slowly to Jordan and put her hand on our baby sister's shoulder. "Jordan, you don't want this to be your story...not this part...not for your babies. Come on, now. Come on," she whispered.

I grabbed her hand that had twisted into a tight fist. She loosened it as Phelps slowly turned to her...ready to justify his hate, ready to show the subject of his hate the wrath of his anger.

"Whatchu got, li'l nigra?" said Phelps with a chuckle.

"That's your problem, Phelps. You don't know what I got," said Jordan quietly...her voice steady with the strength of David before bringing Goliath down.

She pulled her hand away from mine and walked out the door. I held it open for a few seconds, staring at them for emphasis, and walked out behind her.

I kept waiting for them to follow us...to light a firestorm...but the parking lot was clear. We hugged goodbye in silence.

I was sure the firestorm would come later. I was sure of it.

CHAPTER 45

Benjamin Meyers

BULLOCK COUNTY HIGH SCHOOL
UNION SPRINGS, ALABAMA

Benjamin Meyers parked directly across from the sign—BULLOCK COUNTY HIGH SCHOOL—with its image of the school mascot, a hornet. A big one, with human fists and a prominent stinger and a scowl on its face.

Meyers checked the time on his car clock. 3:29. Almost time for the bell.

While he waited, Meyers studied the exterior of the building. The one-story structure was in a state of disrepair. Student body was small—less than one hundred per class—and enrollment was declining. He'd done some research. The school had a demographic mix of races. Achievement test scores were nothing to brag about. Occasionally, BCHS lucked into a winning athletic team.

They'd won a state championship a while back, got a new gymnasium built in the flush of that achievement. It was the only construction update the building could boast.

Meyers heard the bell ringing inside. He stepped out of his car. The students were coming out, walking in clusters. He looked for groups of boys. Didn't want to approach any girls. Ben wasn't inclined to land himself in a jail cell.

Meyers knew that BCHS students were required to wear uniform polos, in class colors. White for freshmen, gray for sophomores, black for juniors, gold for seniors.

The color-coding made his prospecting a little easier.

Meyers let the clusters of tall guys in gold pass him by. He had a feeling they wouldn't engage. At seventeen or eighteen, males weren't likely to confess to activity that would constitute a crime. Especially a sex crime. Especially a sex crime involving a minor.

Meyers let the freshmen pass, too. They wouldn't be at the top of the information pyramid.

He aimed for the middle.

There!

He spotted a small group of boys, some in gray shirts, some in black. They were walking fast, jostling and shoving one another. Meyers had to jog a bit to catch up. When he got within hailing distance, he called out, "Hey! Can I talk with y'all a minute?"

The guys kept moving, kept talking. But one turned around, checked Ben out. "Yeah? What do you want?"

"Wanna ask you about a girl."

That got everybody's attention. The whole group stopped and turned around. Meyers pulled out his cell phone and pulled up an image from Instagram. It was Nova Jones's eighth-grade school picture. No telling who'd originally posted it.

He held up his screen. "Y'all know this girl?"

They all leaned in. One kid — short, with a high-pitched, pre-pubescent voice — spoke up. "Aw, shit, man — that's Nova Jones!"

His friends groaned, made weird faces and guttural animal sounds. Ben had to speak up to be heard. "Any of you ever hang out with her?"

"Hell, no." A Black dude in sophomore gray, the tallest in the group. Rail thin, wearing a pair of high-water khaki pants he'd outgrown. "I wouldn't screw that girl with somebody else's dick."

Meyers kept a poker face. Interesting that "hanging out" went right to sex. "Who do you see her hanging out with? Partying with?"

Meyers saw another kid sizing him up. White guy, a junior in a black shirt. Blond hair, athletic build. Had a suspicious air.

The kid narrowed his eyes. "You a cop or something?"

"No, I'm the opposite of a cop. I'm a lawyer. I'm just trying to find out about Nova."

The blond kid had a swagger. "If you're not a cop, maybe you shouldn't be hanging around a school. Asking weird questions."

The blond kid had a sidekick. Shaggy-haired, squirrelly, with a case of cystic acne. "Yeah, why you hanging around here?"

The tall Black guy looked around, like he was checking for a camera. "You on TikTok? Is this for a podcast? I don't hang out with Nova, she too young. Too thicc, got that big back. Not hot enough for me. But she'll do it with anybody. That's what I hear."

Again with sex, Meyers thought. These guys seemed to have a one-track mind, at least where Nova Jones was concerned. "Okay, but who's she with? Specifically?"

"Everybody!" The short kid stepped close to Ben. His face was lit up. "Go ahead, dude! Put me on the podcast. Nova Jones sleeping with everybody! She don't care if she even knows their name!"

"Ever seen her at a party?" Meyers asked.

A bunch of the kids chimed in all at once. "What party?" "Where's the party?" "I wanna go!"

Meyers was getting nowhere. He needed to pin something down. *Anything.* "Okay. Let me get specific. Do any of you know of anyone who says he had sex with Nova Jones last year?"

The blond kid in the black shirt started smirking. "I heard she went down on the whole basketball team."

Another kid scoffed. "That's a lie, that some crazy bullshit. Nova Jones always babysitting, dragging these brothers and sisters around. How she gonna hook up with everybody on the basketball team?"

Blond kid said, "I heard it! I swear!" He raised his right hand, like he was taking an oath. Meyers caught a brief glimpse of a symbol burned into his forearm but couldn't make it out. Looked like a letter.

"I heard that, too," added another kid. "Nova Jones, she's the biggest whore in town."

"Thanks, guys." Meyers turned back toward his car.

Thanks for nothing.

He was halfway down the sidewalk when one of the boys shouted after him.

"Hey, dude! You want Nova's number? Just call 4-1-7-I-M-A-H-O!"

Meyers unlocked his car, slid into the driver's seat, and started it up.

The boys were still shouting. A couple of catcalls reached him. Suggestions of what Nova would do for a price.

"Shit," Meyers muttered. He put the car in gear and pulled out. He was relieved to have the BCHS hornet in his rearview mirror.

He wished he'd never visited the school. It left him with a bad feeling. Like a storm was rolling in. The kind that turned the sky green and made even Alabama gators run for cover.

CHAPTER 46

Mary Stone

UNION SPRINGS, ALABAMA

By Saturday, it seemed like Mason Phelps had invited the whole damn town to his rally.

And I couldn't stay away.

I know my decision to show up was foolhardy. Hotheaded. And injudicious—a troubling quality for a judge.

But I had to stand up, see it for myself.

I begged off from cleanup after breakfast on the farm, left it to my sisters to wash pots and pans and clear away the trash. Nellie wasn't happy. She demanded to know why I was cutting out.

So I lied. I came up with some bullshit excuse about a meeting of the area bar association and just took off.

I needed to do this alone. I didn't want my sisters with me in Union Springs that day. I had a feeling. A bad one.

When I turned onto Prairie Street, it was already crowded.

Judge Stone

Vehicles lined the road, taking up every available parking space. I turned into my designated spot behind the courthouse.

At least the sign RESERVED FOR CIRCUIT JUDGE MARY STONE still counted for something.

As I opened my car door, I could see the crowd pouring in from the side streets and moving toward the main drag. The sheer volume amazed me. Made me nervous.

But I'd come this far. I had to see what was cooking at the pro-life, white-supremacy get-together. Who *were* all these people? Where were they coming from?

I walked around the courthouse, shouldered my way through the mass of humanity on the sidewalk, and climbed the front steps to get a bird's-eye view. The pro-life protesters were out in force, milling around in front of the courthouse with signs like the ones I'd seen before.

LIFE BEGINS AT CONCEPTION

RIGHTS BEGIN IN THE WOMB

A CHILD, NOT A CHOICE

No surprise in that message. Nothing surprising about the messengers, either. In fact, the pro-lifers looked a lot like the people I'd seen the other day, when I ended up face down on Prairie Street.

What I hadn't expected was the counterprotest. A pro–reproductive rights group had assembled. Mostly young people. But definitely not locals. I was nearly blinded by the intense hues of their hair dye. I saw a lot of hot pink, some purple, some green, some blue. Their signs were just as colorful. Lots of neon-bright lettering.

ABORTION IS HEALTH CARE

BANS OFF OUR BODIES

OUR BODIES, OUR ABORTIONS

PREGNANT PEOPLE HAVE RIGHTS

I shaded my eyes with my hand and scanned the whole crowd. I was searching for a familiar face. Looking for a single person I knew. Sounds crazy, but I swear—I couldn't find one.

I'd never seen so many white people in my life.

Union Springs, Alabama, is a Black-majority town, and it was startling to see that the Black people in this public gathering made up such a small minority. I expected Black folks to spurn the pro-life party; after all, it was organized by redneck racists. But why hadn't they shown up for the counterprotest? Why were there no Black folks carrying pro-choice signs?

Was it old-time religion? Or was it fear?

I noticed something else. There were no babies in strollers at this protest. No kids in wagons. No tots on parents' shoulders.

Everybody had left the kids at home.

As I watched, the two groups started surging toward each other, shouting and screaming, with hate in their eyes. I saw a few local cops trying to maintain order, but it was a losing battle.

A shiver ran right through me.

This was no longer a rally. It was a fight.

Suddenly, I heard the sound of truck engines roaring from around the corner. And I realized that things were about to get a lot worse.

CHAPTER 47

I stepped down onto the crowded sidewalk just as a fleet of pickup trucks turned onto the square, honking their horns and forcing their way through the throng. Each pickup was covered with oversized images of pregnancies in utero. Confederate flags were draped across the truck beds.

The pro-life side greeted the caravan like a conquering army. Just then, the lead vehicle started blaring music from roof-mounted speakers at a deafening volume.

The tune was "Dixie."

That song always gave me goose bumps, in all the wrong ways.

It wasn't just the lyrics that riled me. It was knowing that "Dixie" had been the anthem of the Confederacy. A song about how great the South used to be. Back when Black people—my ancestors—were enslaved. And when the economy of the South rested on the flayed backs of their forced labor. To me that was what "Dixie" celebrated.

I was not a fan.

As the tune played, I saw a man across the street remove his ball cap and place his hand over his heart. Like he was hearing "The Star-Spangled Banner." Or watching US soldiers raise the American flag.

I sidestepped some people on the sidewalk as the fleet approached. I wanted to cuss out the driver playing "Dixie." Was ready to shake my fist, flip him the bird. I'm aware that would be behavior unbecoming of a candidate running for reelection to the office of circuit judge. I didn't give a damn.

When the lead pickup pulled close enough for me to see through the windshield, I froze for a second. I shouldn't have been surprised. It was that goddamn Mason Phelps, the Grand Whatever of the local racist society. *Shit.*

I stepped back. I didn't want to give Phelps the finger or shout the F-word at him. He'd regard that as a win. I refused to let him think he had that kind of power over me.

But he'd caught sight of me. As I tried to press back into the crowd, he peered out the driver's window and our eyes met. I caught it, a flash of pure hate in that look. Replaced by a grin, scary as hell. He drove by slowly. I saw those brown teeth flashing at me, as Mason Phelps started laughing. Like he knew some ugly joke I wasn't clued in on.

I shivered, right there on the street. A chill ran all the way down my back. An omen, Mama would say. Like somebody was walking on my grave.

As the line of battered pickup trucks moved through town, a handful of people in the pro-life crowd gave them some patchy applause. Not many, though. I saw a number of people in pro-life shirts who looked visibly uncomfortable. It seemed like not all the pro-lifers were down with the Confederate flags. I saw that as a positive indicator. Calmed down a hair, caught my breath.

The pro-choice response was much stronger. Young people

wearing ROE and PLANNED PARENTHOOD shirts elbowed me as they moved into the street, booing the parade.

A young man used his BRING BACK ROE sign to whale away at the Confederate flags waving from the truck beds. "Fascists! Fucking traitors!"

Other counterprotesters followed suit, shouting at the trucks as they passed.

The kids with neon hair didn't seem terribly frightened or intimidated. Some of them were even laughing. Making fun of Mason Phelps. Openly mocking him.

And I saw pro-lifers who weren't overjoyed to have Phelps as the leader of their movement. Some of them were packing up, moving on.

The sight gave me a lift. I was glad to see people mocking Phelps. I relished the insults they threw at him. But still. It wasn't smart for those protesters to disregard Mason Phelps and his friends. It worried me. They hadn't been exposed to him for years, like I had.

A young woman stepped off the curb and flung an egg at the cab of one of the dusty pickups, shouting, "Hey, Dixie! That all you got? Bunch of losers!"

I had to smile at that. At that point, I even thought maybe I was wrong to have worried. It looked like the white supremacists' attempt to lead the abortion protest was fizzling.

That was when I spotted the last vehicle in the motorcade. A huge box truck. Plain white, no flags, no slogans, no markings. It lumbered slowly up Prairie Street and came to a stop about a block from where I was standing.

The door of the cab opened. I watched the driver hop out. Aside from being white, he looked nothing like Phelps or his shaggy crew. No long, greasy hair. No baseball cap.

This guy was fit and muscular, with a short military haircut. Dressed in immaculate khaki pants and a red polo shirt.

He jogged to the back of the white truck and opened the doors.

"It's Patriot Front!" someone called out. "They're white nationalists!"

Suddenly, two dozen men jumped out and moved into formation.

To me, they didn't look homegrown. Probably from out of state. Guests of honor, invited by Mason Phelps. He was probably thrilled to see them.

They were all fit white guys, dressed in the same red-and-khaki outfit that the driver wore. Some kind of uniform. Their faces were covered with white gaiters, like the face coverings during the height of COVID. These days, in my experience on the bench, those face coverings were used by people who were trying to avoid identification.

The men were all armed with assault rifles.

"Sweet Jesus," I whispered.

I overheard frantic voices nearby. The neon-haired young people were all shouting, "Call the cops!"

One young woman followed behind the formation, screaming at them. "You can't do this! It's illegal!"

Clearly, the woman wasn't from Alabama. If she was, she'd know that the men with assault rifles were not breaking any law. Alabama was an open-carry state. No permit required.

As the armed, masked men began their march down the street, I heard more frenzied shouts.

Sure enough. The "Dixie" melody started up again from Phelps's truck speakers. He must have been expecting the reinforcements. At the sight of all the guns, people on the sidewalk started to scatter.

I'd seen enough.

Judge Stone

It was time to get the hell out of town.

As I headed for the back of the courthouse, I was getting pushed and shoved from all sides. There was panic in the air—the kind of hysteria that gets people trampled and killed.

No way I could get to my car. The crowd was too thick. Instead, I grappled my way up the stairs of the courthouse and forced my way to the main entrance. Fumbled in my bag for the key ring. I was one of a handful of people in Bullock County entrusted with the key to the courthouse door.

When I got the key in hand, I got shoved so hard that I dropped the keys on the ground.

"Back off!" I shouted. Bending down, I picked the keys up. My hands were shaking as I jammed the key into the dead bolt lock and turned it.

As I grabbed the handle, I felt a crush of bodies behind me, pushing toward safety.

I was still holding the door when I heard the gunshots.

And the screams.

CHAPTER 48

BULLOCK COUNTY SHERIFF'S OFFICE
UNION SPRINGS, ALABAMA

Two hours later, I was sitting in the sheriff's office, giving my statement to Deputy Lonnie Sparks—another cop I'd known since he was a kid.

It felt like the shooting had gone on for an eternity. In fact, it had lasted about ten seconds. Nobody was killed, thank God. Multiple hospitalizations, mostly from folks getting trampled when the shooting started. The bullet wounds were mostly grazes.

I related all the information I could recall. Every detail of my observations on the street. I shared descriptions and names of the people who sought shelter at the courthouse when the rampage began. I was talking so long and so fast that my voice was getting raspy.

Lonnie stopped taking down what I was saying. "You need something to drink, Judge Mary?"

"I could use a Diet Coke," I croaked.

He smiled. "Be right back."

As Lonnie walked down the hallway, I looked around the office. The whole force had been mobilized for the rally, and now they were trying to sort out the aftermath. But this was a lot bigger than the Union Springs PD. No disrespect, but most of these officers were used to dealing with domestic disputes and drunk-and-disorderly calls. They'd never seen anything like this.

Neither had I.

"I hear you're thirsty." I turned around. Mick Owens was standing there, dangling a frosty can of Diet Coke. "Come talk," he said. "You can finish your statement later."

I grabbed the can. "You got a deal."

I followed him into his crowded office in the corner of the floor. He looked back at me.

"You owe me a dollar for that Coke, Mary."

"I don't owe you shit, Mick." I popped the can and took a long, deep gulp.

He propped his boots up on his desk. "I just got back from the hospital. Taking statements, getting information. Records of injuries. Seeing who had video or pictures on their phones."

"It's a miracle nobody died out there," I said. "Why weren't you more prepared? You knew it was brewing."

"I surely did not."

"The hell? This has been stirring up for months. Shoot, the governor has been threatening to send in the National Guard since the Bria Gaines case was filed, seems like. So why wasn't the Guard called in today?"

"Nobody could've foreseen this, Mary. It's not our people raining shit down. It's outside agitators. We wouldn't be having these problems if publicity wasn't dragging in a bunch of crazies."

He was right, in part. But he was leaving something out. "It wasn't only out-of-towners. You can't blame a faceless enemy for this. I know what I saw. You saw the same thing. Mason Phelps was leading that Dixie demonstration. He's been hyping it up for weeks."

Mick waved me off with a hand. "Don't you worry about Mason Phelps. Couldn't organize a keg party."

"You telling me not to worry? This was his party, he could've wiped out our town today. I know he planned it. He was over at Coley's after Cocheta's funeral, handing out Replacement Theory flyers."

Mick sighed and wiped a hand over his face. "Mary, Mason Phelps is a worthless shithead, everyone knows that. And a true Alabama cracker, racist to the core. I don't fool myself, I know what he's capable of, where his sympathies lie. But I've come down hard on him. Kicked his ass more than once. He doesn't mess with me. Trust me, I've got Phelps and his buddies under control."

"You call what happened today under control?"

"Look. I talked to Phelps at the scene. He said it wasn't him that was doing the shooting. He said one of the guys from out of town brought a defective firearm. Went off accidentally. Then people went nuts. Shoving and running and knocking each other down."

"That's bullshit." My prom date was no Sherlock Fucking Holmes, but he wasn't that stupid. "You were out there, Mick! Did those guys look like the types to carry defective firearms?"

"Mary, take it easy."

"I don't think anything went off accidentally. Do you have anyone in custody?"

"We're a small force, Mary. We're working on it."

I could tell that I was getting under his skin.

Good. I decided to burrow a little deeper.

"Working on it? Just like you're working on solving Cocheta's murder? Was that just an accident, too? Did Cocheta accidentally get lynched in her own backyard?"

"Goddamnit, Mary!" Mick swung his right arm and swiped everything off the top of his desk. Coffee cup, papers, pens, pads. His nostrils were flaring. "I don't answer to you!" he shouted. His chest was puffed out, voice rumbling. "I'm an elected official—just like you. The voters gave me this position. I answer to the people."

"Yeah, well, the people are wondering why you can't solve a case."

I stood up. He still towered over me. "Get out of my office," he muttered. "Before I lose my temper."

I looked down at the mess on the floor. "I think you already lost it."

"Fuck you!"

"Thanks for the Coke."

"Leave!"

Whatever. I was tired. I wanted to go home, anyway. I picked up my bag and turned to head out the door. When I was almost there, Mick called after me.

"Hey, Mary! You wanna know what the people are saying to me? What I hear is they want to know why Judge Mary Stone won't get that goddamn abortion case over and done with! Try the fucking case! Then everybody in Bullock County can put it behind us."

I paused for a second. Was that really what folks were saying about me? Maybe so. But I'd never admit it. Not here. Wouldn't give Mick Owens the satisfaction.

As I walked out into the hallway, he had one more thing to say. He shouted it so loud everybody in the office could hear it.

"If anyone gets killed over this abortion case, Mary—that's on you! It'll be your fault! Blood on your hands!"

CHAPTER 49

His words stayed with me. The accusation preyed on my mind. I kept thinking about what he'd said, that I was the one responsible for damage being done. I was to blame for the harm that folks were suffering.

Paying mind to Mick Owens's judgment was a novel circumstance. I'd never held his opinion in high regard. Not even back in high school, when we were going out. I wasn't attracted to his brain back then, as I sat in the wooden bleachers. Watching him run down the court in a Hornets uniform. Leap into the air and dunk the ball.

But even Sheriff Owens could be right on occasion. Like a broken clock, twice a day. So I'd been turning an idea over in my head. Something that might reduce the probability of violence and unrest in Union Springs. I was almost convinced that it was the best option.

That, or the worst. There was a possibility that it would hasten the demise of the community. There was that, too.

Judge Stone

I hustled past Luna's desk on Friday, so deep in thought I forgot to say *Good morning*. She jumped out of her chair and followed me.

"Judge? Got something you need to see."

I pulled my suit jacket off, hung it on the coatrack, right by my black robe. "Somebody file something? I've been waiting for confirmation of a settlement from Barry McCurry. Has he called?"

"No, no court business. It's a media thing."

A wave of irritation rolled, almost making my skin itch. "Stop right there!"

I extended my hand, like I was face guarding her.

"Luna, don't devil me with the nonsense you see on social media. I'm determined to keep far away from that. If I don't read it, don't see it, it can't ruin my day."

"Judge, I think you should check it out."

I leveled a look at her. "Luna. Is it something on social media?"

"Yes, it's on social. But that's not the only place."

"What did I just say?"

Luna's shoulders straightened. She turned her back on me. Returned to her desk, then marched right back into chambers with a stack of newspapers clutched to her chest. Which she dumped directly onto my tidy desktop.

"Someone left these right in front of the courtroom, all of them. Ross found them when he unlocked the courtroom door this morning. I promised him I'd show them to you."

She made a quick exit. Had her hand on my door, ready to shut it. "And yeah—the pictures are on social media, too. Facebook, X, Insta, and TikTok. I checked this morning."

Before she slammed the door, she stuck her head back in. "I'll hold your calls."

I lifted the top newspaper. It was a supermarket tabloid. When I leafed through the stack, I counted a dozen copies.

My picture was on the front page. Sweet Jesus—I saw my face above the fold.

The photo was fairly recent; I wore a sweater I'd ordered online. It was a shot of me and Loucilla sitting at a bar in Montgomery. Loucilla was holding a martini glass. My beverage wasn't visible. The readers wouldn't know I'd been drinking iced tea.

But the picture didn't bother me much. There's no prohibiting a grown woman from occupying a barstool. Not even in the Black Belt of Alabama.

No, it was the headline that unnerved me. In bold caps, it jumped out at me.

GAY AGENDA IN ALABAMA ABORTION CASE

I felt the preliminary jab of a headache. I slid into my chair, pulled a pair of reading glasses out of my desk drawer.

There wasn't much of a story. Hell, what could they actually substantiate? After rehashing the facts of Dr. Bria Gaines's charge, the tabloid detailed my regular dinners with my best friend—whom they described as a "well-known lesbian activist from Montgomery."

As for me? "Circuit Judge Mary Stone, who has been assigned the criminal trial, is running for reelection on the Democrat ballot. Judge Stone is single, never been married."

That was all true. Hell, I couldn't even sue the tabloid for defamation.

I stared at the newsprint littering my desk. Other stories in the tabloid were devoted to actors in rehab; the breakup of a major star's marriage; a rapper sued for harassment. I wasn't just a local officeholder anymore. I'd joined that cluster of tabloid fodder.

Somehow, I'd become a public figure. The kind of person people could feel free to insult and deride. The object of unbridled speculation and scandal.

Damn, I wasn't looking for that kind of notoriety when I signed on for this gig. I wanted to dispense justice. Decide cases, resolve conflicts. But here it was. Staring me in the face. Literally.

The shit was getting deeper around here with every day that passed. I had to make a call. Couldn't sit around feeling sorry for myself. I was not the person most wounded in the scenario. Not by a long shot.

I hit Loucilla's name in my contacts. She picked right up. Didn't say hello.

"I've already seen it," she said.

"Damn! I didn't know you were a subscriber. No wonder you always know all the dirt on everybody."

"I don't subscribe," she said, her voice dry. "I was at the grocery store. In the checkout line. Buying tampons."

"Girl! You still using tampons?" I asked, sounding impressed.

"Yeah. Just like I'm younger than springtime. Maybe that detail will make the next issue. I could earn a buck that way. You think a well-known lesbian activist can get an endorsement deal from a company that makes feminine hygiene products?"

It wasn't funny. I could hear that edge in her voice. I know Loucilla. She was shook. Much more troubled than she'd let on.

"I'm sorry, Lou. So sorry to drag you into this."

"The hell you say? I'm just fine. Maybe I'll write a book about it. Now that you've made me famous, I could get a publisher to respond to a query for a change. What about you, Mary? How are you getting along down there?"

I had to think about it for a minute before I answered.

"I'm fine, too. More than fine, actually. I checked my calendar and a special setting is opening up on my docket. Maybe we can get this case moving, have us a trial."

The prospect of a speedy trial was sounding better all the time.

Loucilla rang off. I shouted through the door, didn't bother to pick up the office line.

"Luna! Get the DA and Benjamin Meyers into court. You tell them the judge says we gotta talk."

CHAPTER 50

BULLOCK COUNTY COURTHOUSE
UNION SPRINGS, ALABAMA

I did that trick of mine. Took my seat at the bench before the hearing was scheduled. I wanted to see them all as they walked in. To get a feel for the situation. See where everyone's head was. It's lots easier to read people when they're not quite ready for you, not prepared to be seen.

The DA arrived a little early. Maybe he was anticipating my move. Reeves walked in with a bounce in his step. Smile on his face. Looked like he'd won a hand pay at the casino.

That was interesting.

I called to him before he took his seat. "Will the AG's office be assisting you today, Mr. Reeves?"

He paused with his hand on the back of his chair. "Why do you ask, Judge?"

The DA was already riling me. Getting my back up, and we hadn't even begun. He was showing disrespect without cause. He had no reason to push back. I'm entitled to know who's appearing in my court. "I want it for the record. The docket entry will need to reflect who's representing the prosecution today."

"Well," he said, setting his laptop on the table. "That would be me."

Then he smiled. Not at me, you understand. A private smile, like he knew something I didn't know.

I was chewing on that, debating whether I should light into him now or later, when Ben Meyers entered the courtroom, with Dr. Gaines following behind.

I almost gawked. Had to pull a poker face, fast. Swiveled my chair to face my computer screen, tapped the keyboard like I was doing court business.

Faking it, in fact. I couldn't even see what was on the screen. The sight of Bria Gaines walking into court was burned into my brain.

That poor woman.

It was crushing her. I could see it from my first glimpse. She couldn't mask it. It had gone on too long, gone too far. Her eyes were swollen and puffy from lack of sleep. She was gaunt, her face hollowed out, cheekbones prominent.

She wasn't eating, that was apparent. The weight loss wasn't confined to her face. Her dress hung off her, like she was a kid wearing her big sister's clothes. Reminded me of Jordan playing dress-up in my church clothes, when I was a teenager and she was in kindergarten.

As the defense settled in, I gave them the side-eye. Sneaked a glance at their table. Bria tried to compose herself, was working hard at it. She sat straight in her chair. Held her head up high.

But when she uncapped her pen, her hands shook so violently that she dropped it on the floor. It rolled under the counsel table. She scooted her chair back, like she meant to get down there on her knees and hunt for it. Her lawyer stopped her. Found her a fresh pen. She shot him a grateful look.

And then both of her hands disappeared from view. Hiding them on her lap, I suspected. She was self-conscious about the tremor.

I caught the DA checking Bria out. I could see his smug expression as he turned back to his laptop.

My face grew hot. I knew what was happening. The DA was easy to read; I'd had lots of practice.

Reeves wasn't blind. He could also observe the physical changes Dr. Gaines had undergone, could see the impact his case was having on the defendant. He viewed it as a victory. He was breaking Bria Gaines down. That was part of his case strategy. To make her crumble.

Bria Gaines is a confident Black woman—or was, when the whole process began.

To somebody like Reeves, a confident Black woman is trouble. It's a character trait he doesn't want to deal with. Makes him uncomfortable. Not just Reeves. All the people who think like him.

They love it when we break.

The vibe in court was confirming my instinct. That this case needed to go to trial. But I needed to see Bria's reaction, hear what her lawyer had to say.

I gave the gavel a rap, to get everyone's attention.

"I'd like to thank y'all for coming in today. You're probably wondering why we're here, since we don't have any outstanding motions."

Nobody said anything. Not a surprise, I hadn't asked them to speak.

I went on. "The case of *State v. Bria Gaines* is on my jury docket, but we don't have a firm date for trial, not at this time. Which isn't unusual. Felony cases of this magnitude tend to languish for a long time before being tried before a jury."

Reeves shrugged. Meyers nodded an acknowledgment. No response from Dr. Gaines.

"It happens, though, that I'm looking at an opening on my trial docket. A case was set for jury trial—a personal injury case, multiple parties. That big explosion on the highway. Y'all surely recall when that happened."

Ben Meyers had caught on. He was whispering to Bria.

"The parties have recently informed me—they've reached an agreement on settlement. Which frees up two whole weeks on my calendar."

I tapped my keyboard, pulled up my court calendar. There it was: a two-week stretch of blank space. No case numbers, case names, notations of matters to be heard and decided. By me.

"So! You know what I'm about to ask."

Reeves jumped to his feet. "The State is always ready, Your Honor!"

Irritation buzzed in my ears. "Excuse me?"

"We're ready for trial at any time."

I snapped. "What are you doing out of that chair?"

He sidestepped, like he had more to say. "I just want to reassure the court that the State can be ready to go whenever the court wishes."

If I were inclined to ask the Lord for favors, I would have sent up a prayer to grant me patience. "Mr. Reeves, I wasn't asking you. I know the State can be ready for trial. Because you have all the power of the government on your side. You have county law enforcement ready to offer whatever assistance you desire. And in this particular case, you have even more power. You got the whole damn state tied up in this case. We've got the Alabama attorney general's office and the governor of Alabama popping up in the Bullock County Courthouse like a Whac-a-Mole game. Governor is saying—again—that the National Guard is on its way."

Reeves sat. *Good.*

I turned to the defense table. Ben Meyers had scooted his chair right next to Bria Gaines's. They sat elbow to elbow. She was wide-eyed. Like she was afraid she'd be the next one in line for a tongue-lashing.

"I need to hear from the defense. The defendant has a constitutional right to a speedy trial. We all know that, right? But I was a defense attorney back in the day. And I know that the defense sometimes prefers delay. Particularly when the defendant is out on bond."

There are a number of advantages to delay, from the defense perspective. Delay can weaken the State's case. Over time, witnesses' recollection may fade. Witnesses might move away, become unavailable to appear at trial. Sometimes the prosecutor's interest in or appetite for the case will fade.

If Ben Meyers wanted more time for Bria, he'd get it. But I needed to see her face. If the waiting was going to destroy her, I had to fight that.

It was a tough call for them to make. Was it more brutal, more painful to proceed? Or to wait around?

Meyers spoke softly to her. I didn't try to eavesdrop. Seemed like she trusted him. I saw her nod a couple of times. She whispered something in his ear.

At length, Meyers stood and said, "The defense has no objection to the trial setting."

I had to be certain.

"Dr. Gaines?"

She looked up, startled. She hadn't expected me to address her directly.

"Your Honor?"

"This setting's just two weeks off. It's unexpected, I know that. You're comfortable with it? You sure?"

I saw her neck move when she swallowed. But her voice was stronger when she answered.

"Yes, Your Honor. I'm ready to have my case heard. I want to take it to a jury."

"All right, then. Mr. Reeves, Mr. Meyers, we'll conduct a pretrial conference the week before jury selection. My clerk will be in contact with y'all, to nail down the exact time for that."

I stood. They stood.

"Court is adjourned."

As I left the courtroom, the voice in my head was loud.

Sure as hell hope this isn't a horrible mistake.

PART
THREE

CHAPTER 51

Bria Gaines

VICTORY BAPTIST CHURCH
UNION SPRINGS, ALABAMA

It was Sunday morning, just eight days before her trial would begin at the Bullock County Courthouse. And Dr. Bria Gaines was late for church.

The timing was intentional. Bria had been a member of Victory Baptist since she'd moved to Union Springs. She'd joined the church straightaway; it was how she was raised, in a family of serious, Bible-thumping Christians.

The congregation had embraced her, back when she joined. They'd praised God for bringing her to town. Flocked to her clinic for medical care.

After the felony charge was filed against her, Bria stopped attending services. She stayed away for a number of reasons, any one of which provided sufficient cause. Fear of rejection, ostracism, the cold shoulder. Or the opposite: She dreaded a verbal confrontation. Accusations, insults. The very real possibility that her church family might kick her out of the fold, excommunicating her from their community of faith.

The prospect of those reactions had been sufficient to discourage her from crossing the threshold. But when she got out of bed on that particular Sunday, with her trial a week away, Bria decided that she needed to return. Her soul felt battered, weary, restless. She longed for the feeling of peace she'd always received when sitting in the wooden pew with her head bowed.

In eight days, when jury selection began, Bria would need courage and strength. The kind of fortitude that only a higher power could provide.

Give it up to the Lord, her heart told her.

She could hear the congregation singing as she left her car and walked up to the front entrance. Bria had missed the call to worship and the responsive scripture reading. They'd moved on to the first hymn: "How Righteous Is Our God."

The timing of her arrival was perfect. Everyone was on their feet. Singing, hands raised. Some with eyes shut, moving with the spirit. She couldn't have picked a better moment to slip in unnoticed.

Or so she thought.

Bria intended to take a seat in the back. Wasn't easy, not that Sunday. The church was packed. Reverend Erskine generally commanded good attendance, but this was a record-setting crowd. Like Easter morning, they'd placed folding chairs at the end of each row, to provide additional seating.

While the churchgoers sang the final verse of the hymn, Bria managed to find a single bare space in the pew, a spot just large enough for her to slide in. That inconspicuous spot in the back was a blessing. She hadn't come to church to be recognized. She wasn't seeking fellowship. She was looking for God.

She wanted to pray. To petition the Lord to give her the strength to withstand the rigors of the trial that she would have to endure in the coming days.

As she slid into the back row, the organ music hit the final notes: *Amen.*

Everyone took their seats. Reverend Erskine had taken his place at the pulpit. He stood there, a forbidding figure in black and white.

His solemn face broke into a beaming smile. "On this beautiful Sabbath morning, brothers and sisters, let's turn to welcome one another, for the passing of the peace."

The sound of pews creaking, bodies moving. A babel of voices rose up as members leaned over for hugs and handshakes, exchanging friendly greetings.

Bria Gaines was seated directly beside a young couple with two children between them. The younger child bounced in his seat, exclaiming, "Mama! It's Dr. Bria!"

That sweet voice made Bria smile. "Good morning," she said to him. She turned to the boy's mother, seated close beside her, and whispered, "A pleasure to see y'all this morning."

The woman would not meet her eye when Bria spoke to her. Didn't even incline her head in Bria's direction. But the woman gave a light touch, a friendly pat, to Bria's arm.

The woman's demeanor made Bria's spirit plummet. Her reaction was physical; she had to clutch the wooden pew in front of her for balance. Why had she decided to attend that morning?

After the volume of voices had peaked, Reverend Erskine lifted a black-bound Bible. "Please stand for the reading from the Old Testament."

Folks took to their feet. A hush fell over the congregation. Bria bowed her head, closed her eyes. Hoped Pastor had chosen an uplifting verse. Something to carry her through the coming days.

"Jeremiah chapter 1, verse 5. 'Before I formed you in the womb I knew you, before you were born, I set you apart; I appointed you as a prophet to the nations.'"

An elderly woman raised her arms, crying out. "Praise be!"

"You may be seated," Erskine said. He waited for the congregation to get settled. Then he placed his hand over his heart. "Brothers and sisters, the words of this book have inspired my sermon for today. God tells us in the Book of Jeremiah that he is the true Creator of every baby in a mother's womb. 'Before I formed you in the womb,' God says. The Lord God made us all! Can I get an amen?"

"Amen!" The chorus of voices was so loud, Bria jerked in her seat.

"The Book of Psalms says the same thing. Gives us the same powerful guarantee! Psalm 139, verse 1—'For you created my inmost being; you knit me together in my mother's womb.'"

A woman across the aisle from Bria jumped to her feet, raising her arms. "Praise Jesus!"

Bria recognized the voice. A knot of dread exploded in her chest as she leaned forward to peek down the row.

It was Starla Jones, occupying the back row, on the opposite side of the sanctuary. Starla's brood took up most of the pew. She'd brought all five children with her.

Nova sat on the far end, near the narrow stained-glass window. Staring straight ahead. Not watching her mother as she danced, moving with the spirit, with her arms reaching up to heaven.

Two of the Jones kids were rassling on the pew, fighting over a paper copy of the church bulletin. Nova didn't shush them, didn't intervene. She sat in the pew like a bronze statue, unmoving, facing the pipe organ.

Reverend Erskine's voice rose. A sheen of perspiration made his face glisten. "The Good Book confirms it. From the Book of Psalms: 'I praise you because I am fearfully and wonderfully made, your works are wonderful.' Do you hear that, brothers and sisters? Each and every one of us, we are fearfully and wonderfully made!"

"Praise the Lord!"

"Amen!"

They were all rising, all getting fired up. Only Bria remained seated, it seemed. She peered around the sanctuary, then peeked down her row, trying to sneak a glance, to see whether other backsliders had kept their seats.

Only one, besides Bria.

Nova Jones.

"The good Lord, in all his wisdom and mercy, has decreed that we humble human beings are his own creation. So! Tell me, brethren. When one of God's people is intentionally murdered; when that life is taken, before it had the chance to begin. When someone kills a precious baby before it is even born—what do we call that, brothers and sisters?"

"MURDER!"

It was a group chant, so beautifully timed, it sounded rehearsed.

Pastor's voice began a crescendo. "God gave us his commandments. He gave them to Moses on the mountain. The Sixth Commandment is clear as day. Thou shalt not kill!"

Bria's mouth was dry, her heart pounding. Nausea was coming in waves. She had to leave. She couldn't bear it, could not remain in that sanctuary any longer.

She stood, tried to scoot in front of the couple who'd made room for her to sit with them. The woman who had reached out earlier to pat her arm made way to let her pass. But the husband was like a column of stone; she couldn't squeeze past him.

Her heart raced, making her dizzy. She moved the other direction, pushed past two old women standing to her left. They didn't try to trap her inside the pew. They scooted back, clutching the pew for support. One of the ladies looked up as Bria surged past. The auntie's eyes were wet with tears.

She stumbled out into the center aisle. She didn't mean to look at anyone. Certainly not Nova Jones, or her mother. Step-by-step, she focused on her escape, keeping her eyes fixed on the brass handle of the church door.

A woman appeared by some bad magic, just as she reached it. The preacher's wife, Doreen Erskine, wrapped her hand around the door handle before Bria could touch it. Bria stumbled back a step. Did the woman intend to prevent her departure? Did the Erskines mean to keep her a prisoner in the church sanctuary?

A hush fell over the sanctuary. She heard bodies shifting in their seats to watch the drama unfold.

Bria's mouth was pressed shut. She sent a pleading look to Doreen Erskine, a silent plea. *Let me go.*

Doreen Erskine's face was a frozen mask of condemnation. The pastor's wife pulled open the church house door, and she uttered two words. "Get out."

Bria bolted. As the door closed behind her, she could hear a wave of voices rise again. She couldn't make out what all they said.

But as she drove away from Victory Baptist, the pastor's words were locked inside her head. Refusing to be silenced.

Murderer. Killer.

CHAPTER 52

Mary Stone

BULLOCK COUNTY COURTHOUSE
UNION SPRINGS, ALABAMA

I rapped the gavel. "Y'all, we're taking a midmorning break. The court will be in recess for fifteen minutes."

Leaving the bench, I moved down the aisle at full speed, determined to make the front of the line to the women's room.

My bailiff stopped me when I reached the courtroom door. "Judge, you're wanted downstairs. County Commission needs to see you."

"Now? Today?" I wanted to snatch those commissioners bald. I had no time to fool with them.

It was six days until jury selection was set to begin in *State v. Bria Gaines*. Folks all over the circuit were tugging on my skirt. I had a shit ton of matters to resolve before Monday rolled around.

Lawyers and citizens were flocking into court, pleading for a moment of my time.

"Ross, I've got five more hearings set before lunch. And the commission needs to see me right now? You serious?"

He held up his hands, like *Don't shoot.* "Judge, I'm just the messenger. But Otis said it's urgent."

"Damn," I said. Whispered it, actually. Since I was standing in the courtroom in my robe, with a dozen citizens of Bullock County within earshot.

I craned my neck to get a look at the hallway near the ladies' room. Six or seven women stood in line outside the door, waiting to get in.

Hell.

"Okay, I'll run down there for a minute. See what the commissioners want. But I'll be back. If I run over a couple of minutes, you let everybody know, Ross. I'm in the courthouse. I haven't run off."

I took the curved staircase so fast, I was in danger of tripping on the hem of my robe as I made my way down. When I reached the commissioners' office, the door was closed.

And locked.

I twisted that antique brass knob while I pounded the wooden door with my left fist.

"Anybody in there? This is Mary! Judge Stone!"

I heard the lock flip when the bolt was turned. The door opened. Otis Post, the presiding commissioner, waved me inside.

"Sorry about that, Judge. We didn't want anyone walking in. Seems like there's reporters sticking their noses into county business these days."

Otis locked the door behind me. An unusual precaution in Union Springs. But times had changed.

Judge Stone

Five men sat at the conference table. Three of them were county commissioners. Otis, Tariq Johnson, and Michael Price.

Sitting at the far end was Reeves, the DA. Which didn't bode well.

And the sheriff. Mick Owens leaned over, pulled out the empty chair next to his. "Sit down, Mary."

I sat on the edge of the seat, as if I was prepared to jump right out of it. Because I wasn't at all convinced that I wanted to stick around.

I looked around that table with my eyes narrowed. "Must be something important going on. Locking yourselves in here. Dragging me off the bench."

"It's a matter of significance," Otis said. He was shiny with nervous sweat, all the way up to the top of his bald white head. "We want you to reconsider a judgment call you made."

"Not a court judgment," Tariq added, speaking quickly. He was young, one of the up-and-coming Black leaders in the county. "Just a lodging arrangement. More like an administrative matter. Which would rest more squarely in the commission's domain. That's what we're thinking."

Michael Price had nothing to add. Par for the course with that dude. He rarely opened his mouth. I often wondered how he managed to get reelected. Maybe it was the passivity. He never said or did anything that could make anyone mad.

"What are we talking about?" I demanded.

Reeves answered. "The jury," the DA said. The commissioners nodded.

Reeves took a breath. "Judge, you indicated months ago that you intended to sequester the jury. We didn't hold a hearing, you just announced it in a conference."

Five pairs of eyeballs on me. I set them straight. "Yeah. I'm sequestering the jury. I've made that clear from the beginning, even when the governor and the attorney general tried to talk me out of it. We're putting them at the Red Cedar Motel. My bailiff has alerted the management. They've set aside enough rooms for us."

Otis Post wiped a hand over the crown of his head. "Don't we have a say in this?"

I made a noise in my throat. Shook my head. "Hell no, you don't. This is not a surprise. I didn't spring it on you. Luna called and left word with y'all when we talked to the motel."

Tariq frowned, looking thoughtful. "Judge Mary, you know our finances in Bullock County. We operate on a fine line. If we have to feed and lodge a jury of twelve during this long trial, it's going to be a burden."

"More than twelve. There will be two alternates," the DA said. "And security, too. Sheriff says he's been asked to assign two deputies to remain with them." Reeves sounded huffy about it, like the money would be coming from his own pocket.

I turned on Reeves. "Why are you discussing this case with me outside the presence of opposing counsel? Where's Benjamin Meyers? Why isn't he here? You trying to woodshed the judge, Mr. Reeves?"

"It's county business," Reeves said. Didn't look a bit sorry.

Shameless.

I turned to the sheriff. "And Mick? You got a dog in this fight?"

The sheriff grimaced, scratched the back of his neck. "I just need to know what y'all decide. So I'll know how many of my personnel I'll be devoting to the trial."

The DA scooted his chair forward. Had the nerve to point his finger at me. "Judge, sequestration isn't just expensive. It's gonna be bad for the trial. Think of all the prospective jurors you're knocking out of contention! Lots of people's circumstances prohibit them from being locked away for a week at a time, or longer. Nursing mothers. Single parents. Farmers with livestock to tend to. You should understand that, Judge. How many head of cattle you got on your place?"

It was a rhetorical question. I didn't answer him.

Instead, I checked the clock on the wall. My fifteen-minute recess was over, and I'd never made it to the restroom. Time to wrap up this conversation.

"Have you men all lost your goddamn minds?"

The swearing jarred them. Even Michael Price's eyes bulged. I was glad to see it. Showed the guy was listening.

I went on: "Y'all know what's been going on in our community since the DA filed this case. The level of press attention it's received. The people marching in the streets. Bullets flying, folks trampled. We have to contain this jury, so we'll know it hasn't been contaminated. The jury must be sequestered. There's no way around it."

"Who's supposed to pay?" the presiding commissioner demanded, raising his voice at me.

I wasn't about to stand for that.

I rose from that chair. Looked down at the shiny dome of his head. "Maybe you can pay by economizing on your personal expenses. Quit turning in per diems. Skip some of the state conferences."

"What?" "You serious?" They were blustering now, protesting, talking over one another.

Meanwhile, outside the courthouse, things were getting loud — again. Somebody talking into a bullhorn, accompanied by a couple of other people. We could see them, right through the window of the commissioners' office. I stepped closer to the window, raised the aluminum blinds to get a clearer view.

While the man talked into the bullhorn, a woman shook out an American flag. A good-sized one, probably three feet by five feet. She handed it off to the guy with the bullhorn. While he held it up with his free hand, she flipped a butane lighter. Set the flag on fire.

"Son of a bitch." Sheriff Owens was out of his chair, looking like he'd be lighting a protester on fire.

Otis pointed toward the window. His face was as red as the flaming flag. "Sheriff, you get out there and put this down! I want that man and woman arrested."

I had to throw cold water on that plan. "Hold on, guys. There's legal precedent for this. The US Supreme Court ruled in 1989. *Texas v. Johnson*. What they're doing is constitutionally protected. First Amendment, it's political speech."

The commissioners weren't persuaded. I appealed to the DA. "Mr. Reeves, am I correct?"

The DA nodded. Looking sulky, like a kid.

Outside, someone on the street was taking issue. Which wasn't a shocker. Not everyone is familiar with the court's decision in *Texas v. Johnson*. The shouting started up. Someone tried to grab the flag away from the guy with the bullhorn—and he used the bullhorn as a club to nail the interloper in the face. Then the fighting started in earnest.

I grimaced. "Hitting people, now that's not covered by the First Amendment."

I turned away from the window, shaking my head. I hated the sight of more violence in the streets of my town. But it certainly reaffirmed my position.

"Damn good thing I'm keeping that jury safely tucked away next week."

Heading out the door, I could feel the burden of that criminal case bearing down. Like the trial, and everything connected to it, wanted to steal my strength away.

CHAPTER 53

STONE FAMILY FARM
BULLOCK COUNTY, ALABAMA

Sitting across from me at the kitchen table, my friend Loucilla Payne studied me. Like she was drilling deep inside my head, determined to read my mind.

"Mary, it's weighing you down. Like you're carrying the weight of the world."

It was Friday evening, and Loucilla and I were having our monthly get-together. But there was no way I could escape to Montgomery for dinner. Thank God, Loucilla had come to me.

I pushed away from the table. Picked up the glass pitcher of iced tea as a pretext. Filled glasses that were still three-quarters full. I knew Loucilla would break through, crack open my secrets if she had the chance.

I said, "It's been hanging over me all this time. I knew the day was coming. Hell, it was my idea to move ahead. I gave them the early trial date. We start picking the jury Monday. Just three more days to wait."

Judge Stone

I set the pitcher down. Stepped over to the sink, washed my hands. Just had to keep moving.

Behind me, Loucilla's voice cut through the sound of running water. "Mary, you're all wound up. Why are you acting like this? Honey, you're not the one who's going to be on trial."

I shut off the water. Dried my hands. A truth was burning in my chest, trying to push its way out.

Loucilla was still trying to reason with me. "You're not the criminal defendant. You're not the State's witness. Mary, you've tried all kinds of cases over the years, presided as judge over murders and sex crimes. This case is big, it's generated lots of attention. But you're experienced. It shouldn't be shaking you up this way. It's getting under your skin."

I tossed the cotton dish towel onto the counter. She'd nailed it, described just how it felt. The facts of the case were under my skin like a bad case of scabies. Burrowing under the surface, laying eggs, making me itch like crazy.

I dragged my chair right next to hers. I didn't want the table to create distance between us. It was likely that I'd need to cry on her shoulder.

"It's strange that I've never told you this before. I know I can confide in you. Tell you anything."

Loucilla's face tensed, like she expected a blow. "Mary. What is it?"

I meant to tell her. And then my throat closed up. I couldn't answer right away. Had to rub the front of my neck before I could speak again.

"I was fifteen. End of my sophomore year of high school."

She saw where it was going. "Oh, no."

The sensation in my throat increased; it felt like hands wrapped around it, choking me. Maybe that was a sign. That I should keep my secret to myself. Keep it locked up.

"Mary? Girl, come on. It's all right." She reached for my hand. "Tell me."

It was that contact—her hand gripping mine. I squeezed her hand back, hard. It gave me strength, helped me to speak the words aloud.

"I was raped, Loucilla."

"Oh, Mary. No, no, no."

Loucilla pulled me to her, hugged me tight, just like my mama had done, years back. Then I heard her growl. "Don't tell me! Was it that goddamned sheriff? Owens?"

I pulled away, leaned back in my chair. "No, Loucilla, wasn't him. Mick Owens was my boyfriend senior year. This was two years before."

"Then who?"

My mind conjured the recollection, the image of his face. I wished I could block it out.

"A neighbor, a grown man. He was a tenant farmer living on the old Hood place. I can barely remember his name."

Liar.

We were still grasping hands, hanging on with a death grip. Lou said, "You want to find him? I'll help you."

I shook my head. "That man's long gone. Dead by now, maybe." Privately, I'd wished him dead for decades. Sometimes I thought about forgiving him. Hadn't gotten around to it yet. "I was cutting through his land on my way home from a friend's house. He came out of his house and chased me down. Said he'd been watching me, that I looked all grown up. He acted like he was drunk, or high on something. Maybe he thought that was an excuse for it."

"Did he go to prison for what he did to you?"

"No! No, nothing like that. He got off scot-free."

Judge Stone

My friend's face was savage. "Your daddy should have killed him."

"Loucilla, my daddy was already dead. Dropped of a heart attack in the pasture behind the barn, years before."

We both fell silent for a minute. I needed something to dull the pain that flared from the recollection. I was thinking about a bottle of Tennessee whiskey I kept in one of my cabinets, behind the Heinz cider vinegar and a tub of Crisco. I wasn't a regular drinker of hard liquor. It was there for emergencies. Like snakebite.

Loucilla had started wiping her eyes. Well. If Lou was crying, it qualified as an emergency. Lord help me, I needed a shot myself. I got up, reached behind the Crisco and grabbed the bottle. Set out a couple of juice glasses. The only barware I owned was a set of wineglasses. Didn't seem right to drink whiskey from a wineglass.

I poured an inch of the whiskey into each glass. Carried them to the table, with the bottle. Loucilla knocked hers back in one swallow. Reached for the bottle and poured herself a refill.

Her eyes met mine. "I don't get it. Why he wasn't convicted."

When I answered that, my voice cracked, like a kid who's about to cry. "Problem was, I didn't tell anybody. Not right away. I was so ashamed. It was my first time. A virgin."

I shook my head as the rage rolled over me. I'd felt it before, many times.

And I recalled the other feelings from my youth. The helplessness, the shame, the fear of judgment. It's no wonder that girls are afraid to talk about it. The world can be a hard, cold place.

"Did you get pregnant?" Loucilla was clutching the juice glass, blinking wet eyes at me.

"No. When my period started, I was so thankful, I took it as a sign. That I could just move on, not tell anybody. But Mama could sense something was wrong. She kept after me. I finally broke down, told her what happened."

"And then? Was he prosecuted?"

I sipped my whiskey before I answered. Grimaced when I felt the fire burn its way down to my belly. It made my shoulders twitch with an involuntary shiver. "There wasn't any physical evidence. Too much time had passed—you know how it works. They didn't do a rape kit. What could they find on a victim who was raped five weeks prior?"

"But your testimony—"

"Would have been all they had as evidence. The sheriff went out and talked to him. He denied it. Sheriff told my mama, it would have been a swearing match. My word against his."

"You would have convinced a jury. Even at fifteen."

I shrugged. No point in arguing what a jury would have made of it. It was ancient history now. "He left the area not long after. So that was the end of it, see? They dropped it."

Loucilla poured more whiskey. We both drank. I confess, with every sip it was getting easier to swallow that liquid fire.

I relaxed in the chair. Let out a deep sigh. That was probably the whiskey. I could smell the liquor on my own breath. Good thing I wasn't driving anywhere. And my chores were done, livestock fed, tractor put away.

"Loucilla, I'll put fresh sheets on the bed in the guest room." Loucilla wouldn't be fit to drive, either.

"Good. I'll help you." She knocked back another swig. "My cat can live without me for one night."

I was glad she was staying. I felt vulnerable, didn't want to be alone.

She got to the heart of it. "So you never got justice. And you never got over it. And this case is triggering you. Because of the child, Nova Jones."

I toyed with the glass. "When I look at Nova Jones? I see myself. Me at fifteen. Nova's younger, but still. The trauma she's going through, I feel like it's me, back when."

That was when I heard my rooster crow. In the twilight, just getting dark. Foghorn did that sometimes, when he was startled. By a predator. Or a light coming at him. Like headlights from a car.

I listened. Got up, walked to the window. Didn't see anything.

I walked back to my chair. Shook off the paranoia. The rooster had a brain the size of two peanuts. No way I'd let him throw a scare into me.

Lou's voice was soft, reasonable. "Mary. Have you ever thought of pulling out of the case?"

I sat up straight in that kitchen chair. "Loucilla! Hell no. I got to see this through."

"But that's just the thing, Mary. My point exactly. You don't have to do it yourself. You are not the only circuit judge in the state of Alabama." She raised her hand, palm up, like she knew what I was going to say. "You're the best, that's for certain! But there are other judges who can step in."

"Well, here's the problem with that. I don't want to turn it over to anyone else. I don't trust anybody in the world with this case. It's got to be me."

"But if it's eating you up, Mary—"

"I'm a grown woman. An experienced judge. I can set my personal feelings aside and do my sworn duty in the courtroom. My duty to all parties involved."

As I spoke of setting feelings aside, I swung my arm, making a dramatic gesture. The whiskey again.

We wouldn't be making a run for dinner, not that night. And there was no food delivery service out in the country in rural Alabama. No Grubhub, no Uber, no rideshare.

I checked the freezer. Two frozen chicken potpies. Kardea Brown's brand, my favorite. Excellent. Good save.

I popped them in the oven on a cookie sheet, because crust browns better in an oven than a microwave. Set the oven at 350 degrees, didn't take trouble to preheat. My oven ran hot.

"We've got forty minutes until dinner is ready." I gave the bottle a questioning look. "You want another drink?"

"Oh, hell yeah."

Good. Me too.

CHAPTER 54

Mary Stone

BULLOCK COUNTY COURTHOUSE
UNION SPRINGS, ALABAMA

*S*howtime.

Standing in my chambers, I opened the door to the courtroom. Ross had been waiting for the cue. My bailiff called out, "All rise!"

Stepping out, I climbed the steps to the bench, took my place. "You may be seated."

The DA and his co-counsel, Eleanor Lindquist, sat at the counsel table positioned closest to the jury box. They gave off a confident vibe in their navy blue business suits, the weight of the cloth and the width of the pinstripes identical. I wondered whether they'd plotted out the color-coordinated clothing. It felt kinda weird.

At the defense table, Benjamin Meyers was projecting positive energy, a noble strategy. But one glance at Bria Gaines confirmed that she wasn't feeling it. Dressed all in black, with her eyes downcast, she looked like she was attending a funeral.

Her own funeral.

I sat up straight in my high-backed chair and surveyed the courtroom gallery, trying to get a feel for the panel we'd summoned by random selection.

Lord have mercy. Prospective jurors were crammed into my courtroom, elbow to elbow, hip to hip. We'd summoned two hundred prospective jurors to the courthouse that morning. Ross had packed about a hundred into the courtroom—a tight squeeze. The remainder waited outside: in the hallways, the basement, any place they could find an empty chair.

There is a set of jury instructions, statements of law and procedure, that the judge is required to read aloud to the jurors, or prospective jurors, at designated times.

"Good morning, y'all. I surely appreciate you coming to the courthouse this morning in response to your call for jury duty. We're set to try a criminal case. The State of Alabama has charged Bria Gaines with the Class A felony of performing an abortion. The case will be tried by a jury. And that's why y'all have been called in. Our justice system can't function without your participation and cooperation."

Some of my lines are written ahead of time. Doesn't mean I can't add my own two cents.

Time to walk around, I thought. The citizens were restless, nervous, edgy. I needed to put them at ease. Otherwise, we'd never find twelve people who were willing to stick around for the trial. Plus two extras, just in case.

Rising, I left the bench and walked down the center aisle that divides the spectator area in half.

"I'm Judge Mary Stone. For the past six years, I've served Bullock

Judge Stone

County as circuit judge. Let me fill you in on my job in this courtroom. It's my responsibility to make sure this case is handled fairly. There are two sides in this criminal case: the prosecution and the defense. Just so you know, my role here isn't to make either side happy."

A pair of young people—one man, one woman—exchanged a look when I made that claim. Then the woman rolled her eyes.

The hell? I paused, waited for her to focus on me. Gave her a stern glare before I moved on. "My role—my only role, you might even call it my obsession—is to ensure a fair trial. To protect the rights of the parties and see to it that the law and procedure are followed. And that's precisely what I'm going to do."

I'd reached the back of the courtroom, near the closed doors. When I turned to face them, most folks had shifted around in their seats, or peered over their shoulders, to see what I was doing.

Good. Loosened them up a little.

Next job: Loosen up their tongues.

"To have a fair trial, we're going to need to pick a jury. And we'll be asking questions to help us do that job. I'll make inquiries. I get to go first; one of the perks of being a judge, right?"

Pause for a chuckle. It got a small laugh, which was fine. I wasn't trying to bring the house down; this wasn't stand-up comedy. A woman's life was at stake.

"The DA and the defendant's attorney will have the opportunity to ask questions, too. It will take a while, so let's all settle in. Try to get comfortable. I know those wooden benches are pretty hard. You'd think after a hundred and fifty years, somebody would've thought about padding the seats."

Another chuckle followed me as I returned to the bench. Instructed the potential jurors regarding voir dire. Placed them under oath. The questions began.

"I'll start. I've already introduced myself. The State is represented by the DA, Robert Reeves, and Assistant Attorney General Eleanor Lindquist. Anybody in this room acquainted with the DA, or his co-counsel? Or related to them?"

We lost some panelists. No surprise there. Reeves was a native of Union Springs. A distant cousin of Reeves was in the room. I excused her immediately. Some neighbors, people who knew Reeves from school, and others who knew his wife. Four guys sitting together, from Reeves's weekly men's prayer breakfast group. Good God, I thought—what were the odds of that? I almost said it out loud.

No one claimed to know Eleanor Lindquist. Same with Benjamin Meyers, the defense attorney from Atlanta. But the defendant herself—a different matter. A couple dozen hands went up.

I called on the nearest one first: a man seated in the second row. "Yes, sir? Your name, please. And the number you were assigned."

"Judge, I'm Abram Wagoner. They gave me the number 17."

"Thank you, Mr. Wagoner. How are you acquainted with the defendant, Dr. Gaines?"

He wore a conflicted expression. "She wasn't my doctor. It was my wife, Charlaine. I took her to see Dr. Gaines two or three times before she passed."

I nodded. "So sorry for your loss, Mr. Wagoner." Watched him as he cut a quick look in Dr. Gaines's direction. She had turned in her seat and faced him. I couldn't see her expression.

I said, "Mr. Wagoner, will the fact that Dr. Gaines cared for your wife keep you from being fair and impartial as a juror in this trial?"

"I don't know. The doctor was mighty good to my wife. Done more for her than anyone else around here."

The DA was on his feet. "Your Honor, the State requests that juror number 17 be removed. Clearly, he can't serve."

I hated to let him go. "Mr. Wagoner. If I instruct you to listen to the evidence presented in this case and base your verdict solely on the evidence presented in court—because that's what the law requires—are you saying you absolutely would not be able to follow the instructions of the court?"

He grimaced, clearly distressed. "I just don't know."

Reeves was already moving my way. "Request to approach the bench, Your Honor."

I waved the lawyers forward. Reeves and Lindquist duked it out with Meyers, in whispers, while the court reporter hunched beside them, taking down every word.

At their insistence, we had to drag number 17 to the bench for further questioning. By the time we were done, Mr. Wagoner was so confused he could barely recall his own name.

I didn't excuse him at that point. Figured if I let Wagoner get away, there would be a run for the door, and we'd lose the entire panel.

As the man returned to his seat, I gave the courtroom a tight smile. "Let's continue, y'all. Refreshing your recollection! The question before you is: Does anyone on this panel know Dr. Gaines personally?"

The hands shot up this time. Twice as many waved in the air. Four dozen, maybe. Almost half of the room.

For the first time, I experienced a panic of self-doubt. Maybe I'd made a mistake. I should have let another judge handle it, let the case go to Montgomery or Birmingham, like the DA had suggested. Keeping it in Bullock County would come at a price.

And that price would be paid by Dr. Bria Gaines.

CHAPTER 55

We broke for lunch shortly after twelve o'clock. Barely three hours into jury selection, and I was already mortally exhausted.

The panelists were dropping like flies. All kinds—Black, white, old, young, male, female. They were snatching at any pretext to be excused from serving on that jury.

Most folks fell into that category: people intent on escape. But I'd picked up on a handful that leaned to the other extreme. Citizens who desperately, fervently wanted to be on the jury. Were overly eager to serve. They had an axe to grind. It was clear to me that they'd already made up their minds, before a shred of evidence had been presented in court. They were determined to snare a seat in the jury box.

I wanted those people gone. They had no business taking part in the case. I couldn't entrust them with any power over a jury verdict.

It was a relief to see the clock tick past twelve. I declared a recess, sent them all away for an hour. Hopefully, they'd be able to get some lunch and be back on time. We didn't have a wealth of dining options in Union Springs, and the streets of town were teeming with people.

I'd anticipated that. Thought ahead and brought my own lunch. I had tossed a couple of hard-boiled eggs into a Rubbermaid container, with an apple and a hunk of cheese. Put that in a grocery bag with two cans of Diet Coke. I was really looking forward to popping a silver can.

I'd barely had time to pull the makeshift meal from the mini fridge I kept in the corner of my office when the door opened. A full camera crew marched into chambers, led by my sister Nellie.

Nellie greeted me with a breezy "Hey, Mary."

"Nellie!" My voice was sharp. "What are you doing back here?"

The smile dropped right off her face. "Isn't it obvious? We're doing the photo shoot."

"What photo shoot?"

She scuttled around my desk, like she wanted us to speak privately, without being overheard. "The one we've talked about for the last six months. You've got to have a TV ad. You know your opponent will. I heard he's already buying up time slots during the evening news hour."

It came to me, then: my campaign. Nellie was right, we'd discussed campaign materials. Just conversation, thus far, about TV, direct mailings, some billboards on the highway. Yard signs. We'd need film to get them made. A photographer, a crew. *But today?*

"Your timing is way off, Nellie. We're picking the jury for the Gaines trial."

Nellie grabbed my robe from the coatrack, shook it out. "Actually, the timing is fortuitous. Couldn't be better. Kenny and his crew, they're freelance. They're at the courthouse today to get trial footage to sell. So they have time to work you in, right now."

I let her help me into the robe and zip it up. She dabbed at my forehead with a tissue.

"You got lipstick?"

"Yeah."

"Purse or desk?"

"Both."

I watched as Nellie pulled my desk drawer open with a jerk. Two lipsticks rattled in the pen tray.

She grabbed one, pulled the top off, squinted down the tube. "This will work. It's a matte, nice natural tone. You don't want anything too bright, too wet. Gotta look dignified."

I didn't argue. Partly because she was right. I needed the footage. I didn't want to look flashy. And the faster we could get around to it, the sooner they'd all leave. I wanted to eat a hard-boiled egg and wash it down with aspartame.

At Nellie's direction, I sat at the bench. The photographer tinkered with the lighting while Nellie worked on my hair. The commercial director walked up to the bench and handed a file off to me.

"Smile!" A young woman was snapping still pictures with a Canon.

I did try to smile but suspected I had a *caught in the headlights* expression.

I was still gripping the file folder I'd been given. I opened it, curious to see what it contained. In truth, I expected to see a bill for services rendered.

But no. It contained a short script. I quickly scanned the lines.

Slapped that file down on the bench. With Nellie's brush tugging at my scalp, I was close to losing my cool.

"What the hell?" I lifted the page, read aloud. "'I'm Judge Stone, and I'm tough on crime.' Who came up with that? It sounds like I'm the county DA's puppet! It's not accurate, you understand me? Because I'm tough on everybody. Everyone! That's what I intend to say."

The director squinted through round tortoiseshell glasses. "Judge, I seriously advise you to just go along. Deliver the script exactly as it was written. Okay?" He waved Nellie away, saying, "Hair's fine. She looks good. Let's see if we can get this on the first take. Judge Stone, are you ready?"

"No. Not ready for this."

Off somewhere to the side, Nellie groaned. I kept my gaze on the man in charge of the ad. "I prefer to be authentic. That's how I want to proceed with this."

He gave me a sad kind of smile. "But do you want to win, Judge? Be reelected? If so, you need to go with the script. Just read it aloud."

"I don't think you know me very well." I was about to say more. He cut me off.

"Maybe not, but I know about political ads. If you want to keep your job, you need to show your support for law-and-order constituents. Businesspeople, property owners. Criminals don't vote, you know what I'm saying? You're going to need the endorsement of the chamber of commerce. You can't win this race without it. In local elections, they control the votes and the money."

I should've eaten that apple. Maybe if my blood sugar had been stable, I'd have held on to my temper and controlled my tongue.

Because I slapped both hands on the bench and said, "Fuck that. People in this county know me. I'm running on my record."

I tore the script in two before walking off the bench and back into chambers.

CHAPTER 56

Picking a jury is damned hard work.

The process took three days. Over that time, we examined most of the prospective jurors we'd summoned to the courthouse. I asked questions. I gave the attorneys for the prosecution and the defense the opportunity to inquire.

We directed the questions to the group as a whole. When it was necessary, we examined jurors individually, separate and apart from the others.

I was careful to listen to the panelists, to take a reasonable approach. If they were sick, or infirm, or had pressing reasons to bow out, I let them go. If they had attitudes inconsistent with an open mind—people who believed, for example, that a person charged with a crime must be guilty of something—I dismissed them for cause. If they'd already made up their minds and wouldn't base a verdict on the evidence alone, I showed them the door.

Finally, we compiled a list of twenty-eight prospective jurors who were competent to try the case. The lawyers came to the bench, and I gave each of them a list of the twenty-eight names.

"Y'all, we'll commence striking the jury. Each of you will have seven peremptory strikes. The district attorney goes first."

Reeves was ready. "We'll strike number 3. Zuri Wheeler."

Not a surprise. Zuri was young, about Bria Gaines's age. College educated. Stated during questioning that she leaned pro-choice, but she would keep an open mind and base her decision on the evidence.

She was an obvious *not guilty* vote for Bria. I knew it, Reeves knew it. He used a peremptory strike to get rid of her. He had the right to remove seven jurors from the strike list without giving a reason. The defense could remove seven people, too.

"Mr. Meyers, the defense shall strike the next name from the list."

Benjamin Meyers held an open file. I glimpsed the strike list inside, emblazoned with scribbles of black ink.

"Garner Lee Bowman."

A good choice, I thought. Bowman had given the defense table the stink eye for the past three days. But he'd never made a statement that could subject him to be removed for cause. So Meyers used a peremptory strike to throw him out.

So it went, back and forth, until only fourteen names remained on the list. We had it then: our jury of twelve, plus two alternates.

Jury selection is a misnomer, an inaccurate term. It's actually a game of Last One Standing.

We announced the list. Let the rest of the panel go. I gathered the jurors into the box and instructed them to raise their right hands.

"You do solemnly swear, or affirm, that you will well and truly try all issues joined between the defendant and the State of Alabama and render a true verdict thereon according to the law and evidence, so help you God."

The response was uneven, but they all answered in the affirmative. "I do."

Next step would be to launch into a series of formal jury instructions. Tell them about their duties, the proper conduct of a jury. What the order of proceedings would be in the trial of the case.

I gave them a close look. They were strung out from sitting in the courthouse for three long days. Anything I said would be promptly forgotten.

A check of the old wall clock showed that it was nearly four o'clock. I turned to the bailiff.

"Ross, it's time to get the reinforcements from the sheriff's office."

"Yes, Judge."

Sheriff Owens was giving us two deputies. One was female — an essential trait. Seven of our fourteen jurors were female. They'd be escorted everywhere — including the restroom — until the trial was complete.

I flashed a smile at the jury box. "Ross is going to show y'all to the jury room — conveniently accessed by a door right inside the courtroom. You're done for today."

They were picking up their purses, their jackets, eager to move on. I held up a hand to halt the activity.

"I need to give an instruction to you before we recess for the day. You'll hear me say this over and over during the trial."

I waited until I had their attention, all fourteen of them. This was important, they were a sequestered jury and needed to remember it.

"Until you have been discharged, it is absolutely necessary that all of you stay together. You must not separate, not even for a moment, unless allowed by me or the bailiff."

Some of them looked shell-shocked by the instruction, as the significance of sequestration registered with them.

I tried to lighten the moment. "When they wrote that jury instruction, I wished they'd have mentioned that you'll have a modicum of privacy. It's not as bad as the military. There are no group showers."

The joke fell flat. Ross escorted the jurors out of the box and to the back of the courtroom, where they disappeared into the jury room.

I turned my focus to the counsel tables. "We'll convene at nine o'clock tomorrow."

They started packing away their files, gathering up the snowstorm of scribbled pages accumulated during jury selection.

While Benjamin Meyers packed his files, Bria Gaines looked up at the bench. As our eyes met, I felt a surge of sympathy for her. I swiveled my chair to the side, hopped up, and hurried away to my office. I would have to combat that natural response, to conceal my sympathies from view. Couldn't let the prosecution or defense or jury think that I was showing preference for one side over the other.

I was fair. Oh, I had my faults. Lots of them. But I ran a courtroom the way the law intended. I didn't show favoritism. No one could say I ran a kangaroo court.

CHAPTER 57

In chambers, it was a blessed relief to shed my heavy black robe. I hung it up, grabbed my bag, and slipped through the back door. I thought I'd make a clean escape. No journalists, no lawyers, nobody asking questions or telling me what they thought about the case.

My car sat in its designated spot. I aimed the key fob at the car, unlocked it.

"Judge Stone!"

I whirled around fast, like I'd heard a gunshot. A man was trotting up the hill, coming toward me. He'd left off his professional attire. No white collar, black jacket, black suit. I knew him on sight, though, even dressed in civvies.

So I couldn't pretend otherwise, couldn't just hop in my car and drive off. I leaned against the driver's door with the fob still gripped in my hand.

He got closer. I could see that the man was sweating. Getting some exercise, I assumed. Probably out for a run in his T-shirt and basketball shorts.

As the pastor reached me, he turned his head, nodded toward the schoolyard. "I was coaching some kids. For the after-school program."

"Is that right? That's commendable, Reverend Erskine. Very generous of you." I saw the kids on the playground at the bottom of the hill. A cluster of children were dribbling the ball, shooting baskets. "I know your time is valuable."

I put my hand on the car door. I wasn't up for chatting with him.

Erskine didn't take the hint. "I thought I'd see whether the jury was picked," he said. "I had a number of parishioners on that panel."

My response was cool, though my hand holding the fob was damp. "All picked, all sworn in. They're sequestered now. You understand what that means, Pastor. You can't have any contact with anyone on the jury."

"I know that. But you'll be guiding them every step of the way." He paused for a moment, as if debating whether to say more. "It's ironic, under the circumstances. Isn't it?"

My heart started hammering. I pulled the door open, turned my back on Erskine, and crawled into the front seat.

He stepped up behind me. Dropped his voice real low, so no one could overhear.

"I haven't told anyone, Mary. You were a member of the congregation, one of my flock. I would never violate your confidence. There's a matter of confidentiality between a pastor and a parishioner."

I tugged on the interior door handle. "We're not having this conversation."

"We have to. Because I don't see how you can be impartial in handling this case. I know you're not pro-life, Mary. Not in your heart."

"You don't know anything about my feelings. What I think, or what kind of judge I am." I wanted to shut him out, but he blocked me, I couldn't close the door. "If you'd kindly get out of my way. I need to get home to my farm."

He grabbed the car frame with both hands and leaned inside the vehicle. The unspoken message: He'd decide when the conversation was over. "Mary, you'll have to face up to this someday. Because a woman who had an abortion, and never repented, will never enter the kingdom of heaven."

He shouldn't have had the power to make me feel bad about myself. Not after all those years. But when he dangled my secret, about an abortion I had at the end of law school, and raised that threat of hellfire, it shook me. It was a shock, to hear it all spoken aloud, when I'd buried it down deep, for a quarter of a century. I wasn't Judge Mary, not in that moment. I was plain Mary Stone, twenty-five years old, revealing my shame to the new pastor, so that I might ask for absolution. We were back on his turf, where he had power—and I had none.

He was still talking. Like he saw my weak spot, knew just where to jab me. "You can't undo that sin. Can't bring that baby back to life, the son or daughter you destroyed. But the Lord is offering you an opportunity to do good. Don't you see that?"

He and I were both sweating now. I felt nervous perspiration beading on my lip. I swiped it off with the back of my hand.

He said, "The Lord is trying to reach you. Can't you see it in your heart?"

I had to get that man out of my space. I started the engine. Erskine stepped back. I was prepared to lean on my horn if he didn't. I slammed the door, shutting him out.

But he had the last word.

"You think you're getting your sin washed away by feeding the poor on your farm on Saturdays? Mary, that's not enough, and you know it."

My hand shook as I put the car in reverse.

The pastor went on. "I've counseled with Nova Jones about her abortion. Guided her through her repentance. She's begged the Lord for forgiveness, and the child is doing her part at this trial. What about you, Mary?"

When I didn't speak, he said, "I remember when you came to me, to unburden yourself. Because you'd killed your unborn child. But you were no girl of thirteen, like Nova. You were a grown woman. An educated woman, about to take the bar exam."

I'd been a fool to counsel with Pastor Erskine all those years ago. I wanted the pastor to understand my dilemma, to know that I didn't make the decision lightly. To tell me I was forgiven. That the Lord understood.

The counseling session didn't go as planned. He condemned me. I walked out of his church feeling bitter, broken. I hadn't gone to Sunday service since then.

It was like my body had a mind of its own. There was no thought process, no impulse control... I just stopped the car, put it in park, released my seat belt, and jumped out.

"I wasn't thirteen when I had an abortion, but I was fifteen when I got raped. You never asked that day. You just condemned! That fifteen-year-old never healed! Never! She shut down in shame waiting for... *anyone* to save her!"

Now I was trembling... I couldn't control my voice.

He just stood there, speechless.

"I came to you as a grown woman who was broken. And instead of seeing me, you broke me down more. And you call yourself a man of God... of love? What the hell do you have to offer Nova?"

I turned to get back in the car and heard myself shout.

"You can shove your holiness up your ass!"

My tires screeched as I drove my car away, not even looking in the rearview mirror. I hated myself for the tears that kept falling.

CHAPTER 58

Nova Jones

BULLOCK COUNTY COURTHOUSE
UNION SPRINGS, ALABAMA

The old brick courthouse in Union Springs was straight ahead. Nova could see it through the windshield. And it was getting bigger and taller, bigger and taller and scarier.

Nova was scrunched up in the back of a police car, next to her mama. Mama wouldn't even look at her. Mama was ashamed. And scared.

So it was Nova and Mama in the back seat, with Sheriff Mick Owens up front driving, *but Nova wasn't there*. Not really. Reason for that was, none of it was real. Nothing felt real anymore, not to Nova. It was all a terrible bad dream.

Not only a dream, though. There were things that had happened to Nova. Things *done to her,* that brought her to that place. That wasn't fair. It was wrong. So, so wrong. She'd been raped. She couldn't forget what they done to her. How they done it. Almost a year gone by. But it was still all locked up in her head. Locked up tight. Because she couldn't tell anybody what happened.

She was so alone. Alone with her secret shame.

The courthouse was getting closer. Too close. If she could, Nova would open the car door. Jump out and run off, as far from that courthouse as she could get.

But there was no way out for her. Outside the police car, angry white people were yelling. Coming off the sidewalk, right up to the police car. They were screaming at her, at Nova. Yelling her name. Yelling bad words.

She clutched her hands together in her lap. She wished she could roll down the car window. Those white people were so close, she could reach out and grab them. She wanted to. Wanted to shake them hard, make them stop.

Nova had never seen so many people in Union Springs. And she'd lived there her whole life. All shouting, angry, cussing. Why were all the people angry—mad at her? They made ugly faces, acted like her name was a dirty word when they said it out loud.

It made her feel dirty. And guilty.

The sheriff said those people out there, they're too close to the car. He flipped a button, and the siren started wailing. Nova clapped her hands over her ears, but it didn't shut out the noise from the siren or the people in the street.

She slid down in the seat. She could see through the front windshield, there were white people holding signs. She couldn't read them, not with the sun hitting the window, making a glare. But she heard more voices. They were chanting together. In rhythm.

"Lock her up! Lock her up!"

Nova felt hot vomit rise up her throat. Thought she was going to puke all over the back seat of the police car. She thought they wanted to lock *her* in jail.

Then she caught a good look through the glass. Saw that one of the signs said Dr. Gaines's name. It was the doctor they wanted to lock up. Not Nova, after all. That made her almost as sick as when she thought they meant her.

She stared at the pushing, shouting people. Wondered what they were doing to Dr. Bria. The doctor helped Nova. Nobody else helped her. Nobody except for the school nurse.

And she was dead.

Somebody killed Nurse Bass.

The sheriff stopped the car right in front of the courthouse. Nova's mama opened her own door, on the street side. Mama got out and disappeared into the crowd.

Nova tried to unbuckle her seat belt. But her hands felt unreal. So did her arms. Her legs were jelly.

The sheriff's face appeared in her window. It surprised her, almost made her pee her pants. He opened the car door. Not talking, didn't say a word. She couldn't tell if the man even saw her, not with his sunglasses. Just held the door open.

Mama was behind him, on the sidewalk. Mama still wouldn't look at her.

The crowd of people edged closer to the car, still yelling, chanting. The screaming and shouting made Nova feel like she'd go deaf. Her face felt like it was on fire.

She didn't know what to do. She couldn't even move, couldn't get out of the back seat. Too scared of what was outside.

Mama finally looked at her. Then Mama stepped over, scooted in front of the sheriff. She reached into the car and took Nova's hand.

"C'mon, baby girl. We have to go inside. We going to court."

CHAPTER 59

Bria Gaines

BULLOCK COUNTY COURTHOUSE
UNION SPRINGS, ALABAMA

On Thursday morning, Bria was watching for Ben Meyers through her living room window. When she spotted his car coming down the street, she locked up the house and hurried down her front walk.

As she slid into the front seat, she looked over at him. "Thanks so much for the ride, Ben. It's really not necessary."

Meyers's face was grim. "I'd say it's *absolutely* necessary."

Bria knew he was right. She was just putting on a brave front. After the first day of the trial, she'd returned to her car to find it dripping and smelling from rotten eggs. Someone had scrawled *MURDERER* on the front window and *BURN IN HELL* on the back.

After that, she'd steeled herself so that no one could hurt her.

That was the plan, anyway.

Meyers put some music on the radio to relax her. By now, he knew how much she loved Brandi Carlile. He cranked it up loud. They made the ten-minute drive without exchanging another word.

When they got into town, it was total chaos. There was no parking anywhere near the courthouse. Too many spectators. Too much press. Meyers took the first space he could find, in the parking lot of LuLu's Diner. CUSTOMERS ONLY, the sign said. Sorry. Not today, LuLu.

As Bria walked with Meyers down Prairie Street toward the courthouse, she could see that a crowd had gathered, filling the sidewalk and spilling over onto the street. Babbling voices were raised—some excited, some angry. The atmosphere was charged with a dangerous kind of energy. The trial hadn't even commenced for the day, and downtown Union Springs was already a zoo.

Bria heard the chant. People were calling "Lock her up!"

She froze for a second on the sidewalk. That was when someone spotted her.

"There she is!"

Meyers grabbed her hand. "Run!"

They took off around the nearest corner, but a few people in the crowd took up the chase. Meyers kept a firm grip on her hand as they managed to dodge their pursuers, running down narrow alleys and then back up the hill to the rear of the courthouse.

An elderly Black woman in a custodian's uniform stood near a back entrance, smoking a cigarette. Bria turned around. The pursuers were just yards behind.

"Aurora!" Meyers shouted. "Open the door!" The custodian yanked on the handle and waved them inside. Bria ducked through the door. She felt Meyers pushing her from behind. The door slammed shut. Bria could hear pounding and shouting from outside.

Meyers walked ahead to check out the hallway as Bria slumped against the wall, breathing hard from the run. Meyers came back and grabbed her arm. "Let's skip the elevator, okay?"

Bria nodded. The outside doors would open soon, and an elevator was not a good place to get stuck with a bunch of haters.

Together, they headed for the back staircase and wound their way to the second floor. When they approached the courtroom, it was still dark. Bria peeked through the narrow glass panes on the double doors. No lights on inside, and she couldn't see a soul. When Ben pulled on the brass handle, she knew the door wouldn't open. No surprise. Just more bad luck.

Meyers looked down the hall. "The bailiff will be here any minute. You need a place to sit?"

Bria shook her head. She felt safer near the courtroom, even though it was the place where her adversaries intended to convict her. Maybe it was Judge Stone's aura. For some reason, Bria really trusted her.

As much as she trusted anyone right now.

Meyers took his place alongside her against the marble wall as they waited. Bria stood quietly, trying to distract herself—until she couldn't wait any longer.

"Ben," she said. "I need to use the restroom. And no, you can't come with me."

She stepped away from the wall and turned left down a corridor. The ladies' room was about halfway down, behind a thick oak door with gilt lettering.

Bria pushed the door open. An automatic sensor turned the lights on. The restroom was empty. She had the whole place to herself. A rare luxury.

Bria opened the first stall and closed the door. She lifted her skirt and slip and pulled down her underwear. As soon as she sat down, she heard the clatter of an elevator door from the hallway, and then the sound of rushing feet and voices.

Shit! They'd let the spectators in!

A few seconds later, she heard the ladies' room door swing open as a pack of women surged in. Bria could hear the other stalls opening and then slamming shut. She could hear faucets turning on. She could smell perfume and hair spray. She could hear snippets of conversation beneath the sound of industrial-strength hand dryers. Some of it was about her.

When she was done, Bria adjusted her clothes, opened the stall door, and moved quickly to the last sink in the row. She didn't look left or right, trying to keep from making eye contact. She kept her head down, not even looking into the mirror. In her peripheral vision, she could see four women reapplying lipstick and touching up their hair.

As Bria soaped her hands, someone shoved her hard, knocking her into the sink. She looked to the right, over her shoulder. In that instant, she felt someone grab her left arm. She saw a white woman's hand holding a red marker. In a flash, the woman made a scrawl on Bria's wrist. Bria jerked away. "Don't touch me!" But the stranger was already gone, the door closing behind her.

Bria didn't take the time to blow her hands dry. She just shook them over the sink, then walked out of the restroom without looking back. As she left, she glanced down at the red scribble on her skin. It looked like an *H* drawn by a child. She pulled her blouse cuff down over it.

Ben Meyers was waiting on the other side of the hall. He briskly walked over to meet her. "Bria, what's wrong? What happened?" Clearly, he could see it in her face.

She pulled him into an alcove and held up her wrist. "Somebody did this to me in there!" She nodded toward the restroom. "They wrote an *H* on me. Like a brand."

Meyers lifted her hand and stared at the mark, his face creased with concern. He looked up. "That's not an *H*, Bria. It's a *K*."

CHAPTER 60

By now the courtroom was open. Spectators were pouring in. Bria held on to Meyers's arm as he led her through the huge double doors and down the center aisle to the defense table.

As soon as they sat down, Meyers shifted in his seat, looking around the gallery. "Is she in here? The nutjob who wrote on you?"

Bria scanned the room. "I don't know." She couldn't tell. She had barely caught a look at her as she disappeared. "Don't make a big thing out of it. I'll just keep my sleeve rolled down."

"I *want* to pick a fight over it," said Meyers. "Nobody gets away with assaulting my client in the damned bathroom."

He wasn't listening to her, she thought. *He didn't understand.* Bria wanted to let it pass. She had to pick her battles. Her reserve of energy was sorely depleted.

But the conversation would have to wait. The door to Judge Stone's chambers opened, and the court bailiff called, "All rise! Circuit Court of Bullock County, Alabama, is in session, Judge Stone presiding."

As Bria pushed back her chair and stood up next to Meyers, she slipped her hands into the pockets of her skirt.

Judge Stone took the bench, carrying a small wicker basket with her. She set it beside her laptop. "Be seated," the judge said.

Bria sat down and put her hands in her lap.

Judge Stone turned to the fourteen people in the jury box. "Good morning! Hope y'all are rested. Are the accommodations okay? Everyone have enough hot water? Beds pretty comfortable?"

The jurors nodded—without enthusiasm. They weren't being lodged in luxury accommodations.

The judge launched into a recitation of the jury's obligations. Meyers bent his head and murmured to Bria. "Put your hands out where the jurors can see them."

Her arm jerked, as if he'd startled her. She bent her head toward his to whisper, "What if they notice the red ink?"

"They have to see your hands. Don't want to leave an impression that you're hiding something."

She didn't counter his advice. Bria knew he was the expert about the courtroom. With a swift move, her hands appeared on the table, folded, as if in prayer.

Judge Stone wrapped up her jury instructions. Bria watched the judge rise from the bench with the wicker basket, descend the steps, and walk over to the jury box.

"I have a tradition in jury trials. As long as I've been on the bench, I like to have a hard candy while I'm listening to the court proceedings. I think it helps me pay attention. Stay focused. Plus, I like candy. Always have, since I was a kid. And if I get to have it, my jury does, too."

Bria tried to smooth the fabric of her sleeve while the judge commanded the jury's attention.

The judge held up a red-and-white-striped peppermint for the jurors to see. "They're individually wrapped. We're not sharing germs, just sharing hard candies! Don't worry about me doing anything that will make my jurors get sick. You're important to me. No way I'd risk your health."

That got a chuckle. The wicker basket was passed from hand to hand, and most of the jurors took a piece. When a heavyset woman passed it along, she said, "I'd love to eat the whole basket, Your Honor, but my doctor won't let me."

The judge slapped her forehead. "What am I thinking? Tomorrow I'll bring in some sugar-free."

More laughter. Bria could tell that the jury was relaxing. And she'd begun to ease up, too. Her hands weren't so tense, the tendons were less prominent. Ben glanced over at Bria. When he caught her eye, she gave him a slight smile.

He scribbled a note on his yellow legal pad. *Judge is warming them up. A laughing jury is good for the defense.*

That made sense to Bria. Sending people to prison was a serious business. No joking around about that.

When Judge Stone returned to her seat, she turned to the prosecution table.

"Is the State ready to make an opening statement?"

Robert Reeves, the DA, stood and buttoned his jacket. "If it please the court."

"Proceed."

Reeves strutted over to the jury box. "Ladies and gentlemen of the jury, this is what the evidence will show."

Bria felt Ben give her a gentle nudge, to remind her: *Don't flinch.*

The DA made the very move that Benjamin had warned her to expect. Raising his voice, he said, "The State of Alabama will present evidence that the defendant, this woman—"

He jabbed his index finger in her direction. And repeated

himself, lest there be doubt. "*This woman,* Bria Gaines, sitting in the courtroom today, committed the Class A felony of performing an abortion on Nova Jones in Bullock County, Alabama."

Bria was prepared. She knew that the DA was likely to kick off his opening statement by pointing a literal finger of accusation at her. She lifted her chin, with a shade of defiance, and calmly returned the stare.

Reeves glanced down at a note card he held. "The State will prove that Nova Jones got pregnant in the back seat of a car when she had intercourse with an unknown teenage boy. She'll testify that she joined a party of other kids—older kids—in Union Springs. Nova will testify that she doesn't recall a lot of the details about that night. There was drinking involved, and marijuana—those gummies that look like candy. She didn't know the boy, doesn't remember who it was."

The DA cleared his throat. He looked uncomfortable. "And she'll probably tell you she didn't consent to sexual relations. Well, not that she recalls, anyway. That fact, though? It doesn't matter, not in the case we're bringing before you, ladies and gentlemen. In this case, her consent to relations, or lack of it, is irrelevant to the charge. Has no bearing on abortion law in Alabama."

He paused, moving to the right and looking out at the roomful of spectators, like he was playing to the whole audience.

"Ladies and gentlemen, in the great State of Alabama, the law regarding abortion is clear. It's simple. We don't penalize the pregnant women who get an abortion. Our law focuses on the people who perform abortions, the ones who actually take the life of an innocent unborn child."

Reeves swung back to the jury. "Under our criminal code, all abortions are illegal unless necessary to prevent a serious health risk to the unborn child's mother. The defendant in this case acted in complete disregard of the Alabama Human Life Protection Act. And the girl, Miss Nova Jones, that the defendant performed the felonious, illegal procedure upon? She was thirteen, ladies and gentlemen of the jury. Thirteen! That abortion, it could have killed her."

She saw Ben Meyers scribble on his legal pad. *13 y/o! PG could've killed her*

He wrote two more words and underlined them.

Reasonable Doubt

CHAPTER 61

Mary Stone

BULLOCK COUNTY COURTHOUSE
UNION SPRINGS, ALABAMA

We hadn't made it through the first morning of testimony, and I'd already grown uneasy about the unrest I sensed in my courtroom.

The spectators were reactionary, volatile. I'd never presided over a courtroom with so much emotional energy. Had never seen it as charged up like that, as a lawyer or a judge. It worried me. I could not—must not—permit the courtroom to spin out of control.

When I broke for a short recess following opening statements, Benjamin Meyers informed me that a woman went after Bria Gaines in the restroom, took a red marker to her wrist while Bria was washing her hands. Well, I wasn't putting up with that. I talked to my clerk; Luna would have to accompany the defendant into the restroom during recess. I'd called the sheriff's office first and told Owens about it, but the sheriff said he didn't have a woman to spare, that his staffing was already stretched from the demands of the trial.

The prosecution had started off with medical evidence. The DA was questioning the ER doctor who'd treated Nova Jones. "Dr. Thompson, what did you observe regarding Miss Jones's condition?"

The witness tugged at his collar, which was too tight for his neck. I could hardly believe that the DA had managed to convince Ron Thompson to wear a suit and tie. He was almost seventy, counting down to retirement, and unapologetically committed to comfort waistbands in his king-size attire.

Dr. Thompson had worked at our shabby hospital for decades. When Bria Gaines came to town, it had felt like progress in our community. People had the option to seek care from a young Black woman rather than an elderly white man. A sizable number of his patients left Thompson for Dr. Gaines's clinic, and he'd cut his hours back as a result, leaving the community with less care. He wasn't a bad doctor, but his passion for the profession had fizzled decades prior.

Thompson said, "The patient was in distress, exhibiting signs of extreme discomfort. She had heavy bleeding from the uterus and blood clots. The attending ER nurse had told me that the girl was miscarrying a pregnancy, but—"

Benjamin Meyers was on his feet. "Objection, Your Honor. Hearsay."

"Sustained." If the DA wanted the jury to hear what the ER nurse thought or said, they would need to swear her in and put her on the witness stand.

I heard sounds of disapproval from the spectators. My eyes scanned the gallery as I cut them a sharp look. It silenced them.

Reeves said, "Doctor, based upon your education, training, and experience, do you have an opinion as to the cause of Nova Jones's condition on that date?"

"I do."

"What is that opinion?"

"She'd had an abortion. Suction curettage—also known as vacuum aspiration. Probably at the end of her first trimester. There are medical risks with the procedure. The bleeding and clots were related to that. And she'd developed a pelvic bacterial infection—not severe, at that point. I treated it with oral antibiotics."

Reeves had strolled over to the jury box. He was leaning against the wooden railing on the far corner of the enclosure. "In your opinion, Doctor, was Nova Jones's pelvic infection caused by the abortion that had been performed by the defendant?"

Meyers on his feet again. "Objection, Your Honor! Calls for speculation, assumes facts not in evidence."

Meyers was right. They hadn't yet put on a witness to testify that Nova's abortion was performed by Bria Gaines.

Reeves waved a dismissive hand. "I'll tie it up later, Judge."

He would, I knew that. But the DA had to play by the rules in my court. "Objection sustained."

An unpopular ruling. The heated murmurs circulated again, rising like a stench in the spectators' section. I tapped the gavel. Shook my head at the gallery, giving them a baleful look, one they couldn't mistake.

The DA knew he had a cheering section out there. He glanced over at them before asking his next direct examination question. "Doctor, what are the medical risks and possible complications of abortion?"

"Objection! Irrelevant, prejudicial—"

He didn't need to continue. Abortion itself was not on trial, not in my courtroom. "Sustained."

"Crooked judge! Let him answer!"

It was a woman's voice, coming from somewhere in the back of the room. I wheeled around to face the spectators. "Who's speaking out? Interfering with this trial?"

The room went dead quiet. I launched out of my chair, was marching down the center aisle of the room, without making a conscious decision to leave the bench.

My voice bounced off the walls. "Y'all think I can't hear you when I'm sitting up there? Think I can't see?"

I stopped midway, to scrutinize the faces in the rows. Hunting for the guilty or hostile expression that would give her away.

It's harder than you think, finding a wrongdoer that way, with the naked eye. I thought about the old saying, a needle in a haystack.

Out of the blue, someone came to my rescue. "It was her! I heard her!"

The finger of accusation was pointed at a woman in her forties, wearing an LSU shirt. *Shit,* I thought, *some outsider from Baton Rouge.* No surprise—another out-of-towner, coming into my town to kick up trouble.

"Out," I said. "I'm removing you from this courtroom."

I threw some dramatic flair into it, lifting my arm and pointing toward the exit, letting the full sleeves of my voluminous robe double my actual size. To handle this crowd, I needed to be larger than life.

Ross Carr was coming down the aisle, ready to back me up. But she didn't put up a fight, maybe because I appeared formidable—I sure as hell hoped so. I watched in silence as she shouldered her purse and departed.

When the door shut behind her, I walked back to the front of the courtroom at a fast clip. Turned to face them all and said, "I don't know where y'all are from, but it seems that there are some people who don't know me. Because folks are acting out. Let's start over, okay? I am Judge Mary Stone, and this is my courtroom."

I paused for a beat. Giving them a moment to see the fire in my eyes. "I have the duty to preside over this trial, and I take that responsibility very seriously. I will not permit these proceedings to go sideways, slip out of control. I understand that court proceedings are a matter of public record. But the right to sit in here and observe can be taken away—by me. I swear, I will clear this courtroom with a new broom if I have any more trouble in here. Y'all understand me?"

My voice grew louder as I spoke. When I was done, I stood there for a minute, to let them know I meant it. Then I returned to the bench.

"Mr. Reeves, you may continue."

"Dr. Thompson, in your opinion, did you see any evidence that Nova Jones had a health emergency or serious health risk? One that might have caused her life to be in danger prior to the abortion?"

"I did not. Aside from her infection, bleeding, and pain, her general health was good."

"No further questions, Your Honor."

I nodded at the defense table. "Mr. Meyers, you may cross-examine."

He was ready, damn near jumping from his chair, he was so enthused. "Dr. Thompson, how many years did you say you've been in the practice of medicine?"

"Forty-three years."

"In your education, training, and experience, what are the risks and dangers of adolescent pregnancies in young girls who are under fifteen years of age?"

"Objection!" Reeves was out of his chair, no surprise. "Irrelevant!"

"Overruled," I said. The doctor shifted in his chair. I gave him a verbal nudge. "The witness may answer."

He was uncomfortable, I could tell. But he didn't violate his oath to tell the truth. "Young adolescents have worse perinatal outcomes than older teens or pregnant adults. That's always been true."

"Specifically, what outcomes are we talking about?"

"Well, let's see. A girl under fifteen, she'd be more likely to suffer from eclampsia. More likelihood of preterm birth—having the baby prematurely. Low-birth-weight infants. Greater likelihood of mortality of the mother."

"Just to be clear here, because we're not all accustomed to medical terminology—a thirteen-year-old pregnant girl is more likely to have a serious health risk, or to die from carrying the pregnancy to term. Correct?"

The doctor wiped his bald head. "Correct."

There was a furious exchange of whispers going on at the prosecution table. The DA was fighting with his co-counsel about something, undoubtedly unhappy over the direction of the cross-ex of their witness. Well, my mama used to say: Tell the truth and shame the devil. I was proud of Doc Thompson for refusing to lie for the DA.

I was letting the doctor's answer sink in, register with the jury, when I heard the crash.

I could hardly believe my own eyes, but I saw it happen. On the left side of the gallery, people shrieked and shouted. They jumped from their seats, brushing glass particles from their clothes, shaking them from their hair.

The source of the broken glass came as such a shock. Someone outside the courthouse had thrown a brick through the courtroom window.

CHAPTER 62

I sat at the bench, doing my damnedest to stifle my impatience. The janitorial team was giving the task their best effort. They'd swept the broken glass away, wiped it off the wooden benches. Two men were securing a sheet of plywood where the big pane of glass used to be.

The janitors' efforts were more commendable than the law enforcement response. Oh, I'd called Sheriff Owens immediately—right after the window was shattered. He'd sent a deputy to follow up. The deputy reported that he talked to the people outside, and many of them speculated about the identity of the troublemaker. People generally agreed that it was a young man. White, wearing a cap or hat of some type, and a KN95 face mask. Pro-lifers thought it was a pro-abortion activist. The Planned Parenthood contingent insisted that the opposite was true. But the deputy couldn't find any hard evidence. And no one could identify the culprit who threw the brick.

Unbelievable. Everyone on those sidewalks had a cell phone on their person. Those devices contained cameras capable of taking still photos and video. But we couldn't run down a picture of the offender.

The door to the courtroom opened and a white teenage boy stepped inside. "When's court starting up?"

I swung around in my judicial chair, inclined to snap at the intrusion. When I saw the boy in my courtroom, wearing a BCHS fleece shirt, I was confused. "Shouldn't you be in school?"

"My journalism teacher sent me over here."

That sent a jolt of alarm through me. "What on earth for? You're surely not putting this trial in the school paper."

That would be horrific for Nova Jones. The middle school also received copies of the school paper.

"No, ma'am." He glanced around the courtroom, like he was checking it out. "I'm covering the trial for my class project. Can I come in and sit down?"

"No. Not right now."

My bailiff was sitting in a chair right outside the jury room, guarding the door. I said, "Ross, has the jury finished eating their lunch?"

"Yes, ma'am, Judge. They're visiting inside the jury room. I can hear it."

I didn't intend to let them dawdle; I was impatient to resume the trial proceedings. The stone-thrower who'd interfered with my courtroom by breaking the window was likely feeling triumphant about his misdeeds. "Ross, you and Luna take the jurors to the restrooms. I'm going to let the lawyers know we'll reconvene in fifteen minutes."

To the high school kid, I said, "Fifteen minutes. Wait in the hallway with the other spectators."

I made the calls myself, since Luna was tied up with the jurors. In a quarter of an hour, we were all back in place. I'd hoped that the head count in the spectators' section would be reduced, that the citizens might be inconvenienced by the delay and move along with their lives.

Sad to say, that wasn't the case. The courtroom was at full capacity, every seat taken. That white boy in the school sweatshirt had found a spot; he managed to squeeze in at the far end of a bench.

Once we were back in trial, the DA called Deputy Wallace Greismer to the stand. After the deputy was sworn in, the DA plucked an exhibit off his counsel table. Something on paper, with multiple letter-sized sheets stapled together.

The DA cleared his throat. The sound served as an alert; it was a nervous tic of his. I edged forward on my seat, wondering what trick he'd try to pull.

The DA said, "Deputy, I'm handing you State's Exhibit number 9. Can you identify it, please?"

The deputy took the exhibit and briefly leafed through the pages. "It's a witness statement. Taken from Cocheta Bass."

Benjamin Meyers was on his feet. "Whoa! This is clearly improper. Your Honor, may we approach?"

"You may." As Benjamin Meyers and Robert Reeves came to the bench, the court reporter positioned herself so that she could hear the conference.

Benjamin Meyers dropped his voice. "Judge, I suspect the DA is trying to slide a written witness statement from Cocheta Bass into evidence. The late Ms. Bass was a school nurse at the middle school in Union Springs. What Mr. Reeves wants to do is a blatant violation of the hearsay rule. The prosecution has prejudiced my client by even making reference to the document."

"Mr. Reeves?"

"Judge, I would argue that the statement must be admitted in

Cocheta Bass's absence. The witness is unavailable. You understand that, right, Meyers? The woman is dead. She can't testify."

I broke into the spat. "Let me see the exhibit."

Reeves retrieved the statement from the deputy and handed it to me. It was fairly lengthy. A question jumped out at me: the deputy asking the school nurse to describe "the abortion plot."

I flipped to the last page. "This is an ordinary witness statement. Not a sworn affidavit or a deposition."

Benjamin Meyers said, "That's my point, Your Honor. The defense was not present. There was no opportunity for cross-examination. There's a Sixth Amendment problem here, a constitutional issue. My client has the right to confront and cross-examine the witnesses against her. But Cocheta Bass isn't available for cross-examination now, and the defense was not present when this statement was taken."

"Counsel for defendant is correct on this issue. The objection is sustained," I said. I offered the stapled statement back to the DA. He snatched it from my hand.

"You sure you don't want to reconsider, Judge? This is the evidence that corroborates the testimony of Nova Jones. Without this statement, the case falls entirely on a child's shoulders. That's a rough burden to bear." He lifted his own shoulders in a shrug. "Hope you're comfortable with the position you're putting the girl in."

There — he'd done it again. Pissed me off, trying to paint me as the oppressor.

I was barely able to keep my voice down as I responded. "Don't you go blaming the weaknesses of your case on me, Mr. Reeves. And don't you dare lay your shortcomings on your thirteen-year-old witness — or the defense, either. You were scheduled to hold a preliminary hearing in this case months ago, which would have preserved your witnesses' testimony. Cocheta Bass would've been available to testify under oath, and subject to cross-examination by the defense. But you persuaded the defendant's original attorney to waive the hearing. That's on you, Mr. DA."

I dismissed them from the bench with a wave of my hand. To the jury, I smiled and said, "Y'all, I apologize for taking so long up here. You'll disregard the DA's last question of the deputy. The defense objection is sustained."

"No further questions." He sounded as snippy as a teenage girl.

I excused the deputy. As he marched out of court, the DA turned his back to me. He walked to the prosecution counsel table and commenced a whispered consultation with his co-counsel.

I let it go on for a minute or so. At length, I had to interrupt their private conference.

"Mr. Reeves, Ms. Lindquist? Is the State ready to proceed?"

Reeves straightened up. Returned to his seat. And then his face lit up with a smarmy grin. In an artificial tone of courtesy, he said, "We're ready, Your Honor."

Something about the look in his eyes gave me a chill.

CHAPTER 63

"You may call your next witness," I said.

Assistant Attorney General Eleanor Lindquist rose from her seat at the prosecution counsel table. She'd switched up her look—no business suit that day. Instead, the woman wore a royal blue belted dress with a double row of bright brass buttons adorning the front, from the collar to the conservative hemline. Made her look more approachable than the drab gray and navy suits. And the dress would photograph well.

Back in my trial practice era, I had to wrestle with those wardrobe issues. Those days were in the past. The black judicial robe I wore spared me all those decisions. Saved a whole lot of my valuable time.

The AAG said, "The State calls Nova Jones to the witness stand."

My bailiff was in position at the far end of the courtroom. He pushed the door open, took a step into the hall. "Nova Jones!"

I fixed my face, schooled my features. I was worried about that girl. Concerned about the impact the testimony would have on her emotionally. It was hard enough to live through the experience. And now the child would be required to relive it in a huge roomful of people. Hanging on every word and judging her actions. But I didn't want to convey that. If Nova Jones walked into court and saw my face all twisted up with sorrow and dread, like I was anticipating a bloodbath, it would scare the child.

I was the judge of this courtroom. I needed to project calm. To help her remain calm.

She stepped through the door and froze, right in the back of the courtroom. Because it seemed like everyone in the gallery had twisted around in their seats to get a look at her.

I could see it in her face; she wanted to turn and run. So I stood up, waved her forward.

"Good morning, Miss Jones! We appreciate you coming to the courthouse today. I expect this is your first time in a court of law. You're going to come up here and sit in this chair."

I pointed at it. And repeated: "You'll sit up here, right by me."

Lindquist, the AAG, was staring at me with a bright, brittle smile. Looked irate. Like I'd stolen her part, by speaking the lines she'd rehearsed for the show.

My bailiff was speaking to Nova, urging her to walk on down and take the stand.

For a moment, I thought she might bolt. I could see it in her eyes. It's happened before, in my courtroom. In an incest case. The little girl took one step inside before she turned and fled. We ultimately had to use video testimony. Which is tricky in Bullock County. We're low-tech. And there's the Sixth Amendment to consider. The Confrontation Clause.

I was thinking of the Sixth as I watched Nova slowly make

her way to the bench. She was required to relate the details of her trauma to all these strangers, and she'd have to tell her story directly in front of Dr. Gaines. That was sure to be hard on the girl, a brutal experience. And then they'd order Nova to point the doctor out in court, identify her for the record.

Finally, Nova arrived in front of the bench. When she looked up at me, I said, "Miss Jones, you'll need to promise to tell the truth in court. Everyone has to do that. The clerk will administer the oath."

Lindquist spoke up. "Judge? I thought I'd ask a few questions first. To, you know, demonstrate her comprehension of the oath. Show the court that she understands the significance of sworn testimony."

I exchanged a glance with Meyers at the defense table. He remained silent. "Ms. Lindquist, the defense hasn't raised an objection to Miss Jones's competence as a witness. She's not a child. The witness is thirteen years old, is that correct?"

Lindquist was still smiling, displaying a shiny mouthful of teeth. "Yes, thirteen, Your Honor. Just a brief exam. For the jury's benefit."

I looked back at Meyers. He lifted his shoulders in a shrug. No objection, then. I thought he might accuse the State of trying to bootstrap their witness's credibility.

"Ms. Lindquist, I want the record to be clear. The court has not required this demonstration. But the defense does not object to it. All right, then, you can proceed."

I turned my attention to Nova. Made sure my voice was warm when I spoke. "Go ahead and sit in that empty chair, Miss Jones. Up here on the stand, by me. You're going to answer some questions before you take the oath."

Nova ducked her head as she stepped onto the witness stand. When she sat, she grabbed the arms of the chair and held on tight.

In a bright voice, the AAG said, "Good morning! Nova, I'm going to ask you questions about telling the truth. Can you look up, please?"

Nova raised her head. Her mouth was trembling. I wanted to reach out, wrap her in a hug, like I'd do if one of my nieces was in that kind of state, upset and scared and shaking.

The lawyer said, "Nova, when people testify in court, they make a promise to tell the truth. Do you know what that means?"

I saw her release the arms of the chair. She slipped her hands under her thighs, hiding them from view. "Uh-huh."

"So you know the difference between the truth and a lie?"

"Yeah."

Her voice was so soft, the jurors might not be able to hear her. I said, "Can you speak up, Nova? I know it's hard, but those folks in the jury box want to hear what you have to say."

She nodded. Repeated it. "I know the difference."

Lindquist said, "Is it wrong to tell a lie, Nova?"

"It's wrong."

The AAG mimed placing one hand on a Bible and raising the other. "Nova, some people put their hand on a Bible to swear to tell the truth. Are you familiar with the Bible?"

"Yes."

"Do you go to church?"

"Yes, ma'am. Victory Baptist."

This line of inquiry was spinning out of control. "Ms. Lindquist, it feels like you're rehabilitating a witness who hasn't even testified yet. Where are you going with this?"

Lindquist resented the interruption. Her eyes were chilly as she regarded me. "Just a couple more, Judge. Nova! Does the Bible say it's wrong to tell a lie?"

"It's false witness."

The girl was demonstrating biblical knowledge that a lot of people lack. But the questions weren't making her more comfortable with the witness chair. She swayed to one side and had to grip the arm of the chair again. I feared she was in danger of passing out.

"I'm cutting this off, Ms. Lindquist." To Nova, I said, "You feeling all right, Miss Nova?"

She blinked rapidly, turned to face me. The girl was breathing fast. I could see the fabric of her T-shirt move in time with her heartbeat, like her heart was pounding so hard it wanted to jump outside her chest.

"Miss Nova, talk to me. Are you feeling faint?"

She clenched her jaw, didn't speak. But she shook her head.

I said, "You sure? I can recess. We can start over again when you feel up to it."

The look of despair she gave me spoke more eloquently than words. She would never feel up to it.

So we needed to proceed, then. I spoke briskly, like it was an ordinary case. "Administer the oath to the witness, please. She's demonstrated that she understands what it means."

Luna stepped up to her. "Raise your right hand, please," she said. "Do you swear or affirm that you will tell the truth?"

"I do," Nova said. She dropped her hand into her lap.

Eleanor Lindquist picked up a legal pad from the counsel table and positioned herself directly in front of Nova, so the jury could see them both. "Nova, please state your age."

"Thirteen."

"And where do you live?"

"Magnolia Apartments. 416 South Street, Union Springs, Alabama."

"Nova, did you learn that you were pregnant in the past year?"

"Yes, ma'am."

A direct jump to the heart of the issue. I was surprised that she dispensed with the buildup.

"How'd you find out?"

I could see Nova swallow before she answered. Wished I had a bottle of water from my chambers; her mouth was probably dry.

"The nurse at school. Miss Cocheta. I kept on having to go to her office, because I didn't feel good. Sometimes I was sick to my stomach. She thought it was a bug at first, a stomach thing. Then she figured it out."

"What did she do?"

"She gave me a test, the kind you take into the bathroom."

Nova glanced up at me. I suspected she wasn't comfortable explaining that she had to pee on the test stick. I gave her a nod, to encourage her to continue.

Lindquist said, "What happened with the test?"

"There were two lines. Two lines meant you were pregnant."

"Did you know you were pregnant? Before you took the test?"

Nova shook her head. She was quiet for so long I thought I'd have to tell her to speak up. Finally, she said, "I didn't want to think about it."

"But you knew there was a chance, right? Because you'd been to a party a few months prior. Where the partying got out of control. Right?"

She didn't answer.

Lindquist waited. Walked closer to the stand. "Didn't you go to a party and have too much to drink? And end up in a car with an older boy?"

"Objection! Leading," Benjamin Meyers said.

I paused for a beat. But he was right, the objection was valid. "Sustained."

The AAG was getting frustrated with her witness. "Nova, just start at the beginning. Tell us about the party. No need to be embarrassed. Please."

CHAPTER 64

Nova Jones

BULLOCK COUNTY COURTHOUSE
UNION SPRINGS, ALABAMA

There wasn't no party.
Nova never been to a high school party.

The lawyer in the blue dress, Miss Eleanor, was bossing her again. "Nova, I'm directing your attention to the night you had sexual intercourse—in December of last year. Tell us what you recall—"

The white lawyer for Dr. Bria got out of his chair. "Your Honor, I object; this is direct examination, and the attorney for the State is leading her own witness."

"Fine!" Miss Eleanor snapped at him. "I'll rephrase. Nova, tell us what happened at the high school party you attended in December."

"I can't." Nova whispered it. She was too scared to speak up.

"I know parts are fuzzy, Nova, because you were drinking. Start with that, explain to the jury. Tell them how you came to be intoxicated that night."

"I can't!" Louder that time, but her voice cracked. Nova was scared, afraid she was about to bust out crying, squall like a baby.

"Nova." The woman lawyer looked stern. "You have to."

Nova wanted to disappear. She wished the floor would open right under her and swallow her up. "I can't. I swore to God. You asked me if I know the difference between the truth and a lie, remember? There wasn't no party, that's a lie. I won't tell a lie when I swore. I don't want to go to…"

Her voice died. She didn't finish the sentence. Not because she was afraid to say "hell" in front of Judge Mary and the jury.

It was because she'd spotted him. He was sitting in there, right out in that courtroom with all those people. His blue eyes were burning into her. Like he was daring her. *Just go ahead and say it. See who they gonna believe. Me? Or you?*

She twisted her head away, so she wouldn't be caught looking at him. But that felt wrong. Because *he* was the one who should've been ashamed. It was his fault.

Dr. Bria had to sit right up front. Because everybody in town, seemed like, wanted Dr. Bria to go to jail. That just wasn't right.

He the one that needed to be locked up. He should go to jail, not Doctor.

CHAPTER 65

Mary Stone

BULLOCK COUNTY COURTHOUSE
UNION SPRINGS, ALABAMA

Sometimes a witness will fall apart on the stand. Nova Jones was teetering on the brink. I could see it coming, like watching a train wreck in slow motion.

The lawyer said, "Let's start with the party, Nova."

"I didn't go to no party!"

Ms. Lindquist said, "These were your words, Nova. The sneaking out, the party, the boy. And it was dark, and you didn't remember? Your. Words."

"Not my words! Someone told me to tell the story that way. And I went along, because everyone wanted me to. I didn't want no trouble."

Lindquist's eyes had narrowed to slits. "You told the sheriff you went to a party and had sex—didn't you?"

Robert Reeves stood, waving his arm like a kid in school. "State requests a recess!"

Benjamin Meyers was also on his feet, shouting over the other lawyers. "Objection, Your Honor—she's badgering her own witness!"

Nova had started weeping. That hard kind of crying, when a person tries to hold it in, and it makes the body convulse.

The spectators' gallery buzzed with noise, people weighing in on Nova's breakdown. More than one person had the gall to pull out a phone and aim it at the witness stand.

The courtroom was veering out of control—again. I slammed the gavel—just once, mind. Rose from my seat and pointed at the courtroom door, straight ahead of me.

I uttered one word. "Out!"

The noise settled down some. Except for the witness stand. The poor child still sobbed like her heart was broken.

But the spectators hadn't followed orders. I needed to provide specificity.

"I am clearing this courtroom."

When I spoke, it came straight from the diaphragm. My voice can be a powerful instrument, and I'm grateful for that, at times. This was one of those occasions.

"By order of this court, all spectators will leave immediately. That includes everyone seated in the gallery. Get. Out."

A white man stood up. "Your Honor, I'm with the local NBC affiliate—"

Sweet Jesus, I recognized him: the entitled little jerk who'd crashed Saturday breakfast at my farm last spring. "Get out of my courtroom unless you want to see a contempt citation. I'm not playing."

That convinced them all, I guess. Folks figured that if I was crazy enough to threaten a TV journalist, I'd certainly rain down fury on a curiosity seeker. The courtroom emptied out, and Ross Carr shut the door behind the last visitor.

"Ladies and gentlemen of the jury, you're excused. I'm sending you off for a break. Ross and Luna will escort you to the jury room."

They didn't dawdle. After the jurors departed, a handful of us remained in court. I stayed at the bench. Bria Gaines and the attorneys for both sides sat at their respective tables. The court reporter tapped her foot on the floor, wearing an uncertain look, like she didn't know if she should stay or go.

And Nova Jones. Huddled in that witness chair, hunched over with shame and defeat, shoulders shaking.

The door to chambers was directly behind my chair. I rose, stepped out of court. In a matter of seconds, I was back at the bench with a cold bottle of water in my hands. A big one, sixteen ounces.

"Nova, honey. Look what I found."

I peeled the plastic off the top, cracked it open. Sometimes those lids are tricky. "You look thirsty, Nova. I got you a drink of water. You see?"

She lifted her head, wiped her eyes with the back of her hand. When she peeked at me, I reached out and handed her the water bottle. She took it.

"I've a box of tissues, right here." I pushed the box closer to her. When she pulled a tissue out, I said, "Take the box."

She did. Blew her nose, wiped her face. Unscrewed the lid and took a long drink of water. The room was hushed, waiting.

I had to hold myself together, too. It was personal for me. And painful, though I was determined to hide that, to project a calm demeanor.

Nova tipped the bottle back a second time. Drank deep, like people do when they've been working in the sun all day.

When she stopped to take a breath, I said, "Courtroom can be a scary place, can't it?"

Nova's eyes turned to me and she nodded, one time.

I kept my voice soft. "That testifying, it's so hard. Especially when everybody starts talking at once. The lawyers and the judge and sometimes the people sitting out there watching. It can be hard to know what to do."

Lindquist was on her feet again. "Judge, the DA and I have had a moment to consult, and we both think it would be appropriate to have some time to talk with our witness. Privately."

I was in no mood. "Sit down, Ms. Lindquist."

"But Your Honor—"

"I won't tell you again."

Pretty sure I was giving her a deadly look. Because she sat, and didn't say another word. When the DA tried to whisper in her ear, she pushed him away.

The girl from the AG's office had some sense. I was glad to see that. I turned back to Nova. "You want some more of that water, Nova? Or something to eat? Sometimes people forget to eat when they come to court."

The wicker basket sat on the bench. I picked it up and showed it to her. "How about a piece of candy? You like peppermint? How about an Atomic Fireball?"

She peered in the basket before she sat back, shaking her head. "No, thank you, ma'am. I'm not supposed to eat candy. I'm the biggest girl in school. At the hospital, that's why they say I got pregnant at thirteen."

That made my eyes sting. I looked straight at her.

I said, "I was the biggest girl in school—bigger than most of the boys. So I got my period in fifth grade, before anybody. When that happened, I was scared to death. Afraid I'd start it in the middle of the school day. I used to lay awake at night, worrying about it."

Nova lost that guarded expression. "I worry about that, the same thing."

"That right? I think we're alike in lots of ways."

She appeared to be considering it as she took another pull on the water bottle.

I took a peppermint out of the basket. As I unwrapped it, I said, "This is a criminal case, Miss Nova. It's important to remember that in criminal cases, the prosecution, Mr. Reeves and Ms. Lindquist—they're trying to put Dr. Gaines in prison. They have accused her of breaking the law. When a person's liberty, their freedom, is at stake, that's very, very important. So it's crucial that every witness tell the truth. The whole truth, while they're in that chair you're sitting in right now."

Nova clutched the water bottle so tightly, I could hear the crackle of plastic. "I swore the oath. I'm trying to do that. Trying my best. To tell the truth."

"The whole truth," I said.

She swallowed; I saw the movement in her neck. "The whole truth. Yes, ma'am, Judge Mary."

"All right, then. You ready?"

She closed her eyes, just for a moment. Opened them and looked up at me.

"Ready," she said.

"Nova, who was the boy you had sex with that night?"

I could see her starting to seize up again. Reeves looked like he was about to raise another objection. I shut him down with a look.

Nova lowered her eyes. She dabbed her nose with a tissue. She stared up at me with desperation and pain written all over her face.

I could tell she was working up to something. Something painful.

"It wasn't one boy," she said. "It was two."

Lindquist jumped up. "Your Honor!"

I rapped my gavel. "Sit!"

Then I leaned over toward Nova. "Don't be afraid. Nobody here is going to hurt you. Just tell us what happened. Everything you can remember."

I could see that she was terrified. She took another drink from her water bottle, then put it down in her lap. "It was two boys. Two white boys. Back in the weeds behind the old gas station. I didn't know 'em. Either of 'em. But they knew me. Called me by my name."

Her voice was trembling, but her words were clear.

"They pushed me down and held me, and then they did it, one after the other. When they were finished, they said I should shut up and don't say anything about it 'cause something might happen to my brothers or sisters, and they knew all of their names, too. They told me they were Klan. That one boy, the big one, show me a *K* mark on his arm, like he was proud of it. And then they run off."

I looked down at the prosecution table and just held up my hand. I didn't want to hear a word from anybody but Nova Jones. Her chin was dipped down to her chest.

"Nova, did they say anything else to you?"

She was sniffling, starting to sob. "Yeah. One of them said I had pretty eyes."

CHAPTER 66

"Your Honor! May we approach?"

Reeves and Lindquist were both on their feet. I waved them over to the side of the bench. Then I looked toward the defense table. "Care to join, Mr. Meyers?" He jumped up and hustled over, too.

I told the clerk to take Nova into my chambers.

Judges learn to be human polygraph machines, so we can weigh the testimony and credibility of witnesses. I have pretty good radar for telling the difference between the truth and a lie. A judge who can't spot a liar should be in a different line of work.

I knew that what Nova had just said was explosive. I also knew it was the truth. I could feel it in my bones.

It took me about five minutes to hear all the objections and arguments about her testimony, from both sides. I listened hard to all three lawyers. I really did. Then I said three words.

"Noted. Step back."

I turned to the bailiff. "Retrieve Miss Jones, and call the jury back in."

When everybody was back in place, I looked down at Lindquist. "Your witness."

I watched her walk up to the witness stand, holding her legal pad in a death grip as she looked directly at Nova. I already knew where her questions would start.

"Nova. On March 23, at midnight, where did you go?"

"I went to the clinic. To Dr. Bria's office."

"Dr. Gaines's office in Union Springs? In Bullock County, Alabama?"

"Yes, ma'am."

They'd established venue with that question and answer. Nova was still speaking in hushed tones, but she'd regained her composure.

"How did you arrive at Dr. Gaines's office?"

"Nurse Bass drove me in her car. I was waiting by the side of the building, our apartment building. In the shadow, so no one could see."

"Why did you wait in the shadow?"

"My mama didn't know about it. I sneaked out the window. Real quiet, so my sisters wouldn't wake up."

"When you arrived at Dr. Gaines's office, what happened?"

"We went in the back door. I put on a blue nightgown thing." She paused for a moment, then added, "Dr. Bria was nice to me. She said she was gonna help me."

Lindquist's voice turned hard. "Help you with what, Nova?"

"I was pregnant. Scared. I didn't want to have a baby. I was so scared."

That lawyer's face was like stone, no mercy. "What happened next?"

"I laid down on a table in her office, the one with a paper cover. Put my feet up." Nova's voice broke then, but she recovered. "Doctor said it wouldn't take long."

"And then what happened?"

"I shut my eyes. I tried to think about something nice. Make pictures up in my head. Flowers. But it hurt, like cramping."

"Did you tell her to stop?"

Sounding defeated, Nova said, "I didn't tell her that. Didn't want her to stop what she was doing. Because I couldn't be pregnant. I couldn't have a baby. I got all I can handle, taking care of the kids at home."

A Black woman on the jury, about my age, shook her head with sorrow. Wiped her eyes. If I could've gotten away with it, I'd have joined her. Wished we could hang on to each other and cry it out.

"What else happened that night?"

"I stayed a while after she was done. She told me some things to do, said I'd need to come back and see her. I didn't pay much attention. I couldn't go back, not without Mama knowing. So I just went home. Crawled back through the window."

"Did you get sick after that, Nova?"

I saw her steal a look at the defense table before she answered. "I kept on bleeding. And then I started feeling bad. But I didn't tell nobody."

"Why?"

"I was afraid people would find out what I done. All in the world I wanted was for nobody to know. So I just kept on going, like usual. Till that day I got sick. And they took me to the hospital."

Eleanor Lindquist stepped back, away from the witness stand. "Nova, the person who aborted your baby at her clinic in Union Springs last March, is she in this courtroom today?"

Nova hung her head and whispered, "Yes, ma'am."

"Point her out for the jury."

Nova did as she was told, but her hand shook when she pointed the finger at the defense table. "That's Dr. Bria. Right there."

Lindquist projected a note of triumph as she said, "Your Honor, may the record reflect that the witness has identified the defendant."

"It shall," I said.

Nova turned to face me. Looking up at the bench with a plea in her eyes, she said, "Judge Mary, Dr. Bria was good to me. It's not her fault I got sick. She helped me. She and Nurse Bass both."

The DA was on his feet, shouting over the girl. "The witness is volunteering information outside of direct examination. I demand that the court instruct the jury to disregard."

"Sit down," I told him. When he remained on his feet, I said, "This is your co-counsel's witness. She's conducting direct examination. You stay in your chair."

I turned to Lindquist, who was staring daggers at Nova Jones. "Ms. Lindquist, you may continue."

"No further questions."

I nodded at the defense table. "Mr. Meyers, you may inquire."

CHAPTER 67

Benjamin Meyers was out of his chair, moving toward the witness stand. I kept a sharp eye on him. There are criminal defense attorneys who view vulnerable young witnesses like Nova Jones as fair game. They'll use cross-examination as an opportunity to scare a girl, confuse her, drag her through the dirt.

Nobody got away with that in my courtroom, though. I didn't tolerate it. And lawyers in my circuit in Alabama are aware of that. But Meyers was from out of state. Maybe he didn't know how I roll.

Meyers stopped a few feet away from the stand. When he spoke to Nova, his voice was soft, respectful.

"Nova, I'm Ben Meyers. Dr. Bria's lawyer. We've met before, some months back. Right?"

Nova sniffled. She wiped her nose with a wad of tissue she held. "I remember you."

"When I talked to you and your mama at y'all's house, I was told you went to a party and had sexual relations, that's where you got pregnant. But that's not what happened, is it?"

"Objection!" It was Robert Reeves. The DA looked nervous. "Irrelevant, immaterial."

"Your Honor," Meyers said, "I may be from Georgia, but I'm licensed to practice law in Alabama. And I know that under Alabama rules of evidence, cross-examination is wide open if it pertains to a material issue. The circumstances regarding Miss Jones's pregnancy are material in this case."

I didn't want the child to be publicly humiliated. But Bria Gaines's lawyer was entitled to raise issues that supported her defense. "I'll allow it."

There was some commotion, movement in the back of the courtroom. I tapped my gavel for silence.

Ben Meyers kept a reasonable distance from the stand. Didn't hound the witness, just asked a direct question. "Do you know who got you pregnant?"

Nova looked out over the courtroom. She squeezed her eyes shut. "No, I don't. Not for sure."

The air in the courtroom shifted, changed. Became charged with tension so thick, it felt like it could deliver an electric shock. I was afraid to make a sudden move. That I might disrupt something dangerous in the atmosphere.

We were waiting for the next question. I wasn't sure what Benjamin Meyers would ask. But Nova Jones stole the thunder from her own examination.

"It could be *him*!" she shouted. "He was there! He raped me!"

Nova lifted her arm and pointed out into the courtroom. Just like the prosecution had made her point the finger of guilt at Dr. Gaines.

There was a scuffle in one of the back rows. I stood, gripping my gavel. A boy wearing a high school fleece shirt was trying to flee the gallery. A couple of citizens grabbed his arms and were doing their damnedest to hold him back.

"Ross!" I shouted. My bailiff ran to the door, locking it tight.

Judge Stone

I banged my gavel down. "This court is now in recess!"

I dropped the gavel onto the bench, pulled the cell phone from the pocket of my robe. Just had to hit one name in my contacts.

When I say I have Sheriff Owens on speed dial, I'm not kidding around. I have that man's personal cell number.

CHAPTER 68

I cleared the courtroom again. Sent the jury out. The bailiff held the kid in the back row while we waited for Mick. It only took two minutes for him to show up with one of his deputies and take the kid into custody.

Now Nova was sitting at a side table with Betty Cooper, the longtime social worker for Bullock County. I could see Starla Jones, Nova's mother, outside the courtroom, peering through the glass. Looking frazzled.

She'd missed the fireworks. Reeves had named Starla as a witness, so she couldn't sit in court during trial. Under Alabama Rule 615, I always order witnesses to be excluded from watching the trial. It's a clean way to ensure that testimony won't be influenced by other witnesses.

Then she walked in.

If I'd ever been inclined to pray, I'd be doing it right then. Praying that Nova's mama had her head on straight. That she would worry about her daughter's welfare, rather than making herself the victim. Because that can happen. I've seen it, in my career.

Starla walked over and put her arms around her daughter, and I saw her whisper in Nova's ear. Nova looked okay, considering the magnitude of the disclosure. She could overcome this, but she'd need a lot of support. I hoped she'd get it.

I rose and stepped down off the bench, eager to get into my chambers. I wanted to collapse in that chair, get ahold of myself.

Nova's revelation had gutted me. My heart bled for the child, what she'd suffered. And her testimony also stirred those old, wicked memories from my youth. When I was just a couple of years older than Nova was now. That rape, it changed the course of my life.

I hadn't even had the chance to hang up my robe when knocking started sounding at the door.

The Kleenex box sat at the corner of my desk. "Just a second." I pulled out a couple of tissues, wiped my eyes. Took a glance in the mirror to see how I was holding up. I didn't want anyone to see me break down. I figured it was just Luna, but still. People think I'm a stoic. I like to maintain that reputation.

I pulled the door open. Observed three lawyers standing on the other side. And they'd brought the court reporter along. *Good Lord!* No rest for the wicked, I guess.

The DA was scowling. "We have to talk, Judge."

"Do we? Now?" He and his co-counsel nodded. Lindquist wore an expression almost as sour as her co-counsel's.

Benjamin Meyers was more congenial. "If this isn't a convenient time, Judge, we can do this later. I apologize for showing up like this, without asking leave."

He sounded contrite. Which made me suspicious. Was the defense attorney able to divine my vulnerable emotional state?

Well, I couldn't allow that.

"Come on in. Let's keep it brief, though. The clock's ticking, and folks got to eat."

I waved a hand at the chairs in front of my desk. "Have a seat." The court reporter and Meyers sat. The lawyers for the prosecution remained standing. Robert Reeves said, "Judge, you prejudiced the State in there."

Didn't see that coming. That man always knew how to gall me. "Did I?"

"Yes, Your Honor."

"Tell me when I did that."

"When you let that girl state in front of the jury that she was raped." The DA's face was turning red. Embarrassment? Anger? It could be either. Or both.

Lindquist picked up the argument. "Judge Stone, Nova Jones's claim that she was assaulted has no legal relevance. The girl is thirteen, so she can't consent to intercourse."

"Not in Alabama," the DA said. His face was scarlet.

Lindquist was quick to respond. "Not anywhere I know of. In the United States, anyway. So it only served to confuse the jury. Any sexual act would be rape, whether she said no or not. But it introduced evidence of forcible compulsion."

I struck a grim tone. "I'm aware. She's your witness. You called her to the stand and questioned her under oath and then prompted her to provide inaccurate testimony. What are you saying that I did wrong in there?" I pushed my chair away from the desk, fixed them with a no-bullshit gaze. "I was sitting right at the bench when the DA made his opening statement. Reeves said the girl had been raped by a teenager in the back seat of a car. Do I recall that correctly?"

"Your Honor—"

It was Reeves, wanting to correct me, as was his habit. I cut him off.

"You prepared the jury for a rape scenario. Said she had sex at thirteen and was incapacitated at the time. But it's first-degree rape in Alabama, whether there's forcible compulsion or incapacitation. Explain how I prejudiced the State's case. I've just been sitting in my chair."

Lindquist murmured it, almost so softly that I didn't catch it. "Not exactly sitting."

"What's that, Ms. Lindquist?"

She only looked guilty for one second. Then she recovered. "I was just observing that you spend a lot of time out of your chair. Leaving the bench, walking around the courtroom. That's not something I've seen before."

"No? Well, welcome to Bullock County." I focused on her co-counsel. "Mr. Reeves, what relief are you seeking? If it's a motion for mistrial, I'm going to overrule it."

His red face had a pinched look. "We want you to instruct the jury to disregard Nova Jones's outburst concerning her accusation of rape. The testimony took the State by surprise. The allegation hasn't been investigated. What's more, it's irrelevant, inflammatory, and prejudicial!"

"Overruled. Is that all? Are we done yet?"

The DA and Lindquist made eye contact, exchanging an expressive look. The kind of look people share when they've been talking shit about you behind your back.

Reeves said, "Counsel for the prosecution demands that you recuse yourself from this case. You're ignoring Alabama law. And your actions make it clear that you are not an impartial arbiter to preside over this case."

I popped my fist on the desktop, using it like a gavel. "Overruled again! I'm on a roll, aren't I? Got any more motions, Mr. Reeves?"

Thought I heard a snicker from Benjamin Meyers right before the defense attorney coughed into his hand.

But there was no levity from the other two attorneys. Lindquist tried to whisper something to Reeves. He shook his head at her, with his jaw tight, like he was trying to hold back angry words.

I checked the time. "I hereby declare this chamber conference is concluded. It's 12:25, and I'm going to eat my lunch."

The court reporter, Marlena, sighed out in audible relief. I'd known Marlena since we were girls in elementary school, and she'd always been at the front of the lunch line.

We're Southerners. Mealtime is serious business.

The court reporter exited first, with Benjamin Meyers holding the door. Reeves and Lindquist stormed out of chambers. I could see sweat dripping down the back of Reeves's neck, revealing a wet ring around his shirt collar.

CHAPTER 69

At the end of court that day, the governor finally acted on his intention to call in the National Guard. I was met outside my judicial chambers by four Alabama Guard soldiers. Two Black men, one white female, and one white male.

The white man appeared to be in charge, but I addressed my question to all of them.

"What are y'all doing hanging outside my door?"

The white man said, "The Guard has been called out. We're assigned to see you safely in and out of court."

Well, that was unnerving. I didn't want them there. I didn't need them.

"Thank y'all so much! But I guarantee, I can get to and from the parking lot on my own."

The white guy held up his hand. Like he was giving me an unspoken order to shut my mouth.

What the hell?

I almost said it: *Do you know who you're talking to?*

But he didn't give me the opportunity. He placed a finger on a bud in his ear and said, "Code 10-44. Status. Code 10-44."

And the guardsman at the rear placed a firm hand on my shoulder. It gave me a jolt when I realized: They were literally restraining me.

I shook him off and then swung around to scold the young Black man. "Where on God's earth did you get the idea you could put hands on me? I'm a circuit judge, and this is my courtroom."

I was about to lay into all of them when the white guard clutched my shoulder, turned me back to face him. "We're clear," he said. "Judge, we've been ordered to escort you safely to the city limits. Once we're sure no one is following you, you'll be free to carry on."

"I don't need to be escorted to the city limits. I know my way around this town."

"We have our orders from the governor's office. To escort you out of the city."

Invoking the governor's authority set my temper to a boil. "I already told you, I don't need an escort to the city limits. You tell the governor, from Judge Stone: This has never been one of his sundown towns. You're in the Black Belt of Alabama. Can't run us out of town. We're everywhere."

One of the Black guardsmen covered his mouth. Looked like someone appreciated my humor.

The guy in charge released his grip. Which was a good thing; I didn't have to bat his hand away.

He sounded more civil when he said, "I'm aware that you're in total control—when you're in the courtroom. Outside of it, though, you're in my domain. And that includes public thoroughfares. Like it or not, Judge, I've got my orders from the governor. We're seeing to it that you make it safely out of town."

I didn't like it.

I searched his face, looking for answers, picking up clues. The guardsman might have been a jerk, but he wasn't there to mess with me. I was curious.

"Why now? All this extra security, walking me out to my car. Following me through town. This trial will be over in a few days. How come you're just now showing up?"

I started walking through the courthouse with my escort, like a rock star surrounded by security guards.

"Chatter, Judge Stone."

That set me back. "Chatter? What's that supposed to mean?"

His voice dropped; apparently, we were discussing some super-secret information. "Chatter."

"Chatter where? Social media? People have been saying reckless things on there, but I don't pay attention to that. Not since I changed my cell phone number, anyway. It's a distraction from my job. I just have to ignore it."

"We recently set up electronic surveillance around town. There's a lot of talk on cell phones, on the internet. About you. You've stirred up a lot of ill will with your handling of this trial."

That sent a live current of panic zinging through me. Automatically, I peered around, looking for danger.

We were marching along at a steady pace, but I felt compelled to speed up. I wanted to bolt, to shove the guard aside and make a run for my car. I wanted to get home. Felt a pressing need to be on my property, inside the safety of my own house. The place that was my refuge. I wanted the normalcy it provided.

I couldn't escape my escort, though. I was trapped in their midst, as they walked alongside me. All four of them in uniform, carrying holstered firearms. With assault rifles strapped around their shoulders, hanging to the waist. It wasn't like a rock star's security team. More like a convicted felon must feel when she leaves the courthouse, to be conveyed to prison.

We fell silent as the guards escorted me to my car in its designated spot, behind the courthouse. I tried to ignore the reporters aiming cameras at me, the onlookers pointing at us, making a high-pitched commentary. Someone in the cluster shouted, "She's guilty!"

For a second, I wasn't sure who they meant by that. Surrounded by uniformed guards, I was uncomfortably aware that my stroll around the courthouse looked like a perp walk, with me in the position of the accused.

While I stood by my car, gripping my key fob, the uniformed white guy laid out my instructions.

"You follow me. Our other vehicle will follow you. If we stop, you stop. Got that?"

Jesus. I didn't put up an argument. Because I wanted to get the hell out of town.

"When we get to the city limits and we have an all clear, the rear vehicle will flash its headlights at you. Then you can pass my vehicle, head on out."

He didn't crack a smile. No surprise. I slid into my car, followed behind his car, just like he'd told me to. Easier to go along. Besides, I thought: I didn't want to give him an excuse to shoot me if I fell out of line. There's always a chance of that.

The area around the courthouse was still packed. Spectators, activists carrying banners, television journalists, and the National Guard. A whole lot of guardsmen, at least twenty or so that I could see. All of them armed to the teeth.

I felt like I was living a documentary. Maybe that was true.

I saw the lights flash behind me and the lead car pulled over to the side of the road, to let me pass. As I left the city of Union

Springs, I glanced into the rearview mirror, half afraid that some bogeyman would be following.

It was all clear, though. The patrol cars blocked the highway. No one would get through that barricade until I was long out of sight.

I was safe.

CHAPTER 70

*C**hatter.*
   The word echoed in my head.

I knew people were cussing me out. Folks all over the country, who didn't even know my name, suddenly had an opinion. About my judicial ethics. My performance on the bench, knowledge of the law. My hair, my weight, my dialect.

They hollered when I entered and exited the courthouse. I supposed some were shouting at me in front of their television sets. Attacking me on social media. Accusing me of misdeeds and villainous motivations. It bothered me. Scared me, if I'm being honest.

But I knew that my discomfort didn't compare with the real victims of the real-life drama that had unfolded. The suffering that Bria Gaines and Nova Jones had to endure put my troubles in the shade. I wasn't facing prison—not that day, anyway. And it had been decades since I'd been subjected to unwelcome sexual aggression. That experience never leaves you, though. You can't bury the trauma deep enough to make it disappear.

Since the first day of jury selection, I'd been ruminating about all these matters, juggling them in my head. And trying to keep my courtroom in line, the trial under control. The dire warning from the National Guard was about to push me over the edge.

I needed to get home.

That was my best method for drowning out the madness surrounding the Gaines trial. For a few hours, I wanted to push the trial to the back of my head and focus on the farm. Think about that instead. *Life on the farm.*

There was work ahead. Livestock to be tended. In the barn, I'd muck out the stalls. Work was waiting for me inside my house, too. My kitchen wasn't up to standard, and I had laundry to do. I'd go from one chore to the next.

Rural life is hard, physically challenging, laborious. It wears me out sometimes, and I even wonder if it's time for me to give it up. But it has its rewards. And the Charolais cattle, my mare Tornado, the crazy rooster, even the bull—they were better behaved than the people currently crowding the Bullock County Courthouse and the streets of Union Springs.

So I was starting to relax as I approached my driveway on the farm road.

When I pulled in, I braked and grabbed a couple of items from the metal mailbox. Tossed the mail on the dash. One of the envelopes was embossed with the business address of that land-grabbing attorney, Arch Pearce. The irony struck me: Why wasn't the world chasing him with pitchforks and torches, instead of persecuting a dedicated doctor and the young girl she'd tried to help? Made no sense at all.

As my car bumped up the gravel drive, the rooster came running around the side of the barn. He was crazier than usual, cackling and trying to fly into my windshield. I didn't even make it up to the carport. When Foghorn flew onto the hood of my car, I stopped the car and tapped the horn. He answered with a squawk.

I turned off the engine, right in the middle of the side yard. I was plumb worn out, tempted to head straight for the house, collapse on the sofa and steal a short nap. But there were creatures on the land who depended on me. I decided to check on the livestock first. See how Tornado was faring.

The forecast had sounded iffy that morning. The cattle could weather a storm, but not my mare. She would be delivering that foal any day.

Foghorn hopped off the hood of the car and followed as I trudged past the barn, gazed out over the field. The Charolais were there. I even did a quick count: twenty—and my bull was corralled, right where he belonged.

Foghorn stayed with me, dashing back and forth and pecking at my shoes. He was bugging me, so I shut him out of the barn. I slipped off my courthouse shoes and tugged on a beat-up pair of chore boots I kept near the door.

I went inside to Tornado's stall, where she greeted me with a soft whinny.

"Hey, girl! How you feeling? You get any bigger, I'm going to have to change your name. These days, you're looking more like a hurricane than a tornado."

Her belly was swollen, getting ready to pop. I'd been giving some thought to names for the foal. As I stroked her along the neck and shoulder, I turned possibilities over in my head. Maybe Thunder, if it was a colt. Or Lightning if she had a filly.

I talked sweet to her, speaking in a soothing tone. I told her to stay calm while I walked behind her and lifted her tail. It was light enough in the barn to get a good look, and Dr. Nelson had told me what I needed to watch for. There wasn't any abnormal bagging up. A little vaginal discharge, but nothing major. I checked her belly. Didn't find streaming milk.

I pulled my phone from my pocket and debated calling the vet, just to check in. Decided to do it later, when I got inside my house. I had a bottle of white wine in the fridge, and I intended to pour a medicinal dose as soon as I made it into the kitchen. I'd put the phone on speaker, talk to the vet while I loaded the dishwasher and sipped that cold wine.

Sounded like a plan.

I was already feeling better, like I'd escaped the grip of that courtroom drama, the unrest in the streets of town. The smell of the barn and the sound of my horse's snuffling, it was a comfort. I mucked her stall out, since I was already in the barn, wearing rubber boots. Put fresh straw down for Tornado's bedding, left her with feed and fresh water. Didn't change into my overalls to do the chores. My courthouse shirt and pants could go straight into the washer.

Before I left the barn, I grabbed a handful of seed for Foghorn. "Crazy bird," I muttered. I remember thinking right then that maybe I was the crazy one. For putting up with a useless rooster, when I didn't even keep hens anymore.

When I exited the barn and walked onto the hard dirt, I could see him, sitting on the porch swing, waiting for me. As soon as he saw me coming, Foghorn started flapping his wings. I'd kept his wings clipped since he was a chick, but Foghorn still managed to fly. Short distances, if he was so inclined.

I tossed that handful of chicken feed onto the hard-packed dirt. The rooster squawked at the sight, came running off the porch to get his supper.

The late-afternoon sun cast a glow in the farmhouse, gilding it in golden light.

Time slowed down for me as I stood in the side yard, watching the rooster. Seeing a strange sight.

The setting sun illuminated a horizontal line, so close to the ground that I'd overlooked it at first. It stretched across the ground, all the way in front of the farmhouse. I could see that line where the steps led up to the porch and the front door of my home. When I squinted in the light, I could see something scrawled on my door in dripping red paint.

A giant letter *K*.

Foghorn hit that shining line before my brain was able to absorb what was happening.

I heard it first, the explosion. The force of the blast lifted me up into the air and threw me backward on the hard dirt between the house and the barn. I landed on my tail, but my head slammed down and took a hit. I guess I blacked out for a time.

When I came to, fire had erupted. I had to crawl away from the house, to distance myself from the heat and the flying ash. Stunned, I watched the flames burn like an inferno. I had my phone with me. My hands shook so violently, it took three tries to make the 911 call.

Wouldn't have made any difference, though, if I'd gotten through on the first try. The old wooden structure had been built one hundred years ago. I sat and watched my house — the house my great-grandparents had built with their own hands — burn like kindling.

By the time the local fire truck pulled onto my property, with lights flashing and siren wailing, the entire house was engulfed, with flames eating through the roof, black smoke rising all around.

There was nothing left to save.

CHAPTER 71

BULLOCK COUNTY HOSPITAL
UNION SPRINGS, ALABAMA

"There's always something to be thankful for."

My sister Jordan stood by the hospital bed, patting my hand. And making the kinds of observations that earned her the nickname "Saint Jordan" by the time she was a second grader.

Nellie sat on the opposite side, in one of those unforgiving plastic chairs you see in hospitals and medical offices. "Jordan, you have lost your damn mind. Somebody just tried to blow Mary into a million pieces. This is not our lucky day."

"But that's my point," Jordan said. "Mary was targeted, but she's alive. Not even hurt too badly."

I wouldn't go that far.

Yes, I was alive. And that was purely a result of luck. I was supposed to trip the wire when I walked up to enter the house. The trip wire had surrounded the house on all four sides, so it wouldn't matter whether I came up to the front porch or went in the side entrance, by the carport.

But despite Jordan's rosy diagnosis, I was hurting. Physically, my back was killing me; my head felt like I'd been bashed with a baseball bat; my tailbone was so sore, I couldn't sit upright. These were just the primary complaints.

And my mental health? Oh, Lord. No blessings to count on that score.

Jordan squeezed my hand too tightly for comfort. I made a face as I disengaged her fingers.

"Oh! Sorry about that, Mary." She looked so crestfallen, I thought I should have borne the pain. Then she tugged my hospital gown into place; it had fallen down on one side, exposing more of me than she was comfortable with.

"And the barn was spared. The fire department couldn't save the house. We're all sad about that. But the barn's still standing. Your horse is just fine, the animals are all right."

"Jordan's got a point," Nellie said. "Tornado was shut inside the barn. If that horse had died, you would've had a hard time with that."

I didn't say it out loud, but I was having a hard time. Yes, I was thankful that my horse had survived. But in the aftermath of the explosion and fire, I felt despair raining down on me. Crushing me under its weight. A black hole was pulling me into the abyss, the gravity flinging me into an emotional nether land.

There was a heavy tread of boots coming down the tiled hallway outside the door. Mick Owens walked into the room without knocking first.

"How you feeling, Mary?"

I glared at him, thinking it was a good thing my little sister had covered me up. "It's a funny thing about hospitals. You forfeit your right to privacy when you check in."

He ignored the set-down. "Nellie, how's she doing?"

"Hard to say." Nellie gave me a once-over. Her eyes were troubled. "I think they ought to give her something. She got blown across the side yard. I know she's hurting. But she won't accept it. Keeps telling the nurse her pain is at the zero to one level. Now, that's a damn lie."

Mick walked over to the bed and stared down at me, frowning. "How bad is it, Mary?"

I wasn't going to detail my pain for him. He wasn't a doctor.

When I didn't answer, Jordan piped up. "Mary is so strong!"

"No pain meds. I'm keeping my head clear," I said, biting off the words. Because it took an effort to speak. "I want to know what y'all are finding out there on my property."

"We're still investigating the scene," he said. "No conclusions yet."

"But what did you see? Did I tell you about the guardsmen, what they told me today?"

I couldn't remember whether I'd passed the information on to Mick. Everything that had occurred over the past hours was patchy. My sharpest recall involved impressions: the smell of smoke, heat of the fire on my face, sound of sirens, flashing red and blue lights. My horse screaming in the barn.

I closed my eyes, trying to block it out. Someone started patting my hand. Not Jordan this time. It was the sheriff.

"You ought to let the nurse give you an injection, or a pill. Or are you staying awake because of a concussion?"

I couldn't even remember. "What about the boy from the courtroom? The one Nova pointed out."

"His name is Elgin Frane. Seventeen-year-old dropout from Russell County. Bad seed. Already has a record."

"What about his pal? The other attacker?"

"Elgin hasn't given him up yet," said Mick, "but he will. When we have 'em both, we'll see which one cracks first."

"If they're sixteen or older, they can be tried as adults, if juvenile court certifies them. Forcible rape is a Class A felony."

"I told you, Mary. We're investigating. It's being handled."

That wasn't sufficient assurance, not for me. I knew Mick too well. "Damn it, Mick! You can't let this shit slide!"

My voice cracked when I screamed at him. He turned and made his way to the door. Without looking back, he said, "I'll tell Dr. Thompson he needs to take a look at you."

Jordan sounded frightened when she said, "Dr. Thompson is supposed to get back to her soon. They sent the X-rays to the radiologist in Montgomery. It shouldn't be that much longer."

Nellie said, "Hey, Mary. You sure you don't want to talk to the nurse about the pain? I know you're tough. You got nothing to prove."

Jordan picked up a plastic cup of ice water and dropped a hospital straw into it. "Mary's so strong! I admire that so much. I aways have."

Nellie nodded. Standing on the other side of the bed, she said, "No matter what happens, Mary keeps on going. Never looks back."

Jordan held the cup out to me. "You want some water, Mary?"

I pushed the cup away.

Jordan set it on the tray table. In a hesitant voice, she said, "I'm sorry about your rooster."

The rooster. Why that did it, I can't even say. Those were the words that broke me. Those tears started coming, wouldn't stop. I tried to wipe them away—with my fingers, and then I used the bedsheet as a Kleenex.

"Mary?" Nellie bent over the bed, looking scared. "You okay?"

The crying intensified. Huge, gasping sobs that choked me. Made me struggle for breath.

Jordan said, "Mary?" Her voice wobbled, like my breakdown was contagious.

"Shut the door," Nellie said. She grabbed the tissues, pressed the box into my hand. And then she stroked my hair away from my face. Like our mama used to do.

When I managed to catch my breath, I said, "I'm so tired."

"Just close your eyes, then," Nellie said.

I shook my head. That wasn't it. I raised my voice, so she'd understand me.

"I'm tired of being strong!"

Both sisters stood by the hospital bed. That was when I melted down again, big-time. Bawled like a baby. Because I was incapable of being strong anymore. I had to release the pressure or it would explode, blow me up just like my farmhouse. It felt dangerous, that grief.

I could let go, with Nellie and Jordan. With my sisters, I was safe.

CHAPTER 72

BULLOCK COUNTY COURTHOUSE
UNION SPRINGS, ALABAMA

Early the next morning, I sat behind my desk in chambers, slumped in my chair. A McDonald's bag containing an untouched breakfast sandwich sat on the desk blotter. Nellie had ordered it at the drive-through window when she drove me to the courthouse. A big plastic cup rested by the bag, still half full of Diet Coke. I picked that up, sucked on the straw.

Tried to figure out where I was going to find the stamina I'd need to make it through the day.

Dr. Thompson released me from the hospital the night before, though he was reluctant to do so, once the X-rays ruled out a concussion. I didn't think I'd ever fall asleep over at Nellie's. I did, finally. Though I wished I'd stayed awake. Because as I slept, I dreamed, my brain creating terrifying snatches of sight and sound. I couldn't remember all of it. But I know that I dreamed about my mama. She was at the farm, still alive. I heard her crying out, and I came running. I couldn't find her, though I hunted for her everywhere. Suddenly, I was standing in the side yard when Mama came tearing out of the barn. She was screaming my name, calling for me to help her. I wanted desperately to rescue Mama, to save her. But I couldn't move. I was frozen in place.

I must've been making noise in my sleep, because Nellie shook me awake. She hugged me, held me. Begged me to stop crying.

That was a shock; the statement penetrated the fog that nightmare left. What did my sister even mean — crying? Twice in a day? It wasn't possible. I almost never cry, I'm no crybaby.

But my face was hot, my nose running like a faucet. When I touched the pillow, it was wringing wet.

For some reason, I tried to deny it. Needed to. "I wasn't crying," I said to Nellie. Like a fool. One look at me put the lie to my words.

Nellie wiped under my eye with her thumb. "It's all right," she said. "You just need to release some pressure, like last night, at the hospital. Do you good. Then you can get some sleep."

Well, I didn't let that happen. I was done with sleeping. No way I'd take a chance on drifting into another nightmare scenario: my mother screaming for help, and me powerless to provide it. That was no place I ever wanted to go again.

I lay in bed, staring at the ceiling in Nellie's spare room until it started to get light outside. Didn't play games on my phone. I wasn't in the mood for games. It was a relief when morning came and I could ease out of that bed.

Sitting at my desk in chambers, I took another sip of that cold McDonald's drink as a soft rap sounded at the door.

I said, "Luna? Come on in."

It wasn't Luna, though. It was Eleanor Lindquist, wearing a black suit and a somber expression. She clutched a file folder to her chest.

"Judge Stone, I heard what happened. I'm so sorry."

Before I had a chance to respond, my throat closed up and I felt my nose sting. I had to blink back tears while I gripped the arms of my chair.

It took a moment before I could trust my voice. "What can I do for you?"

She slipped into the office and shut the door. Stepping up to my desk, she looked down at me with a sorrowful face. "Robert and I have been talking it over this morning, Judge. The burden on you. It's too much to bear. Too much for anyone to bear, but especially someone in your circumstances."

The words were like a verbal slap. I sat up straighter in my chair. "Excuse me? Someone in my circumstances?"

She let out a sympathetic sigh. "A single woman. Living alone, in the country. Now your home has been destroyed. Robert and I understand, Judge—really. There's no way you can continue to preside over this case. Just pull out. Disqualify yourself. No one will think less of you. No political fallout, I guarantee it."

She was trying to put me in a spin. "We're in the middle of a felony trial, Ms. Lindquist."

"Exactly. A very important case. The judge needs to be 100 percent present. And we understand, Judge. There's no way you can perform up to your standards. Your house burned down last night! You lost everything!"

She did it, then. Glanced down at my clothing. I was dressed in Nellie's schoolteacher clothes. Because my entire wardrobe was reduced to ash.

Nellie was taller than I was. Stouter, too. I was wearing a printed orange tunic over a pair of black jeans that were too long in the inseam. I'd rolled up the cuffs of the pant legs, pushed up the sleeves to my elbows.

She couldn't make me self-conscious about my borrowed clothes. Not after what I'd been through. "Ms. Lindquist, my house didn't just burn down. It was blown up."

"Riiight," she said, stretching the word out.

I sucked down some more Diet Coke before I cleared my throat and spoke again. "So! Thank you, Ms. Lindquist, for your sympathy and concern. I appreciate that. But there's too much at stake here for me to just quit. I can't walk away. Do you want to make this proposal on the record? Because you know that ex parte communications between counsel and the judge are prohibited. You want to call defense counsel in here? Get the court reporter?"

"No," she said. "No, absolutely not."

She squeezed her eyes shut. Dropped her head, so I was staring at the part in her hair. She let out a long groan before she spoke.

"Oh, God. I hate to have to do this."

CHAPTER 73

I tensed, waiting for the shit to fall. I didn't even know what to steel myself against.

One thing, though. They probably weren't trying to take my property from me today. That was yesterday's move.

"I've been sent by the attorney general. To show you this." She finally lifted her head. Opened the file folder she'd been clutching. She pulled out a document. Handed it across the desk to me.

It was a copy of an old medical record.

I recognized it, of course. From the first glance. Tried to keep a poker face as I looked at it. Total fail.

My voice was hoarse when I asked: "How'd y'all manage to get ahold of this? What did Dick Winston do to get my medical information? You know that the AG's possession of this record is a violation of federal law. It's protected by HIPAA. People's medical records are private."

She lifted her shoulders with a helpless look—that *don't blame me* expression people try to use when they're part of a group of wrongdoers.

"I know," she said.

"So how'd you get it? Who turned this over, gave y'all access to my personal business, my medical history?"

"Oh, Judge. You know I can't reveal that. We have to protect whistleblowers. It's important, we believe, or they'd never come forward. But that's not the point."

"It's not?" I sounded deadly. Scary.

"The significance of this document is obvious. It demonstrates that you absolutely cannot preside over the case. You can't be a fair and impartial judge for both sides in this matter. Because you had an abortion yourself. In your twenties. Which you did not disclose to the parties."

My eyes dropped to the document. It was the record from the abortion clinic I'd gone to in Birmingham. Even all those years ago, when *Roe v. Wade* was the law of the land, it wasn't easy to find professionals willing to perform the procedure. Not in the Deep South. Alabama, Mississippi, and Louisiana had a scant handful of clinics between them.

The AAG was talking to me, using an urgent, persuasive tone. "My boss says we can keep this a secret. Really, Dick gives his word on that. No press conference, no leaks whatsoever. There's no reason why the public has to know about it. You just step away from the case. In light of yesterday's attack, no one will question the decision. Announce your recusal today."

I picked up the record. Gave it a final look before I slid it back across the desk. "The AG and I go way back. I practiced criminal defense in the state capital at the same time your boss served as DA of that district. When Dick Winston was rising in the political ranks. His hands are filthy. Does that surprise you?"

The phony look of sympathy dropped from the woman's face. "I don't know what you mean."

"Oh, come on. I bet you've heard it. Seen it. When Winston was a prosecutor in Montgomery, he sexually harassed his employees. Secretaries. Interns. Assistant DAs. Women in the circuit clerk's office. The man was a menace."

She'd gone pale, her face white as chalk. I kept on talking.

"One of the women came to me about it, asking for legal advice. She had a tape recording she'd made. Alabama is a one-party consent state for recording a conversation. You're aware of that."

She gave me a stiff nod.

I continued, "I met up with him at a bar. We had a few drinks before I confronted him. He made damaging admissions. That man never could hold his liquor."

I tipped back in the chair to ease the pressure on my tailbone, grateful that my sister wore queen-size jeans. "I recorded that conversation. Still have it, even though my client decided against bringing suit."

Lindquist couldn't meet my eye. I observed that she didn't register shock or surprise. Didn't defend Winston against the accusation. So he was still playing the same game, in a position where he had even more power, and a larger staff.

I kept my eyes trained on her. That was when I knew. I should've realized it sooner.

"Oh, my God," I said. "He did it to you."

She didn't deny it. Said nothing at all.

"Son of a bitch." I shook my head. Hating the man for all kinds of reasons. Resenting that I had to feel sorry for the white woman in my office who'd come in there to blackmail me.

"I'm not trying to push you into confiding in me, Ms. Lindquist. Keep it in your heart, if you prefer. Women been doing that since the dawn of time. But about this."

I reached for the medical document again and smoothed the paper on the desktop. "Here's my message back to y'all. You want to expose me? With this piece of paper? There was nothing illegal about the abortion I got, years ago. I had a constitutional right of privacy to get the procedure done. But your boss? The dirt I have on him will get him disbarred."

She snatched the paper off the desk, shoved it in the file folder. Didn't meet my eye as she headed for the door.

And she left without speaking a word.

CHAPTER 74

Presiding at the bench that day, I was in rough shape.

Sitting on a broken tailbone was no picnic. Dr. Thompson told me the night before that it was a miracle that my only fracture was a broken coccyx. He had remarked that I was lucky—that chorus again, telling me to count my blessings, it could've been worse.

He said there's nothing you can do medically for a fractured coccyx. He handed me an Rx for oxycodone, which was still in the bottom of my purse. Told me to sit on an ice pack.

Right.

I was sitting in my usual seat behind the bench. Not the hardest surface I've perched upon, but it felt unforgiving that day. No ice pack, I'd disregarded that medical advice. I didn't intend to make that walk from the bench into chambers looking like I'd wet myself. An ice pack would surely make a wet spot on the back of my robe.

The defense was presenting their case, starting with an expert who flew in from out of state to testify—another reason for me to show up and tough it out. Benjamin Meyers had called Dr.

Steinfeld to the witness stand as his first witness. The doctor was a female OB from Virginia with an impressive résumé. During direct examination, she'd outlined a clear description of the health risks of pregnancy for adolescent girls.

Benjamin Meyers said, "Dr. Steinfeld, you've testified that teenagers have higher risks of eclampsia, puerperal endometritis, and systemic infections than women over twenty, is that correct?"

"Yes. That's well established in the literature."

"Can you describe these complications in everyday terms, for the benefit of the jury?"

The doctor explained the perils in plain language. I checked out the jury. They were paying attention.

"Dr. Steinfeld, for a female pregnant at the age of twelve or thirteen, are there any additional dangers?"

"Certainly. Pregnancy and childbirth at such an early age is especially dangerous, for both the adolescent mother and for the infant. The pregnant adolescent of twelve or thirteen is at a greater risk of death or disease due to varied causes. Bleeding during pregnancy, hemorrhage. Toxemia. When a child of twelve or thirteen gives birth, labor is prolonged and difficult. What am I forgetting? Oh — severe anemia, that's more likely. And young adolescents are five times more likely to have eclampsia than older teens."

"In your opinion, are the conditions you've described severe risks to the health of the pregnant adolescent?"

"They are. And there are risks to mental health as well. Greater likelihood of postpartum depression and suicidal ideation."

"What are the risks to the infant born to a mother who's twelve or thirteen?"

The witness was solemn as she turned to face the jury. "Much higher risks of prematurity. Of birth defects. Low birth weight. And neonatal mortality."

Meyers wrapped it up pretty fast after that. I caught him exchanging a satisfied look with Bria Gaines at the counsel table; their expert had performed well on the stand.

I said, "The prosecution may inquire."

The DA stood up, stepped around the counsel table. "Doctor, you just testified that a baby born to an adolescent mother has a higher risk of death. Correct? Higher risk of mortality?"

"Yes," she said, nodding. "That is a well-established fact."

"But let's get something straight. If a doctor aborts the baby of an adolescent mother—that increases the risk of death all the way up to 100 percent! Am I wrong about that? Because the abortion kills that baby. Correct?"

The doctor paused, frowning. "I would take issue with the characterization inherent in your question. You refer to the unborn fetus as a baby. An abortion terminates a pregnancy, it doesn't kill a human baby."

Robert Reeves did a turnaround for the benefit of the whole audience: jury, spectators, his co-counsel. So that they could see the incredulous expression he wore.

"So you don't think a pregnant woman has a baby in there—is that right? When my wife was nine months pregnant—because she delivered ten days past her due date—she didn't have a baby in her womb? That's what you're saying? Because my wife sure thought she did."

"Objection, argumentative," Meyers called out.

"Sustained," I said.

Dr. Steinfeld answered, despite my ruling. "It was a fetus. Until the pregnant woman gives birth, she carries a fetus."

Reeves rubbed the back of his neck. He was heating up—literally—just as I've seen him do in court for years. "Doctor, when you told us all of your education and experience, you left something out, didn't you? You've worked for Planned Parenthood up in Massachusetts, isn't that right?"

Someone in the jury gasped. The DA had struck a nerve, scored for his side. There are folks in Alabama who think Planned Parenthood is the devil incarnate.

And plenty of other people who support their work. A white man in the gallery with longish black hair unfolded a sign and lifted it over his head. In bold black print on a pink background, it read SAVE BRIA GAINES.

In the blink of an eye, my courtroom was out of control again. A woman sitting in the row ahead of the sign bearer grabbed the banner and tried to tear it into pieces.

"Ross!" I called, but he was already on the move. My bailiff and a deputy hustled the battling activists out of court, but the noise level had risen—with chatter, I guess you'd call it. I stood up, slammed my gavel. Called for order in the court.

Stood there until the room was silent. Then I dropped back into my chair.

Oh, Lord. I'd forgotten the tailbone. Should've eased into the chair. A bolt of pain ran through my backside and up my spine. I had to clench my jaw to keep from howling.

As the cross-examination resumed, I wished I'd filled that prescription. If I had a bottle of those pills, I'd have popped a dose, and dry-swallowed right up there on the bench, in front of everyone.

I did keep a bottle of ibuprofen for emergencies. And this certainly qualified. As the expert testified, I eased open a drawer at my right hand. The small plastic bottle was there.

It was empty.

Shit.

CHAPTER 75

The defense had called a solid assortment of upstanding citizens from Birmingham and Montgomery to testify about Bria Gaines's good character and professional ability. Two locals had taken the stand on her behalf, patients who literally owed their lives to her care.

The final witness for the defense was Bria Gaines.

I watched closely as she took the stand and testified in her own defense. After a short time, I was able to relax. She was doing a good job of it.

That's not always the case.

When providing testimony in court, some folks are their own worst enemy. Even when they're intelligent, educated. Not everyone comes across. Some get angry, act defensive. Others freeze. I've seen nice, amiable people get on that stand and lose their likability factor.

And if the jury doesn't like you, and you're the defendant in a criminal court case? That happens. Happens a lot in criminal cases.

When it does—you should've stayed in your seat at the counsel table. Let your lawyer do the talking for you. That's what advocacy is all about.

But Dr. Gaines was handling it. She and her attorney had a good back-and-forth on direct examination.

"Dr. Gaines, was the Union Springs health clinic your only option for employment after completing your residency?"

"No. I practiced in a primary care clinic in Birmingham. And I'd received offers of employment with health facilities in Alabama, Georgia, and Louisiana."

"Why did you decide to open a practice in Union Springs?"

"Because I know there's a serious shortage of health care providers in small towns and rural communities; it's true everywhere in the US. And I can't fix that, but I wanted to be part of the remedy by providing professional care where it's needed most."

It was a good point, and she delivered it well. Not overly pious, wasn't demanding gratitude. Just stating the facts.

"Dr. Gaines, did you in fact perform a procedure that terminated Nova Jones's pregnancy last spring?"

"I did."

Just two words. Straightforward, no hesitation. I kept an eye on the jury. They were listening, waiting to hear more.

"And why did you terminate her pregnancy on that date?"

"She asked me to. Cocheta Bass—the middle school nurse, she's deceased now—brought Nova Jones to my office. Nova asked me to help her. The help she needed was termination of pregnancy."

There was a hush over the courtroom. I glanced over at the spectators, making sure that no one was getting ready to raise hell.

"Dr. Gaines, were you aware that state law in Alabama prohibits doctors from performing abortions?"

"Yes, but there's one exception. In the language of the statute. It says that an abortion is permitted if the doctor determines that the abortion is necessary to prevent a severe health risk to the pregnant mother. I honestly and sincerely believed that the pregnancy was a severe health risk to Nova Jones. Due to her age, her circumstances, the circumstances surrounding the very fact of her pregnancy. I still believe it was the correct action."

Ben Meyers turned to face the jury before he said, "No further questions."

Eleanor Lindquist hopped out of her chair and advanced on Dr. Gaines. Initially, it surprised me to see Lindquist come forward, rather than Reeves. I'd have assumed that the DA would want to personally conduct cross-ex of the defendant, especially before a national audience.

But it made sense, tactically. One of the reasons Reeves had brought Lindquist on board was to eradicate the impression that the male DA was bullying a woman. When one woman cross-examines another, it improves the optics for the prosecution.

"When you aborted Nova Jones's baby, it wasn't due to a medical emergency. Right?"

"I believed there was a health risk…"

"Answer the question, Doctor. You know the difference between a medical emergency and a health risk. Was she suffering a medical emergency?"

The doctor took a moment before she replied. "I believed that her health—"

"It's a yes or no question. Was there a health emergency?"

"In my opinion—"

"Yes or no, Doctor!"

"Objection!" Ben Meyers was on his feet, pointing at Eleanor Lindquist. "This line of questioning is argumentative!"

Well, it was. "Ms. Lindquist, give the witness time to answer."

The AAG narrowed her eyes as she turned back to Bria Gaines.

"So! Dr. Gaines, you were aware that your patient Nova Jones was a thirteen-year-old girl. And she was pregnant."

"Yes, of course I was aware of that."

"Did you know the circumstance of the sexual activity that resulted in the pregnancy?"

"The rape? No, she didn't inform me. I didn't know any of the details."

"But you knew that, at her age, the law would view her as a victim of rape — regardless of the particulars."

"Yes. I knew that."

"Dr. Gaines, you've told this jury that you wanted to help Nova Jones, correct?"

"Yes! That was my motivation, the reason I got involved."

"If you wanted to help her, why didn't you report her sexual abuse to the police?"

Bria looked like she had taken a punch to the gut. "I didn't know—"

"Didn't know what? The particulars? You knew some male had trifled with that girl, got her pregnant! But instead of calling the police, you killed the baby and left Nova Jones in the same situation you found her in, vulnerable to abuse and unprotected! Didn't you?"

Dr. Gaines opened her mouth, then shut it. As if she was searching for words.

But Lindquist was triumphant, she had her in a headlock. "You are a mandated reporter! The law settles responsibility on you, to sound the alarm when you know or suspect a child is being abused. But you didn't make a peep! For all you knew, you sent her back for another round of sexual assault the next day!"

"I had to choose!" Dr. Gaines said. Her voice was a desperate whisper.

"What did you say? You had to choose? So you chose to kill a baby and send Nova out, vulnerable for more abuse, is that right?"

She was louder when she answered. Dr. Gaines gave Lindquist a level look. "I had a choice. I could perform the abortion, or I could call law enforcement. I couldn't do both. And if I'd called the police, they would have made her carry the pregnancy to term."

Lindquist paced from the witness stand to the jury box, her whole body rigid with righteous indignation. "You want these jurors to believe your heart bled for Nova! You wanted to help Nova, save Nova! But you didn't protect her. Didn't tell her mother, or alert a social worker, or let the DA know that a person in the community had impregnated a thirteen-year-old girl. You did nothing to prevent her from being raped again."

Eleanor Lindquist turned to the jury box. Huffed a humorless laugh and shook her head in disgust.

Two of the jurors in the box turned to each other, to exchange a look. Then one of them crossed her arms on her chest.

That meant something, definitely. But what?

CHAPTER 76

STONE FAMILY FARM
BULLOCK COUNTY, ALABAMA

It was dusk when I pulled into the drive. I hit the brakes when Nellie ran out of the barn, waving both arms.

Made no sense for my sister to be hanging out in the barn. She'd come to the farm that day to await the delivery of my new living quarters. And it had arrived: A single-wide mobile home with skirting and temporary stairs was already set up between the barn and the bands of yellow police tape that surrounded the burned-out shell of my ancestral home.

I'd be living in a trailer for the time being. Despite the protests I'd received from friends and family, who believed I should be bunking with them in town. Because, as I repeatedly explained to those who tried to argue with me, I had a farm to run.

A farm that was dragging me down. I had to admit it: I felt weary, burnt out by my family farm obligations. It felt like I was carrying the world on my shoulders. Can't do that forever. How much longer could I manage the physical labor required in the daily grind of farm life? My back and my joints were bothering me already.

I rolled down the window as Nellie reached the car. She was all worked up and breathing hard.

"It's Tornado! She's having that foal."

I was out of the car, fast as my battered body permitted. "Are you certain?"

She made that face—the one that warns a person not to cross her. "I saw a tiny hoof poke out of her vulva. What do you suppose that signifies?"

With that report, I took off for the barn. Inside, I saw Tornado pacing in her stall. Her coat was drenched with sweat.

Nellie came up behind me. "When I saw how she was behaving, I got things ready. Mucked the stall and sprayed it with vinegar mix. Put down fresh straw."

I was grateful for Nellie's help. It wasn't my first time witnessing the foaling process, but it was Nellie's first. I was nervous as hell.

"The hoof, when did it poke out?"

"I don't know. Ten minutes ago?"

Ten minutes was a mite too long. It worried me. "Was it a front hoof? It should be a front hoof."

"Damn it, Mary, I don't know. I wasn't expecting to see anything. Didn't you tell me she had another week to go?"

I thought she did. Maybe I'd missed the signs, too caught up in the Gaines trial to pay close attention.

I pulled out my cell phone, found the vet in my contacts. It was a relief to have him pick up on the first few rings. But when he answered, I could barely hear him. I bumped up the volume.

"Troy! It's Mary Stone. Tornado is foaling, I need you over here!"

There was background noise on the other end of the call. Laughter, loud talk, dinging sounds. I thought I heard him say: "Can't get there!"

"What?" I was shouting into the phone, determined to make him hear my end of the conversation. "Did you say you're unavailable? We need you, Troy. She's having that foal right now."

His voice was clearer.

"It's going to be okay, Mary. The mare knows what to do."

I looked down at Tornado. She had dropped to the floor of the stall and was lying on her side. I could see that she was straining, trying to push.

"You can assist her, Mary, if she needs it. Go to the house and scrub up your arms. Then rub some lubricant all the way up your arms. You got K-Y Jelly in the house?"

Invoking the image of the smoking remains of my family's home made my throat tighten. I coughed to clear it. "I don't have a house. Got water and soap out here by the barn, though."

"No house? What do you mean?"

More dinging on his end, and the sound of a happy shriek. "Troy, are you sitting in a casino?"

"It's our thirtieth anniversary, Mary. I took Charlene to Gulfport to celebrate."

My luck couldn't get much worse. The vet was down in Mississippi, way out of pocket. Probably drunk. The drinks are free in those Gulfport casinos.

Overheard a shrill voice on his end of the call. "Troy! This is the one day of the year that your wife comes first. I swear, if you don't hang up, I'm filing for divorce."

Despite his wife's threats, Troy hadn't hung up on me yet.

He said, "If the foal won't come on its own, you can help. You said one foot is out?"

Nellie was squatting behind Tornado. She heard the vet's question. She gave me a thumbs-up.

"One hoof," I said.

"Reach in there and see if you can grab the other one."

In any other circumstance, I'd have been down in the straw with Tornado, doing it all myself. But the injury from the explosion inhibited my ability to move. I'd barely managed to sit in a chair all day.

Nellie followed Troy's instructions. "I've got it," she said, her voice triumphant. She looked up at me, smiling. Then her face fell. "Oh, my God."

I watched my mare seize with a powerful contraction. Nellie cried out, and I stuffed the phone in my pocket.

"Oh, Lord, Nellie. You gonna be okay?"

If someone's arm was going to be broken during the delivery of the foal, it should be mine.

Nellie's eyes were squeezed shut, her mouth open with a silent scream of agony. Then, slowly, gradually, her face cleared, eyes opened. Tornado's contraction passed.

Nellie pulled her arm out. She wiped the bloody fluid from her skin and gingerly felt along the forearm, assessing the injury.

"Is it broken?"

"No. Gonna be sore as hell though." She heaved a weary sigh. "Mary, I'm never doing that again."

I couldn't ask her to repeat it. But maybe Nellie's assistance had done the trick.

We watched as Tornado strained with another contraction, and the foal started to appear. The hooves first, both front feet, soles down. When the nose appeared, my heart started pounding with a mix of joy and anticipation.

My mare kept on straining, moving that foal through the birth canal. Once the head and shoulders were out, Tornado stopped to rest.

We were watching, waiting for nature to do its job, bring the foal the rest of the way. Tornado was taking too much time.

"I got to make sure the airway's not blocked," I said.

Nellie groaned. "You want me to blow?"

"I'll do it. Help me get down on my knees, Nellie."

It hurt, but with my sister's assistance, I got down on the floor of the stall. Covered one of the foal's nostrils with my hand, placed my mouth on the other and blew.

Not a pleasant task; the foal's head was sticky with blood. But it was effective. Once my air passed into the foal, it breathed on its own.

Just a few strong pushes after that, and the foal was born.

My chest tightened with emotion as Tornado sniffed the foal. Started to nuzzle it and lick it.

"Look at that," Nellie said. "She knows her baby." Nellie wrapped her sticky arm around my shoulders and hugged me.

We got on our feet and leaned on the side of the stall, watching the mare and foal form their bond.

Within a few minutes, the foal made its first attempt to stand. Unsteady and unbalanced, it started with its hind legs, and then pushed up, one front leg at a time.

"I believe that's a boy," Nellie said.

"Looks like it," I agreed.

As if overwhelmed by the news, the foal fell sideways with a grunt, landing by his mother in the hay.

Within minutes, he was up on all fours again, starting to take a few steps. After a few tries, he managed to find his mother's udder and commenced to suckle.

"Definitely part of our family," Nellie said. "Gets right down to eating."

We laughed. It's funny because it's true. I nudged Nellie.

"I was considering calling him Thunder. What do you think?"

She scoffed. "You and those weather names. Tornado, Thunder. Foghorn."

Foghorn. It was the first time all day I'd thought about my rooster.

I was quiet for a bit, contemplating that. My close call. The dangers the trial created. The uncertainty of the outcome, for everyone touched by it.

Then Nellie spoke. "This is what I miss about the farm. Times like this. Seeing nature at work, you know what I mean?"

I did know. Watching Tornado and her colt, it felt like I'd witnessed a miracle.

So miracles did exist. That was a good thing.

We'd need one in my courtroom.

CHAPTER 77

BULLOCK COUNTY COURTHOUSE
UNION SPRINGS, ALABAMA

Counsel for the State and the defense were making their closing arguments to the jury.

Robert Reeves kicked it off. The DA always goes first in closing, because they have the burden of proof. It's the job of the prosecution to prove that the defendant committed the crime.

But the DA gets the last word, too. I give the State and defense equal time for closing. In this case, thirty minutes each. But the State always has the option to reserve part of that time to make a rebuttal when the defense attorney's argument is done. That day, Reeves was breaking it down twenty-five/five. So the DA would speak first, for twenty-five minutes. The defense would have thirty. After Benjamin Meyers completed his argument and sat down, Robert Reeves would have the last five minutes to poke holes in Meyers's summation.

Reeves did a reasonably good job in the initial portion of his argument. He summarized the State's case, talked about the evidence that proved the elements of the crime. He checked off all the boxes, raised his voice a time or two, pounded his fist on the wooden lectern he stood behind. Pretty standard performance.

Then Benjamin Meyers had his turn. He outplayed Reeves from the start. He bypassed the lectern, stood directly before the jury box. Commanded the attention of all of the jurors.

"The prosecution, in the DA's argument, recounted the testimony of the witnesses for the prosecution. He took twenty-five minutes to do it. But he left out some extremely significant statements. Swept past crucial pieces of this case without a mention."

Meyers took a step to the right, gripped the edge of the jury box. "The DA talked about the testimony of Dr. Thompson, who examined Nova Jones when she fell ill and was brought to the hospital. But the DA made no mention of the dangers that Dr. Ron Thompson, the State's own witness, told you that Miss Jones would have faced if she'd carried that pregnancy to term. Do you remember that? Dr. Thompson said Nova Jones had a greater risk of death or disease. He cited multiple health risks. It's in the record of his testimony!"

He paced to the other end of the jury box, directed his argument to the people sitting there. "The same complications Thompson named were raised in the defense case by our expert witness, Dr. Steinfeld. So the State's own evidence corroborates the defendant's expert witness! The State's case supports the defense we've raised! You heard that, ladies and gentlemen, in this very courtroom."

He paused, looking up at the ceiling for a couple of moments, before turning back to face the jurors. "Here's another thing. Something curious about this case, just can't stop thinking about this."

He sounded sincere, looked genuinely baffled.

"The prosecutor, in his argument, brings up the work of the

investigators. The testimony of the sheriff and his deputies, people in law enforcement. Ladies and gentlemen, those so-called investigators — the people charged to enforce the law, to serve and protect the citizens of this community? The investigation was so misguided, they failed to uncover a gang rape! At the heart of this case is a child who was raped in public by two teenage boys, in broad daylight!"

"Objection."

"What kind of law enforcement is that? They're chasing down the medical doctor who cares about the health of people living in this community! Your sheriff and DA are too busy persecuting Bria Gaines to uncover the gang rape of the child who's their own prosecuting witness. Can't see a violent felony happening right in front of their faces!"

"Objection, Your Honor!"

Both attorneys at the prosecution table were on their feet, demanding my attention.

Eleanor Lindquist said, "Judge, this behavior of the defense is outrageous. Instruct the jury to disregard. And order defense counsel to confine his argument to the relevant facts and law."

Before I spoke, Benjamin Meyers swung around to confront her.

"Relevant facts? Are you claiming that the circumstances of Nova Jones's rape are irrelevant? You're the ones telling this jury a phony story from the start. Who you covering for, Ms. Attorney General? How many times did you talk to that girl? How many opportunities did you have to get the truth from her?"

He turned back to the jury box. "Do you see, ladies and gentlemen? The prosecution doesn't care about the truth in this case."

"Judge Stone!" Lindquist was yelling at that point.

"Approach the bench," I said.

All three lawyers stood before me. Lord almighty, emotions

were running high; somebody might throw a punch any minute, and Lindquist was likely to take the first swing.

"Basis of the State's objection?" I said. Speaking calmly, trying to smooth this over.

"Relevance, Your Honor. Rape doesn't create an exception to the Alabama abortion law."

"Overruled. The State did mischaracterize the circumstances of Nova Jones's pregnancy. During opening statement and in direct examination. It's fair game for the defense to point that out."

"It's also inflammatory, Your Honor," Lindquist said. Her eyes were flashing, her dander was up. "The defense accusations have crossed the line of proper argument. I request that Benjamin Meyers be reprimanded and censured."

"No reprimand," I said, still trying to remain chill. I didn't want wild, hair-raising closing arguments from either side. They might rile up the community, unleash further violence. "Bring it down, counselors, keep your arguments civil. Confine them to the evidence and credibility of the witnesses. Apply law to the facts. Don't go off half-cocked, Mr. Meyers."

Everyone returned to their respective places. Meyers switched topics, talked about Bria Gaines's good character, her positive contributions to the community. He pointed to the expert evidence, pounding home the physical dangers of the pregnancy for a thirteen-year-old, the peril it posed for Nova.

I interjected at the twenty-nine-minute mark. "You have one minute remaining, Mr. Meyers."

And he went back to the forbidden waters. "You know, the defendant in a criminal case doesn't have the obligation to prove anything. It's the prosecution that has the burden of proof. But in this case, the defense has proven that Dr. Bria Gaines was doing her duty toward Nova Jones when she terminated the pregnancy.

You know what's really a crime? Making that girl carry her rapist's child. Anyone who had anything to do with that ought to be behind bars. But that doesn't include Dr. Gaines."

"Time."

Meyers paused. Took a moment to make eye contact with everyone in the jury box before he returned to his seat.

I said, "Mr. Reeves, you have five minutes."

He'd had time to recover, to collect himself. The DA returned to the wooden lectern and grasped it with both hands.

"Some cases are complex, ladies and gentlemen. Because laws can be complicated, or the facts can be unclear."

He let go of the lectern. He folded his hands on the wooden surface. "This isn't one of those cases, though. The case of *State of Alabama v. Bria Gaines* is simple. It's open-and-shut."

Finally, he stepped away from the lectern. Slipped his hands in his pockets.

"There's no dispute—none—that Bria Gaines aborted the unborn child of Nova Jones at her medical office in Bullock County, Alabama."

He lifted both shoulders in a shrug. "Doesn't matter how Nova came to be pregnant. Not in our state. That's the decision made by our state legislature."

His voice grew testy when he said, "And no matter how they try to twist it, we all know that the abortion wasn't performed due to a medical emergency, not as that term is defined by Alabama law."

I could see the back of him. His neck was fiery red. "So, ladies and gentlemen, there's only one decision that you can legally and rightfully reach in this case. I ask that you return a verdict of guilty against Bria Gaines."

He stood up straight before he added, "And I want you to send a message to the community with your verdict. A message to the whole country, watching this case here in Union Springs, Alabama. Return a verdict swiftly. And recommend the maximum sentence of imprisonment."

He didn't expand on just what that would be. He didn't have to, everyone knew.

It was imprisonment for ninety-nine years or life.

CHAPTER 78

The jury was deliberating. They'd been at it for two whole days.

Just before sending them into the jury room to deliberate, I excused the two alternates, so we had a jury of twelve to decide the case. The twelve jurors — seven women, five men; eight white and four Black — had been shut up in the jury room for so long that a languor lay over the courtroom. The DA and his co-counsel retreated to the prosecutor's office. Bria Gaines and Benjamin Meyers remained close to the counsel table, but he'd removed his jacket, loosened his tie. She had a book with her; I couldn't tell what it was. But whenever I was in the courtroom, I noticed she didn't turn many pages. No surprise there. A defendant waiting for the jury verdict wouldn't be able to concentrate on the text.

I spent the majority of the long wait in my chambers. And because the jury's extended deliberation afforded me the luxury, I was sitting on an ice pack, as the doctor advised.

Luna tapped on the door and stuck her head through. "The jury has a message, Judge."

"A message?" I repeated.

I pulled my robe on, zipped it up. I'd been waiting for someone to announce: *We've got a verdict, Judge.*

Hearing that the jury had a message was a distinctly different matter.

I stepped carefully up to my seat at the bench while Meyers pulled on his jacket. Reeves and Lindquist came running through the doorway, hurried down the aisle.

I nodded at Ross. He walked up to the bench and handed me a folded sheet of white paper.

I opened it, read the words. Looked up and said to the parties, "They say they're deadlocked."

Bria Gaines's eyes shut; she covered her face with one hand.

The DA said, "The State requests to see the message, Your Honor."

"Certainly. I'll read it aloud first. 'We can't agree on a verdict.' It's signed by the foreperson."

I handed the note to Reeves. Meyers joined him at the bench.

"The language is clear," I said. "There's no indication of which way they're split, or how many votes are on either side."

Reeves was back at the counsel table, consulting with Lindquist.

Meyers had an arm around Dr. Gaines, was whispering urgently in her ear. I sent him a silent message, telling him to urge her to stay strong. The battle wasn't lost, not yet.

Reeves faced me and said, "Your Honor, the State requests the dynamite charge."

He wanted me to bring the jury into court and read an instruction to them that would encourage them to continue deliberations. Advise them of the importance of reaching a verdict.

We called it the dynamite charge in Bullock County. Some places, they call it the *Allen* charge. Named for the old case *Allen v.*

United States, where the Supreme Court approved the use of such instructions when juries hang up.

I looked over at the defense table. "Mr. Meyers, what is your position?"

He stood and said, "The defense doesn't oppose reading the *Allen* instruction."

He must have thought he had one or more jurors on their side.

That was my answer, then. I told Ross to bring the jury into the courtroom. It was the work of a moment; they were shut in a jury room that adjoined the circuit court.

They filed into the jury box, and I gave them the instruction: Alabama's version of the dynamite charge. They wore sullen faces. They all looked tired—plumb worn out, even the younger ones.

After Ross escorted them back to the jury room, I returned to chambers. I wouldn't do the dynamite a second time. Some people are critical of judges who use it. They say it's inherently coercive, and pressures jurors to give in to the majority.

When Luna pounded on the door an hour later, it appeared that the dynamite was effective.

"Verdict, Judge!"

Back into the robe. I waited for a bit before I entered. Let the parties and the press and the public settle down first. Luna rapped on the door. That was my cue.

After I settled into my chair, I directed Ross to bring the jury into court. That gave me a moment to check out the courtroom. The press was there, in full force. We'd lost some curiosity seekers, but the most dedicated activists on both sides were present. Ready to blow up if they didn't like the outcome.

As the twelve jurors filed into the jury box, I focused my attention on them. Out of long habit, I tried to read their faces.

Old-timers claimed that you can predict a jury's verdict if you correctly read the signs. But I didn't know about that. Seemed like there was a fifty/fifty chance.

I hoped they'd taken the case to heart, that they'd done the right thing. But it was hard to predict.

And in any case, we'd know in a moment.

The foreperson was female. You'd think that would be a good sign — a positive omen for the defense. Experience had taught me not to rely on that. Although women were inclined to acquit in general, female jurors were often unsympathetic to their own sex in criminal cases.

"Members of the jury, have you reached a verdict?"

The foreperson spoke up. "We have, Your Honor."

She was holding a sheet of paper: the verdict form. I nodded at Ross Carr. The bailiff took the paper from her and handed it to me.

I read it silently first. Rubbed my eyes and read it again, though there was no mistake. It was set down before me, in black and white. And signed by the jurors.

I took in a deep breath. Read the verdict aloud.

"We, the undersigned, find the defendant, Bria Gaines, guilty."

The ink on the page commenced to swim before my eyes. I blinked and read: "We recommend a sentence of imprisonment of ten years."

So they'd compromised on the penalty. The jurors who had been hanging up on Bria's behalf switched their votes to guilty in exchange for the minimum penalty of ten years' imprisonment. They split the baby, like King Solomon.

The courtroom was buzzing; faint cheers from one section, indignant voices all around. It didn't seem that the compromise verdict satisfied many folks. The DA was on his feet, shouting to make himself heard.

"Your Honor! The State hereby requests that the defendant's bond be revoked and that she be taken into custody pending sentencing in this case!"

Ten years.

Even with early parole consideration, she'd be locked in prison for years. Her medical license would be revoked. The course of her life irretrievably altered. Her liberty stolen from her.

Because she wanted to save Nova Jones.

The noise level was rising. Both of the lawyers at the prosecution table were on their feet, demanding that I put Bria Gaines behind bars immediately.

I picked up the gavel. Slammed it hard. Cut my eyes at Reeves and Lindquist.

When I spoke, everyone could hear me.

"Sit down."

CHAPTER 79

When I'd first opened the verdict form and read the jury's decision, it was a shock to my system. Felt like I'd stuck my finger in a light socket, that kind of jolt.

I hadn't realized how much I'd counted on that Bullock County jury doing the right thing.

A person might argue that as a judge, I shouldn't have been naïve. Judges have a front-row seat to the jury process. We know how wrongheaded the jurors can be. Just takes one or two strong personalities in that box to turn everything upside down.

The DA hadn't taken me at my word, apparently. He was still on his feet. I repeated the order, louder this time.

"Sit. Down."

He sat.

But the courtroom still buzzed with reaction: whispers, sobs, some laughter. I was not having that. I refused to speak until the room was silent.

Looking out at the spectators, I lifted my right hand, palm up. Put my left index finger to my lips. Shook my head. Hoped my eyes were scalding the offenders with a look that told them they should not be messing with me.

I caught a glimpse of Bria Gaines. No tears. Just the appearance of someone who was shattered. Who had lost everything.

That was when the inspiration struck. I knew what would come next, what I'd do. It felt like that emoji where the icon's brain blows up. But in a good way.

When the courtroom was quiet, I spoke to all of the people assembled before me.

"In the case of *State of Alabama v. Bria Gaines*, the jury has returned a verdict of guilty against the defendant. After the verdict is returned, Alabama law states under Rule 20.3..."

The DA was sitting at the counsel table with his head cocked and a confused expression on his face. But his co-counsel was sharper; she could see what was coming. Eleanor Lindquist lunged out of her chair.

"No! Your Honor, I object!"

I raised that voice of mine. It soared like a jazz singer's, drowned the other woman out. "Under Alabama Rule of Criminal Procedure 20.3, after a jury verdict, the court on its own motion may grant a judgment of acquittal. I'm taking the action authorized under Rule 20.3 in this case, setting aside the guilty verdict and entering a judgment of acquittal."

The noise from the gallery was rising. I smacked the gavel to give a warning.

"The defendant and her attorney shall rise. Please."

Bria Gaines exchanged a look with her lawyer as she and Benjamin Meyers pushed their chairs back and stood.

I said, "It is the decision of this court that Dr. Bria Gaines is acquitted—found not guilty—of the charge against her. I have that authority by state law in Alabama. The rule says, and I quote: 'After a verdict or the entry of a judgment of conviction...the court, on its own motion, may grant a judgment of acquittal.' Are we all clear on that?"

It appeared that a large number of people in that courtroom were not clear. I said, "Just so everybody understands. Rule 20.3 of Alabama Rules of Criminal Procedure means that when a jury hands down a guilty verdict, the judge has the power to do whatever she thinks is right in the case. The judge has the right to throw out a jury verdict. That's what I have decided to do in this case. I'm throwing out the guilty verdict. And I'm finding the defendant not guilty. This is a final judgment and may not be appealed or overturned."

To drive that point home, I stood and pointed at Bria Gaines with my gavel. I said, "Dr. Gaines, you are free to go."

Journalists were scuttling down the rows of benches and running out of the courtroom, eager to be the first to break the story. The general public remained in court, raising their voices to weigh in on my decision. Some shouted in protest, others in triumph. The noise level grew to a cacophony of sound that blistered the ear.

But I was watching Bria, seeing her transformation. The shattered posture changed first to disbelief as she absorbed the import of my words. Her lawyer whooped and grabbed her in a victory hug; her head tipped back and I saw that expression of joy. Her body sagged with relief when the full impact of the decision struck. Her lawyer was holding her up, keeping her on her feet.

Seeing the joy of freedom wash over Bria Gaines was a profound experience. Gave me tremendous satisfaction. Made me proud. *It was worth it,* I thought.

But a price would be paid. By me.

My judicial career was over.

CHAPTER 80

STONE FAMILY FARM
BULLOCK COUNTY, ALABAMA

The autumn season was hot that year. Second summer stretched all the way through October. That spell of dry fall weather would be a big help for a political campaign. Plenty of good weather to go politicking door-to-door, put up yard signs, hold a local rally to drum up enthusiasm.

But I wasn't campaigning. It wouldn't accomplish anything, other than wasting my time. And wasting money, when I didn't have much to spare. The insurance on the farmhouse didn't begin to cover the replacement of everything I'd lost in the explosion and fire.

So on the Saturday after Halloween, I spent my afternoon sitting in the trailer, in front of a television set. I'd given up the traditional Saturday breakfast. Couldn't host that breakfast any longer, not without a proper kitchen and seating for guests. There was no need to spend the day in the barn. The horses were out in the field, enjoying the sunshine. I could see Thunder prancing in the grass, but he never strayed far from his mother.

And there was no need to spend my weekend doing judicial work. I was a short-timer, everybody knew that. I'd blown the upcoming election by tossing out a jury verdict. Spitting in a jury's eye was political suicide.

Since my decision in the Bria Gaines trial, money had poured into my opponent's campaign. His staffers had been busy planting yard signs. They'd sprung up like weeds, all over town. And the TV ads were running hourly, it seemed like. All negative ads, focused on me.

Mary Stone doesn't respect the American tradition of trial by a jury of our peers! She thinks that she alone should make the decision of guilt or innocence! She threw out a jury verdict—and she'll throw our constitutional rights out with the garbage!

While the voice-over defamed me, the ad ran a series of hideously unflattering photos. Candid shots in which I looked angry, unkempt, and unbalanced. The last image was the worst: I was standing in front of the Bullock County Courthouse with a snarl on my face. Just before the ad's final line, they popped a cartoon golden crown on my head, tilted it sideways.

Don't let Mary Stone rule the 3rd Judicial Circuit of Alabama!

I sat in that stiff new recliner, staring at the ugly ad, when I heard a tap at the trailer door. A tap so soft, I thought I might have imagined it.

I muted the television. The knock sounded again, a light, tentative rap. Not the decisive knock of a friend or family member.

I was tempted to ignore it. I wasn't expecting any visitors—and certainly wasn't hungry for company. I thought the intruder might just give up if I remained in my chair.

Changed my mind about that pretty swiftly, though. I'd survived an attack recently, right on that piece of land. If someone was coming on my property uninvited, I damn well needed to know about it.

I stepped up to the door, turned the lock. Pulled it open so suddenly, it must have startled her.

Nova Jones stood on the makeshift steps to my trailer door, clutching a plant in a terra-cotta clay pot. When I'd flung the door open, she'd backed up and almost fallen down the steps.

"Nova!" I peered around her. There was no car idling in my side yard, no adult waiting at the bottom of the steps. "What you doing out here, honey? You surely didn't walk all this way. I'm five miles outside the city limits."

"No, ma'am, I didn't walk. Social worker dropped me off at the gate after our meeting today. I'm supposed to wait for her down there on the road. She be back to get me in a minute, drive me home."

"I see," I said, studying her. That was a falsehood on my part. I didn't see, had no clue what the child was doing here.

Nova looked down at the pot she clutched to her chest. "I brought you something, Judge Mary."

The pot held a blooming mass of purple pansies.

I tried to catch her eye. Nova pulled out a bit of dirt and rubbed it between her thumb and fingertip. "These are yours, Judge Mary. I saw the pansies down by your fencerow wasn't doing so good, didn't have enough color, enough bloom. So I dug some up and repotted them in fresh soil."

"I see," I said again.

"It's a good time to plant them now. Weather's cooling down. Or you can keep them in the pot if you want, on your steps. You used to have pretty pots of flowers on your porch when we came to Saturday breakfast."

She handed the pot to me. I said, "Nova, thank you. That's real thoughtful."

Hesitantly, she said, "I know you're awful busy, being a judge at the courthouse. But if you pull off the old flowers, it helps new ones to grow."

"I'll remember that, Nova. That's good advice."

I saw Nova's eyes cut over to the patch of bare ground where the farmhouse formerly stood. "There's no Saturday breakfast anymore."

My throat grew tight. "That's right. My house burned down, and the fire took all my good old pots and pans. This little kitchen in the trailer is too small to feed a crowd."

I stopped talking, aware that I was making excuses. But then, I couldn't think of a way to explain it to this young girl—that I didn't have the fortitude to host those community breakfasts anymore.

I was too tired. Tired and beaten down.

I shifted the weight of the clay pot to my hip, trying to think of a way to break the silence. But then Nova spoke again.

"Dr. Bria's office got a sign in the window."

"Yes! That's right. I hear it's for rent. Somebody told me she's moving to Chicago."

"Chicago?" There was regret in her voice, deep sadness. "Is she coming back?"

A car pulled into the drive. Betty Cooper sat behind the wheel. The social worker tapped the horn and waved.

Nova didn't turn to go, not then. She stared down at her feet. "Ms. Cooper says it wasn't my fault what happened. Those boys following me, what they did."

My heart twisted in my chest. "Your fault? No, Nova, nothing was your fault. Not a thing."

My voice was strident, too loud. Nova took a step back, descended one stair. "She thinks I don't have to worry about seeing them anymore."

My heart was pounding. "That's right," I said, striving to sound calm. Mick Owens had kept me informed. The boys had broken down and confessed. They were being confined in the juvenile detention facility in Birmingham. The juvenile case was still ongoing; there would be proceedings to determine whether they'd be tried as adults. Whether it was handled by the juvenile court system or criminal courts, I believed they'd be penalized. And I was glad. I wanted them to get what they deserved. In a recent interview, one of the boys revealed a connection to local white supremacists. Mick said he'd turned the information over to the feds.

Betty called from the driver's window. "Nova? I need to get you home. Your mama's waiting!"

Now that Nova was about to depart, I found that there was much I'd like to say to her. Give some wisdom, maybe. Give encouragement, words of hope. I set the pot of pansies by the door as I struggled to summon the right words.

But no eloquent words of comfort came to mind as we stood on the makeshift steps. Nova looked down, wouldn't meet my eye. She shoved her hands into the pockets of her jacket and hunched her shoulders. I heard a sniffle, and I wondered whether she was about to cry.

Wondered whether I'd cry with her.

I was about to speak, to break the uneasy silence, when Nova turned and hopped off the steps, walking quickly to Betty Cooper's car. I just stood there, watching her go.

And then she whirled back around and ran back to the trailer. Stormed up the stairs and hugged me, tight. I wrapped my arms around her and held her, rocking from side to side. Neither of us spoke. Didn't need words, not in the moment. We were bound by a shared history. United by a painful experience that surpassed understanding.

Nova pulled away, and I let her go. She ran to the car, got in the passenger seat. I waved at the car as it turned around on the gravel, but Nova never looked back.

CHAPTER 81

BULLOCK COUNTY COURTHOUSE
UNION SPRINGS, ALABAMA

When you think you're going to a place that you'll be leaving soon, it feels really special to be there again. It's kind of like you're seeing it with fresh eyes.

I felt that way walking into the county courthouse.

My other home.

It was a Monday morning, warm and sunny. When I got to the front door, Aurora was there to hold the door open for me. "Good luck with the election, Judge Mary."

"Thanks, I'll need it." I didn't tell her I knew it was already a lost cause.

I walked through the doorway. My footsteps echoed down the hardwood floor of the hall. Along the way, one by one, people started peeking out of their offices.

Dead woman walking.

I was sure some of them would be voting for me. But I was also sure most of them expected me to lose. Probably thought that after my term expired in January and my opponent got sworn in, they'd never see me again, except down at the Winn-Dixie.

I took the elevator at the rear of the building. The one that opened up right next to my chambers. I walked in. Looked at my desk. What a mess. I had half a mind to start cleaning it up. Put everything in boxes. Take my diplomas and certificates off the wall. Save myself the time after the votes were counted.

I took my robe off the hook and slipped it over the dress I'd borrowed this morning from Jordan. I hadn't managed to replace my wardrobe yet, so I was taking turns wearing clothes from my sisters.

I looked at the clock on the wall and paced back and forth until the minute hand moved to 10. I took a deep breath and opened the door that led from my chambers to the courtroom.

Showtime.

Ross Carr, my bailiff, called out, "All rise!" Felt like he put a little something extra into it this morning. The clerk announced the case as I stepped onto the platform behind the bench. She ended with "the Honorable Mary Stone presiding." I realized that I was really going to miss hearing those words.

I sat down and looked out over a full gallery, dozens of people whispering in low tones. The whole town had an interest in this case, even though this was just an arraignment.

I banged my gavel. "Be seated." The crowd settled. I looked to my left. DA Reeves stood with his hands folded in front of him. He gave me a respectful nod. Then I looked down to my right.

"We are on the record," I said. "Will the defendant please rise."

Reluctantly, slowly, Mason Phelps stood up. No baseball cap today. No Confederate tee. Just an ill-fitting suit and a fresh shave.

Mick Owens stood behind him alongside a court security guard. A public defender stood at the table beside him. It was

Scotty Whelker. Local attorney. Former high school wrestler. Good kid. I'd known him for years.

In court, it's customary for the clerk to read the charges. Not today. I wanted to read them myself.

I didn't even need notes.

"The grand jury of Bullock County in the State of Alabama charges that on or about September twenty-third of this year, Mason Euell Phelps did unlawfully and with malice aforethought, deliberately and willfully take the life of Cocheta Ann Bass, in violation of Alabama Code Title 13-A."

I paused for a few seconds to let the words sink in.

"Mr. Phelps, how do you plead?"

He gave me a sneer with his answer. "Totally not guilty."

Immediately, Scotty Whelker jumped up. "Your Honor!"

I knew what was coming. I was fully prepared for it. "Counsel?"

"Your Honor, in light of the Court's connection with a previous case in which the deceased was an expected witness, the defense intends to file a motion for recusal, demanding that you remove yourself from this case."

The gallery started buzzing. I rapped my gavel.

"Mr. Whelker. I'm way ahead of you. You are absolutely correct. I knew Ms. Bass. When I heard about her death, I went to the crime scene. Saw her hanging from that tree."

Not a whisper in the room after that announcement.

"So there is no way I can be objective in this case. No need to file a motion. I'll make the ruling from the bench. I hereby recuse myself. The clerk will handle the paperwork. This case will be assigned to another judge."

I could see Mason Phelps smirking as if he'd just won a big bet.

I looked right at him. "Before I adjourn, however, I have one more question for the defendant."

Phelps shifted his feet. His smirk faded a little.

"Mr. Phelps, did you or did you not set a dynamite charge and trip wire on my property in an attempt to blow up my home with me inside it?"

Phelps went pale. The gallery went crazy.

"Your Honor!" Scotty Whelker shouted.

I held up a hand to signal the public defender. "I acknowledge, Mr. Whelker, that for me to ask that question was totally out of line. And a judge who has crossed a line must recuse herself. But I already have, you understand?"

I rapped my gavel again and pointed the mallet at the defendant. "No need to answer, Mr. Phelps," I said. "We both know the truth."

With that, I stood up and walked out of the courtroom. Back in my chambers, I pulled off my robe and tossed it onto a hook on the coatrack.

Dug an empty Banker's Box from a closet. Looked around the room, wondering where to start. Which piece of my judicial career I'd toss away first. But I was frozen. Couldn't do it, not yet. *Later*, I thought.

Five minutes later, I was back in my car, heading for home with the window down, country air in my face. There were plenty of good judges in the Black Belt of Alabama. I had faith that Mason Phelps would get a fair trial, and that he would soon receive the justice he deserved.

But for right now, I tried to put all that out of my mind. I was taking the rest of the day off.

I had a new foal to care for, and cattle to feed.

CHAPTER 82

STONE FAMILY FARM
BULLOCK COUNTY, ALABAMA

It was the first Tuesday after the first Monday in November. Election Day in Alabama.

In prior weeks, I anticipated that I'd be mournful when November finally rolled around and made my judicial demise a definite outcome. Thought I'd be depressed, blue. I was about to find out whether my supposition was accurate.

I checked the time on the stove as I walked to the kitchen for a refill of ice water. It was 8 p.m.; the polls had been closed for an hour. But as I returned to that stiff new chair in the trailer's living room, I didn't feel blue, exactly. More like aimless. Uncertain what the future held, and what my role would be. If I wasn't Judge Mary Stone—who the hell was I?

A familiar voice popped into my head: sounded like my friend Loucilla. *You don't base your identity on your occupation!*

She'd said that to me repeatedly, particularly in recent weeks.

I wasn't convinced. It was easy for Lou to say. She was a tenured professor at the university.

I was afraid I'd start talking to myself, sitting alone in that trailer on election night. The trailer was too quiet, eerily so.

I'd turned the phone off. I didn't want any sympathy calls. And the TV was off, too. I didn't have cable or a dish, could only pick up local stations. And local stations would be running election results on the screen all night, on a banner during regular programming, leading up to the ten o'clock news. I was making a conscious decision to avoid the heartache of seeing the count roll in, watching my opponent win by bigger and bigger numbers.

No damn way. I'm a realist—I knew I'd lose. But I'm no masochist.

I expected that time would be hanging on my hands that night, moving slow. So I'd dragged a box of hard files home from the courthouse. I pulled a stack of manila folders out of the box and set them on one of the TV trays I used as all-purpose furnishings these days. TV trays served as dinner table, coffee table, desk, nightstand.

I was reviewing those files, trying to sort out the cases I'd try to complete before my judicial term ended in January. I was making progress, too, emptied the box about halfway, when I heard a car engine, and gravel crunching under tires.

I closed the file folder, pushed the TV tray to the side. A surge of impatience rolled through me when pounding sounded at the door. Even in defeat, they wouldn't leave me in peace.

"Mary!" The pounding doubled in volume. I stepped up to the door, unlocked it, and pulled it open.

Both my sisters stood on the top step, arms around each other, like they were holding each other up.

And I thought: *Oh, God, no.*

CHAPTER 83

I pulled the door wide open, certain that some new catastrophe had befallen our family. "What on earth? What's happened now? Is something the matter?"

They laughed. Laughed loud, like a couple of kids at the circus.

Jordan said, "Nothing's the matter! But you gotta go!"

"What? Go where?"

"To the party. The watch party over at the community center, at Oak Grove Park."

"Oh, hell no." Waving off that suggestion, I flapped a hand in front of my face, like insects were buzzing around me. "I'm not going anywhere."

"You have to!" Nellie said.

"No way. I told you. I'm staying in tonight."

Nellie grabbed my arm. "Mary. You're in the lead."

Maybe I didn't hear her right. She sounded kind of drunk. Looked it, too, to be honest. But when I sniffed her to check for alcohol, I didn't smell anything.

"Is this some kind of joke? Are you messing with me?"

Jordan grabbed me, wrapped me in a hug. "You're winning, Mary! Everyone in the county is there—you've got to see it."

"They're asking for you," Nellie said. "Chanting your name."

I was almost speechless. "My name? Bullshit," I said.

They both broke into peals of laughter, like I was the funniest thing they'd ever heard.

"Come on, Mary. Loucilla's been calling you, we all have, can't get you to pick up. She's driving in from Montgomery. She'll be at the watch party any minute. Everybody wants to talk to you!"

I let them lead me to the car. My mind was so muddled, I didn't even stop to think about what I was wearing. Showed up at the watch party in my overalls. People didn't seem to mind, though. When we walked in, all conversation stopped. There was an instant of silence.

And then the cheering began.

I couldn't believe it. It sounded like a roar, bouncing off the walls of the multipurpose room. Joe Turner, the local party chair, ran up to congratulate me, shake my hand. It was dreamlike. I didn't trust it to be the truth.

"Show me the numbers, okay?" I said. "What the secretary of state's office is showing. And the county clerk."

Joe pulled me over to the screen where the current results of the races were on display. They did indeed show me to be in the lead. With 45 percent of the returns counted, I was beating my opponent, 61 percent to 39 percent.

I stared at those figures, trying to get my head around the unexpected outcome. "Not possible," I said.

Joe was ebullient. "Mary, it's solid. We're taking the numbers from the official websites. It's absolutely accurate. Your lead has been consistent since the returns started rolling in."

Squinting, I checked the voter turnout column. "But look at the voter numbers. There's gotta be a mistake."

"No mistake!" That was from Nellie, who'd joined us. "They're sky-high, right? Those returns rolled in, showing that the community turned out to vote in numbers way bigger than anyone predicted. You did that, Mary! You got everybody off the couch and into the polling places today."

"It broke a record," the county chairman said. "We haven't had voter turnout this high in this century."

"More returns coming in!" somebody shouted, and the chairman ran off. People from the courthouse pushed through the crowd to say hello. The associate judge from the circuit ran up to congratulate me, said the turnout I'd instigated was helping him, too.

The room in the community center smelled of spice; a big delivery of barbecue had arrived at a food table, and they were serving up pulled pork sandwiches. Someone handed me a cold beer, and I drank it, straight from the can. In front of God and everybody.

The party got so crowded, I started to perspire, had to wipe sweat from my forehead with a paper napkin. Loucilla arrived, pushing through the crowd to hug me around the neck. And my sisters stuck close by me, leading the cheer every time a new round of numbers was posted on that screen. My lead inched up. By ten o'clock, I was staring at the new percentages—63 percent to 37 percent—when someone tapped me on the shoulder.

I turned around and saw Bria Gaines standing there, with Benjamin Meyers.

"Dr. Gaines!" I exclaimed. "And Ben Meyers. This is such a surprise, it's nice to see you."

There was a cheer in the room, a babble of excited voices. Bria Gaines had to speak up to be heard.

"I had to see you before I left. I want to thank you."

I brushed it off. "No need, Dr. Gaines. I was just doing my job."

She shook her head decisively. "Judge, I know what you did for me. The risk you took on my behalf. I'm so grateful to you. From the bottom of my heart."

Ben Meyers shook my hand. "Congratulations on your victory, Judge. This is a monumental win. The best thing that could happen for the Third Circuit and Bullock County."

I checked the results again, like I was afraid the lead might have disappeared. It was still hard to believe it was happening. "I got lucky this time, didn't I?"

Bria gave me a knowing smile. "Luck? Judge, you know it's not luck. We always have to work twice as hard—to get anything."

The county chairman pushed through the crowd, called out to me. "Judge, you got to do an acceptance speech! The Birmingham TV news is here. Your opponent just conceded!"

Television? A speech? I was wearing overalls. "You mean right now?"

"Yes!"

Joe was pulling me away from Bria Gaines. Before the crowd swallowed her up, she waved at me, shouting, "Look me up in Chicago!" And then I was up on the makeshift stage, with white lights blinding me. The chairman's voice blared through the speakers. "Judge Mary Stone has won reelection to her seat as circuit judge for a second term!"

Folks were whooping, applauding, stomping their feet. I was teetering once again, in danger of a crying breakdown. I didn't let go, though. Took a deep breath. Thought about my mama. Making her proud. My people, generations of them buried in the soil of the Black Belt.

And I knew what to say.

"Friends, thank you for your support. I'm proud to serve for another six-year term. My roots are here, my heart is here. One thing you never have to doubt, that I swear to you tonight. Sitting at that bench, I'll do everything in my power to see that justice is done in my courtroom in the state of Alabama."

People cheered, some of them screaming at the top of their lungs.

And in the corners of the hall, I observed a few frowning faces. One man muttering something to another, with a formidable expression.

That was sobering. But I'm glad I caught it. It served as an important reminder.

In this job, I can't make everyone happy. It would be dangerous to try.

A judge who wants to please everyone won't bring justice to people in the Black Belt.

They need a judge who's willing to fight.

Born and raised here, I'm as much a part of this community as the famous soil we stand upon. I understand the challenges we face; the injustices we've suffered. When I die, they'll bury me on the land my great-grandfather bought, scores of years ago. That's why I'll never leave this place.

The people need me.

We need each other.

ABOUT THE AUTHORS

Viola Davis is an internationally acclaimed actress, producer, *New York Times* bestselling author, and EGOT winner – only the fourth person to do so exclusively via performance-based awards. She is the cofounder of JVL Media, a full-service production/media packaging firm and independent publisher.

In 2025, the Golden Globes honoured her with the Cecil B. DeMille Award for 'outstanding contributions to the world of entertainment'.

Davis is known for her exceptional performances, such as her Emmy-winning role in television's *How to Get Away with Murder*; her Academy Award-nominated movies *Doubt*, *The Help*, and *Fences* (for which she received the Oscar); her Screen Actors Guild Award-winning role in *Ma Rainey's Black Bottom*; her two Tony Awards (for *Fences* and *King Hedley II*); and as a Grammy winner for best audiobook narration and storytelling recording for her bestselling memoir, *Finding Me*.

James Patterson is one of the best-known and biggest-selling writers of all time. Among his creations are some of the world's most popular series, including Alex Cross, the Women's Murder

About the Authors

Club, Michael Bennett and the Private novels. He has written many other number one bestsellers including collaborations with President Bill Clinton, Dolly Parton and Michael Crichton, stand-alone thrillers and non-fiction. James has donated millions in grants to independent bookshops and has been the most borrowed adult author in UK libraries for the past fourteen years in a row. He lives in Florida with his family.